DESIRE

"I'd see you, Gilliane." Richard's voice was almost a whisper, as his hands worked to loosen the soft sheet she wore.

"I—I cannot," she gasped, clutching at his hands, holding them still.

His lips found her neck, kissing lightly down to her bared shoulder, sending waves of excitement coursing inward. She held her breath and let the sheet fall away, sliding over her bare skin to land in folds at her feet. For a moment, he stood very still himself. Then his palms moved over her breasts, cupping them, caressing them.

Agony . . . ecstasy . . . she knew not what she felt, as her protests turned into a floodtide of need she could no long deny. . . .

HEARTS OF FIRE

Anita Mills

AN ONYX BOOK

NEW AMERICAN LIBRARY

ONYX TRADEMARK REG. U.S. PAT. OFF. AND FOREIGN COUNTRIES
REGISTERED TRADEMARK—MARCA REGISTRADA
HECHO EN DRESDEN, TN, USA

SIGNET, SIGNET CLASSIC, MENTOR, ONYX, PLUME, MERIDIAN
and NAL BOOKS are published by New American Library,
a division of Penguin Books USA Inc.,
1633 Broadway, New York, New York 10019

First Printing, June, 1989

1 2 3 4 5 6 7 8 9

PRINTED IN THE UNITED STATES OF AMERICA

For my husband,
Larry Mills,
whose faith in my abilities
both inspires and prods.

Foreword

In December of 1135, Henry I died, plunging England into a civil war that would last nineteen years. Earlier, after the death of his only legitimate son and heir, Henry had chosen his daughter, Mathilda, to follow him on the throne, and he had forced a reluctant baronage to swear fealty to her on two separate occasions. Unfortunately, when she'd been widowed as Holy Roman Empress, he'd contracted a second marriage for her with Geoffrey of Anjou, a marriage that was highly unpopular in both England and Normandy. And, on his death, there were few who wished to be ruled by her Angevin husband.

This set the stage for the rise of other contenders for the English throne, most particularly two of Henry I's nephews, Theobald, Count of Blois, and his younger brother, Stephen of Blois, Count of Mortain and Boulogne. Some of the baronage even preferred Henry's favorite bastard son, Robert, Earl of Gloucester, over "the Empress," as Matilda was usually called. The strongest personal rivalry existed between Stephen of Blois and Robert of Gloucester, the two greatest land-holding magnates in the realm, each of whom possessed nearly one-half million acres of English land, and each of whom had loyalists ready to argue his claim.

My story opens as the Norman barons were preparing to bypass Mathilda and offer the crown to Count Theobald. But Stephen, not to be outfaced, had rushed to England, enlisted the aid of yet another brother, Bishop Henry of Winchester, taken possession of the royal seal and treasury, and persuaded the Curia Regis, a body comprising for the most part ranking clergymen, to declare him king. He was helped immeasurably by the perjury of another baron, Hugh Bigod, who swore that the king had repudiated his daughter on his deathbed and named Stephen as his heir. Robert of Gloucester, the one man who could refute his testimony, remained in Normandy with his father's body.

Almost immediately, the rival factions supporting Stephen, Mathilda, and Robert quarreled over the Curia's selection, and Stephen began his reign over lands fast dissolving into anarchy. The England which had been for the most part at peace during Henry I's long reign was wracked by the armed conflict of those who supported causes and those who sought merely to profit from the unrest. It was the beginning of what one chronicler called "nineteen long winters" of civil war.

1

Castle of Beaumaule
Kent, England–December 10, 1135

Pushing the castle tiring women aside, Gilliane directed her brother's men-at-arms toward the front of the chilly chapel. She stood back to let them carry the heavy wooden box past.

"Lay him before the altar," she ordered. "And I would have you remove the lid ere you go. Garth, seek out Master Bodwin from the priory that a cast may be taken."

Tears flowing unabashedly down their faces, the men nodded silently. To a man, there'd not been any who'd not loved his young lord, who had not been willing to follow him anywhere. And follow him they had, riding blithely into William of Brevise's ambush. The ensuing battle had been one-sided but intense as Geoffrey de Lacey had attempted in vain to slash down his attackers, only to fall himself, victim to the overwhelming odds. Two men had perished with him and seven others nursed their wounds, severely depleting Beaumaule's defenses, but none felt the devastating loss so much as the young girl before them.

"I'd be alone with him," she whispered, holding her arms against her both for comfort and for warmth against the cold of the freezing rain that struck the chapel windows.

Geoffrey's captain, Simon of Woodstock, raised his hand toward her and then let it drop helplessly at his side. There was nothing to do, nothing to be said. Two blows of a battleax had not only snuffed out a man's life but also thrown them all into a precarious existence. As Geoffrey de Lacey's lifeblood had soaked the wet ground beneath him, the fortunes of everyone at Beaumaule had ebbed with it. The young lord's death was an ill omen, he believed, for it followed within days of the old king's demise, and reflected the lawlessness of a disputed succession. In the interim, evil men like William of Brevise had already benefited from the anarchy. Sighing, Woodstock acceded silently to the girl's wishes and gestured to the others to follow.

Gilliane de Lacey waited until all of them, even her own women, had filed soberly, uneasily past her brother's funeral bier, their shared apprehension apparent in their faces. Slowly, gingerly almost, she approached the wooden coffin, fearful of what she would see.

His wounds had been cleansed and wrapped in fine linen before the woman Alwina had dressed him in his best blue tunic, but nothing could hide the agony of his death. Instead of his ready smile and his laughing blue eyes, he carried his final grimace into eternity. For a long moment it was like staring down into the face of a stranger—marble white, cold and set, drained and bloodless. The memory of how he'd looked when he'd ridden out flooded over the girl—he'd sat his saddle tall and straight, his handsome profile silhouetted against the early dawn, his red hair made even redder in that faint orange light. He'd been on his way to Winchester after receiving the news that King Henry had died in Normandy nine days earlier. It stood to reason, he'd told her, that the baronage would rebel at the thought of the Empress Mathilda as queen, and he meant to be there in support of Robert of Gloucester, Henry's strongest bastard son. After all, with Gloucester king, the sagging fortunes of the de Laceys would again rise. But Geoffrey'd never reached Winchester—he'd fallen but twelve furlongs from home, victim of Brevise's vicious attack.

The tears which had refused to come in the numbing hours since they'd carried him home flowed freely now, coursing unchecked down her cheeks, spotting the blue silk of her brother's tunic, as she remembered how vital he'd been. Reaching to brush a drop from his face, her chilled fingers felt the even greater coldness of his skin, and the last of her composure crumbled.

"Oh, Geoffrey!" she wailed, casting herself onto his rigid chest. Her hands clutched at the silk, drawing it into clenched fists as her whole body was wracked with sobs. "Oh, my brother!" Words which had been few since morning now tumbled almost incoherently, choked out in the anguish of unbearable loss. "I . . . I'll see his h-head on a p-pike for what he has done—I swear it, Geoffrey! I swear it! He'll not live unpunished!" Raising her head, she looked about the small chapel wildly until her glance chanced upon the wooden statue of Christ behind the altar. She stared at it for a moment before pushing away from the bier, and rising, she groped past Christ's table to look up into the painted bloodstains. "As you are my witness, William of Brevise will die for what he has done to my brother!" she cried out to the statue. Still sobbing, she unhooked the small door at the base and drew out a jeweled gold box said to contain a relic of the True Cross. "I swear it!" she whispered vehemently as she lifted it upward. "On the Cross, I swear it!"

"Lady."

She spun around at the sound of Simon of Woodstock's voice, whipping the gold casket behind her guiltily. The eyes that met hers were troubled. Quickly brushing her wet cheeks with the back of her other hand, she tried to regain her dignity.

"I . . . I was but bidding him farewell, Simon," she managed to explain through twisted lips.

"Aye. The monk comes with the wax, that he may cast the death mask," he told her quietly. "Perhaps some warmed wine—"

"I do not wish any wine!" Her famed temper flared, then faded pitifully against the man's diffident recoil. "Oh, Simon, what will we do *now*?" she wailed.

It was not an easy question to answer, yet one that begged a response. He shifted uncomfortably in his heavy, water-soaked boots and looked away. He knew what she wanted—she wanted him to tell her they would seek revenge—but they lacked both the men and the power to attempt it. "Ask for the king's justice, Lady Gilliane," he answered finally. " 'Tis the murder of a Norman lord—there is no presentment of Englishry, after all. It cannot be said he was English, and therefore you have a right to seek punishment for his murderer," he reminded her, citing the Conqueror's law that had protected the nobility since the Conquest.

"A Norman murdered by a Norman!" She spat out the words with renewed fury. "At best, Brevise will be but fined! And to whom do we appeal—the Empress? Or Gloucester? Or Stephen even? King Henry is dead—we have no king, Simon!" She paced angrily before him. "Were I a man, I'd carve Lord Brevise's liver from his carcass—I'd cleave him from his neck to his manhood!" Bringing up the relic, she held it in front of her defiantly. "But I swear I'll not let him go unpunished—d'you hear me? I swear it!"

" 'Tis blasphemy for a maid to swear that which she cannot do," he muttered, reaching to wrench it from her clenched fingers. "Nay, but there will be another king soon enough, I'll warrant, and you will be his ward. You must appeal for justice, lady."

"Justice! Justice?" Her voice rose to an indignant

screech. "Nay, but there is no justice! My brother is dead, Simon—dead by Brevise's hand!"

"The old king—"

"The old king is dead! And the thing Geoffrey feared is like to come to pass—Stephen of Blois will rule!"

"Then we must appeal to Stephen. From all I have heard, he is a generous man," he reasoned aloud, not daring to meet her angry glare. "There is naught else to be done, my lady—we are powerless to take vengeance on Lord William."

"Jesu! Are we cowards all that we cringe before Brevise?" she demanded. "The man wants our land, Simon! He murdered my brother for this one small piece that sits as a thorn amongst his roses! Appeal to Stephen?" she demanded sarcastically. "Nay, but he is Lord William's own liege! What justice will we have of him, I ask you? I'd see Brevise dead—not fined a pittance for this!"

He watched her restless, almost frenzied pacing with unease. Her face flushed with impotent fury, her eyes flashing, her red hair streaming in tangled disarray down her back, she reminded him of a snarling caged animal, a thing caught yet unwilling to accept defeat. It was an impossible promise of revenge she made, but reasoning fell before her raging grief, and he was wise enough not to attempt again to mollify her when only he and Bodwin could hear her dangerous words. Instead, he let her vent her anguish through her temper and waited for her rage to abate. Replacing the relic, he straightened up, feeling every one of his thirty-six years. Aye, it was hard on all of them—William of Brevise had not only struck down his lord but also imperiled Simon's future, for it was by no means certain that the girl before him or her weak, spineless half-brother could further afford his service. The thought crossed his mind that Gilliane de Lacey should have been a son, for the girl had been born with more spirit and a greater will than any of her brothers.

"Demoiselle . . ." He spoke tentatively. Moving closer, he touched her shoulder clumsily with the grasp of a hardened warrior unused to female company.

"Oh, Simon!" Her faced contorted piteously as she turned into his arms. Startled by this unseemly behavior, he nonetheless attempted to smooth her bright hair with his callus-roughened hands.

"Oh, Simon, what will befall me now?" she cried. "I have no wish to be ward to Stephen—or to anyone else." Sniffing, she tried to hold back the tears that still overflowed her eyes as she buried her head in his woolen tunic, heedless of the smell of the sweat and blood that permeated it.

He stood very still. "Mayhap you should have taken the husband offered you." Almost as soon as the words had escaped him, he wished them back, for he could feel her stiffen against him. And the responsibility was not hers alone—Geoffrey de Lacey had not truly wanted to lose this sister who ran his household so well, and he had found it easy to refuse the aging Lord Widdemer's suit. His excuse had been that he'd not see her wed where there were already legitimate sons to inherit, but that was all it had been—an excuse—for in truth Geoffrey could not expect much more for her. He had not had the land to dower the girl properly—nor the money either, for that matter. It was as though he'd meant to keep her at home forever, squandering what little he had in dowries for the younger girls, ensuring that Gilliane would not be taken. And in his own selfishness, de Lacey had now ensured her certain poverty.

"I was ungrateful," she sniffed into the rough wool. "I am accursed for what I would not do."

"Nay, Demoiselle—Geoffrey did not think it," Woodstock consoled her. "Your brother valued you higher than Widdemer's offer. He loved you right well, lady, and would have seen you here to the end of your days." Privately he'd thought de Lacey a fool for it, but it served nothing to say so now.

"Do you think the new king will send me to a convent?" she asked suddenly, daring to voice the fear that he would.

Simon looked down on the flaming red hair against his shoulder and sighed. The girl was comely and her birth gentle, but there was no dowry, making her a liability to whoever became king. Without money to be made in her marriage, who could say what would happen to her? There'd be none to clamor for her wardship—nay, not even Gloucester would wish to be guardian for naught.

"I know not," he admitted finally.

"I know not which is worse—to languish under an abbess's rule or to wed a stranger and never see Beaumaule again," she added haltingly.

She'd stopped crying, but the seeming resignation in her voice was even more pitiable than her tears. Despite his own hardness, he could not bring himself to tell her that there was naught for her now.

"Nay, but as old as you are, you are not too old to bear, and the young wives, many of them, have borne babes too early and died, Demoiselle. Mayhap the king in his pity will seek one who has no need of land for you—someone who keeps his first wife's dowry."

"I'd rather stay here with Aubery than be wed to a man who found no value in me. What life would there be for me if I brought no land to my husband?" she countered bitterly.

"Nay, but you cannot stay. You cannot hold Beaumaule, and as for your brother—there will be a guardian for him, for he at least can claim Beaumaule."

"Sir—"

Simon dropped his hands and stepped back, red-faced and self-conscious at the sound of Master Bodwin's voice. "Aye," he muttered gruffly to hide his discomposure at being caught touching the demoiselle of the house.

"Is my lady wishful of casting the death mask in wax—or is the likeness to be carved from stone?" the rotund monk continued to address Simon.

"I . . . I'd have it carved, I think," Gilliane answered. "That is, I should like it done, if 'twill not beggar Aubery. I'd not squander what little remains of his patrimony."

"Nay, Demoiselle, I'd do it for naught but the stone itself," Bodwin offered. "Your brother was a good lord who supported God with what he had." Lifting the bucket of steaming wax, he turned to his task. "But 'twill be difficult to make him seem at peace."

A lump formed again in her already aching throat and threatened her composure once more. Nodding, she could barely whisper, "So be it."

"Lady Gilliane! Sir Simon!"

They turned at the sound of running footsteps, sharing a common dread at the urgency in the boy Garth's shouts. And even before he reached them, he confirmed their fears.

"Riders!"

"Jesu!" Gilliane gasped, the color draining from her face. Beside her, Simon of Woodstock exploded with a string of oaths that would have shocked her under other circumstances. "Whose?" she demanded, her pulses racing at the same time her heart seemed to have stopped in her breast.

"How many?" Simon asked curtly.

The boy gulped for breath and sought to answer both at once. "Thirty or more—and they carry no pennon—nor any device that could be seen. He said he was fortunate to see them at all in this weather."

"William of Brevise." It surprised Gilliane that she could say the hated name so calmly, but in her heart she'd expected he would come to take Beaumaule. And the wood-and-stone stockade would be no match for his pitch torches now, for the storm that raged outside now had but blown up and the timbers were not yet soaked. Geoffrey's words that "With the old king dead, we are no longer safe until there is another" echoed in her mind. Only last week he had spoken of finishing the curtain wall in stone. "Brevise comes for Aubery's land," she sighed heavily, "and we cannot stop him."

"Aye. Not even the weather will halt him," Woodstock muttered, echoing her own pessimism. "I'll warrant he means to strike whilst there is no king." The captain's scowl deepened as he considered the possibility that Brevise would finish what he'd begun. Aye, a ruse was to be expected of Lord William, for had he not taken Geoffrey de Lacey's life through ambush? "I suppose we had best treat with him," he mused aloud.

"Nay! So that he may kill Aubery also? And what of the others—and of you?" she questioned hotly, disputing him. "The dead carry no tales to Winchester!"

"He'd not kill a maid—not even Brevise would kill a maid. And I see not how—" Simon stopped, well aware that, made bold in the absence of royal protection, Brevise would not stop at taking the castle—he'd want none left to carry the tale to the next king.

"Can we not take him by deceit? Simon, can we not best him through trickery?" She spun away and began to pace anew in front of her brother's funeral bier. "Oh, would that I were a man! I'd—"

"He'll burn us out ere he leaves." Simon shook his head, not daring to meet her eyes. "Nay, but we are no match for him. There's not above twenty-five men in this keep, and seven of that number are wounded."

"As if we are lost already! Nay, but if only . . ." Her voice trailed off as she appeared to consider the matter, and then she whirled on him. "Simon, what if he thought we meant to surrender? What if we lowered the gates? He'd not burn us then surely—he'd not burn Beaumaule if he thought it to be his." The blue in her eyes sparked martially at the idea newly forming in her head.

"Nay, but—"

"We lower the gates," she continued, ignoring the negative shake of his head. "And when they are almost to the bridge, we loose the arrows. We take

them even as they took Geoffrey, Simon." She stopped
pacing and faced him, her chin set with determination. "But we wait until Brevise himself is on the
bridge. I'd not let him escape justice—nay, I'd not."
Her voice dropped to a fierce whisper as she met his
eyes. "Aye, I'd see Lord William's head above this
gate—I would."

" 'Twill be said we acted dishonorably," Garth
protested.

"And what honor was there to my brother's death?"
She rounded furiously on the boy. "Nay, we will take
him as dishonorably as he took Geoffrey's life! Simon, do you think 'tis possible to draw him in?"

Geoffrey's captain stared hard at the statue of the
bleeding Christ before them, as though to seek the
answer. "Your brother always said you had the mind
of a warrior, Demoiselle," he conceded with grudging admiration. "Aye, I think it possible—I think it a
risk worth taking." Turning back to her, he fixed
her with eyes as blue as her own. "But if we fail, I'd
have you save yourself to tell the tale. I'd have you
hide from William of Brevise's wrath."

"His men will take the women, and there's naught
we can do to prevent it. At least my name protects
me from that."

"Nay—he'll have no care what they do with you
ere you are killed. I mean to put you in the scullery
as a boy and hope he spares those who would feed
him. I doubt he would think to look for you there."
His expression still grim, he nodded acceptance of
her plan. "I am ready to do your bidding in this,
Demoiselle, but you will swear to do mine if we are
lost."

"We dare not lose, Simon."

"I pray God you are right," he muttered under his
breath, turning away. "Garth, see that every man
and boy breathing in this keep has a bow."

2

The rain froze on the steel helmets as soon as it hit, leaving a shiny glaze that dripped to form icicles over the men's faces. As Richard of Rivaux lifted his mail-encased arm to brush at his face, the ice cracked like eggshells at his shoulder and elbow.

"God's bones, Everard, but can you see anything? I'd thought to be to Beaumaule and a warm fire by now."

"Nay, my lord." The captain's breath was white like hoarfrost before him, crystallizing almost immediately. His fair eyebrows glistened with shaggy bits of ice as he lifted his head to stare through the pelting sleet at the hill ahead of them. "I pray 'tis but beyond that, for I am nigh frozen to my saddle," he muttered.

"Aye—as are we all," his young lord agreed. "But I've no doubt that de Lacey will bid us welcome, and we shall break our journey there." Shifting his stiffened body uncomfortably, Rivaux rose in his stirrups to study first the road and then the heavy clouds. " 'Tis too far to press on to Winchester in this storm, anyway. And if we cannot travel, then neither can Gloucester's enemies." Settling back, he clicked his reins and urged his horse onward.

"Myself, I'd as lief we'd waited for Gloucester and made the crossing with him," Everard of Meulan grumbled. As captain to Guy of Rivaux's son, he served one of the greatest families in the Anglo-Norman baronage, and therefore he'd expected a

life of greater ease. But Count Guy had asked him to
serve Richard well, releasing him from his earlier
oath to the father. And his heart, if not his loyalty,
was oft torn by the conflict between them, for he'd
soon found that his new lord chafed under the weight
of Guy of Rivaux's glorious reputation. Aye, at twenty-
three, the young man sought to separate himself
from Count Guy, seeking his own way, his own fame.
Like the Alexander of the Greeks, he wished to
conquer something for himself, and now King Henry's death gave him the opportunity he sought: he'd
speak before the Curia Regis on Robert of Gloucester's behalf—even if it meant setting himself against
his father, who could be expected to honor his oath
to Henry's daughter.

Aloud, Everard muttered through teeth clenched
against chattering, "I am glad you are certain of our
welcome, my lord, for we sent no word."

"Nay, I dare not—'tis Kent. If you do not count de
Lacey, we are among Stephen's vassals now."

"And I like it not."

"Without pennons and devices we risk no recognition," Richard reassured him. "Aye, Gloucester's enemies will not expect us to come this way."

"Still, I cannot like it."

Rivaux's ice-caked black brow rose despite the
weight on it. "Everard," he said with deceptive patience, "there's none to guess we are here, I'll warrant. Nay, but they all warm themselves by their
fires."

The captain fell silent, knowing this argument
would but provoke his lord's already strained temper. It had all been said before they'd left Normandy, and naught had dissuaded him—not Gloucester's bastardy nor Guy of Rivaux's expected support of Mathilda.

"My lord, look ahead!" Walter of Thibeaux, Richard's squire, edged his horse even with them at the
crest of the hill, while every man in Richard's mesnie
tried to follow where he pointed. Even before their

lord decided, "Aye—'tis Beaumaule, I'll warrant," shoulders that had been hunched against the cold were squared in anticipation of mulled wine and warm beds. The news spread down the thirty-man line, picked up and passed on eagerly, brightening the grim mood immediately. "Should we sound the horn, my lord?" Walter inquired.

"When we are closer. De Lacey'll not think we are come to make war on a day like this." Richard chafed his hands in his heavy mailed gloves as his dark eyes studied Beaumaule, a small stone-and-wooden stockade built on a motte of packed rubble. He'd been told once that it stood on the site of an ancient hill fort, but this was the first time he'd actually seen it. For a moment he was disappointed by the meanness of it, but reason reminded him that not all who fostered with Robert of Gloucester were sons of wealthy men. Indeed, Geoffrey de Lacey had been in the lowest ranks, trained because his late father beggared his patrimony for the honor. 'Twas said at the time that the old man wished to secure Henry's favor through the influence of Gloucester, but it had not happened. The young de Lacey had spent his years with the earl as squire to a lesser knight rather than Gloucester himself and had not gained much notice.

" 'Tis misnamed—there's naught pretty about the place," Everard complained under his breath, echoing Richard's own thoughts. " 'Tis a wonder it still stands, for I doubt it could withstand a siege with those timbered walls."

"They have been at peace." Irrationally, Richard felt the need to defend de Lacey. "The king's justice forbade petty quarrels amongst the baronage here, and 'tis not so unsettled as in Normandy—or at least it has not been until now. But with Henry dead and a crown to be had, I expect 'twill change even in Kent." He pressed his mail-clad knee against his horse's side to urge it up the ice-packed trail that passed for a road. "Jesu, but 'tis long since I last saw him—nigh to three years, I think."

"Aye, and you scarce knew him then—he was but another mouth at Gloucester's table."

"I pray we are welcomed." Richard's young squire pulled his heavy woolen cloak closer about his frozen face.

"Aye. In three years, he could have become Stephen's man," Everard observed sourly.

"Nay—I was not his enemy either. And there's none who have served Gloucester as would be against him. You may sound the approach now, Walter."

"God's blood, but his lips will freeze to the horn, I fear."

Richard smiled to himself. There was that eternal pessimism about Everard of Meulan that belied his true character, for despite his apparent dissatisfaction with everything, he was an outstanding soldier, always ready to ride into the thick of battle, always ready to lead his men where few would go. Brave, utterly fearless in the face of death, Everard seemed nonetheless unwilling to tempt fate with boastful words. He always expressed the worst fears about everything, possibly in hopes of being proven wrong. And to Richard, his captain's bravery more than compensated for his tendency to grumble. Everard was one debt he owed his father.

"My lord, there is no need—they wave us in." Walter raised his arm in an answering salute to the men who peered over Beaumaule's wall.

"Aye, they lower the bridge—though God knows they cannot recognize us through the storm." Everard raised his hand to signal those who rode behind to fall into line. "Jesu, but what I would not give for a warm bed and a wench to heat my blood."

"Mayhap they take pity on poor travelers on such a day," Walter guessed. "Were it not unseemly haste, I'd race to the bridge."

"Your animal's too tired," Richard answered with

a glint of mischief in his eyes. "A mark says you cannot make it before me."

"Aye, and you'll both break your necks." Everard's face broke into an answering smile that lightened his usually serious mien. "But I'd put my money on Walter—as squire, he carries less weight and less mail, my lord."

"You'll pay me a mark this day, my lord!" Walter shouted at Richard, kicking his horse so hard that it nearly reared. "I'll drink the first wine to be had in Beaumaule!"

A cheer rose behind them as Rivaux spurred after him, and the entire column joined in the pursuit, riding haphazardly despite the roughness of the road and the ice. The bitter cold and the harsh, pelting sleet were forgotten at the thought of shelter. The man and the boy were nearly even when Richard's horse slowed on the precarious footing, and his young squire was first on the bridge. At almost the same time that his horse leapt to clear the gap, Walter's shout of triumph died in a hail of arrows. And as his mount lost his footing, the boy pitched like a sack of grain to the other side and lay inertly in the ice-crusted dirt. The bridge, which had been lowering, stopped with a lurch as someone on the other side reversed the pulley before the heavy wooden platform could touch the frozen ground. The ropes creaked and groaned, drawing the bridge upward, obscuring the squire from view.

"Walter! Nay! Sweet Jesu—nay!" Richard cried in dismay and horror. Despite the arrows that fell around him and glanced off his own helm, he drew his sword and spurred his mount furiously, forcing it to jump onto the rising bridge. The animal neighed frantically as it reached the wooden floor and skidded downward. Richard, braced backward from his saddle pommel, managed somehow to keep his balance on the frightened horse. Shouting, "For Rivaux! For Rivaux!" he brought down the man who worked the gate with a single blow that cleaved him from the

side of his neck to his breastbone. Dark crimson
spurted from the man's wound, spraying Richard's
heavy fur-lined cloak as the young lord leaned to
strike at the heavy rope, sundering it. The fellow on
the other side of the gate fell back, cowering against
the wooden wall, while the rope next to him unrav-
eled, letting the bridge fall.

Shouts of "For God and Rivaux! For Rivaux! For
Rivaux and Saint Agnes!" followed Richard as his
men whipped their horses across the icy wooden
platform.

An arrow struck and lodged harmlessly in the
thickly padded leather and mail that encased Everard's
shoulders. Cursing, he raised his sword to strike the
second gateman.

"Mercy, sweet lord! Have mercy!" The fellow extended his hands outward as he pleaded.

Above them, there was pandemonium on the wall
as the defenders realized their mistake. Someone
shouted loudly, "Holy Mary—'tis Rivaux!" and cries
of "Sweet Jesu!" mingled with "God aid us—'tis
Rivaux!"

Still cursing, Richard's captain contented himself
with a kick of his heavy boot that sent the gateman
sprawling. Seeing that there was no further resistance to be had in the small courtyard, he rode to
where his lord had dismounted over the body of
Walter of Thibeaux. Tears streamed down Richard's
face as he tried to raise his squire, and Everard, who
thought himself inured to the sight of death, watched
with a painful catch in his chest while Richard removed his gloves to feel along Walter's jaw for a
pulse.

" 'Twas treachery, my lord." The gruffness in the
older man's voice betrayed his own grief. "By the
looks of it, there are not many defenders—would
you have us storm the archers?" Already the men of
Rivaux were climbing the walls in search of revenge.
And above them a man, apparently Beaumaule's seneschal, shouted down his surrender.

"Aye." Looking upward to the wall, Richard's eyes went hard and the muscles in his jaw tightened visibly. "I'd punish them all for the insolence—bring them down that I may hang the one who ordered this." Resting his weight on the hilt of his bloody sword, he exhaled heavily and turned again to Walter. "Sweet Jesu, but I'd not have had him harmed. I swore he would come to no harm in my service."

"Nay, you cannot be blamed, my lord." Clearing his throat to relieve his own aching, Everard shouted to the others, "Tell them to throw down their weapons!" Shaking his head, he muttered to Richard, " 'Twould seem de Lacey welcomes us not."

"Aye, and for this he will pay." Richard's voice was low, but there was no mistaking the set of his face. "He learned no such treachery from Robert of Gloucester." He felt again along the fallen boy's jaw, tracing downward from the ear, but could not be sure he detected a faint beat. In a final desperate effort, he struck a blow to Walter's chest, expelling the air there. The boy choked, retched, and began to regain his color. "Thank God he lives, else I'd kill them all," Richard muttered under his breath. "Walter . . . Walter . . . can you hear me?"

"He lives? God be praised! But I thought—"

"So did I, but I can see his breath now also. Mayhap he was winded when he hit the ground." For answer, Walter of Thibeaux's eyes flew open and fluttered to focus on his lord. "Nay, do not speak—save your breath," Richard urged him. "I can see you live."

"My arm . . . Jesu . . . my arm," the boy gasped.

"Cover him ere he freezes. Everard, do not let him rise ere you see what injury he has taken." Already the men on the walls above them were hastily surrendering their weapons to Richard's men, but he wasn't attending. He eased Walter into another man's arms and stood, staring across the small yard at the keep itself. "I'd go first to be certain there's none to resist in there."

"My lord! My lord! 'Twas a mistake!"

Richard turned back but briefly, noting the faded wool cloak and the poorly patched mail on the man who called to him. "Aye," he growled, " 'twas that, I'll warrant. I'd have justice for the treachery you offered me."

There was such contempt in Rivaux's face that Simon of Woodstock felt a surge of impotent anger. Turning instead to Everard, he addressed him. "As seneschal to Beaumaule, I submit and ask your terms." Even as he spoke, he unbuckled his worn sword belt and proffered his sheathed weapon hilt-first.

"Terms!" Everard spat viciously at the ground and snorted derisively. "Art a fool to ask—'tis Rivaux you have attacked!" The wall emptied behind them and he counted the defenders who now filed soberly to flank their captain. "I see but seventeen here, my lord. I'll warrant—" But Richard had already left them, moving in long strides toward the hall of the keep. With a sigh he turned back to Simon of Woodstock. "Art a fool," he repeated. "Rivaux brooks no challenge. He'll have Geoffrey de Lacey's head for this."

"De Lacey's dead—felled by the blow of an ax yesterday. 'Twas thought you were Brevise come to finish the task of taking Beaumaule."

"Holy Jesu!" Everard spat again, this time to hide his shock at the news. "Then these are all that are left?"

"Aye."

Richard paid no attention to the protests of Beaumaule's defenders, ignoring the cries of those who were shoved against the walls. He'd been fired on without reason, and he did not mean to be merciful. His sword in his hand, he approached the timbered building that obviously housed Beaumaule's hall. Aye, if he met any further resistance, he'd burn the place down about their ears. He raised the heavy blade, holding it before him, and kicked the iron latch upward viciously. The force sent the door banging inward to reveal the long, seemingly empty room.

He was unprepared for the scene that greeted him as his eyes traveled warily along the soot-blackened walls. Unlike his own keeps, this one was sparsely furnished with rough-hewn tables and benches gathered close to the central fire pit, giving the place an even poorer appearance. The remains of the morning's blaze smoldered and sent black smoke curling upward to the vent hole in the cross-timbered roof. Edging warily now, he entered the hall, half-expecting to be set upon, but he was alone. His nose wrinkled at the stench of the fire, for it was not unlike what he'd smelled before when he'd come across the burned-out hulls of peasant cottages. He moved closer, drawn by the strange odor, and he could see now what smoldered in the brazier—it was human hair. Bright, coppery human hair, so hastily dumped that it overflowed the metal grate and spilled onto the floor, lay in a heap beside the fire pit. One hand still on his sword hilt, he leaned over to lift a handful of it. It was long—more than an ell, he guessed—and as red as any he'd ever seen. He let the strands slide like so much silk through his bloodstained fingers before bending to retrieve a lock and tuck it into the purse that dangled from his belt. As he straightened, he thought he noted movement behind the faded arras that hung at one end of the long room.

"Who goes there?" he demanded loudly, raising his sword again.

His voice and his footsteps echoed eerily in the open room as he advanced on the tapestry. Pulling it aside, he discovered the sleeping area beyond, also empty. Mother Mary, but he could not like the feel of the place. The wind from the storm outside whistled through two narrow high windows, blowing the heavy material beside him. With his free hand he signed the Cross over his breast before exploring the doorway that led to a narrow passage, probably to the kitchens, he supposed.

"Jesu," he muttered under his breath. From the courtyard he could hear Everard demanding answers of Beaumaule's men, but inside, it appeared the castle was deserted. The smell of the burning hair lessened in the passageway, replaced with that of baking bread. Reassured somewhat by the change, he eased his tall frame, stooping to clear the doorway, into the narrow hallway.

3

Gilliane waited in the scullery, not knowing how her ruse had fared. The shouts in the courtyard seemed far away as she strained to hear anything, to gain some sign that Brevise had been taken—or, failing that, that he had fled. Heavy, booted footsteps sounded outside the kitchen door, sending a tremor of apprehension through her body, tightening the knot that gripped her insides. She pulled her hood forward and bent her head low over the pot she stirred. And under her boy's tunic, her heart thudded painfully, almost drowning out her swift, silent prayer.

The door burst open, admitting a stranger, and Gilliane knew fear. It was as though in one brief moment everything stood still. A complete hush descended over the kitchen as the tall, scowling knight stepped in, bringing a sudden chill with him.

"Do not move—any of you," he ordered harshly, his dark eyes scanning the wide stone-walled room warily.

For answer, the cook, a stout florid woman, turned to face him, while a scullery wench continued to chop onions on a board and two spit boys turned meat over a fire. Their faces flushed from the heat and shiny from the grease, they stared apprehensively at the armed man who loomed over them with his sword in his hand.

And then Richard noted the boy who sat at the steaming pot. Despite the warmth of the kitchen, the boy's hood fell forward, the coarse wool shadowing all but the lower part of his soot-streaked face. But the hands that ceaselessly, rhythmically stirred the thick stew were strangely clean and white.

"I'd have food for thirty men," he announced as he advanced into the kitchen, sheathing his sword. "And I'd have the fire tended in the hall—my men are nigh frozen." He walked slowly, deliberately toward where the iron caldron bubbled over the fire, and as he stopped there, he thought he could hear a sharp, collective intake of breath that seemed to come from every peasant there. The spit boys ceased their endless turning, and the scullery girl was suddenly very still. But the boy he faced still stirred with an even, deliberate motion, ignoring his presence.

"How are you called?" he demanded.

Gilliane's heart jumped in her chest, beating against her ribs painfully as she kept her eyes averted. To hide the terrible fear that stabbed at her chest, she dipped the heavy wooden spoon to scrape the scorched bottom of the caldron before daring to answer, "Erman."

"Stand up, Erman, that I may see you."

"Nay." The instant the word escaped her, she knew she'd made a mistake. Out of the corner of her eye she saw the knight's jaw harden and his dark eyes flash ominously above the nasal of his helmet.

Richard's free hand snaked out to grasp the coarse wool of her hood, yanking it forcefully, pulling her to her feet. She stumbled, nearly falling into the pot, and the rough material which had been merely wrapped and hastily secured with a rope gave way, suddenly baring her. "You forget your manners, Erman—scullery boys do not gainsay their betters," he growled—and then saw she was not a boy at all. "Holy Mary!" he breathed as he looked at her bared white breasts, and his jaw hung agape. Her face flushed a dull red beneath her cropped red hair as he stood transfixed for the moment.

Furious at discovery, she took advantage of his

surprise by flinging a full spoon of hot stew at his face. He turned his head, and the gravy spattered harmlessly against his helmet, while the vegetables dripped down onto his bloodstained cloak. He recovered, reaching for her again, swiping at her over the steaming pot.

"God's bones, but you would scald me!"

Instead of backing away, she grasped the hot vessel by the serving rings, burning her hands, and threw its contents at him. As he raised his mailed arm to shield his face, she dodged beneath him and ran, clutching Erman's poor tunic about her.

The fiery mess scalded the flesh on the back of his hands and clung to the links in his mail before slowly sliding down his ruined mantle. Through his burning fingers he saw her take the stairs behind the kitchen, and, still wiping the hot mess off him, he started after her, the fury in his face sending the others scurrying out of his way.

Seeking refuge in the storeroom, thinking to hide among the foodstuffs stored there, Gilliane crouched beneath a row of barrels containing salted meat and tried to relap the rough wool across her breasts. Praying silently that he would not find her, she held her breath and waited. Her worst fears had been realized—Beaumaule had been taken and they were at the mercy of Brevise's men. Aubery would fall into the hands of her brother's murderer, and she . . . She dared not think what might happen to her. She willed herself to remain very still as the invader's footsteps neared her. A rat, disturbed by her presence, skittered past her so close that she felt it brush against the tattered tunic.

It was dark and dank in the storeroom, and Richard was at a disadvantage from a lack of familiarity with the place. He stood for a moment, letting his eyes adjust to the darkness, and then he walked slowly, keeping his body between the stores and what he suspected was the only exit.

"You'd best come out before my patience is at an end," he called out in the darkness.

She flattened herself against the floor and held her breath at the sound of his spurs clinking as he walked. His heavy boots crunched on spilled grain, moving with deliberation, drawing closer. To her horror, it appeared that he meant to walk behind the barrels.

He edged along the standing casks until his spur caught in something. Bending over in the darkness, he felt along the ground until he touched the coarse woolen cloth. It moved in his hand as she shrank further back.

"I'd see the rest of you, I think," he murmured, knowing he'd caught her.

But as his hand grasped the hem of the tunic, Gilliane sank her teeth into the soft web between his thumb and forefinger, biting until she tasted the salt of his blood. "God's bones!" he gasped from pain. "Art a vicious witch!" Groping for what was left of her hair, he found it in the dark and pulled hard. " 'Tis enough of this, I'll warrant."

Tears welled involuntarily in her eyes, but she kept her teeth embedded in his flesh. Furious, he released her hair to deliver a resounding slap to the side of her head, and as she cried out, he disengaged his bleeding hand. Jerking her upward, he pulled her toward the slit of light that illuminated the stairway.

"Wait!" She tried to wrench free, but found she could not. Her stomach knotted with fear, she nonetheless managed to dig in her soft slippers against the packed earth floor, slowing him. "I . . . I claim the protection of the Crown!" she spat out defiantly. "You dare not ravish me!"

"There's none to wear the crown," he gibed scornfully. "And I'd sooner beat you!" He half-turned to look down at her, his contempt evident on his face as his eyes traveled from her cropped hair to where the woolen cloth pulled tight over her breasts. "Though you'd be comely enough if you were cleaned," he decided as his eyes raked her in the faint light.

"Beast!"

"Beast?" His black eyebrow rose, disappearing behind his helmet. " 'Tis you who have the fangs!"

"If you think to lay your great bloody hands on me, I'll—"

Shaking her until her neck nearly snapped, Richard tightened his jaw in an effort to control his already short temper. "I've borne enough of this!" he snarled. "If you would not tempt me to violence, you'll hold your tongue, girl! 'Tis not I who have burnt and bitten you." With that, he wrenched her in front of him and gave her a push up the steps.

"What do you think to do with me?" she choked out, still fearing the worst.

Ignoring the question, he kept a tight grip on her elbow, steering her ahead of him. She tried to look back up at him as they emerged again into the kitchen, but all she could see was his mailed arm where the soiled cloak fell away. When he relaxed his fingers slightly, she twisted to turn around. She lifted her eyes slowly, noting his red-and-black embroidered surcoat, the heavy gold clasp at his shoulder, and the polished nasal of his helm that extended over his nose, dividing his face into two equal parts above a firm, clean-shaven chin and a well-formed mouth. The fleeting thought that she might be in the hands of Brevise himself crossed her mind. The dark eyes that met hers were distinctly unfriendly.

"I claim protection of Beaumaule's liege—I claim protection of the Earl of Gloucester," she managed finally through suddenly parched lips. "Nay, you would not dare harm me."

"Think you Gloucester would have a care for one wench?" he taunted back. "You overvalue yourself then, for the earl attends more important matters now." Gripping her elbow again, he pushed her past the staring kitchen servants. "And I'd have justice ere I think on you."

He walked quickly, still forcing her ahead of him as they traversed the length of Beaumaule's deserted hall. And each time she attempted to stop or pull away, he wrenched her shoulder painfully and gave her a shove that threatened to send her sprawling. Knowing herself in the hands of an angered enemy, she bit her lip to stifle the cry of pain. If the fellow thought to see her cower before him, he was doomed to disappointment. Nay, but she'd not give him that satisfaction at least—he might take de Lacey land, but he'd not destroy her pride.

A strong gust of icy wind swirled about them as he thrust her through the door and into the courtyard. Abruptly he released her, flinging her to the ground in front of him. She grasped at a horse rail for support and pulled herself up. "I will tend to you later," he promised grimly.

The harshness in his voice foretold a fate that sent another shiver down her spine. Nay, but she'd not die tamely, ravished by this giant of a man. She scrambled after him, catching him by the arm, and as he spun around, she raked his face with her fingernails, clawing at him, kicking at him with her soft leather shoes. It was like attacking a tree. He brought up his elbow to shield his face, and caught her hair with his free hand, pulling her head back with such force that she thought he'd snapped her neck. His eyes glittered darkly as he forced her to look at him. " 'Tis enough of this, I said." Slowly, deliberately, he raised his open palm and brought it across her face with such force that she fell in a heap at his feet.

Tears of pain and anger welled in her eyes, but she would not let him know how badly he'd hurt her. She stared mutely at the man who towered over her, his hand still raised as though to strike. For a long moment their eyes met, and then he dropped his hand.

"I am unused to the attacks of scullery wenches," he muttered. He reached to touch the exposed portion of his cheek and then held out his fingers to look at them. "Twice this day you have drawn my blood, girl—God's bones, but you would tempt me to violence."

"You will kill me anyway," she answered evenly. "And I'd not die tamely."

His gaze dropped lower to where her breasts still heaved from exertion, and a slight smile quirked the corners of his mouth. "Nay—'twould be a waste to kill you." He watched her blanch and nodded. "Aye—to the victor comes everything, does it not?"

"I'd kill you first."

"My lord, there's naught but these and some wounded. And, by the looks of it, Walter's arm is broken from his fall." Everard strode toward them, his face stiff and ruddy from the cold. "Jesu, but what happened to you?" he asked, stopping short at the sight of Richard's soiled cloak and his bleeding face.

Gesturing at the rising Gilliane with his thumb, Richard muttered succinctly, "I found a she-wolf in there."

"Were there any others—or is this the only comely one? God's blood, but she does not look big enough to warm both our bones," Everard decided regretfully, peering more closely at the sullen girl. "Any more men inside?"

"Nay—naught but scullery, and few enough of them."

Everard's gaze reluctantly returned to his lord. "By the looks of the place, de Lacey does not prosper."

" 'Tis not so! If my brother had little, 'twas because my father left him little! My brother—" Gilliane started forward, bristling at the knight's tone.

"Hold your tongue. Jesu, but was there never woman born who did not speak too much?" Richard snapped at her. "I said I'd tend to you later."

Aware now of the interested looks cast her way by the mailed men who gathered before their leader, Gilliane bit back a sharp retort and hugged her arms to her, both to draw warmth in the icy rain and to cover herself. It was not unknown for castle wenches to be passed around amongst the victors when a place fell. Her own eyes searched the glistening yard for Simon of Woodstock, even as she knew in her heart that he could not aid her now. She shivered from both fear and cold.

The man she judged to be Brevise's captain jerked his head toward where the Beaumaule men had been herded. "What would you we did with them, my lord? That one is Woodstock—he says he is seneschal here."

"Nay, but you cannot—" Gilliane gasped, suddenly fearful for the men who'd defended Beaumaule.

"Silence!" Richard commanded without looking at her. "Nay, but afore God, I'd punish them all."

"Nay, but you—"

"God's bones!" Richard roared at her again. "Do I have to beat silence into you? Everard, if you cannot find de Lacey, bring me the captain—his head can hang over this cursed gate first if I like not his answers."

"My lord, de Lacey—" Everard began.

"Nay!" Gilliane cried out again.

Ignoring her, two men in red cloaks thrust Simon of Woodstock forward. Gilliane could see they'd bared his head, and for the first time in her memory she saw fear in his eyes. The lord who'd brought her out stepped forward to demand of him, "Who gave the order to fire on us—whose was this treachery?"

Simon's eyes dropped, but he did not hesitate to answer. " 'Twas I, my lord—as captain of Beaumaule, I gave the order."

"Simon!" Gilliane screeched.

"Then you hang."

The pronouncement was swift and succinct. Gilliane gaped first at one man and then the other as it sank in what Brevise's men meant to do to her captain. Stunned, she watched Woodstock exhale sharply.

"Nay! Nay! I'll not let you do it! Simon, tell him the fault was mine! Tell him!" She grasped the mailed arm of her captor, pulling it to draw his attention back to her. "You cannot! Nay, you must not—if any bears hanging here, 'tis I!" Panic choked her as she sought the means to stop him. "I . . . I gave the order to trick you, my lord!"

"Lady—nay!" Simon protested.

Swallowing hard under the tall lord's incredulous stare, Gilliane raised her eyes to his. "You killed my brother, Lord William," she managed, despite the awful sickness in her stomach. "I did but seek revenge for your treachery."

"Lady, 'tis not—nay, he is not Brevise," Simon sought again to explain, and then realized that she was not attending him.

But Richard's eyes were intent on the girl before him. "You mistake me—I am not William."

"Then you do his bidding," she spat back, unable to hide her hatred further. "You were well-served for the murder of my brother—our mistake was that we did not kill you!"

" 'Tis Rivaux," Simon interrupted again, this time more forcefully. " 'Twas a mistake we made."

"Rivaux?" For a moment Gilliane could not assimilate the full import of her captain's words, and then as she realized the enormity of their error, the color drained from her face. "This is *Rivaux*? Nay, it cannot be. Rivaux is older than—" She stopped, compelled by the sober expression in Woodstock's eyes. "Holy Mary . . . oh, Jesu!" The words formed slowly, silently, escaping involuntarily. She turned, her own eyes widening in horror as she stared into the dark, unfathomable depths of her captor's. And then she did the only thing that came to mind—she sank to her knees before him and bowed her head. "Had I know 'twas Rivaux who came, my lord, I would have prepared more suitable welcome," she whispered. "I pray you forgive us for our folly."

Richard stood over her, for once at a loss himself. His fury faded, cooled by the icy wind, as he stared down on the cropped red hair that bent to touch the sleet-covered ground. Clearly a mistake of some sort had been made, a mistake that had nearly cost him a boy he'd valued highly, but he could scarce execute a mere girl for it. The awful thought that she was a gentlewoman crossed his mind, shaming him.

"I am Richard of Rivaux," he admitted when he found his voice. "How are you called, Demoiselle?" he asked finally.

"I am Gilliane de Lacey, my lord."

"Sister to Geoffrey?"

"Aye."

She dared to raise her head above the hem of his mantle, where a piece of boiled onion still clung to the streaked and spotted cloth. "I . . . I will make you another cloak with mine own hands, my lord. You find us in disarray, unable to offer you the hospitality your rank commands, but—"

"Geoffrey is dead then?" It seemed impossible that the boy he'd remembered could have been murdered. "Sweet Jesu, but why did you not tell me earlier? Why did you not tell me in the kitchen?"

"I knew not who you were!" she snapped with asperity, remembering her earlier humiliation—and then she recalled whom she addressed. " 'Twas but yesterday that he died. I pray you will forgive me, but I—" The cold and the day's horrors were taking a toll on her nose, forcing her to sniff deeply since she had no rag. "Well, I can scarce believe him g-gone."

Her voice broke, effectively rendering even the last vestiges of his anger impotent, and he felt a surge of sympathy for her. Reaching a gentler hand to lift her by her elbow, he pulled her up to stand before him. "The sorrow is mine also, Demoiselle. Indeed, I'd not tarry but for the storm."

"Oh, nay—you must not think me inhospitable, my lord," she hastened to reassure him. "If you would share what there is, you are most welcome to stay until the weather clears. 'Tis just that—"

"I'd leave you gold to pay."

"Nay, I'd not take it. Geoff would not wish it."

Richard eyed her curiously now, much struck by her stubborn pride. And then he noted the already purpling bruise that darkened her cheek. "I am heartily sorry for this, Demoiselle."

"Aye." She felt suddenly shy and self-conscious before this man she'd only heard about from Geoffrey, this son of Guy of Rivaux. "The fault was mine also, my lord." And as she looked once again at his ruined mantle, she hung her head and murmured, "Alas, I regret that there will be no stew to sup."

4

The Beaumaule man worked patiently to start the fire in the brazier that was supposed to heat the lord's bedchamber, while Richard gazed down through the gap between the shutters of the small window in Beaumaule's single square tower. Still helmeted and in his full mail, he watched the smoke from the kitchen ovens waft horizontally against the pelting sleet and disappear eventually into the overall grayness of the air, and he wished he'd stayed in the warmth of the kitchen. It would be a while—if indeed ever—before the small chamber he'd been offered warmed. As it was, it was still so cold that he could see his breath before him in the room.

When he turned back, the fellow who'd toiled with the fire had managed to blow and coax the hot coals from the scullery into a small flame that licked valiantly at the broken tinder sticks. The bark on the logs above them sizzled and popped. As he looked around the sparsely furnished chamber that had belonged to Geoffrey de Lacey, he could not help contrasting it to that of his parents at Rivaux or even to his own chamber at Celesin. A pang of homesickness assailed him as he remembered the warmth and the luxury of what he'd left.

But he could not stay at Rivaux—he was too much his parents' son. He shared the tempers of the fiery Cat and Guy of Rivaux. Was it any wonder that he could not sit idly by, living the life of a rich young lord waiting for his father to die? The familiar guilt washed over him, the guilt of a man who was son to a strong and powerful sire. For twenty-three years he'd heard again and again how 'twas Guy of Rivaux who'd brought the infamous Belesme to justice, how he'd fought in Wales, how he'd wed Roger de Brione's daughter to become one of the richest, most powerful men in all of Normandy. Aye, and therein lay the strife between them—Guy would extend his power over his only son, bending him to his own will or breaking him.

Not that he himself was not equally stubborn. From the first day he'd been fostered with Robert of Gloucester, that long-ago day when he'd arrived as an eight-year-old boy at Robert's castle at Bristol, he'd been determined to make his own way, to gain royal favor on his own, to create his own wealth and power in England. So he had turned eagerly to the earl, the most powerful tenant-in-chief in the realm, learning the art of war while earning Gloucester's affection and approval. And to that end, he had been rather successful, for had he not enlisted the earl's aid in gaining his father's reluctant approval of Cicely of Lincoln for wife? Had he not forced the betrothal to the heiress? And if he were successful on Gloucester's behalf at Winchester, would he not have the new king's ear and his favor? King Robert— aye he liked the sound of it even. Nay, someday the bards would sing of *Richard* of Rivaux even as they sang of Guy now.

"My lord—" Gilliane de Lacey cleared the last step and stopped. "Oh. I did not think that you would still be armed . . . that is, I thought you'd be . . ." Her voice trailed off uncertainly as she noted the helm and mail.

He turned and saw her. "You thought to find me undressed, Demoiselle?" His eyes raked her, remembering what he'd seen in the kitchen, and he felt a surge of desire for her. To stall, to keep her there, he favored her with a smile. "And I thought you'd mislike me since—"

"Not once I discovered you were not Brevise." She held out the folded garments she carried. "I thought mayhap you needed a clean tunic, and Geoffrey had some warm woolen ones. But," she added quickly, suddenly afraid that she should have sent Alwina in her stead, "I can see they will not fit. I had not noted it earlier, but you are bigger than he was."

"By several stone."

Nonplussed by the presence of such a great lord, she stared at the rush mat on the floor, mumbling lamely, "If you will give over your cloak, I will see if I can remove the soil—when you are warmed, of course. You may send it down with Algar."

"I thought 'twas your promise to make me another."

Her eyes widened warily for a moment as she wondered if he ridiculed her, and then she contemplated the task. "Well, and I will, my lord, but 'twill take weeks to obtain the cloth even. Alas, we have naught so fine here."

" 'Tis of no matter—I can get another in London."

"Oh, no! That is, 'twas I who ruined it, after all," she admitted honestly. "And 'tis the least I can attempt for amends." Moving closer now to study the ruined garment, she noted the richness of it and shook her head. "But I cannot obtain the vair, my lord—'twill have to be rabbit."

She was so solemn, this girl who faced him offering her humble substitute for what she'd damaged. He took in the plainness of her bright blue woolen gown, its simple lines devoid of the gaudy embroidery and trim that one expected of a girl of noble birth, and he felt an unexpected surge of sympathy for her. As a de Lacey, she deserved better and probably had no hope of getting it. Glancing down at the jeweled embroidery that outlined the black hawk of Rivaux across the front of his tunic and then back to her face, he matched her soberness. "Nay—spend your gold on yourself."

She'd followed his gaze from her gown to his chest and she mistook his meaning. For a moment her temper flared and her eyes flashed. "I assure your lordship that you need not be ashamed of my work! I am thought to sew a fine hand! And . . . and even if you do not want it, 'tis my honor that makes me replace the cloak! Until then, you may wear Geoffrey's! I am not so poor that I . . . that I—"

"Lady Gilliane, I did not accuse you of poverty," he interrupted. "You mistake the matter. I fostered with your brother in Gloucester's household. Indeed, if there is aught that you need—"

"Beaumaule supplies our needs," she snapped, and then collecting herself, realized how she must sound. "Your pardon, my lord—'tis my accursed tongue."

"I would that you learned to curb it better ere you are beaten for it." He moved closer, and for a moment she feared he meant to strike her, but then his expression softened somewhat as a faint smile played on his lips. "Nay—I'd cry peace with you."

There was something in his dark, flecked eyes that made her uneasy—as though she had more to fear from the warmth than from the coldness there. "Nay, but you cannot understand," she whispered hollowly. Clasping her hands together before her, she turned to the window. For a time, she stared, not seeing the ice-glazed grass or the rough cobblestones in the courtyard. "Nay, you cannot understand, Richard of Rivaux." Her voice low with suppressed emotion, she added bitterly, "You cannot know what it is to lose all you have come to love. My brother lies dead in the chapel, his wounds so terrible that even his death mask cries out for vengeance, dead by the hand of William of Brevise, killed by greed over this small, hilly piece of land, simply because it stands in the midst of Brevise's estates." Her shoulders shook slightly before she managed to compose herself. "And Geoffrey's heir is but a minor, a boy of but eleven years, a boy lacking in both the temperament and the ability of fight for what is his. Jesu, but I would that I were a man!" she finished forcefully.

"Aubery will be taken under wardship until he is

able to rule Beaumaule," he murmured, coming up behind her.

A harsh, derisive laugh escaped her. "And who names his guardian? Stephen of Blois? My brother's murderer is Stephen's man! Nay, willy or nilly, William of Brevise will have Beaumaule, my lord, and my last brother will perish in his care." Her back still to him, she supported herself against the wooden window casing. "Once we were eight—three daughters and five sons born to two wives of my father. Hugh was the eldest—he died of a fever when I was yet small. Humphrey fell fighting for his king in Wales, and Esmond drowned crossing a flooded ford—I think 'twas that that killed my father—but no matter," she digressed with a sigh. "My sister Ela died birthing her lord's babe when she was but fourteen, and Alys lives in Provence with a husband who values her not. So now there are but Aubery and myself left to care about Beaumaule. Truly we have offended God, my lord, but I know not how."

"Nay." The rush of desire he'd felt earlier faded as he tried to discover some words of comfort. "God does not punish men like Geoffrey, Lady Gilliane," he said quietly.

"Then *why*? Why must my brother fall and a man like Brevise live?" Her voice rose and broke.

"I know not. My sisters and I all live, and I cannot say we are any more pious than another—less, more like." A helpless silence descended between them, hanging like a curtain wefted of the warm, smoky air that now emanated from the brazier, spreading through the chilly chamber before wending upward to the small chimney hole. Out of the corner of his eye Richard could see that the Beaumaule man had departed. Walking to stretch his hands toward the fire, he motioned to her, speaking finally. "Come warm yourself, Demoiselle, and speak with me whilst I divest myself." Unclasping his soiled cloak at last, he flung it into a pile in the corner.

"I thought great lords had body servants for that."

She mastered her sniffles, ashamed suddenly that he must think her weak. Trying to show him a calm that she did not feel, she wiped her damp cheeks with the back of her hand and turned around, managing a small, twisted smile. "You must think me a poor chatelaine, my lord, when I can but weep and complain. If you would sit before the fire, I would take your helm."

But he'd already loosened the helmet, working it upward with an effort until it came off to reveal the mailed coif beneath. She hastened to take it from him, setting it down on a table nearby. Always fascinated with the trappings of war, she turned to watch him work the hooks at his neck.

"I could aid you—I have watched Geoffrey divested of his armor," she offered, despite the awkwardness that had sprung between them with her tears.

"Aye, and my fingers are so cold they are clumsy."

"Sit you down then, that I may reach you." Even as she spoke, she moved closer, and he dropped his tall frame to one of the two crude benches drawn before the fire. Looking at the broadness of his shoulders, she could see he was a big man, one whose size was not much augmented by the heavy garments he wore. Leaning over his shoulder, she deftly unhooked the seven hooks that fitted the metal coif to his neck. He reached to push it back from his head until it came loose, revealing the padded leather cap that cushioned blows. With a quick upward motion from his hands, that too gave way, exposing thick, glossy black hair beneath. He leaned back, craning his neck to look at her, and her breath caught in her chest with the realization of his extraordinary handsomeness. Stunned, she could only stare—she'd not expected such wealth and looks in the same man. He was possessed of the most arresting face she'd ever seen. Despite the deep lines imprinted by his coif along the edges of his face and by the nasal over his cheeks, he was truly beautiful. Of all Geoffrey had

ever said of Richard of Rivaux, he'd failed to tell
that. The eyes that met hers now, no longer shadowed by the helmet nasal, were a rich brown, warmed
strangely by faint flecks of gold that deepened as
they radiated from the pupils until they disappeared
in an almost black ring at the edge of the irises.

"God's blood, but your stare disconcerts me, Demoiselle," he muttered, looking away.

Startled to her senses, she colored as the blood
diffused hotly through her cheeks and her pulse
pounded in her temples. She stepped around to face
him and waited for him to raise his arms, which he
did without prompting. She hesitated, embarrassed
by her own foolishness and self-conscious at the
thought of undressing her first stranger, but then
she reminded herself that true chatelaines even bathed
their guests. Pretending she'd done it dozens of times,
she grasped the edge of his embroidered surcoat
and pulled it upward. It caught briefly under his
chin and then came over his head, ruffling the black
hair. He reached up to smooth the thick, straight
fringe back from his face, while she folded the richly
embroidered garment before her and laid it aside.

The flickering yellows and reds of the popping
fire reflected in the gleaming steel links of his mail
shirt. Unlike Geoffrey's, it was new and unmended.
But then, she supposed that if one were heir to Rivaux,
Harlowe, and numerous lesser possessions, one could
buy anything, even the best armor. In all of her
nineteen years, she could not remember ever being
in the presence of any as rich or powerful as he.

"Start at the neck," he advised, leaning forward to
rest his elbows on his mailed thighs.

She considered leaning over to reach him and
realized that his head would be thrust into her breasts.
"Nay. You will have to sit up, else I cannot do it," she
murmured, her face flaming anew at the thought.

At that moment, he looked forward, directly into
the rounded mounds beneath her simple gown, and
desire coursed through him, warming his blood, re-

minding him how long it had been since he'd had a woman. As her hands touched him again, he looked up at her through a veil of dark lashes half-lowered to conceal his thoughts. She was taller and fairer-skinned than his mother and sisters, and her hair, which must have been glorious before it was cut, now hung at her neck, brushing at her shoulders like a peasant boy's. It was bright like polished copper, a rich hue that brought out the deep, clear blue of her eyes. And while he would not go so far as to think her a true beauty, there was something infinitely pleasing about her. Again his thoughts strayed to how she'd looked when the wrapped tunic had parted. And then, reminding himself that she was more than a castle wench, he straightened his back. "Oh, aye," he managed through suddenly dry lips. Silently, his rational mind shamed him for the thoughts that had sprung unbidden to quicken his blood, and he forced himself to remember Geoffrey. Only a true lecher would seek to lie with a girl whose brother had just died.

Her fingers were cold, nearly as cold as his own, where they brushed against the plane of his cheek, seeking the fastenings of the mail shirt, but they heated his blood where they touched him. There was a hesitation, a tentativeness that made him wonder if he were the first man she'd ever undressed. "Art betrothed?" he asked curiously, revealing he'd been thinking of her.

"Nay."

" 'Tis a pity you are not."

Her fingers stilled and her body stiffened in front of him. While she had often reflected in much the same vein, going so far as to dream of a strong, handsome husband sometimes, she had no wish for this stranger's pity in the matter. "My brother let me refuse a match, my lord—he did not wish to marry me where I would not."

"Art dowered?"

"Nay." She unhooked one of the fastenings before

adding defensively, "The crops were poor these three years past, and there was no money. King Henry took much of our land when he said my sister Ela was wed without his consent."

"And yet your sisters wed, Demoiselle," he persisted. "How is it that the younger girls were given husbands first? I'd think 'twas the eldest who should have whatever dowry there is."

To him, it was perhaps pleasant discourse, or mayhap but idle curiosity, but he'd touched on something painful to her. Keeping her voice even and toneless, she unworked another hook as she answered, "Mayhap they were comelier than I—or mayhap my brother liked his comfort and was not inclined that I should wed."

"There is nothing uncomely about you."

His words, spoken low, sent a rush of warmth through her whole body, threatening her already shaky composure. "My lord of Rivaux, I have no wish to speak of this," she retorted, hiding her pleasure that he found her appearance pleasing. "If you would have me divest you, you will not ask of my marriage or lack of it."

"Your pardon, Demoiselle. I did not mean to pain you," he apologized hastily. " 'Twas but curiosity that prompted me to ask."

"Aye, and if you think me vexed that I have no husband to beat me or to use me like a breeding sow, you mistake the matter," she retorted tartly, ignoring his attempt at amends. "There—you are undone." She stepped back and waited for him to lift off the heavy shirt.

He stood to disencumber himself from his steel casing, peeling the soiled links away from the stiffened leather garment beneath. The distinctly male odor of oiled metal and leather wafted past her nose, prompting another look at him. Her gaze flitted to his face, taking in the high cheekbones, the slightly hawkish nose, the dark eyes that seemed to mock her predicament, and she had to force herself to look away. Her next words slipped out unbidden.

"And you, my lord—art wed?"

"Nay."

" 'Tis a pity you are not, then," she mimicked to hide her embarrassment. "For you have not my excuse, I'll warrant—'tis well-known that you are heir to much."

"Aye, but my father was not eager to ally himself with anyone," he admitted candidly. " 'Twas I who pushed the matter, Demoiselle. I found mine own heiress, and am betrothed to Lincoln's daughter."

"And King Henry allowed it?" she asked incredulously, somehow disappointed that this man was already taken. "Nay, but I thought he wanted none to rival his power. It surprises me that he would risk adding Lincoln to Rivaux and Harlowe. 'Twill make you as rich as Gloucester and Stephen one day."

"I had Gloucester's aid in the matter." He dropped back to the bench and leaned back. "Are you not going to unlace me?"

"Nay."

His dark, flecked eyes gleamed wickedly as he openly grinned at her now, favoring her with a slow, lazy look that seemed to mock her. "What—now that you find me betrothed, you cannot bring yourself to minister to me?"

" 'Tis no matter to me whether you are wed or betrothed," she retorted stiffly. "I did but ask to serve you from the same cup—'twas you who pried in my affairs first."

His grin faded at the tartness in her voice, and he sobered. "I wished to know how Geoffrey left you, Demoiselle—whether I should ask Gloucester to intercede on your behalf, or if you had a husband to hold for you."

Unmollified by the change in his mien, she snapped, "There is naught to hold but this—this keep at least is Aubery's."

"Aye, but he can seek wardship over you and your brother," he reminded her.

"From Stephen? You jest, my lord."

"Stephen is not king yet."

"Nay, but he will be," she muttered bitterly. "Do you think the baronage will remember their oaths to uphold a mere woman? Nay, they will not—they cannot wait to offer King Henry's crown elsewhere."

"The Empress is no mere woman, Demoiselle," he answered dryly, "and there is more than Mathilda to stand in Stephen's way."

"Gloucester?" she asked with a faint lift of one eyebrow.

"He is one."

"Aye—Geoffrey died because he would declare for Robert of Gloucester," she acknowledged bitterly.

He nodded. "As king, Robert would be kind to your family."

"He swore to the Empress! Jesu, but you are like Geoffrey, my lord, if you would follow a forsworn liege! Nay, but the Empress Mathilda has the right!" she declared passionately. "Nay, even though Geoffrey believed him an honorable man—loved him for it—I find it curious that Gloucester's honor lets him forget his sister."

"Demoiselle, 'tis beyond his hands now," Richard protested, stung by her attack on the man who'd fostered him. "Aye, if the Curia should choose him, he could scarce refuse, could he? And the Empress is not well-liked, after all."

"Bah! He still swore to her. If you persist in his ambition, you will cause bitter war in this land, my lord."

"Nay—we stop it. More than half the baronage hates the Empress for her overweening arrogance, lady, and they will not follow her. And while Stephen wants a crown, he lacks the wisdom to rule." He leaned back to watch her, and his irritation faded, replaced by a faint smile that lifted the corners of his mouth appealingly. "But I'd not tax you with what you cannot understand, Demoiselle. Just now, I am more concerned with food and warmth."

"What I cannot—" She gaped in astonishment at the effrontery in his words, and then caught the mischievous glint in his eyes as his smile broadened to a grin. "Sweet Mary, but you mock me again."

"Mayhap," he admitted. "Art quick to temper, Demoiselle, when I mean no real harm. As son to the Cat, I know a woman's worth."

"The Cat?"

"My mother—Catherine of the Condes. No man dares meet her and think a woman weak or foolish. Nay, but both she and my grandmother Eleanor are strong of will, Lady Gilliane."

"And wed to men who keep their oaths, I'll warrant. If I have heard aught else of Guy of Rivaux and Roger de Brione, 'tis that they are honorable, truthful men, my lord."

He sobered at the tone in her voice, and his eyes grew hard. "I did not swear to Henry's daughter, Demoiselle—I was in Normandy when the English barons swore and in England when 'twas Normandy's turn."

"Oh." She was conscious of a desire to placate him, this powerful noble who sat before her. " 'Tis no concern of mine," she conceded. "I am naught to any of them—'twill make no difference to Beaumaule whether 'tis Stephen or the Empress or Gloucester even who rules England—we will be the victims in any event." Sighing, she leaned over him and began to unlace his leather shirt.

She was so close he could smell the faintly sweet and slightly musty odor of dried roses that emanated from her clothing. Either she wore a sachet bag between her breasts or she had packed her gown in the dried petals to gain the scent. Where her wide sleeve fell away from her wrist, he could see she was fine-boned for a tall girl, and her fingers were white and slender. He closed his eyes and remembered the full white breasts he'd seen in the kitchen, and desire washed over him again.

"Scratch my head, I pray you," he murmured.

"Art full of lice?" she asked curiously, wondering if she should get the grease to smother them.

"Nay—'tis but where the coif fit tightly."

Her hands left the leather laces to touch the black hair, gingerly at first. It was thick and heavy—had it been long like a woman's, it would have taken a day to dry it. But it was neither greasy nor smelly, and its glossiness shone in the firelight. She slid her fingers through it, working along his scalp, feeling strangely drawn by the unseemly intimacy of touching him, of feeling the warmth of his skin beneath hers. He was so vital, so alive, so near that it felt almost sinful to stand there, to feel his breath against her arm. And yet she was loath to move away.

He opened his eyes to watch her, enjoying the feel of her hands on his head. There was something infinitely pleasant about her touch, something intensely intimate. His renewed desire made him bold.

"You do not have to look to Stephen for protection."

He spoke quietly, but his words penetrated her momentary reverie as though he'd shouted. She froze, her hand still in his hair, and cautiously looked down into his now intent gaze.

"Aye—nor Gloucester even," he added softly.

A knot formed in her stomach as she feared what he would say, but she willed her tongue to silence and waited to hear it. Without a dowry, she was unmarriageable, and therefore more like to get offers she did not want. But the pleasure she'd had in this man's company had fled, replaced by the sickness she felt.

"I'd take you under my protection," he found himself saying to her. "You'd want for nothing." His hand reached to clasp hers and pull it down from his head. His thumb stroked the smooth cup of her palm, sending a sudden, visible shudder through her. "Aye—there'd be none to gainsay me now, and later . . ." His voice dropped to a husky, coaxing whisper. "You behold before you a man able to give you anything—I'd see you wanted for naught," he repeated. "I can give you the silks and velvets that befit your station, Gilliane."

She jerked her hand away as though he'd burned it. Two red spots flamed in her cheeks, and her eyes flashed. "The station of a whore? Nay, but you cannot give me a marriage bed, can you? 'Tis shame you would offer me, Richard of Rivaux!" she spat at him. "Fie on you—I am as gently born as you are!" Turning on her heel, she marched from the room as stiffly as if she were the Empress herself.

He stared after her, aware he'd done the unpardonable. He opened his mouth to protest she'd misunderstood him, but he knew she hadn't. He wanted to call after her that he'd meant her no dishonor, but he'd be lying. But he'd not meant to be so precipitate about it—his passion for her had come upon him quickly, unbidden almost, and certainly without reflection. He lifted his hand as though to order her back, and then he dropped it, sighing. There was no denying he wanted her, but somehow the thought shamed him. Unlike the women he usually took to his bed, this one was neither a whore nor baseborn. This one was sister to a man who'd fostered at Gloucester's castle at Bristol with him. This was a girl he ought to protect. Resolutely he forced the heat from his body and resolved to offer Gilliane de Lacey no further insult. Aye, he'd seek her pardon when her temper cooled, and he'd bed a wench who knew what he was about. He'd think no more of the fiery-haired Gilliane who smelled so enticingly of dried roses.

Slowly he rose and finished unlacing his leather shirt, pulling it over his head and discarding it in a heap at his feet. The quilted wool gambeson underneath itched his skin, and he indulged in scratching where it had rubbed against his sides. He moved closer to the fire to heat his still-stiff arms, and he extended his hands over the blaze. The smoke curled around his fingers and wafted upward to the vent hole in the ceiling.

"My lord, we found the boy—we found young de Lacey."

"Where?" Richard did not turn around at the sound of his captain's voice, but continued to warm himself.

"In the stable loft. Had we been this Brevise, he'd have been cooked alive, no doubt." Everard stepped into the small chamber and pulled off his dripping helmet, setting it on a low table before he too sought the fire. "Jesu, but 'tis cold."

"Aye, but the ice stops, I think," Richard observed, looking up at the hole in the ceiling.

"But the wind does not. I gave orders that we billet in the common room below, and everyone was glad enough for the fire there."

"What did you do with the boy?"

"Gave him over to his sister just now—and to Woodstock. 'Tis certain he would beat him if he dared—he'd told the boy to hide beneath the bier in the chapel."

"God's bones, but young Aubery is a fool," Richard muttered, shaking his head. "Geoffrey should have fostered him ere now, for by my count he is old enough."

Everard shrugged expressively and hunched closer to the blaze. "Mayhap they were too poor to send him—by the looks of it, Beaumaule has not prospered —or mayhap 'tis because the boy has little taste for war. I had it of Woodstock that he's more suited to the Church than anything—he says the boy's not got one-tenth of the girl's spirit." Rubbing his hands to warm them over the flames, he added, "What think you will happen to them now? There's not much to be bled from this place, and I doubt that whoever is king will want the bother of it."

"Nay," Richard agreed readily, his mind turning once again to Gilliane. "And there'd be little quarrel if I took them under my protection, I'll warrant."

"Them?" Everard cocked his head sideways to stare quizzically at his lord. "Why would you wish such a thing? Beaumaule's naught to you either—naught but a small stinking pile of sticks and stones."

"Geoffrey de Lacey fostered with me—'twill not be remarked if I accept wardship of the girl and her brother," Richard mused almost to himself, making up his mind with a suddenness that startled even him. "Aye—I mean to do it."

"You scarce knew de Lacey!" Everard protested. "And if you take wardship, you will have to protect this place. Sweet Jesu, my lord, but we have not the men to leave here now."

But Richard's enthusiasm warmed for the newly formed idea as he continued to consider it. "I'd have Woodstock raise my pennon above—not even William of Brevise dares the wrath of Rivaux."

Everard stared, uncertain as to whether his lord jested, and then, perceiving that Richard was indeed serious, he sought to dissuade him further. "With Stephen king, 'twill make him bold. Nay, I'd not do it—'tis too distant from any lands of yours, and—"

"Stephen is not crowned yet!" Richard retorted sharply, unwilling even to admit the likelihood of its happening. "Nay, but I'd see Theobald rule me ere I'd swear to Stephen, and that's not to say he's any more like to best Gloucester in the matter."

He spoke so emphatically that his captain hesitated, still doubting Richard's motives in the matter, and then shook his head. "But ..." He paused, eyeing his young lord warily, and then blurted out, "'Tisn't as though you know the whole, is it? The girl and her brother may have a kinsman to stand for them."

"Nay. My mind is set in the matter," Richard announced flatly, ending any further thought of protest. "And now, Everard, I'd have you tell Lady Gilliane that I'd have a bath."

"You'll die from lung fever." But there was no mistaking the impatient set of the younger Rivaux's jaw—it reminded Everard too much of Count Guy's to brook further complaint. Sighing, he capitulated. "Aye, I'll tell her, but she will think you mad."

After his man left, Richard paced before the fire, waiting for her, composing his apology for his lapse. His offer of protection was genuine, he'd tell her, and was made with chivalry. It was his regard for Geoffrey de Lacey that had made him speak, and she must not think he meant any dishonor. But she could not remain at Beaumaule—the place was too unprotected for her safety. Aye, that's what he would say to her. And in time . . . well, it was not as though she had hope of any other, he rationalized.

It seemed like time crawled while he waited for her return. The smaller logs in the brazier burned through, letting the larger ones fall with a rumble and a bump. He picked up the iron rod and poked the pieces back into the fire, then added two more logs to the top, hoping they'd catch soon. Jesu, but what kept the maid? Did she think to make Rivaux wait forever? The gleam of red hair trailing from beneath his discarded cloak caught his eye, and he walked to retrieve it, idly wondering what it would have looked like in its glory, streaming from her head, spilling onto his pillow. It gleamed like bright silk in his hand, its strands reflecting the firelight so richly that he thought again that it had been a travesty to cut it.

He spun around eagerly at the soft scuffing sound of a woman's footsteps on the stairs, and his pulse raced with desire. But the woman who entered the small chamber was neither red-haired nor young. "God's bones! Jesu!" he muttered under his breath before allowing himself to address the old woman. "I sent to the Lady Gilliane."

"Aye, and Old Alwina is come to tend your lordship at your bath."

"By whose authority? Did she send you to me?" he demanded.

"I did. Lady Gilliane attends Sir Geoffrey's bier in

the chapel, my lord." Simon of Woodstock stood behind her, one foot remaining on the winding stair, and spoke with an edge to his voice that brought Richard up short. Leaning against the doorway, the older man met Richard's eyes coldly. "She has but lost her brother," he reminded Rivaux.

The desire and anticipation cooled under that cold stare, replaced again by shame for what he would have of the girl. Turning back to the fire, he muttered tersely, "You exceed your authority, Simon of Woodstock."

"I guard Beaumaule and its people—as I am sworn to do, my lord."

"Do you hold lands of de Lacey? Is Beaumaule patrimony to your overlord?" Richard demanded, knowing full well that it was unlikely that the small fief could in turn enfief another.

"Nay."

"Then your oath died with Geoffrey, did it not? You were bound to serve the man rather than the land. Nay, but you will tell the Demoiselle that I am taking wardship over her and Lord Aubery until such time as the king deems it meet that they go elsewhere. If you would stay here, you answer to me now."

The muscles in Simon's jaw worked, and temper flared in his eyes for a moment before he recalled himself. As a landless knight, a mercenary, he had no claim to either Beaumaule or its people. And there was naught to be gained by disputing the authority of Guy of Rivaux's son, but he could not quite hold his tongue. "By whose writ?" he managed to ask, knowing that a man like Rivaux needed none when there was no king to gainsay him.

"By right of conquest if any dares dispute it. I take Beaumaule, holding it forfeit for the injury to Walter of Thibeaux. Later I will return it to Geoffrey's heir."

"Nay, you cannot—you are not overlord here," Simon spat out.

Richard's eyebrow lifted at the unexpected challenge to his authority. "And who is to refuse me? An uncrowned king? You?"

Simon looked away, stung by the tone of Rivaux's voice. "Nay," he answered low.

"Think on it—Gloucester will stand for me." Richard walked to the doorway to face the older man. "You will fly the hawk of Rivaux over this keep, Simon of Woodstock."

"I'd not stay—my oath to Geoffrey de Lacey lies dead with him."

"You have my leave to seek service elsewhere, if 'tis your wish."

"Aye."

"So be it then. I go to Winchester as soon as the storm clears, but I mean to return this way. Until that time, I hold you responsible for the safety of Gilliane de Lacey and her brother."

Woodstock turned and started down the stairs, his heavy steps reflecting the anger he dared not vent openly. Above him, Richard turned away, wondering how Gilliane de Lacey would react to her captain's news.

5

*God aid your sweet soul, Geoffrey, and grant you peace in
His care. As you have died for naught, so must Brevise. I
will not rest, my brother, until he is dead. I will do anything, everything to see you avenged, Geoff.*

Gilliane knelt on the cold stone floor, her head
bowed and covered with her dead mother's sendal
veil, and tried vainly to compose words for the re-
pose of her brother's soul. But no matter what came
to mind, it was soon obscured by the bitter thoughts
of revenge, thoughts that tumbled, crowding all piety out. She was consumed by the helpless realization
that if Stephen became king—nay, *when* he became
king—he would surely protect his liegeman. Aye,
'twould be a small fine at most that Brevise paid for
her brother's death. Mayhap Geoffrey and Richard
of Rivaux were right—mayhap in Robert of Gloucester lay her greater hope of justice. And certainly
she'd never sworn to the Empress.

She drew her cloak closer and tried again to pray
over Geoff's body. In the chill, damp duskiness of
the chapel, there were but two of the precious wax
candles flickering, one at each end of the wooden
box, casting strange shadows on the embroidered
satin de chine that draped the catafalque on which
Geoffrey's bier rested.

Her reverie broken by the sound of bootsteps on
the stone, she hastily bent her head and signed the
Cross to again compose her mind for prayer. Her
heart thudded as he grew nearer. His walk was heavy,

deliberate, the sound reverberating through the emptiness of the chapel, sending a chill racing down her spine. Powerful both physically and politically, he gave her a sense of unease, frightening and fascinating her at the same time. Even in the duskiness of the room, he cast a long shadow over her as he came to stand behind her. Her heart caught painfully for a moment while he hesitated, and then he dropped to his knees beside her and leaned to rest his elbows against the chapel rail.

Stealing a covert glance through the softness of the tissue sendal, she could see that he'd closed his eyes and that his lips were moving in his own prayers. Strangely drawn by the almost echoing silence now, she cocked her head to study him again. The profile was fine and even, with firm, straight chin, nearly hawkish nose, and a forehead almost concealed by black hair that although combed still hung like black fringe above his dark eyes. Gone were the mail and the other trappings of a warrior, replaced by a heavy velvet tunic girded with a thick gold chain, and where the wide sleeves feel away from masculine wrists, the gold embroidery on his silk undertunic gleamed, catching the candlelight. He must be immensely wealthy to wear such clothes, wealthier than nine-tenths of the lords in England, she suspected, for not even the old king had dressed so finely when he'd passed by Beaumaule hunting. The Black Hawk of Rivaux, they called his father, an appellation that seemed equally well-suited to the son. Aye, he was as handsome as she'd first thought him. What had be called his mother? The Cat? Son to the Cat and the Hawk—sweet Jesu, 'twas small wonder Richard of Rivaux was such a man.

An ice-covered branch brushed against the small window as the wind came up again. She shivered anew, this time from the cold, tried yet again to turn her mind back to her prayers, forcing herself to realize that they would bury Geoffrey beneath the floor on the morrow. This time, her eyes sought to commit her brother's face to memory, and all thoughts of Rivaux left her mind as she considered the finality of the parting she faced. Deep melancholy descended, tightening the hollow ache in her breast. Slow tears trickled in rivulets down her cheeks and spotted her old cloak.

" 'Tis difficult to pray when the heart is empty," Richard of Rivaux murmured aloud beside her, revealing that he had been watching her also from beneath his lowered lids. " 'Tis easier to ask why than to accept it."

"Aye," she sighed in agreement. "Geoffrey was blameless." She looked up and her breath caught in her throat. Sweet Jesu, but mortal man ought not to look on one quite like that. The flecks seemed to have disappeared from his dark eyes, leaving them almost black, and the faint light played off the angles of his face, giving it a harsh strength. She averted her gaze, staring at the even pattern of the stones on the floor. "Aye," she sighed. "There can be no reason why Brevise lives and my brother dies, can there?"

"I do not know—the will of God, perhaps, but I would doubt it. 'Twas blind fortune, more like."

" 'Tis blasphemy to say that," she murmured.

"But 'tis something that you think also."

It was the truth—she could not deny that. Instead, she traced the polished wood of the rail with a fingertip. "I know not what to think, if you would have the truth of it. Sometimes I believe the de Laceys are truly accursed, and other times I believe we will prevail—that somehow Aubery will grow strong and regain what we have lost."

"Demoiselle . . ." He hesitated, his heart racing as hard as it had in his first calf-love, wondering if she would rail at him when he told her what he meant to do. "Demoiselle," he began again, "I ask your pardon for the offense I offered you. 'Twas not my intent to insult so much as to protect."

She felt as though her whole body had turned to stone, that all time stood still as she waited for what else he would say. Her fingers curled over the railing, holding it.

The girl gave him little encouragement. Sweet Mary, but he was not born to grovel before a woman. He sucked in his breath and tried again. "The storm has passed—I leave as soon as Geoffrey is interred on the morrow." Rising to stand above her, he looked one more time at her brother's bloodless face. And then he leaned to draw the sign of the Cross over him, intoning, "May God in His gentle mercy love and keep you forever and ever, in the name of the Father and the Son and the Holy Spirit. Amen."

When she looked up, he appeared to be a giant from where she knelt. Reluctantly her eyes traveled up the length of him to his seemingly impassive face. "Then I wish you Godspeed, my lord."

"Nay, but I return here within the fortnight." He had the satisfaction of seeing her eyes widen in surprise. Apparently Simon of Woodstock had not yet told her of his plans. "My mind is decided, Demoiselle—you and your brother are under my protection. You will return to Normandy with me."

"Sweet Mary—nay," she gasped. The words escaped her involuntarily, and she had to swallow hard to hide the panic she felt. "But *why*?"

Ignoring the question, he continued, "Aye, I leave your Simon of Woodstock here to hold the place under my banner in my absence. I doubt even Brevise will be so bold as to challenge Rivaux, and when it is known I have taken the boy for ward, he has naught to gain in besieging the place."

"But you cannot. You have not the right—"

"I have every right!" he snapped, irritated at her consternation over his news. "I won Beaumaule this day, Lady Gilliane."

"But Aubery—"

"I mean to hold it for him."

"But why must we leave—why must I go?" she protested, her voice little more than a whisper. Her heart seemed to have quit beating, held in abeyance for his answer.

"Your walls are timber, your keep too small to provision—think you that you could hold it against the likes of Brevise?" he countered, not answering her question directly.

"Nay, but—"

"And if that gown you are wearing is your best, you have my leave to bring it. You'll need naught else but your cloak. I'd buy you clothes more fitting your gentle birth, for I'd not have it said I mistreated you."

As her blue eyes widened and she sought to comprehend that he meant to wrest her from the only home she'd ever known, he turned aside, genuflecting slightly before the altar, signing the Cross again, this time over his own breast. His back to her, he added with unwarranted harshness, "Nay—I'd not hear it. We are late to sup."

She gaped after him, barely aware of the sound of his footsteps on the stone floor, and the blood drained momentarily from her face. Why would he do this? He'd asked her pardon for what he'd said earlier, but could she trust him? And even if she could, what made him think he had the right to declare himself Aubery's guardian—or hers? Two spots of high color rose in her cheeks, fired by her rising temper. Heedless of where she was, she gathered the long skirt of her gown in clenched fingers and ran after him.

"Nay! I'd not go! I'd stay at Beaumaule with Simon!"

He'd emerged into the deserted, ice-glazed courtyard, striding so rapidly away from her that he was nearly across it before she caught up to him. They were alone, save for the sound of his heavy boots cracking the layer of ice and the rattle of the tree limbs.

"Wait!" she shouted furiously.

The wind ceased in that moment, and the whole yard was suddenly silent when he turned back to her. She shivered, sending a puff of frosty breath

into the icy air. Pulling her cloak closer, wrapping
her arms against her breasts, she faced him. His eyes
seemed to rake her, and her arms tightened.

The gesture was not lost on him—it was one of
defense—and for some reason it angered him that
this girl would fight him. "Nay, I'd not harm you—
you are safer with me than with Woodstock," he
offered curtly.

"You cannot force me to go with you, my lord.
You are not my liege lord, and these are not your
lands." She tried to keep her voice from shaking
despite her anger and the bitter cold. "I shall remain
at Beaumaule with my people."

"Do not be a fool!" he retorted. "Would you go the
way of your brother? Would you fall into your enemies' hands for your overweening pride? *I* can hold
his patrimony for Aubery de Lacey—you cannot."

"You cannot just come here and impose your will—
surely. We are naught to you, my lord." Her whole
body now racked with shivers, she wished she'd caught
him inside the hall itself instead of in the open yard.
"Aye, and I'd not—" She stopped. She could not
very well accuse him of base motives when he had
but apologized, and besides, she had no wish to put
such thoughts into words again. "Nay, but you have
not the right," she finished lamely.

Her cheeks were ruddy with the cold, and the
wind had whipped her cloak and her veil back from
her incongruously short hair, but there was something that brought him a grudging admiration of
her, something beyond mere desire. His answering
scowl softened as he stared down into her flushed
face. "Do not be a fool, Demoiselle—I can protect
you and your brother, whereas Woodstock cannot."

"Sweet Mary, but will you not listen to me?" she
demanded in exasperation. "I said I would not go
with you! I am a gentle-born woman. You have not
the right—"

A wry smile lifted one side of his mouth. "Aye, I
will concede that you came more gently into this

world than I did, Demoiselle, for you speak to one born on a muddy riverbank, received into Robert of Belesme's bloody hands, and cut from my mother's cord by his sword."

"Holy Jesu!" she breathed, temporarily diverted. "And he let you live?"

The smile broadened. "As you can see, I am flesh and blood."

"But from all I have heard, he was the devil come to life—I mean, he was . . ." She recoiled visibly at the thought of the hated name of Belesme.

"Aye, he was, from all I have heard also, but he breathed his own breath into me, and for that I cannot curse his memory, however cruel he may have been." He watched her whole body shudder with revulsion. "But we tarry where 'tis cold, Demoiselle, and I have no mantle," he added pointedly. "Come, I'd not die of lung fever." He slipped his fingers beneath her elbow and guided her toward the hall.

She was acutely conscious of his hand, and even though his fingers were separated from her flesh by the layers of her clothing, she thought she could feel a warmth that could not be there. "Wait." She hung back for a moment, resisting the pressure on her arm. "You would not dishonor me?"

The eyes that searched his face were intent, beseeching and seeking her answer. For a moment he was torn between truth and falsehood, for he could not deny he meant to have her. He stared at her upturned, wind-reddened face and then looked away to where the icy tree branches raked the small chapel walls.

"I'd do naught with you that you did not will—you have the word of Rivaux for that."

"Then you'd let me stay here, my lord."

" 'Twas not what you asked just now, Demoiselle." His jaw tightened perceptibly. "Do not be clever with me, Gilliane de Lacey, giving one question and taking the answer for another. I mean to take you to my keep at Celesin for your safety."

There was no use arguing. Richard of Rivaux had the greater force and obviously he was accustomed to being obeyed in all things. Wordlessly she allowed him to draw her toward Beaumaule's single stone tower. At the doorway, he stepped before her and pulled the heavy iron ring. As the door groaned open, a gust of warm air carried the intermingled smells of smoke, food, musty rushes, and oiled leather past her. And across the sooty, rush-strewn hall, Simon of Woodstock looked up, frowning.

Reluctantly handing her cloak to Alwina, Gilliane pulled her veil back over what was left of her hair and moved to take her place on the small dais that oversaw the room. Her gaze traveled over the blackened walls critically, making her all too aware of how mean Beaumaule's hall must seem to a man like Rivaux. No doubt he was used to palaces and could not value her home at all. Look at him in all his finery, she told herself—his rich, deep red velvet tunic, with its wide sleeves bordered in costly vair, was worth more than Geoffrey's armor, and the blue silk undertunic, embroidered with gold thread and winking jewels at his wrists, would have bought clothes for Beaumaule's entire household for two years and more. Her eyes dropped to her own simple gown, and she felt as though she must appear to him as little more than a serving wench who would be treated as a lady.

It was as if he shared part of her thoughts, for he leaned from the seat beside her to murmur, "You will be pleased with Celesin, I think, Demoiselle—it lies well-situated above a pretty valley, and it has its own manor house within." Reaching to trace the edge of the plain sleeve of her overgown, he added, "And there are few to compare with the seamstresses there, for they are skilled in all manner of embroidery. Once you are made new clothes, you'll forget the harshness of your life here."

"Forget my birthplace? Nay, never," she retorted stiffly. "Beaumaule may be naught but a stinking pile to you, but we cannot everyone be born to wealth and power—what appears as poor to Rivaux is the reward given my great-grandsire for following the Old Conqueror into this land. Ere King Henry confiscated my brother's fields, we were rich in crops, and this keep, ancient even in Saxon times, once commanded the old coastal roads."

"Nay—have done, Gilliane. Art too quick to offense," he protested, reaching to touch an errant strand of copper hair.

"You may have the means to force me from here, my lord," she said harshly, turning away from his hand, "but Beaumaule is de Lacey land—and I will return to it."

"I would you had not cut it," he murmured, leaning closer, brushing the strand of hair back from her temple and tucking it beneath her veil. "Aye, I've never seen the like of the color."

But she was not to be so easily diverted. Instead she pulled further away from him and stared fixedly to where Simon of Woodstock sat. "Had you been any other, you'd not dare to do this to us, but I suppose the great son of Rivaux does as it pleases him," she observed woodenly.

He leaned back, but the flecks in his eyes were warm as he continued to gaze at her proud profile almost lazily, and then his mouth broke into a decidedly sensuous smile. "Always," he murmured. "Aye—always."

6

Richard brushed the melting snow from the hair that fell over his forehead and rubbed his hands together to warm them as he waited to be ushered into Henry of Blois's presence. It had been a cold ride from Beaumaule, and the fire in the antechamber was a welcome one. He was tired, so much so that Everard had urged him to seek his bed first and speak with the bishop on the morrow, but frustrated with the delays of weather and Gilliane de Lacey, Richard had chosen to seek the late audience. He paced restlessly, his eyes scanning the rich hangings that shut out the winter drafts and muffled the sound of the wind outside. Jesu, but the bishop's palace at Winchester reflected the occupant's love of luxury, Richard decided as he observed the exquisitely worked tapestries and the polished dark woods that lined the inner walls.

A sense of unease stole over him as his spurs clicked noisily, rhythmically against the hard stone floor. The good bishop was, after all, Stephen's brother, and therefore possibly dangerous. Not that blood meant everything, he reminded himself, for Henry of Blois had been known to quarrel with both of his powerful brothers. And he shared blood with Count Theobald also, that brother the Norman barons were already prepared to approach with England's crown. Nay, but if he could but persuade Henry to remain neutral, Richard considered it possible that he could sway the Curia Regis to support

Gloucester. England and Normandy needed the earl, needed a strong and capable soldier rather than either the affable Stephen or the high-handed Empress —aye, that was the argument—there was none more capable, none more respected than the old king's eldest bastard. As for Theobald, the danger from Anjou ought to be enough to keep him in his own lands. Aye, if only the good bishop could be made to see that . . . if only he could be brought to lend his support to Gloucester.

"This way, my lord."

He spun around to see a page in Winchester's colors waiting diffidently to escort him into the reception room. A cursory glance revealed the boy to be liveried in velvet and gold braid. Richard smiled to himself, thinking the churchman lived like a king in royal splendor. Aye, he could be bribed with gold if necessary.

He followed the boy, pausing in the doorway of the long chamber whilst the page announced importantly, "Richard of Rivaux, Lord of Celesin and Ancennes, warder of the royal keeps of Ramsey and Stanford."

For a moment Richard's palm sought the rounded pommel of his sword in a gesture he'd unconsciously learned from his father. Then, swinging his scabbard backward and out of his way, he stepped into the room. Owing to the lateness of the hour, the bishop was almost alone save for the page and a clerk, sitting in a chair before the fire. At the sound of Richard's boots on the flagged floor, he rose and moved forward to extend his hand.

Keeping his sword back with the pressure of his palm, Richard dropped to one knee to kiss the episcopal ring. Henry of Blois's fingers closed over his briefly, gesturing him to rise.

"You have the look of your father, my lord," he murmured, stepping back. "Art Rivaux in deeds as well as appearance also, from what I am told."

It was an encomium that should have made him

proud, but Richard was restive with being compared to his sire. The more he heard it, the more he wanted to shout, "There is but one Guy of Rivaux—'tis Richard you face," but he held his counsel and schooled his face to pleasantness. "You honor me."

Henry lifted the other beringed hand to beckon the page while addressing his guest. " 'Tis cold this night, my lord—I pray you join me for a cup of mulled wine." His black eyes were intent as he contemplated the younger man. "Aye, and you must tell me how 'tis I am to serve you."

"I would address the Curia—and I'd seek your aid."

The bishop's eyebrow lifted, betraying surprise, and then his eyes were veiled. "I see. 'Tis a matter of some import then." Turning briefly, he took a steaming cup from the boy and handed it to Richard. " 'Twill warm your blood, my lord."

"Aye." Richard sipped it and burned his lips.

Henry took another cup for himself and settled into a seat by the fire, gesturing to Richard to sit. His eyes narrowed shrewdly for a moment as the younger man sank into the seat opposite, and then he spoke with an uncharacteristic bluntness. "And how do you think the Curia can serve you where the king's council cannot? You came from Normandy, did you not? The lay barons meet even now, I am told."

"Aye, they meet to choose your brother Theobald in the Empress's stead."

"I see." Henry set aside his cup and pressed his fingertips together over his rounded stomach. "And your father would plead for the Empress—did he send you here? Can it be that he does not know the old king—may God have mercy on his soul—that he changed his mind ere he died?"

"Where had you that story?" Richard asked with a start, unprepared for the news.

"Hugh Bigod has sworn that he heard King Henry's last words at Lyons."

"Sweet Jesu—and were there any to believe him?"

"I believe him, my lord, for he swore before the Curia on the most sacred of relics that he spoke naught but the truth. Aye, there were few who chose to dispute him." Leaning forward, he reached to take another sip of the warm wine. "Your father is too late, if he would argue for the Empress."

"I do not come from my father, Excellency—nor from my grandsire of Harlowe. I would address the Curia as lord of Celesin and Ancennes."

"Norman lands," Henry reminded him silkily. "You cannot speak as an English lord before us."

It was clear that they played a game of cat's-paw between them. The bishop leaned forward, watching his guest warily, waiting. And there was something in those black eyes that made the neck hairs stand on the back of Richard's neck. He drained the fiery liquid in his own cup, letting it heat the path to his stomach, and then leaned back.

"Aye, but I hold English lands also—and you forget I have wardship of royal castles." As though to adjust it for his comfort, he grasped his pommel and shifted his sword in its scabbard, moving it against his leg.

It was a gesture reminiscent of Guy of Rivaux, one that reminded Henry of Blois that regardless of the extent of his land holdings, regardless of what he would in time inherit, the young man before him was already a power to consider. "Aye, 'tis your right, my lord—there's none to dispute that," he conceded quickly. "But if you are come to argue the succession, you are too late. We were met two days before and have offered the crown to my brother Stephen."

"Jesu!" The word escaped him involuntarily, but Richard recovered his composure on the instant. "And none disputed that?" he found himself asking almost casually.

"How could they?" Henry relaxed as his guest sat back, and he proceeded to tell the tale. "Aye, with Bigod swearing that the king repudiated the oath he made the baronage give the Empress, 'twas plain to all that another must be chosen quickly to prevent anarchy. And since Bigod clearly heard Stephen named with King Henry's blessing, there was naught else to be done."

"It was unanimous then?" Richard found himself asking with sinking stomach.

The bishop shrugged expressively. "When is a crown bestowed to everyone's satisfaction? Nay, but they could not quarrel when 'twas made known that Roger of Salisbury yielded my brother the keys to the treasury and King Henry's seal."

So the king's justiciar, his regent in his absence, had sided with Stephen. That was a circumstance that Richard had not foreseen. "The Empress will make war."

Again the older man shrugged. "Nay, but her husband of Anjou has little interest here."

"There is her son—there is yet another Henry."

"A babe of some two years." Henry dismissed the matter with a wave of a beringed hand. "Babes make poor kings, my lord, and there's not a man in either England or Normandy to want Geoffrey of Anjou for regent in the boy's stead." Henry of Blois gripped the arms of his chair and leaned forward again, confronting Richard with the thought. "Would you? Think on it—would you have the Angevin over you?"

"Nay."

Satisfied at Richard's easy capitulation on the matter, the bishop relaxed, unbending enough to explain further. "In the absence of the lay magnates, the Curia has but exercised its ancient right of choice, my lord, and we have chosen Stephen of Blois as rightful king. And all London has hailed him for sovereign, as there is no other with a better claim."

"There is Gloucester."

Henry's head snapped back, and his eyes glared at his guest for a moment. He shook his head as though the very idea offended him. "Earl Robert is a bastard," he pronounced firmly, "and therefore unable to succeed."

"William the Conqueror was bastard-born. And Robert of Gloucester carries his grandsire's blood as surely as I carry Rivaux's."

"Alas, but 'twas 1066 then, and the Church had not ruled on the matter. I doubt even Old William would be accepted in these times." Henry rose, signaling that the interview was at an end. "How long are you in England, my lord?" he asked abruptly. "My brother's coronation is at Westminster on the twenty-second—just before Christmas feast. He'd have the barons renew their feudal oaths then and when he keeps Easter feast, mayhap at Oxford."

"Nonetheless, it seems precipitate, Excellency," Richard murmured, rising also. "Aye, there will be those who will dispute Stephen's claim."

"Then why did they not present themselves before the Curia?" Henry snapped. "Why did not Gloucester himself come, if he would claim England's crown? And what of the Empress—what of Mathilda? Nay, but 'twas only Stephen who dared to come."

"Earl Robert executes King Henry's wishes, remaining at Lyons-la-Foret with his father's body."

"Then perhaps he does not truly wish to be king. But if 'tis Gloucester you favor . . . But if you are yet wishful of speaking before the Curia . . ." The bishop allowed his voice to trail off deliberately, conveying the impression that Richard's appearance would be useless, that there was no more to be said to England's independent-minded prelates.

"Nay." With a heavy heart, the younger man hid his disappointment, realizing that he was too late and that he could only gain Stephen's hostility by speaking openly now. Nay, it was better to return to Normandy and seek Gloucester's counsel in the matter. One thing he did know, however: the earl had little love for Stephen, and his dislike was returned in full measure. Aye, there would be bad times ahead between them, but even a newly crowned king would not dare move against England's most powerful tenant-in-chief. And all England would watch what

Robert of Gloucester would do. Richard bent to kiss the bishop's ring again, and Henry murmured a brief blessing over his head.

"Do you take your oath to the king at Christmas?" Henry asked as Richard straightened up.

"Nay, I am for Normandy now. Mayhap at Easter court."

"Then I bid you Godspeed on your journey, my lord."

It was over, his bid to make Gloucester king—over before he'd had a chance to present his arguments, over even before he'd arrived in the country, Richard reflected bitterly as he stepped out into the cold winter's night air. Aye, he'd ridden through a storm and nearly lost a man for naught. A sense of intense frustration gnawed at him—it was an injustice to even think of Stephen as king. Bigod had lied—he'd not even been at the old king's bedside at the end—but what was that to the purpose? The handsome, fickle Stephen had stolen a march on everyone, taken the royal treasury, and had himself named ruler whilst the baronage quarreled in Normandy over who should have the crown.

Stephen. To Richard, it was a cruel jest. Stephen, he snorted derisively to himself, lacked the temperament to control anyone. Aye, he'd seek to rule by his smiles and gifts, no doubt. Jesu, what would Gloucester do? Would he swear to his cousin of Blois—or would he support his half-sister now? Or would he raise his own standard?

An ostler held the bridle for his prized Spanish stallion, and billows of foggy breath spewed forth from its nostrils. Richard swung up into his saddle and grasped the reins, clicking them as he nudged the horse with his knee.

Everard's mount fell into pace beside him silently. One look at the set of his lord's jaw had been enough to tell the captain that all had not gone well with Henry of Blois. He waited, keeping his own counsel, until finally the famed Rivaux temper exploded.

"God's bones! The fools would crown Stephen! Can they not see him for the affable fool he is? Jesu! Do they think he can stand against Anjou's wrath? Nay! And he'd have *my* oath at Christmas or Easter!"

"They chose Stephen then?"

Ignoring Everard, Richard muttered tersely, "There will be hell on earth ere I swear to him." Then louder, "Hell on earth—d'ye hear!" The winter wind caught at his words, swirling them with the light snow, carrying them until they were swallowed in its howl.

His captain shook his head and held his tongue. It was better to let his lord vent his anger where there were none to hear him now. Stephen as king. The older man sighed heavily and wrapped his cloak closer to his body. Jesu, but it did not bode well for any of them, not when 'twas known Richard of Rivaux would have stood against him. Aye, there would be war, but for whom? Would Gloucester declare for himself, pitting Rivaux against Rivaux—or would he uphold his half-sister, sending them all forth beneath her standard?

Behind them in his palace, the Bishop of Winchester took another cup of mulled wine and stared into the crackling flames, trying to reassure himself that Gloucester would come to terms with Stephen. It would take time, but even a powerful earl like Gloucester must surely see there was no use fighting what was already done. Aye, the judicious award of a few choice manors should soothe the bastard's anger.

But the hotheads like young Rivaux worried him— 'twas always those who believed in causes who made the greater trouble. Perhaps Lord Richard's passage to Normandy should be delayed until after Stephen was crowned—just long enough to ensure that Robert of Gloucester remained unaware until the deed was done. But no harm must come to the boy—he'd not have it said that he plotted against Guy of Rivaux's son. A brief sojourn with Warenne—or Brevise mayhap. Nay, 'twould have to be Warenne, for he could not trust Brevise not to harm him.

7

The fire crackled and popped in the brazier, sending sparks that flew harmlessly into the air, drifted, and then landed as small black specks on the woven mat beneath her feet. Gilliane's hands unworked a knot in the long strands of hair while she uttered a mild oath of frustration and wondered why silk tangled less. At her feet lay a spool of precious gold thread, thread she'd been hoarding for use in Geoffrey's chairing gifts. Aye, and for embroidery on his Christmas robe. The cloth itself had come from the Flemish clothmakers and had cost her the silver marks her mother had left her, and now there was none to wear it. There would be no chairing of the lord this Christmas, for Geoffrey lay beneath the cold slabs of Beaumaule's chapel floor.

Above her, the chimney hole revealed that the weather had cleared and the sun shone brightly in contrast to both the cold air and the chill in her heart. The knotted hair stretched and broke in her hands, prompting another oath. Reluctantly she turned her full attention to the task, carefully tying the coppery strands. Would Rivaux think a sword belt a poor gift, an unsatisfactory substitute for his fancy cloak? she wondered. The image of the great lord floated before her, and she saw again those strange dark eyes and that faintly mocking smile. Her palm tingled as she remembered anew the feel of his thick, shining black hair, and she found herself reaching to touch the blunt ends of her own. It had been her best claim to beauty and it was gone, reduced to the few long tresses that she'd retrieved where they'd spilled from the hearth, the tresses she now worked into the belt. Ah, but if he could have seen it as it was . . . Her thoughts trailed off, and she forced herself to deal with the present.

Richard of Rivaux was not the sort of man one dared dream of. Nor was he even one it was safe to dream of, for he could not bring her anything but shame. And yet she had dreamed of little else in the days since he'd left Beaumaule for Winchester. Aye, when she was not mourning Geoffrey, she was left wondering what Rivaux truly meant to do with her. One part of her fervently hoped that he would forget his promise to protect her and Aubery, that he would leave them be at Beaumaule, but another part of her wanted to see him again, to see if her memory had somehow played her false, to see if he were indeed as handsome as she remembered him.

Leaning to pick up the thin multicolored strips of bright silk, she continued the painstaking process of weaving the long, brightly colored band. Drawing an end from the spool, Gilliane's fingers moved deftly, intertwining silk, hair, and gold thread, braiding them into a pattern that was pleasing to her eyes. If she could not give him a fine cloak, she reasoned, she would give her self-appointed guardian something he could not obtain even in London, and mayhap she would gain his goodwill for it.

But would he return anytime soon? Or would he spend days, weeks even, at Winchester? If the magnates and the clergy could not agree on Mathilda or Stephen or Gloucester, they could well argue a month and more. But he would come back—she was certain of that at least, for Walter of Thibeaux mended at Beaumaule. And from all she had seen of Rivaux, he bore affection for the boy who served him. Nay, but he would come back for the squire at least. She finished one end of the belt and held it up to admire how it caught the light from above. 'Twould be like

Joseph's coat of many colors, the only one of its kind.

"My lady . . ."

She looked up, surprised to see Simon of Woodstock standing in the doorway of the small solar, for he usually sent a boy first to ask her permission for admittance. She'd often thought it his age or an old wound that troubled him, as he seldom came all the way up the steps. But as the light from the partially shuttered window caught his fair hair and his unlined face, she realized that he was by no means as old as she had thought him. Aye, the white hairs that mingled with the gold were few enough and almost beneath notice. That he'd been a man as long as she could remember did not necessarily make him more than thirty-five or thirty-six years old.

He stepped the rest of the way into the small chamber. "There is the merchant come with his wares below, Lady Gilliane. Would you have me send him away?"

There was so little money, scarce a pound of pennies to be had in the keep, but Gilliane could not resist the thought of seeing and touching the pretty things most of the traveling traders brought with them. "From whence does he come?" she asked, hoping it was from Flanders.

"France—he but stops here to warm himself."

"There can be no harm in seeing, do you think, Simon?" she ventured wistfully.

"There is no money here," he reminded her.

"Still, I would come down to the hall to inspect his wares." She made up her mind to do it, laying aside her nearly finished work. With a disgusted shrug at her foolishness, the captain turned to leave. "Simon," she asked, "how many years do you have?"

He stopped, one foot on the stairs, and turned back to her with seeming impatience. "I am six-and-thirty."

She'd not guessed wrong then. Curiosity prompted her to blurt out, "Why have you never wed, Simon?"

His blue eyes grew so hard, so embittered, that she almost recoiled. "When I have thought to take a wife, I am reminded that I have no property, something not easily forgiven by any maid's family. Alas, I have nothing, Demoiselle."

"Yet you do not seek service with Rivaux."

"Nay."

"But why?"

"I'd not serve him," he answered simply, turning back to the stairs.

"Wait . . ."

He stopped and waited, his irritation at her questions barely concealed. His head and shoulders were still visible at the top of the stairwell. Impulsively she picked up the belt she'd been working and held it out. "Come tell me what you think of this."

With seeming reluctance he came back into the room to take it from her. As he turned it over in his callused palm, he nodded and an appreciative smile lightened his usually sober face. "I think it quite pretty, Demoiselle, but if you have done this for me—"

"Nay," she cut in hastily, realizing now she'd made a mistake, " 'tis for Rivaux."

His smile faded abruptly, replaced by a bleakness that chilled even his eyes. "Aye, Rivaux. 'Tis the Rivauxes who gain all and leave naught, isn't it?"

"You mislike him."

"I mislike those who have everything, Demoiselle. What can he wish from a small place like this? Nay, he is as greedy as Brevise, but in a different way."

His tone angered her unreasonably, and she felt an inexplicable need to defend a man she'd alternately cursed and hailed herself. "Nay, but he would protect Aubery and me against Brevise, Simon."

"Why?" he asked bluntly. "It cannot be that you are a wealthy heiress or that Aubery's patrimony can be bled. Look around you, Demoiselle—is there aught of worth here?"

"Beaumaule has succored you these nineteen years

past, and I've not heard you complain ere now," she snapped. "You have been content enough to eat at our table, have you not? You have wanted for naught here, Simon of Woodstock."

"Aye, and I would have died protecting Beaumaule for you, Demoiselle, but I am not given the task. Instead, you would turn to Rivaux."

Taken aback again by the harshness, the suppressed anger in his voice, she was at a loss for words for a time. And then she sought to placate him. "Simon, there is so little left of Aubery's patrimony that I have no choice but to turn to him. I have prayed it be otherwise, but it is not."

"There is this knight before you, but you have never thought of me, have you, Demoiselle?" He watched her eyes blink in surprise as though she had not heard him aright, and then he turned away. "Aye, but I am a nithing in your eyes, Demoiselle— naught but a landless knight who eats at your table."

"Sweet Mary, but you mistake the matter, Simon. I'd have you stay, but I have not the land to—"

"You could wed with me."

She stared, unable to believe her ears. "Holy Jesu! Simon, you know not what you ask. I—"

"Aye. You think yourself above me, but had I the land, I could be lord to you." His back to her, his voice low, he leaned against the cold stone wall and nodded. "It surprises you that I have dared to think thus of you, Gilliane de Lacey, but I've thought of naught else since we were in the chapel at Geoffrey's bier."

"I have no dowry, and I'd not—"

"There is Beaumaule."

"And there is Aubery," she reminded him softly. "Simon, I have to hold Beaumaule for the son of my father's blood."

"A weak fool!" he spat at her viciously, turning back to face her. "Aye, a boy more a maid than a man! A boy unfit to rule!"

"My last brother, Simon—only he has the right to

rule Beaumaule. Nay, but he cannot be set aside, and I'd not will it if he could."

"You are more a man than he! Send him to the priests and rule in his stead! There will be a new king—receive this fief in my name! 'Tis I who have held it for all of you these nineteen years past!" He took a step toward her, his hands outstretched, his voice pleading with her. "Aye, we could hold Beaumaule, Gilliane!"

"Jesu! 'Tis wrong what you would ask me to do, Simon! The land is not mine to give you—'tis Aubery's!"

"And you would let Rivaux make you his leman to keep it for one who does not value it! Nay, but 'tis wrong what you would do also!"

In all of her years as daughter of the house, she'd never been addressed thus. Bright spots of anger heightened the color in her cheeks as she groped for words of denial. Nay, but she did not have to answer to him. Slowly, ever so slowly, she mastered her temper, drawing it in tight check. The man before her was a sudden stranger.

"Look at me." He held out his scarred hands in supplication at her silence. "Do you not see the blows I have taken for Beaumaule? Look at this face—can you not see the lines of years I have spent in service here? And 'twas all for naught."

"You swore to my father, Simon, and to my brother after him, but your oath gave you not Beaumaule or me," she said finally. "And 'tis insult to say that I would be leman to any man." Drawing herself up to her full height, she met his eyes squarely. "But for the service you have given Beaumaule, I will forget what you have asked—I'd not part angered with you."

"Gilly?"

Both of them spun around at the sound of Aubery de Lacey's thin, reedy voice. Simon raked him contemptuously with eyes that betrayed his impotent fury, and then he pushed past the boy without speaking. Gilliane sighed heavily and shook her head.

"God's blood, but what ails him?" Aubery demanded plaintively.

"Rivaux, I think."

"I am glad enough he leaves us, Gilly. He faults me for what I cannot become."

Gilliane took in her brother's slight form and wondered if he were the changeling Alwina had always claimed, for there was so little resemblance between him and the tall, stalwart brothers she'd lost. There must have been something wrong with Morwenna's blood, or else her father's seed had weakened before his last marriage. But it did not matter—he was in truth lord of Beaumaule now. Aloud she merely answered, "He would have you be a warrior, Aubery—'tis all that he asks of you."

"Aye—and I cannot even bear the weight of the lance without pain."

"You are young yet."

"Nay, but I do not grow as the others," he added sorrowfully. "And I cannot stand what he would inflict on me. I would that Geoff had not died, Gilly, that I could give myself to God."

"Beaumaule has the greater need of you, Aubery."

"Aye, but I'd not—"

"Well, 'tis no matter now, lovey, for we go with Rivaux, and Simon leaves us. 'Twill be some years ere you are called to rule here."

"I am glad for that also." He walked to the loosely shuttered window and peeked out the crack in the middle. "Do you think Rivaux will despise me also? Will he care that I would rather copy verses than fight?"

"I know not what Rivaux will think," she admitted. "I know him even less than Simon." Reaching to ruffle his bright orange hair above his pallid face, she managed to smile. "But I have not given up hope that you will grow tall and strong. Come, let us go see what the cloth merchant brings."

"Nay. I did but come to see why Simon shouted at you. I thought he meant you harm."

"Well, as you can see, I am whole. 'Twas over naught," she reassured him. "He is but disappointed to leave Beaumaule, I think."

Gilliane stroked the gray-and-white softness of the fur, admiring the warm luxury of it, before reluctantly pushing it away and turning instead to the bolts of cloth the peddler had brought. Her woman's heart yearned for these silks that had come from the East, some shimmering from the metallic threads woven within them, others embroidered by Flemish artisans in the *orfrois*, or French style, with ornate designs worked in gold and silver. But she dared not even ask the cost of any of them for fear her shock would betray to the peddler how little she had to spend.

"Perhaps my lady would look again at the vair," he suggested, lifting the precious fur before her eyes. "A hard winter such as this one makes it thicker."

"Nay."

His blunt fingers ruffled the fur to show its beauty again. "Seven shillings a skin, my lady."

"Nay." The price he asked was one-quarter of all the money in Beaumaule. Turning away from the silks, she noticed a roll of lustrous crimson velvet, and she could not resist asking, "How much for that?"

"The red?" He shrugged expressively and appeared to be figuring the cost in his head. "Red is most expensive—the dye is not plentiful—but for you, lady, five shillings to the ell."

It was much like the velvet of Richard of Rivaux's ruined mantle, yet another reminder of just how very wealthy he must be. Her fingertips touched the softness gingerly, wondering how it would work beneath her needle. And she remembered the way he'd looked at the meanness of Beaumaule's hall. *Spend your gold on yourself*, he'd said. Impulsively she rose, ordering the merchant to wait for her, and hastened to rummage in her mother's meager jewel chest. Drawing out a golden buckle set with bright blue cabochon stones, she held it to the light. It was the finest thing to be had in Beaumaule, having once belonged to the grandsire who'd come to England in the Conqueror's train, and she'd thought to use it on the sword belt she was working. Pocketing it, she hastened back to the hall.

"How much would you give me for this?" she asked, laying the buckle on the table before the peddler. When he did not pick it up right away, she hurriedly added, " 'Twas a gift from the Conqueror himself."

"A pretty bauble—twelve shillings at best."

"Nay. See for yourself, Master Galeran—pick it up," she urged. " 'Tis of gold and set with stones from Byzantium. I'd have twelve ells of the cloth and six skins of the vair for it." Her heart pounding at her own daring, she waited.

" 'Tis but a buckle!" he snorted.

"Nay—hold it in the palm of your hand . . . weigh it."

"You would beggar me," he grumbled, lifting it and balancing it, testing its weight for the gold. "But mayhap a pound—"

"There will be many lords at Christmas court eager for such a buckle—I'll take no less than the cloth and the fur for it."

"Byzantium, you say?" He squinted, holding the jeweled ornament up to the light and looking for cracks in the blue stones. Aye, there'd be a market for such a piece. "The cloth then," he offered.

"And the fur."

"Jesu, but you would rob me," he complained.

"Very well, then." She reached to pluck the buckle from his hand. "If you cannot see its value, Master Galeran, then I shall use it on the sword belt I am making—'twill make a fine Christmas gift for a fine lord." With a wave of her hand toward the cloths he had spread over the rough tables, she shook her head. "You may repack these, as my mind is set on the velvet and vair and naught else."

"Six ells of the cloth and four skins then," he negotiated grudgingly.

"Nay. 'Tis for a big man, and six ells would scarce cover him."

"Six ells will cover anyone," he sniffed. "Sweet Jesu, but is he a giant?"

"I'd have it reach his ankles—I'd not make a short one."

"Six ells—"

"Twelve," she repeated definitely. "And the vair."

He could see she was adamant on the amount. Mentally he calculated how much he thought a wealthy magnate would pay for the buckle. It was, after all, exquisitely wrought. "Aye." He sighed grudgingly. " 'Tis not often Galeran is robbed by a mere girl." Reaching for the heavy cloth shears, he turned to the velvet.

"And I'd not have it stretched until it tears, either," she warned him, her heart beating rapidly at thought of the staggering price she'd just paid.

Later, as she climbed the solar stairs carrying the precious material and fur in her arms, she worried if she had the skill to work it into anything Rivaux would wear. The lowering thought that she should have put the buckle on the belt instead came to mind. But nay, she'd promised him a cloak, and by the blessed saints, 'twould be a cloak he'd have. She would have liked to line the entire garment with the vair, but 'twas impossible. Nay, inside where it would not show, she'd use plain English rabbit.

It was only when she reached the small solar that she actually realized the enormity of what she'd done—she'd all but beggared Beaumaule to make a cloak for a man who could buy a hundred such garments for himself. She stared at the shimmering velvet, wondering if the devil had prompted her to squander such a sum. It was her honor that had demanded such sacrifice, she told herself. And this time, Richard of Rivaux would not think her so very poor.

After availing himself of the keep's slim hospitality, the peddler led his packs out of Beaumaule, still wondering at the Lady Gilliane's extravagance. Sitting astride the lead ass, he picked his way over the narrow road that wended through the chalky hills, until he reached the appointed place where a band of mounted men waited.

"Did you sup inside?"

"Aye."

"How many are there?"

"I counted but twenty-five, my lord, and of that number, several are sore wounded and unable to bear arms. And there are mayhap another twelve or thirteen women."

"Did you see the boy?"

"Aye."

"And his sister?"

"Aye."

A slow smile spread over William of Brevise's harshly lined face as he stared upward toward Beaumaule's single stone tower. Too long that small castle had stood in the midst of Brevise lands, a thorny reminder that he was not lord of all he could see. The red-and-black pennon that flew above it had worried him at first, but then he'd seen Rivaux pass by close enough to determine that it was the son rather than the father. And now, by the time that young lord gave Beaumaule another thought, it would belong to Brevise. Aye, Stephen would see to that— he'd confirm what William meant to take.

"My lord . . ."

William looked across to where the peddler had his hand outstretched, and his face hardened. "What?"

"There is the matter of money between us."

"Nay, there's no gold spent in hell," William retorted coldly, signaling to one of his men, who raised his sword to strike. Spurring his mount aside, William turned back to the rest of his mounted knights. "We return with sufficient men that we shall not fail."

8

With the help of Alwina and the girl Annys, Gilliane spent the early afternoon pressing, stretching, and cutting the costly velvet, taking great care to keep it as clean as possible. Smooth boards had been laid across three trestles, and the floor had been swept bare and washed as an extra precaution, so great was her concern that the cloak be perfect. Even her needles were tossed in sand and vinegar to remove any hint of rust that might spot the softly shimmering fabric.

One of Geoffrey's well-mended cloaks was taken apart, each piece pressed, measured, and laid on stout English wool, where it was used for a pattern. The wool was cut carefully, allowing several inches around each piece to make it bigger, before the new pattern was transferred to the velvet itself to avoid soiling even the underside of the cloth. It was a painstaking process that would yield two cloaks, one for Richard of Rivaux and one for Simon of Woodstock to ease his parting. No matter what he'd said to her, she did owe him for nineteen years of service to her family, and a mercenary knight would have need of a warm woolen cloak. Perhaps the gift would aid in easing his bitterness.

While Annys and Gilliane cut out each piece of the velvet, Alwina measured and trimmed the vair, cutting it into strips for use around the edges of the cloak itself and for lining the hood. And all the while, she muttered to herself that 'twas foolishness to squander gold on one who did not need it.

"Be still, old woman," Gilliane ordered her finally. " 'Tis a matter of honor—I ruined one far better."

"Aye, and he probably has ten of them, if the truth were known," Alwina complained. " 'Twould be more useful to have gotten cloth for yourself."

"You've no cause to carp—Geoffrey saw that all had new Christmas robes."

Unmollified, the old woman bent her head to her task and continued muttering as to the folly of giving to them that already had. Gilliane chose to ignore her this time and returned to her own work.

A stack of rabbit skins was brought up from the storeroom, and soon Alwina had enough to occupy her thoughts as she brushed and trimmed them into strips to add length and breadth to the lining she'd already pieced for Lord Geoffrey's Christmas cloak ere he died. That task done, she threaded her needle and stitched them together until they added to the chessboard pattern on the skin side so neatly 'twould be thought the whole had been done at once. Turning it over from time to time, her gnarled and veined hands smoothed the fur until it lay soft and flat.

When Annys would have sewn on the velvet, Gilliane shook her head, saying that if 'twas to be ruined, she'd ruin it herself. With a disappointed shrug, the girl turned to the plain brown wool, muttering that naught was wrong with Sir Simon's old mantle.

They worked far into the evening, long after the light from above turned to black, starry sky. The work was tedious and meticulous as each woman stitched, her head close to her work beneath the smelly tallow candles. The yellow light smoked and flickered, while Gilliane silently thanked her patron saint for the fact that a man's cloak had few pieces to it. She and Annys were done long before Alwina, who had the greater task. Dismissing the girl, Gilliane turned her attention to the hood, lining it carefully with the pieced rabbit the old woman had sewn, and then framing the edge with the gray-and-white vair. Looking up as she put in the last portion, she noted that Alwina dozed over her blanket of fur.

"Alwina," she began softly. "Alwina, get you to your pallet."

"Unnnnuhhhhh."

"Alwina!"

There was a pause in the low, sonorous breathing as the old woman roused slightly. "Eh?"

"Get you to bed."

"Nay, but . . ." Determinedly the Saxon woman turned back to the skins on her lap.

" 'Tis all but done." Gilliane rose and walked to pick up the neatly stitched fur, holding it up to the brazier light, where the reds and golds of the fire made it look more brown than gray. "Aye—'tis warm and well-made, Alwina," she observed with satisfaction. "He cannot fault it for that."

"Humph! 'Tis fit for a royal prince, if you was to offer it there," the old woman sniffed as she also rose and flexed stiffened fingers. "Aye, and a prince'd have as much use for it as Rivaux, too. Alms begins with them that need it, my lady."

"I ruined his cloak—I can do no less." Turning aside to lay the fur on the underside of the velvet mantle, Gilliane measured it against the outer garment. " 'Tis of a size," she murmured almost to herself.

" 'Tis you as should be in bed also," Alwina muttered.

"Nay, I'd finish the task. I cannot depend on when he will return, and I'd have it done ere he comes."

"If he comes. He might send for the boy, and be done with Beaumaule."

"If he comes not, I will send it to him."

"Where?"

That gave her pause, for he'd merely said he was going to Winchester. If he did not return to Beaumaule, he had so many possessions that 'twould be difficult to know where to send it. And she had not a man to spare to carry it, anyway. "Nay, he will come," she declared with a conviction she did not truly feel. "Get you to bed."

She waited until the old woman left before turning her attention back to the cloak. They thought her a fool—Alwina, Annys, Simon—all of them. They could not see it was a matter of pride to give back what she'd destroyed, no matter what Richard of Rivaux's wealth—she'd not have him forgive the debt out of pity. And besides, she'd look on him again.

The task of fitting the lining was a slow one, requiring small neat stitches despite the heaviness of both cloth and fur. From time to time she stopped and sucked on her tender fingertip, reddened and swollen from forcing the needle through the layers, and then she resolutely began again. Thrice the smelly tallow candles were gutted and had to be replaced on their iron spikes. The area between her shoulders ached all the way up into her neck, and her eyes watered from the smoke and the strain of the faint light, but she was too nearly done to quit.

A distant cock crow sounded even as she finished the last stitch and tied it off. She stood, letting the sumptuous velvet flow off her lap to fall into rich, dark red folds at her feet. It was the finest thing she'd ever done, she admitted to herself as she held the shoulders out in front of her and admired her handiwork. The hood, with its checkered gray-and-white vair border to frame and shield his face, fell back to reveal the warm rabbit inside. She could not resist burying her face in the richness of it, feeling its softness. Still rubbing her cheek against the thick velvet, she carried it to the window, and with her free hand she unhooked the shutter, letting in a blast of cold air. The pale, still hazy light of dawn illuminated the mantle, proving it as fine as she thought it.

Impulsively she slipped it around her own shoulders to savor the feel of it, letting it gather at her ankles. Pulling it closer against the cold, she snuggled into the thick fur lining and stared out into the peaceful countryside below Beaumaule. Naked, spreading branches were heavy with icicles where the ice and snow had tried to melt, only to refreeze into crystal daggers pointed toward the frosted earth. It was both barren and beautiful. Her eyes scanned the silent, hoary land as though seeing it for the first time, marveling at the wild, empty look of it in the early dawn. And then she noted the movement on the far horizon.

Across the glistening chalk hills, the morning light reflected off a row of polished helmets like mirrors. Her heart leapt as she strained to identify the riders, and then sank when she caught the blue-and-yellow pennon that floated above them. Sweet Jesu!

The cloak forgotten, she let it slide to the floor while she looked again, and then she spun to run as fast as her weary, cramped legs would take her down the narrow stairs. Shut away from the outside, they were dark and dangerous, and she fell the last several steps. Righting herself by clawing at the uneven stones, she groped her way into the curtained end of the hall, where Beaumaule's men-at-arms slept.

"Simon! Simon! Sweet Jesu, but we are attacked!" Grasping the blanket that wrapped him, she unceremoniously uncovered him. "Mother of God! Do you hear me? 'Tis Brevise, Simon!"

He sat up, heedless of his nakedness, and shook his head to clear it. "Wha . . . God's blood, Demoiselle, but you would wake a dead man," he complained. Then her words sank in. "Brevise? Art certain?"

"Aye, I have seen them. They ride from the north, Simon, and there is no mistaking his colors."

He let out a string of oaths that would have made her blush at another time and lunged up from his straw-stuffed pallet. His scarred body was covered with gooseflesh from the cold. "Hand me my garters," he ordered tersely as he reached for his chausses. "Aymer! Baudwin! Hugo! We are attacked! Build the fire for the pitch! Aye—and man the arrow slits! Holy Jesu, but there is no time to dally!"

Even as he drew on his chausses over his nakedness, he was barking out commands to the meager garrison. She stared in fascination at his man's body, realizing it was the first one she had ever seen in the whole. His was marked in numerous places, bearing mute testimony to a hard life of continual fighting. It wasn't until he'd pulled on his rough woolen tunic that he noted her again.

"God's bones, Demoiselle, but 'tis no place for you."

Blushing at what she'd seen of him, she turned to where he stacked his mail. "Tie your garters, and I will vest you, Simon."

" 'Tis unseemly."

"There is no time—let your man arm himself."

Nodding at the sense of that, he bent to fasten the leather bands across his calves. When he straightened, she already had his much-mended gambeson ready. Slipping it around him, she fastened it quickly, lacing it beneath his arms. When she would reach for the boiled leather shirt, he shook his head. "Nay—if you have seen them, there's no time for that. Get me the mail and be done."

Wordlessly she helped him don the mail shirt, pulling the kinks in the links out until it hung below his knees. All around them, there were the scuffling sounds of men arming themselves frantically. Even the scullery had come to life, and men and boys and kitchen wenches struggled to drag pitch vats out into the yard. Fastening every other hook of the mail shirt, Gilliane's fingers worked quickly. Simon reached for the leather cap that protected his head, fastened it beneath his chin, and worked the mail coif up over it. She stood ready with his helmet.

"You would make a good soldier's wife, Demoiselle," he murmured as he took the helm. Even before he had the heavy steel nasal positioned over his face, she was looping the frayed leather sword belt around his waist. "My thanks."

"Nay, 'tis nothing. Here . . ." She lifted the heavy broadsword from where it had stood against the wall, and struggled to sheathe it. "Sweet Mary, but I know not how you carry this."

"Leave it out." For an instant his blue eyes met hers. Leaning over to pick up something from beneath his pallet, he drew out a sharp dagger. Weighing it in his palm, he proffered it. "Do not use this unless you need it, Demoiselle, for 'tis good only one time. Once a man knows you have it, 'tis of no use to you. Do not strike until he is as close as I am to you—closer even. Do you understand me?"

She passed her tongue over suddenly parched lips and nodded. His meaning was clear: if they could not hold Beaumaule for her, she'd have to defend herself. Her hand closed over the dagger's hilt.

"Aye."

"And if I should fall, I am sorry for the quarrel between us. I did but think to make a bargain useful to both of us."

Armed now, he started toward the curtain that separated the men's sleeping quarters from the hall. At the faded tapestry itself, he stopped and turned back briefly. "Put Aubery in the chapel—and you take refuge again in the scullery. Tell him that if he chooses the stables again, I will whip him, lord or no, if we both live."

"Aye. Simon . . ."

"What?"

". . . I am heartily sorry I could not . . . that is, I'd not have you think me ungrateful for all I owe you." She rose on tiptoe to straighten a kink in his hauberk. "May God aid you now, Simon of Woodstock."

"Aye," he muttered gruffly, thrusting her aside. "Get you to the kitchen while you can."

Judging from the sounds above her, the men of Beaumaule were making a valiant stand. The smell of pitch intermingled with the smell of burning thatch, and the whinnies of terrified horses drowned out the sounds of men shouting and the thuds of rocks hurled against the timber outer walls. The courtyard was alive with running feet as everyone from the cook to the alewife to the lowliest spit boy darted with buckets of water from fire to fire. Finally Gilliane could stand it no longer.

She emerged into the courtyard just as a flaming section of wall gave way. The burning logs, their crossbars already gone, fell over the ice-filled ditch. And while the archers on the other wall were still able to harry Brevise's men away from the smoking gap, it was obviously only a matter of hours until Beaumaule fell. Aye, and even if they could last until nightfall, they would not be able to defend themselves in the darkness against a direct assault.

Smoke burned her eyes and choked her as she made her way to the wall where Simon of Woodstock shouted curses and orders at the same time. Two men, their hands black with soot, carried a caldron of hot pitch closer, ready to fling it on any brave enough to breach the gap, while boys scrambled about the yard, picking up Brevise's arrows for use by Beaumaule's archers.

"The stable's afire!" someone yelled behind her, and as she turned around, she could see the flames shooting up from the roof. Inside, the trapped animals banged against the walls and neighed hysterically.

Gathering the loose-fitting boy's tunic about her, Gilliane ran toward the burning stable, shouting for someone to aid her. She and an ostler reached it at the same time, and both heaved against the bar to open it, while another rushed in to drive the frightened horses out. She screamed a warning as a section of burning thatch fell like a great coal at her feet. The rush of hot air from within scalded her throat and lungs.

"Demoiselle!"

She did not know who called to her, nor did she see who pulled her away from the stable before it collapsed inward with a resounding crash. Sparks shot from the burning building and fell like rain onto the small sheds around it, sizzling against the ice crystals in the thatch and then catching in some of the drier places. In a matter of a few minutes the sky was orange and black, thick and choking, as Beaumaule's granary and the armorer's shed caught fire also. It seemed as though burning projectiles were everywhere.

"Get you inside, Demoiselle!" Simon of Woodstock yelled at her from his place on the wall.

"Nay, I'd not be burned like bread in an oven!" she shouted back.

"Then go to the chapel!"

"Nay!"

There was no time for him to say anything more. A knight in Brevise's colors jumped the burning timbers in the drainage ditch and cleared the break in the wall. Gilliane watched in horror as he struck down a kitchen boy struggling with a bucket of water. Blood spurted as the child collapsed into a pile of red-soaked rags. Running to what was left of the armory, she grasped a practice lance and pulled off the wooden end with an effort. When she turned around, the Brevise knight was riding through her courtyard, taking his sport unmolested, striking down any in his path. She stood rooted with the lance as he noticed her, and her heart seemed to stop as he spurred toward her, his bloody sword in his hand.

Numbly she stood, time suspended, and then she remembered watching Geoffrey practice using the lance. As the horse bore down on her, she dropped to the ground, and at the last minute she raised the lance. The horse reared too late, and the lance shattered from the force as it impaled the animal. Gilliane rolled from beneath its flailing hooves and lay still from the impact. The Brevise knight flopped wildly in the saddle and then lost his balance entirely, falling beneath his mount as man and horse came down together.

She knew she was alive, but she couldn't breathe.

Her legs and arms were like meat jelly when she
tried to move them. She could see Simon come off
the wall and run toward her. At the same time,
Brevise's men poured through the breach, cutting
off help for her. Slowly her breath came back into
her body, and as the melee raged around her, she
crawled toward the hall, thinking to seek refuge in
the tower. Her fingers closed on Simon's dagger,
seeking reassurance from it. If she were going to die,
she hoped she would take William of Brevise with her.

9

It was the acrid smell of smoke and burning pitch that first alerted Richard of Rivaux to trouble. He'd been lost in his own thoughts, scarcely aware of the body that ached from the jarring, slow trot of the horse beneath him, cursing himself for a fool over seeking out Bishop Henry. He ought to have gone before the Curia itself, but he'd been too clever for his own cause, thinking that Henry would wait to see how the baronage went. And who could have known he would support Stephen? Jesu, but they'd quarreled often enough before, after all, for a man to think blood made no difference between them. Aye, he bitterly regretted his hasty journey through the cold and ice, a journey that had yielded him naught but two wards he did not need. He sighed, drawing in a deep breath, and realized he smelled something other than hearthfire.

Pitch. It had a distinct odor, one he associated with war and siege. And even as he noted it, Everard drew closer and pointed toward the black column that climbed like a tall billowing cloud into the morning sky. It gave meaning to the smell.

"By the looks of it, 'tis Beaumaule that burns, my lord."

"Aye."

Gilliane de Lacey. A chill went through him as he thought of her and her young brother. And Walter—Walter was in there also. He rose in his stirrups to better see the deserted road ahead, and then looked

upward at the smoke in the sky. Wordlessly he sank
back in his saddle and spurred the big black Spanish
horse forward. Behind him, Everard shouted to his
men to follow.

At the crest of the hill across from Beaumaule,
Richard reined in just long enough to assess their
chances. From where he sat, it appeared that the
whole motte and bailey were on fire, that the wooden
walls had been breached, and that a small army
overran the keep itself. Besieged on the walls were
the few Beaumaule men, fighting valiantly, literally
kicking at those who sought to pull them down.
Somewhere inside the inferno was Gilliane de Lacey.

He had but thirty men, but there was something to
be said for surprise—and he was of the blood of
Rivaux, after all. He raised his hand, giving the battle
signal for charge, and Everard followed his lead.
Unhooking his heavy mace from behind his saddle,
he shouted, "For God, Saint Agnes, and Rivaux!"
and dug his spurs against the big black's flank.

They streamed down the small hill and up the
road to the packed-earth mound that was Beaumaule,
charging across the little valley to cries of "For Saint
Agnes! For Rivaux!"

The fire and the fighting both raged with an intensity that obscured their approach until Simon of
Woodstock, having retreated to a section of burning
wall, caught sight of the red-and-black banner of
Rivaux. Kicking viciously at a blue-shirted man who
sought to pull him down, he took up the battle cry.

"For Rivaux! Sweet Jesu, 'tis Rivaux! God aids
us—'tis Rivaux!"

His shouts momentarily panicked Brevise's knights,
who were now riding pell-mell through the bailey
and yard, cutting down anything that dared move.
The archers atop the single square tower joined in,
chanting, "Rivaux! Rivaux! Rivaux!" while fitting their
arrow notches in their crossbows and renewing their
efforts, firing into the melee in the courtyard.

The Brevise men, under a new hail of arrows,

sought cover beneath the tower itself, while a few attempted to take the structure. Inside, on the narrow stairs, could be heard the shouted insults of those holding positions above. Made bold by Rivaux's sudden appearance, they now taunted their attackers.

Richard did not have time to count the enemy before he stormed the place. Miraculously, someone inside cut the ropes to the bridge, and it came down with a resounding thud. Everard took half the column and thundered across it, sounding for all the world as if they were a hundred men. Richard sought to cut off any retreat by going through the broken and burning wall.

Swinging the heavy mace at any who would stop him, he cut a swath through the melee before him. Across the small yard he could see Everard stun a knight, who was immediately pulled down by a stout peasant woman and spitted with a pitchfork by an enterprising ostler. His mace caught in some burning thatch, flinging it in the face of a man who sought to cleave him with a battleax. One of his men swung wide with a broadsword, and the Brevise knight took a look of surprise into eternity.

"For God and Rivaux! For Rivaux! For Rivaux!"

It seemed that every living occupant of Beaumaule crawled or ran into the yard, carrying any weapon available, picking up the battle cry. Above Richard, a sooty, bloodstained Simon of Woodstock shouted, "Aid the Demoiselle!"

Richard cupped his hand to shout back, "Where?"

"The hall!"

The battle still raging around him, Richard reined in and dismounted. A blow from behind glanced off his mail, and as he turned around to counter it, his foeman was felled by a blow of Everard's broadsword. Unsheathing his own, Richard cut his way across the courtyard toward the hall, where the timbered roof was already ablaze. He kicked open the door and waited cautiously before stepping inside. His heavy boots crunched on the rushes, and the cross timbers above popped loudly. Instinctively he knew where she'd be if she were yet alive.

The hall appeared deserted, as though it were aloof from the violence outside. He crossed the long room quickly, found the sleeping area empty, and passed on into the kitchen behind it. A low moan sent a shiver of apprehension through him, but then he realized that it came from a Brevise knight who lay doubled up from a wound in his stomach, the sort that one died from slowly.

"Sweet Jesu, aid me," the fellow groaned. "I am stabbed—the wench stabbed me."

Richard leaned over him. "What wench?"

The knight groaned again and groped for his weapon at the fury in Richard's voice, but he was too late—Richard kicked it out of reach. "What wench?" he repeated awfully.

"Thought she was a boy . . ." came the thick reply. "Oh, Jesu, aid me. Ought to have killed her first." The bloody hand that held his abdomen reached out in supplication now. "Aid me—"

"Aye."

It was nothing he took pleasure in, this sort of killing, but there was no help for the man. Richard's blade flashed in the dim interior light, coming down with such force that the breastbone shattered beneath it. It was a sickening sound, that final expulsion of air. The knight's head lolled and blood trickled from a corner of his mouth. Richard hesitated before giving him the final blessing and signing the Cross over his chest. If he found Gilliane de Lacey harmed, he'd regret the service.

The stairs were steeper and darker than he remembered as he descended them. Closing his eyes tightly and reopening them in hopes of adjusting to the blackness, he edged off the last step. A sudden rustle of clothing alerted him, and he barely had time to raise his arm to shield himself from the blow. The dagger cut through the silk sleeve of his surcoat and glanced off his mail. He swung wildly with his free hand and caught the rough wool of a tunic. His sword arm came around and imprisoned his attacker, pinioning arms, and he knew he'd found Gilliane de Lacey. She struggled furiously, kicking and biting.

"God's bones, but you are a fierce maid, Demoiselle," he murmured softly in the darkness.

She went suddenly still, rigid in his arms, and then sagged against him, clutching his surcoat for support. "Art Rivaux?" she asked in the darkness.

"Aye."

"Oh, sweet Mary," she whispered, choking on tears. "I'd thought to die this day, my lord." All of the horror of what she'd witnessed came home to her as his hands circled her, holding her in the roughness of his mail-clad arms. She leaned into him gratefully, choking and crying from the horror of what she'd seen and done. His height and his strength seemed to envelop her, providing far more comfort than words.

"There's no time to weep," he acknowledged grimly, setting her back from him. "Aye—already the hall's timbers are burning, and 'twill not be long before the fire spreads to the kitchen roof."

As if to bear testimony to his words, one of the cross rafters broke in the hall and sent part of the ceiling crashing down. Gilliane bit her lip hard for control and nodded.

"Aye."

"Come on then." He grasped her arm with his mailed glove and pushed her before him toward the dim light of the stairwell. At the foot of it he stopped and stepped in front of her. "I'd best go first, lest any of Brevise's men yet live."

The smoke on the stairs stung her eyes and choked her. Gasping for air, she stumbled behind him and nearly lost her balance. He half-turned and caught her elbow. "Would you that I carried you?"

"Nay, I am all right." A paroxysm of coughing gave the lie to her words, and she had to clutch at his surcoat for support. Her throat burned and her lungs suffocated in the hot, pungent air.

It was stifling for him also. Bending low to catch what breath he could, he tried to fill his chest with it before pulling her into the kitchen. "Lie down and crawl," he rasped. "There's less smoke on the floor." Dropping to the ground himself, he twisted his hand into the woolen tunic she wore and dragged her after him. She crouched on all fours, keeping her head down, and scrambled dog-fashion after him. Above them, sparks from the igniting roof fell like hot coals. Both of them were coughing and gasping when they crossed the threshold of the kitchen into the covered passageway between it and the hall. Ahead of them, one of the roof supports collapsed. Panicked, Gilliane clawed her way through the burning debris, nearly leaving her tunic behind. Thinking his lungs would burst, Richard heaved himself after her, clearing the doorway. Through the smoke and flames he thought her clothing was afire, and he lunged to cover her with his body, and both of them rolled into the courtyard.

Amid the cries of the wounded and dying and the frantic shouts of those who fought the fires, he stood shakily and gave her his hand. She grasped his fingers, stumbled, and pulled herself up. For a moment they stood coughing, surveying the death and destruction around them. Much of what could burn was already on fire, and the valiant efforts of Beaumaule's inhabitants to control the spreading flames were useless. Gilliane's whole body quivered as she again fought back tears. Turning away blindly, she nearly tripped over the Brevise man she'd killed earlier. She caught at a still-standing post and, overcome by the horror around her, leaned against it, her shoulders now racked with sobs.

"Sweet Jesu, b-but we are ac-accursed!" she burst out.

"Demoiselle—" Richard came up behind her and turned her around. "Aye, you can weep now," he whispered huskily as his arms closed about her shaking body. They stood, knight and girl, locked in an embrace that gave comfort to each. She burrowed her head against his shoulder and clutched the embroidered silk of his surcoat in her fists, twisting and balling it in her hands, while his steel-plated gloves snagged in the rough wool of Erman's tunic.

Even when her sobs subsided, she was loath to raise her head. She could feel the cold, hard links of his mail through the stiff silk, and she could smell the oil and the boiled leather beneath, and they were oddly reassuring smells. It was not until she heard the crunch of heavy boots behind her that she reluctantly raised her eyes to his.

"You must think me a silly fool," she managed tremulously as she attempted to wipe the sooty tears from her cheeks with the back of her hand.

"Nay." His dark eyes warmed as they looked down on her, and one corner of his mouth twisted downward in a crooked smile. "Nay, I think you a warrior maiden." Raising his mailed arm to show her the rent in the sleeve of his embroidered surcoat, he nodded. "Aye, two men you would have slain this day, Demoiselle."

"Three." She looked down at the dead horse and rider beside them, and then looked away. "God aid me, but I killed this one also."

"My lord! Sweet Jesu, but I thought we were done!" Walter of Thibeaux loped toward them, his broken arm tied against his chest, his good arm still brandishing a sword.

Richard's eyes misted over at the sight of the boy, and he released Gilliane to clasp the squire against his breast. "Aye, I promised your father you would come to no harm, Walter, but you are determined to prove me wrong."

"My lord . . ." Everard hesitated to intrude on Richard, but there were things to be done. "The tower is all that stands, I fear. Would you that—"

"The tower! Oh, merciful Mary!" Gilliane gasped,

remembering the velvet cloak she'd sewn. Without a word of explanation, she turned on her heel and ran for the stone tower.

"Demoiselle! Nay, but do not go unattended!" Swearing under his breath, Richard started after her, fearful that there might still be a Brevise man hiding there. "God's blood, Demoiselle, wait!"

"My lord . . ." It was useless. Everard raised his hand to protest and let it fall in disgust. Turning back to a begrimed Simon of Woodstock, he exhaled and shook his head. "I'd suppose he means to take all of you with us now. Have you counted your wounded?"

"Aye—there are but four of us whole."

"Jesu! And how many cannot sit a horse?"

"Six. I do not expect Hugo to live until 'tis noon, so I do not count him."

"And the prisoners—are there any that can ride?"

"Nay—those that cannot are dead."

"Well, I know not what Lord Richard would with them, but none can stay here." Everard surveyed the smoldering ruin of what had been Beaumaule. "And you, sir—do you serve Rivaux now?"

"Nay. I am for Clifford's keep—there's room for a man to earn his bread there."

There was an emptiness in Simon of Woodstock's voice that drew the other man's sympathy. "You have served this family many years, then?"

"Since the Demoiselle was a babe."

"Oh—aye. 'Tis difficult to leave such service."

Beaumaule's captain turned and walked away. As Everard watched him, he kicked savagely at a charred log in his path. It was hard being a landless man in a world where land was everything. Sighing heavily, Everard looked toward the tower, a lonely sentinel over the blackened skeletons of Beaumaule's buildings, and felt a sense of foreboding. War was simmering, waiting to break out in a peaceful land. 'Twas no time to become nursemaid to a homeless girl.

And in the tower, Gilliane de Lacey picked up the magnificent red velvet mantle where she'd dropped it. As she inspected it to see that it was still whole, Richard rounded the stairs after her, his sword drawn. She rubbed the soft fur against her cheek and then held it out to him.

"I . . . I have replaced that which I ruined for you, my lord. See—'tis vair and velvet, as was yours." When he did not take it from her, her disappointment was evident. "You do not like it," she whispered through the sudden constriction in her throat. "If 'tis unworthy—"

"Nay."

He stood there watching her, an odd expression arrested on his face. Above the steel nasal, his dark eyes were sober.

"Take it, then!" she choked out. " 'Tis the finest these hands could work!"

He stood his sword in the corner and pulled off his gloves with his teeth, discarding them at his feet, before lifting his hands to dislodge his helmet. Working it off, he let it fall to the floor beside him and pushed back both mail coif and leather cap. His hands stretched toward the cloak and then stopped.

"Nay, I'd have you lay it on me—mine hands are too bloodied to touch it."

His voice sounded oddly strained, but the red-and-black streaks where blood and soot had mingled on his palms were evident. She wiped her own soiled hands on her clothing before lifting the precious velvet and moved behind him to settle it over his broad mail-clad shoulders, letting it fall to his ankles. Moving to the front, she pulled it close over his battle-stained surcoat and stepped back, suddenly shy.

" 'Twill need a clasp," she offered lamely, waiting for his reaction to its warmth and beauty.

He glanced down, taking in the rich, lush crimson velvet and then noting the neatly patterned vair trim. She must surely have beggared herself for it. "Why did you do this?" he demanded harshly. "You've enough need—you've naught yourself."

Her face fell. " 'Twas a matter of my honor, my lord. I am sorry it displeases you," she answered simply.

"It pleases me well, Demoiselle." He sighed, and his voice softened. "You mistake my words, Gilliane— 'tis you who should have the fine things." His blood-ied hands sought hers, clasping them strongly. "Nay, but 'tis strange for me to find a woman who thinks of honor as a man does. Most would take what I offer rather than give. You behold a wealthy man, Demoiselle."

" 'Tis of no matter, my lord—I did but replace what I destroyed." She dropped her gaze to study the woven reed mat at her feet, unwilling now to meet the warmth in his eyes. And then she remembered the sword belt, which lay folded on a bench behind them, and pulled away from him. "When I did not think to find the cloth, I made this instead." Quickly bending to pick it up, she held it out also. "I used the hair for luck, but I cannot say it worked."

"Nay." He reached to lift her chin with his knuckle and stared into the deep blue eyes. "If it brought no luck, 'twas because I did not wear it. I would that I had some gift for you in return."

The sudden warmth in his voice was matched by the lightening of the flecks in his otherwise dark eyes. To hide the flood of emotion that threatened her composure, she pulled away, turning her head, that he could not see. " 'Tis as Joseph's coat, my lord—made from bits of colored silk."

" 'Tis beautiful, Gilliane." He reached to take it from her hand and held it to the light. "I cannot say I have ever had another like it."

Uncertain whether he mocked her with his words, she dared to look at him, and again what she saw in his eyes disconcerted her. "Truly? You will wear it?"

"Aye." To show her, he shrugged out of the velvet mantle and laid it gingerly across the bench. Then he drew the belt around his waist, holding it above his own stamped leather sword belt. His pleasure in the gift evident in his smile, he nodded. " 'Twill fit as soon as I get a buckle."

"One would think you like it best."

" 'Tis the first I have had made of your hair—I can see the copper of it. Aye, I think 'tis the finest sword belt I have ever had."

A tremor passed through her as she realized he was looking at her rather than the gift, and his mood had shifted suddenly. She swallowed at what she saw in his eyes, and when he took a step toward her, she forced herself to back away.

"Art afraid of me, Gilliane?" he asked softly.

Sweet Mary, but there'd been none to look at her like that before, and for that brief moment she'd felt both a sense of power and a sense of fear at the same time. She could not play his game—she dared not. But his eyes were warm, the gold flecks lightening the brown, and they never left her face as he stepped still closer.

She passed the tip of her tongue over strangely parched lips, almost unable to speak for the nearness of him. "Nay, 'tis not that I am afraid . . ." She moved back again, and he followed. " 'Tis what you . . . 'tis how you . . ." She almost stumbled, realizing now that her back was but a handsbreadth from the wall. "Sweet Mary," she breathed, "but—"

"Gilliane."

His hands came up to clasp her shoulders, making further retreat impossible, and he held her still. As she looked up into those gold flecks, her heart pounded, thudding almost painfully against her ribs. She sucked in her breath and held it, not daring to breathe, both afraid he meant to kiss her and afraid he would not. His head bent closer until she could feel his breath against her skin, and a shiver of excitement coursed down her spine. And then, just as she closed her eyes, his head snapped back at the sound of running footsteps on the stairs.

"Demoiselle!" One of her men rounded the last step, breathless, and held on to rough stones for balance. "There is ill news. . . ."

They'd found Aubery de Lacey's body in the ruins of the stable. At first Gilliane refused to accept that it was he, but a search of the chapel and the surrounding burned-out buildings failed to yield the boy. And Simon of Woodstock identified Geoffrey's seal ring, which had been given Aubery on his brother's death, beneath the charred body.

In the yard the survivors worked with scarves tied over their faces to combat the stench of burned flesh as they attempted to sort their fallen comrades. And peasants, who had fled at Brevise's approach, returned to struggle with the frozen earth, digging with picks to make a common grave for all the dead save Aubery de Lacey, who was to be hastily wrapped and set beneath Beaumaule's chapel floor.

It was Richard who had pulled the grieving girl from her brother's body, enfolding her in his own cloak. She was strangely silent and rigid, unable to weep now, as she stood like stone beside him. And for a time he feared her mind had broken from this final horror. When she finally did speak, she turned to stare at those who worked to bury the bodies.

"I would that they be left out for carrion." She spoke tonelessly.

There was no doubt as to whom she meant, but he shook his head. "Nay, but 'twould ruin the water to let them rot. 'Tis enough that they die unshriven."

"And who gave Aubery his final blessing? Who commended his soul to God?" Her voice rose suddenly, almost hysterically now. "Nay, but—"

" 'Twas done, Demoiselle—I spoke the words myself."

"And Brevise?"

"Brevise escaped."

"Aye, Brevise always escapes, does he not?" she

cried out bitterly. "Who's to punish him? How is it that he lives and my brothers die?"

"I will."

"My lord . . ." Everard interrupted them reluctantly, his own heart heavy over the loss of the boy. "My lord, Sir Simon identifies Brevise's captain, who yet lives. What would you we did with him? Would you ransom him?"

Richard looked down to where Gilliane stared at the open burial pit. "Nay—dispatch him. And post his head above the gate on a pike." Behind him, he could hear the man cry out, but his jaw hardened. "Aye—I'd have William of Brevise know he has gained me for enemy this day."

Gilliane shook loose from him and shrugged out of his mantle, handing it to him. Clasping her arms across her chest, she walked to the chapel, which had survived somehow. Its small windows were cracked and shattered from the heat of the fires that had burned around it, and the cold sunlight streamed down to the rectangular stones that covered the floor before the altar. Already, two men labored to pry up a couple of them while another waited with a shovel to dig beneath. And on a makeshift table of boards between trestles, Alwina sewed Aubery in his shroud. The old woman's shoulders shook and her fingers trembled, but she stitched as carefully as if it had been his Christmas robe. Richard watched helplessly as Gilliane stared down into the unrecognizable charred flesh. And then she covered her face and stumbled away.

He caught her, shaking her to force her to cry, but she remained dry-eyed. Finally, overcome himself by the bleak anger in her eyes, he attempted to cradle her against him. "Demoiselle . . . Gilliane . . ." he murmured soothingly, feeling in her rigid body an anguish more intense than if she'd torn her clothes and wailed outright.

She stood unyielding within his arms for a moment, and then pushed him away. Raising her set

white face, she met his eyes. "I'd see him dead, my
lord—I'd do anything to see Brevise dead. If I were
a man, I'd hunt him down, dog that he is, and I'd
face him this day."

"Nay—I will see him punished."

"I'd see his soul burn in hell," she whispered with
suppressed violence. "I'd not see him fined for this."

"He'll die," Richard promised grimly.

"Will you swear it? Will you swear it to me now?"
There was an urgency in her voice, and her hands
clasped his mail-clad arms tightly as she looked up at
him. "Will you?"

"I swear it."

"On the Holy Rood?"

He disengaged her hands and drew his sword.
Holding it so the tang and quillon of the hilt made a
cross before him, he held it to the light. It cast the
image of the Holy Rood in shadow over the smooth-
hewn flagstones of the floor. His face grave, he in-
toned clearly, "I swear before God and Saint Agnes
that William of Brevise shall not go unpunished."

"Nay, he shall not live," she protested.

"That I will seek justice . . ."

"That he will not live," Gilliane insisted, her voice
low, her eyes on him rather than on the shadow of
the Cross.

"That I will seek justice through his death," he
finished. Sheathing his sword, he returned his attention to her. "Art satisfied now, Demoiselle? Sweet
Mary, but you are a bloodthirsty maid."

Thinking he mocked her, she lifted her chin defiantly. "Nay, my lord. Naught but the spilling of
William of Brevise's lifeblood will ease the pain I
feel."

"So be it then." Irrationally, he felt bound to her
now, bound by an oath that gave them a common
cause. He reached to grasp her elbow and turn her
away from the horror of what Alwina did. "Come,
there's little time, Gilliane, and I'd have you pack
whatever you can find to take."

"Aye." She sighed, exhaling heavily. "There is not much to take, is there? My family is gone, and my home is burnt."

"You are mistress of Beaumaule."

"Aye—mistress to naught but rubble." The toe of her leather slipper drew a half-circle in the sooty dust that had descended like a blanket over the floor. "Nay, but there's naught left here for me."

"I will see it rebuilt, Gilliane—'twill rise again in stone," he promised. "But for now, we must leave ere the sun reaches its height." His hand still clasping her elbow, he guided her out. "Come."

Simon of Woodstock paused from the grim task of raising the grisly pike above what was left of Beaumaule's gate, and watched Rivaux lead Gilliane de Lacey from the chapel. For a moment his eyes narrowed and his jaw tightened. Then he turned away to drive the supporting stake into the frozen earth with unwarranted viciousness.

10

Gilliane's spirits ebbed further with each passing furlong as her horse plodded beside Rivaux's. She had bidden all she knew farewell, and despite assurances that it was not so, she was certain she'd never see Beaumaule again. And even if she did, it would not be the same. Her brothers were all dead, her men either buried in a common grave or scattered to seek service elsewhere—even Simon of Woodstock was gone now, gone to Thomas Clifford's keep. She was numb, unable to feel, unable to cry for her losses, and yet unable to turn her thoughts elsewhere.

"Demoiselle, if you tire, we will stop again."

Rivaux's voice was kind, intruding on her reverie almost apologetically, as though he knew her pain. She looked up and realized he'd been studying her with troubled eyes. But neither kindness nor rest could ease the terrible emptiness she felt.

"Nay, I am all right, my Lord. I'd not delay you further."

There was nothing to say to her, nothing to do save wait for time to heal her heart and spirit, he realized, and yet he felt the need to try. As inured to death and battle as he was, he also could not forget the horror they'd left at Beaumaule. Aye, it had been a long time ere he slept at the monastery where they'd rested for the night, for every time he closed his eyes, he could see again Aubery de Lacey's frail, charred body, could smell again the stench of the seared flesh. If there ever was an act that demanded vengeance, it was the burning of Beaumaule.

He sucked in his breath, thinking to cleanse his mind with the cold air, and smelled instead that last curling, spiraling smoke that had followed them more than an hour after they'd left the place. He glanced sideways at Gilliane de Lacey, wondering if she shared his thoughts. Where the hood of her woolen cloak fell back to reveal her face, he could see her stony profile, white and set, in contrast to the bright copper hair that brushed against her high cheekbone and fluttered in the chill breeze. And once again it came home to him that she was pretty in an unusual way—not breathtakingly beautiful like his mother and sisters—just pretty. If only she could recover . . .

Aye, that was the question, wasn't it? There was a time yesterday when he'd feared for her mind, feared that the horror of what had passed had broken her will to survive. She'd ridden so silently, so stiffly, for hours on end, until at last she'd slumped forward in her saddle, and Everard had had to brace her quickly to break her fall. For once he'd not complained, calling out instead for aid, and they'd halted to lift her, senseless, to the ground. She could go no further, and they could not stay in the cold. And while they disputed among them whether she'd swooned from hunger or whether her mind had gone, the old woman had insisted that 'twas because her mistress had had no sleep. It had been the crimson mantle he wore—she'd stitched all night on it, old Alwina had said. Aye, 'twas what had saved those who survived— Gilliane had been the first to see Brevise's approach.

He pulled the warm fur-lined garment closer and remembered the feel of her. They'd placed her before him, and he'd wrapped her in it, holding her whilst she slept. Sweet Jesu, but the maid had been tired—she'd not stirred even when carried to bed. He flexed his sore arm as best he could. It was stiff still, both from wielding his sword at Beaumaule and from holding her steady on his horse, so stiff in fact he'd forgone his mail this day in favor of his *cuir bouilli*. He turned to look again at her, wondering if she was worth the pain and effort he'd expended on her behalf. A lock of her red hair spread in the breeze, catching the sunlight like spun copper, and he knew somehow she would be.

"Sweet Mother of God! 'Twould seem we are awaited, my lord!" Everard pulled his reins so sharply that his horse reared.

Brought up sharply by the urgency in his captain's voice, Richard jerked his head to stare where Everard pointed. A long, unsatisfactory string of oaths sprang to his lips as he cursed himself for a fool. He was caught in the open, unmailed and hampered by women and wounded, with nowhere to flee on the chalky ridges.

Gilliane's heart tightened as she clutched at the pommel of her saddle and leaned forward to see where they looked. "Is it Brevise—do you think 'tis Brevise?" she asked fearfully, knowing they had not the means to fight.

"Nay."

It was Richard who answered her. He stood in his saddle and tried to make out the colors on the pennon that flapped in the wind above an armed column. His eyes narrowed for a moment, and then he sat back. " 'Tis Warenne—and he is Stephen's man."

"Then mayhap they do not wait for you at all," she offered, relieved.

"They wait for me." His voice grim, he considered whether he dared attack, leaving her, her women, and Beaumaule's wounded behind. But he had not the time to armor himself—although the column was halted as the leaders conferred, they were still mounted.

"How do you know?"

He knew. He knew instinctively that the good Bishop of Winchester had alerted his enemies, and now they lay ready to take him. Why had he not considered that they'd not want him to warn Glouces-

ter? He'd been so certain of his own power, a power
secured by the old king's grace and his father's reputation, that he'd scarce given a thought to his vulner-
ability under a King Stephen.

"They do not want me to warn Gloucester," he
answered her finally, his mind racing through his
choices even as he spoke.

"They have the greater number, my lord," Everard
muttered as he attempted to count the shining helmets in the valley below. "Would you that we turned
back? I do not think we are seen yet."

"To what? There's not a keep within a night's ride
now that does not call Stephen liege lord," Richard
retorted, barely controlling his anger with himself.
"Nay."

"We cannot fight—there's the maid, and the
wounded from Beaumaule."

Gilliane listened to the captain's nearly dispassionate assessment of their chances. Without thinking,
she blurted out, "But if they await Rivaux, if 'tis
Rivaux they would stop, then let them pursue him
back from whence we have come."

"Jesu!" Everard's expression became one of complete disgust. "And then they take him."

"Nay." Her melancholy forgotten in the face of a
new threat, she leaned forward, straining for a better look. The men below were still little more than
shining specks in the morning sun. "Aye, they see us
not." She turned in her saddle to face Richard, reasoning, "And one helmeted man is much like another from the distance, is he not? Had it not been
for the pennon, you'd not have identified Warenne,
would you?" Seeing that he eyed her impatiently, she
shook her head. "Nay, but were I a man, I'd fight as
they have—I'd save myself by ruse."

"The maid thinks herself a warrior," Everard
scoffed.

But Richard was considering, ready to listen to
anything that might offer a better outcome. "Speak

your ruse, Demoiselle—and quickly. Nay, I'd listen," he silenced the incredulous captain.

His eyes narrowed intently beneath the shadow of his helmet, watching her and waiting. She drew her breath and nodded. "I'd flee, my lord, but I'd have this Warenne pursue another. If you but gave one of the men that which marks you, you could escape. In your helmet and cloak, he could be mistaken for you, and—"

" 'Tis cowardice!" Everard fairly howled.

"Is it bravery or vanity that makes men fight when they are outnumbered?" she countered. "Mother Mary, but I do not understand the lot of you! My brother rode to his death rather than run, and he—" she caught herself and appealed instead to Richard of Rivaux. "If you fight, my lord, what happens to us?" With a sweep of her hand she indicated Alwina and the wounded who rode at the back of the column.

"You will be captured."

"Aye, and Brevise is Stephen's man also—think you he will not seek me? Nay, but if we run and are caught, 'tis the same, but at least—"

"Aye," he cut in curtly. Turning to Everard, he murmured, "They do not intend to harm me—they'd not risk my father's certain wrath, I think. At worst, they will but seek ransom from him, and I will see that 'tis paid. What say you—would you be taken for me?"

"What of the others? You cannot take them also, else Warenne will suspect," Everard pointed out.

"I'd have you tell him that I will ransom them also." His dark eyes searched his captain's face. "But if you do not wish to do this—"

"Nay." A wry smile twisted Everard of Meulan's face as he shook his head. "You are unmailed, my lord, and the leather will not take many blows. Besides, Warenne's keep is warm, I'll warrant."

"They move," Gilliane noted with alarm. "Sweet Mary, but you have not long to decide!"

"What say you—would you go willingly in my place?"

Richard asked again, his gaze still on the older man.

"Aye."

"So be it then," Rivaux murmured with a sigh, reaching for his heavy helmet. "We are not of a size, but if you sit tall and ride my horse, mayhap they will not know of the deception until 'tis too late." Reluctantly he dismounted and waited for the other man to swing down also. Unclasping the red velvet mantle at his shoulder, he lifted it off. The boy Garth hurried to take it, while Everard handed over his own plain woolen one.

"I shall be considerably warmer than you, my lord," the captain murmured, settling into the fur-lined cloak. "Aye, 'tis overlong, but that cannot be seen when I am in the saddle." He stepped into the stirrup and eased his mail-encased body onto Richard's favorite horse. "Gently, you black beast, gently," he soothed the animal as it stepped sideways. "I think he knows I am not up to your weight, my lord. Who goes with you?"

"Can we not take Alwina at least?" Gilliane asked hopefully.

"Nay. Were it not for his arm, I'd take Walter." He looked down his line, considering. "We dare not draw attention if we are to succeed. You, fellow," he addressed the boy Garth suddenly, "would you ride with me?"

"Aye."

Richard pulled the stiff woolen cloak closer and swung into his captain's saddle, nodding. "Then I take the demoiselle and the boy. Everard, once you are taken, we shall strive for the nearest port where Gloucester has ships. Tell Warenne to send to Celesin with his demands for your ransom."

The captain nodded grimly now and jammed Richard's helmet on his head. It was too loose for battle, but he meant to surrender anyway. Kneeing the black horse, he saluted his lord and urged the big animal forward.

"Wait." Gilliane hesitated, aware that they'd done this for her, and then blurted out, "The mantle—have a care for the mantle, good sir. And . . . and I wish you Godspeed—all of you."

Everard of Meulan nodded and raised a gloved hand to signal the column to fall in behind him. The boy Garth edged his horse closer to Richard and waited. As the men of Rivaux and Beaumaule slowly descended, their wounded behind them, into the valley, Gilliane and Richard and the boy watched. From the distance, they could see Warenne's mounted troop draw nearer. Their leader, mayhap Rainald de Warenne himself, rode forward to greet Everard, who remained helmeted. After the exchange of some words, Richard's captain drew his sword and proffered it in surrender.

It was then that Richard truly cursed. Gilliane's eyes widened nearly as much at the vehemence in his voice as at the blasphemy. "Holy Jesu, but what ails you?" she had to know.

Richard's fingers closed over the hilt of his own sword, grasping it in his palm. "If you'd pray, pray that we can outride them, Demoiselle," he muttered, kicking his horse and cutting wide of the halted column. She and the boy had to spur after him.

"Wait. I don't understand—"

"The sword. I forgot the sword—he will know 'tis not mine he takes!" he all but shouted at her. "Come on!"

As if to give credence to his words, she could see several men detach themselves from Warenne's column and ride toward them. "We are seen!" she called out to Rivaux.

"Aye, but we are unmailed and lighter!"

She did not have to be urged twice. She dug her heels into the flank of her horse and gave it its head. It stretched its neck into the wind and pounded the hard, frozen earth in pursuit of Richard of Rivaux. Garth kicked and shouted at his own beast until it too ran as though hell pursued them.

"Archers!" he cried out in dismay. "Lady, there are archers!"

Two bowmen, their aim hampered by the movement of their own horses, tried to draw within range. An arrow fell, its flight spent, in front of her, and she spurred her lady's horse even more furiously. But they had little interest in her. Richard, whose stronger mount easily outdistanced all of them, turned back at Garth's frantic shout, slowing to reach for Gilliane's reins. At that moment, the bowman who had been shooting at the boy loosed an arrow that caught Richard in the shoulder with a whooshing thud. He swayed slightly from the sudden impact as the metal tip cut through the boiled leather, pinning his cloak to the *cuir bouilli*. Gilliane, without thinking, leaned to grasp both sets of reins from his hand. As a red stain spread, seeping through the mantle, Warenne's archer reined in in horror, and Gilliane took the lead, drawing the big bay beside her.

"I thought you said they would not harm you!" she shouted at him.

"Nay—'twas not I he attempted." Richard of Rivaux leaned froward in his saddle, braced against the pain. "Nay, do not stop," he gasped through clenched teeth.

Whether it was because they thought him done or because they were afraid of the consequences of shooting Guy of Rivaux's heir, the riders drew off. Gilliane, leaving nothing to chance, knotted his reins around her wrist and kicked her mount harder. The bigger horse jarred the earth beside her, and the man held on to the pommel of his saddle. His face was contorted, his skin pale beneath his black hair, but somehow he managed to keep his seat.

She did not look back until they'd crossed the breadth of the valley and climbed the next hill. Then, when she perceived they were no longer pursued, she reined in shakily. Garth dismounted and walked to stand beneath her.

"God's bones, Demoiselle, but 'twas a ride!" he breathed.

"Aye."

It was more of a groan than an acknowledgment, but admiration mingled with pain in Rivaux's dark eyes as he looked at her. Gilliane cast a furtive look behind them, and then slid out of her saddle. Her legs felt strangely weak and her heart beat apprehensively as she stared upward to where the arrow shaft pinned the cloak to his shoulder. A sudden wave of nausea engulfed her, forcing her to swallow hard or disgrace herself. "Sweet Mary," she breathed, closing her eyes against the sight of it.

"Nay, I am all right. I . . ."

When she managed to look up again, he weaved before her, giving lie to his words, and she feared he would fall. "Do you think you are able to dismount, my lord?" she asked anxiously.

"Aye." He leaned precariously over her, swaying in his saddle, and then murmured thickly, "Nay."

"Garth, can you take him down?" she asked, knowing in her heart that he could not.

The boy eyed him doubtfully and shook his head. "Nay, but he is fourteen stone clothed at the least. If he fell on the arrow—"

"Aye."

"I'd ride—whilst I can." Richard spoke through clenched teeth. His gloved hands held tightly to his pommel for balance as he tried to fight the burning pain in his shoulder. "If I am taken down, I'd not be . . . able to remount," he gasped.

"And if you fall—"

"Tie me on." He closed his eyes, and she feared he would swoon. With an involuntary "Sweet Mary," she lunged to catch him, but he rallied and held on. "Tie me on," he repeated. " 'Tis not far to the sea."

"I can smell the water now, my lady," Garth said hopefully.

Gilliane sniffed deeply and smelled nothing, but she was loath to dispute it. If Rivaux could but hang

on until they reached a port, she could get aid fo
him. "All right, but there's naught for rope—I'd tr
to hold you."

"Nay, I am too heavy." He groped at the arro
shaft, and then shook his head. His hand fell awa
his glove covered with his own blood. "Break it off
he ordered Garth.

"Holy Jesu!" the boy breathed. His own face wa
pale, greenish-gray almost, and his eyes were wid
with horror. "Nay, but I cannot—I cannot even reac
you, my lord."

Rivaux's eyes mirrored the pain he felt as he leane
toward Gilliane. Numbly she shook her head also
He exhaled visibly and reached again to the shaf
stopping midway. "Take the glove, Demoiselle." I
was as much a groan as an order, but Gilliane reache
to pull the heavy blood-reddened glove from h
hand. His breath was uneven, coming in white puff
of steam that dissipated into the cold air. "Aye, hol
me steady—that I do not fall."

As he loomed above her, his eyes closed for
moment, she attempted to reach him. Finally sh
stood on tiptoe to press against where his leg strad
dled the horse. " 'Tis the best I can offer, my lord."

He raised the bared hand again, grasping the ar
row shaft, and blood seeped between his finger
dripping onto his saddle in front of him. He gr
maced as he attempted to dislodge it, and then, wit
an effort, he broke the slender wood between hi
thumb and forefinger, twisting it as he did so. H
slumped forward to catch his breath, swaying agai
Alarmed, Gilliane ordered Garth, "Help me to moun
that I may hold him."

The boy stood transfixed, his throat visibly swa
lowing the gorge that rose at the sight of the arro
stump. And then her words took on meaning fo
him. Wordlessly he cupped his hands and move
next to Everard's bay. Gilliane lifted the skirts of he
gown and undergown and stepped into the interlace
palms, swinging up as he boosted her. She threw he

eg over the width of the animal's back behind Rivaux's
saddle, and leaned forward to slide her arms around
the man.

"Hand me his reins."

"Aye, Demoiselle."

"Nay—you cannot . . ." Richard of Rivaux weaved
unsteadily in her arms, protesting weakly.

"Be still, that you may breathe, my lord," she muttered into the breadth of his back. "Garth, you will
have to guide us, as I cannot see around him. My
lord, can you use your knees?" she addressed Rivaux.

It was an important question, for any horse capable of going into battle had to be directed by its
rider's movement rather than his reins. In front of
her, Richard managed to nod. Gilliane waited for
the boy to remount, and then she slapped the bay's
rump. Its braided tail swished, but it moved slowly
forward. Rivaux pressed his knee into its side, directing it toward the road that was little more than a
path.

Gilliane knew not how long or how far they rode,
bobbing and weaving, jarred until their bones ached,
but it seemed an eternity. She leaned her head against
his back and prayed silently that he could keep his
seat. He spoke not at all, and she feared he had
swooned, but she held him tightly encircled and willed
him to live.

When they came over the last chalk hill, the busy
port bustled before them, its narrow streets teeming
with the sounds and smells of vessels being laded.
Rivaux kneed the horse forward into the first lane.
They must have been a strange sight, a wounded
knight and a girl, for people immediately began to
collect around them, walking beside them.

"My lord of Gloucester's ship—I'd seek Gloucester's ship," she announced boldly. "I'd seek aid for
his man."

Rivaux straightened up and rallied with an effort.
"Aye—a silver mark to any who leads us there."

"My lord Stephen—" One man looked up at them doubtfully, reaching for the reins.

"Nay, he is Gloucester's man," she interrupted quickly. "He is his lord's responsibility, for he i hurt."

"There is a physician—"

"Nay." This time it was Richard who spoke, brush ing aside the man's words. "Gloucester."

The fellow shrugged and grasped the leather line that encircled the bay's nose. " 'Twill fester, sir." He looked up at Richard's plain cloak and the well-battered helmet that hung from his saddle pommel and surmised that perhaps the knight could ill-afford a physician. "I'd not take your money."

"See us to one of Gloucester's ships, and 'tis yours," Gilliane promised. "I'd have him tended in Normandy."

"And he lives."

The man's words sent a chill shuddering through her, but she dared not discourage Rivaux. "Nay, he will live."

They wended, a strange procession, through the cramped streets of the city, drawing everything from the derisive jeers of those who instinctively hated mounted knights, to shouts of encouragement from those who didn't. Many stood watching in silence, unwilling either to aid or to stop them. As the way grew narrower, she considered the possibility that they would be robbed and left for dead in some dank alley. The stench of offal and rotting fish assailed her nose and nauseated her, but she managed to hold the man before her steady on his horse. Finally there was the unmistakable salt scent of the sea, and the crowded wharves lay ahead of them.

"Give him the money—'tis in my belt."

Nodding, she pulled back his cloak and felt along the stamped leather that girded his waist, moving her hands over his flat abdomen, finding the soft leather pouch that hung there. As she loosened it and drew it out, a collective gasp escaped the crowd massed around them. It was suddenly realized that

he wounded knight was a man of substance, and
whatever sympathy his plight had gleaned for him
faded. Several people pressed closer, reaching out
their hands to rob the fat purse.

" 'Tis a rich lord—aye, he's a lord!"

The red silk gleamed bright with gold embroidery
on the surcoat that covered his *cuir bouilli,* but the
black hawk was for the most part obscured by his
bloody cloak. One of the bolder men sought to pull
the wounded man down, frightening Gilliane, who
kicked furiously at him.

"Nay—'tis Rivaux!" she cried out in alarm. "Aye—
you'll be punished if you touch him! 'Tis Rivaux!"

"Rivaux! Rivaux? 'Tis Rivaux?"

Doubtful murmurs swept through the crowd as all
eyes suddenly studied him intently. The mood, which
had grown ugly, eased almost to awe. The man who'd
led them looked up at him curiously. "Nay, but you
are too young to be such a one as he."

"He is Richard of Rivaux, son to Count Guy,"
Gillian hastened to explain before they turned on
him again. "Aye, but his father punished Belesme."

Belesme. It was a name that could bring fear and
loathing into the hearts and minds of Norman and
Saxon, peasant and lord alike, despite the fact that
he'd been gone from the earth almost twenty-four
years. Even now there were the superstitious who
feared that he would incarnate himself yet again and
return to wreak death on them. But it was Guy of
Rivaux who'd taken him, Guy of Rivaux who'd finally ended the terror Belesme had visited on Normandy and England. And it was of Guy of Rivaux
that every bard sang in the halls of both lands.

"Art truly his son?" a ragged beggar who'd followed them asked.

Richard leaned forward, swaying in Gilliane's arms.
"Aye," he whispered. "Jesu, aid me—"

A dozen hands grasped at him, easing him down as
he fell, almost taking her with him. "Sweet Mary, but
he bleeds to death!" she cried. "Can no one aid us?"

They'd gathered around him, bending over him obscuring him from her sight. The one who'd le the horse straightened up before the others an shook his head. "Nay, he is but weakened from th ride. We can take him to my lord of Warenne—"

"Nay! He is Gloucester's liegeman. Is there no shi of Gloucester's here?"

"Aye, but—"

"If you love his father, if you love Guy of Rivaux I pray you will take us to one who serves Gloucester— pray you." Gilliane managed to slide from the b bay's back into their midst. "Garth, tell them—te them that Gloucester will reward them." She rounde frantically on the startled boy, who stood tongue-tie behind her now. "Garth!"

"Aye, D-Demoiselle," he answered finally, stam mering at the suddenness of her plea. "Aye." Facin the curious onlookers, he managed to tell them, " 'Ti as the Lady Gilliane says—'tis Rivaux's son."

"And we'd see him to Normandy before his ene mies overtake us!" Gilliane begged them. "I pra you—aid us!"

For answer, one of the burlier men knelt besid Richard and wrenched at the stub of the arrow shaf where it still protruded from his chest. Richar groaned, biting his lip until it bled, and then hi head lolled as flesh and leather yielded the metal tip

"Oh—nay, but you would kill him!" Helpless tear rolled down Gilliane's cheeks.

But the men ignored her as one tore at his ow undertunic to provide a piece of cloth. The fellow who'd pulled the arrow free laid his head close t Richard's bared head and listened for his breath Satisfied, he sat back on his haunches and rolled th dirty cloth. Loosening the lacings of the stiffene leather *cuir bouilli,* he thrust the wad beneath th hole and then pulled the leather thongs tight agair Rising, he wiped his hands on his own tunic.

"He swoons, but he breathes strongly," he addresse Gilliane, stating the obvious, and then he adde

Our lord serves Stephen, lady, but we'd not see harm come to Rivaux's son—nay, but 'twas he who took Belesme." He paused to sign the Cross over his breast at the hated name, as though doing so would protect him from some ancient curse, and then he turned back to the others. " 'Tis Guy of Rivaux's son—would you carry him to Gloucester's ship?"

Nodding assent, several of the men attempted to stand the unconscious man up, bracing him between two of them. As he sagged, others formed a human bed with their arms beneath him and lifted him. Gilliane followed as they carried the unconscious man, praying silently that he'd live and that they'd not betray him.

The captain of the *Windrunner* received them, and after listening to Gilliane's plea for Richard, agreed to lift anchor early for the crossing. In their haste, they'd found a cargo vessel more used to carrying barrels of pickled fish and lampreys than people. Gilliane huddled in the cold, dank, rancid hold, covering Richard with Everard's bloody mantle, hovering over him anxiously. It was dark, and the air was unbearably foul, but she didn't care. Once she heard what sounded like a great sigh, and fearful, leaned close to listen for his breath.

"Demoiselle," he whispered in the darkness. "I am in your debt this day."

Tears stung her eyes, scalding them, as she gave a silent prayer of thanksgiving that he would rally. God in His mercy had not abandoned her entirely.

"I thirst."

"There's naught—Garth, ask if there is water to be had for my lord."

"Aye, Demoiselle."

She could hear the scuffle of his boots as the boy scrambled toward the faint light at the other end of the hold, and then there was only the sound of

Rivaux's breathing and the movement of the rats a
they scampered along the ribbed timbers.

"I . . . I feared you would die, my lord."

"Nay."

"You cannot ride to Robert of Gloucester."

There was a heavy sigh in the darkness as h
acknowledged the truth of her words. "Nor even
Celesin," he admitted reluctantly. "Nay, but Rivaux
is closer—though I am loath to go there."

Rivaux. For some reason the idea of going int
Guy of Rivaux's great keep lowered her spirits, which
already seemed to rise and fall with the seas beneath
them. What would they—Count Guy and his high
born countess—think of her? She'd be a nithing t
them, one scarcely above a serving maid, she sup
posed, and they could not be expected to welcome a
homeless, undowered maid.

"Gilliane?"

"Aye, my lord?" She leaned closer to listen to hi
harsh whisper.

"I'd have you lay your head down again, that I
may smell the rosewater in your hair—it eases me."

His mind must be wandering. She started to retor
that 'twas smoke he'd smelled, but the words died or
her lips. If in his confusion he turned to her, wha
harm could there be in comforting him? She lay
down beside him, stretching her body against hi
greater length and curving her arm over his chest
feeling the bulge in the torn leather. He sighed and
turned his head against hers.

His breath was warm against her face, reassuring
her that he would live. He had to. Her hand sough
the hard muscle of his arm, closing over it, as she
eased her head to rest against the stiff leather of
his *cuir bouilli* on his good shoulder. The though
crept into her mind that, for good or ill, his fate wa
hers.

It took Garth a long time to beg wine and a suit
able drinking vessel of the ship's captain, and when

he returned, he discovered his mistress and Rivaux
both asleep, twined together in Everard's cloak. After sitting for a time huddled against the cold, he
drank the wine himself and eased his body against
theirs. The three of them lay close, taking and giving
warmth in the cold, dank hold.

11

It was obvious by the time they reached Dieppe that Richard of Rivaux could travel no further. The shipmaster had him carried to a wharfside inn, and Gilliane drew upon Richard's purse to buy lodgings for them despite the meanness of the place. With great misgivings she sent Garth to carry a message to Guy of Rivaux, hoping against hope that the boy could find his way in a strange land—and that the great lord would believe his son lay grievously wounded in Dieppe, unaided by any but a maid.

She knelt in the small sleeping loft over the inn stable that Rivaux's silver had bought them, and tended him anxiously. He'd lost far too much blood, and his mind wandered often, alarming her greatly. And now he complained of the cold also, shivering mightily within Everard's cloak, but when she touched him, his brow was hot.

"I th-thirst," he croaked for the fourth time in a short while. With an effort, his eyes opened to stare at her as though she were a stranger, fluttered, and closed again.

Her hands shook from the cold as she poured sour wine from the skin the innkeeper had sold her, taking care to strain the debris with her fingers. Lifting Richard from the straw pallet, she braced his shoulder against her knee and held the crude cup to his lips. He drank deeply and fell back sighing.

"J-Jesu, b-but 'tis c-cold."

Laying aside the cup, she drew the woolen cloth

closer to his shoulders, pulling it up to his chin, but the chills continued to rack his body. In desperation she scooped straw from the floor around them and piled it on him for warmth, and still he shook. She pinned him down, lying over him to try to stop the awful shaking, but he moved beneath her like a quivering horse until she could stand it no longer. What if he died in her care? What would his family do to her then?

Finally she left him then to seek out the innkeeper. Afraid to reveal 'twas Richard of Rivaux she tended, afraid she might be among his enemies, she begged for a blanket for her husband. The innkeeper's eyes raked her boldly, scoffing at her claim of marriage, but she no longer cared about that.

"Tumble you for it," he offered, his eyes on the swell of her breasts beneath her plain mantle.

"Nay."

"Then let him freeze." He shrugged and moved away.

"Wait. I have silver . . ."

It was a mistake. She could see the gleam of avarice in the man's eyes as he turned back to her. "How much?"

"A little," she lied, wishing she'd not come down from the loft. "I gave you most of it for the pallet."

"Give me the rest."

"Aye." She nodded, running her tongue over suddenly parched lips. "I will get it of my husband."

"Husband?" He sneered, taking in the plainness of her clothing and her short, blunt hair. " 'Tis plain to me that you are naught but a harlot shorn for her sins. But if you would seek the knight's protection, you'll find yourself alone." His eyes lingered insolently on her breasts again. "Aye, for he won't live long with a wound like that."

Her heart tightened painfully in her chest, but her fear did not betray her. "Nonetheless, sir, I'd have a blanket for my husband," she repeated coldly.

"Get me the silver then."

"Aye."

She returned to the loft afraid—afraid that the innkeeper spoke the truth, afraid that Richard of Rivaux's life ebbed, afraid that when night fell they would be robbed or worse. She picked up the purse and moved to where the shutters let in a sliver of light. Opening it, she counted out the contents. It was the equivalent of a fortune to her, but she dared not spend any more of it without risking losing it entirely. She drew the string reluctantly and carried it back to where he lay, his eyes closed, his teeth chattering, beneath the pile of straw.

Nay, but 'twas not just another blanket he needed, she had to admit to herself. Even as unskilled in simples as she was, she could see he had to have a physician or die. But she knew of none in the strange place, and she'd not risk approaching the innkeeper again. Mayhap a priest could direct her—aye, a priest—he'd need one anyway if she could not find help.

She bent over to brush back the thick black hair from the hot, dry skin of Richard's face. His eyes fluttered but did not open.

"My lord, can you hear me speak?" she asked, placing her mouth near his ear.

"Aye."

"I leave to seek aid for you—I will return," she promised him.

"Nay."

"I must."

The straw rustled beneath her as one of his hands wriggled free of the cloth and reached to grasp hers. "Nay," he croaked again. "I'd h-have you w-warm me, G-G-G—" He abandoned the effort to speak and pulled her hand closer to his breast.

Gratified that he knew her at least, she lay down beside him again and spread her cloak over both of them, waiting for him to sleep. His breath was harsh and labored beneath her head, so much so it was difficult to tell if he slept or swooned. She waited until she could stand it no longer.

This time she did not tell him she was leaving, but rather stole down the ladder with his purse tucked beneath her mantle. The stableyard was busy enough that none took note of her. Approaching an ostler scarcely older than herself, she told him, "A priest—I have need of a priest. Do you—?"

"Aye." He stopped untying a horse and turned to her sympathetically. "God's mercy on your man."

"Nay, he lives."

"Then I'd not have the priest—'tis a monk you need."

"Where?"

He turned and pointed vaguely toward the south. "But 'tis a league and more."

"Jesu. I'd have the priest, then—where is he?"

For answer, the ostler drew the streets around them with a stick, scratching in the hardened earth and then gesturing toward the town itself. Without waiting to thank him, Gilliane picked up her skirts and ran through the narrow, cramped streets, trying to remember the direction. She was rewarded when the unassuming spire of a small church loomed before her.

Breathless, she pounded on the door until the iron ring reverberated against the thick carved wood. When she stopped, she could hear muffled voices within and then the scraping of shoes against the hard floor. The door cracked slightly, letting out warm air that turned white when it mingled with the cold, and a short, rotund priest peered out.

"Ho, now—what's this?" he demanded, opening the door wider at the sight of the slender girl shivering on the stoop. "Child, 'tis too cold for you to be out like this."

The kindness in his voice caused her to burst into tears, and for a time she could only stand there. "Hugh, get the child some mulled wine to warm her," the priest in the doorway ordered. Reaching out to her, he caught her elbow and drew her inside. "Nay, daughter, but there's naught that God cannot mend if we trust Him," he consoled her.

Almost immediately a cup of steaming wine was thrust into her hands by a thin-faced man wearing the cassock of a monk. His tonsured head gleamed beneath the smoking torch that hung in the rung above him as he hovered solicitously over her. Gilliane wiped her wet cheeks with the back of her free hand and took a sip of the hot liquid. It burned, warming her as it slid down her throat. The priest behind him waited until she'd calmed down. She swallowed more of the wine and then met his eyes.

"I am Gilliane de Lacey, good father," she began. "I . . . that is, I am mistress to Beaumaule, a small keep in England," she hastened to add, fearful that he would not believe what she would tell him. "And I seek aid for the son of Rivaux."

The priest's eyes widened perceptibly, but it was the monk who turned to ask, "The son of Rivaux, you say? By the Holy Mother, where is he?"

When the words came, they spilled out, one on top of the other, until she'd poured out the whole story so quickly that it was unlikely it could be followed, but neither man questioned her until she reached the point that she'd left Richard of Rivaux unattended in the cold and drafty loft of a waterfront inn. Then the brother called Hugh cut in, "He is there yet? Nay, but 'tis not safe, Demoiselle."

"I could not move him, Father, and he is too weak to walk himself."

"Aye—of course you could not," the priest said soothingly. "But if he is indeed Count Guy's son, 'tis most important that we attend him as quickly as 'tis possible. I'd not have it said that I failed to aid Guy of Rivaux's son."

Almost immediately word was sent to the Cistercian abbey nearby to prepare to receive Richard of Rivaux, and three menservants with a litter were dispatched to the inn. The monk went with Gilliane, ready to do battle with the lecherous innkeeper if the need arose. While Gilliane sought to explain the extent of Richard's wounds, the fellow listened, his thin face grave, and then when she paused to catch her breath, he explained that he had some skill in tending the sick. "Indeed, 'tis the reason I was with Father Herve—his joints pain him in the cold."

They found Richard lying naked, robbed of every shred of his clothing, and freezing in the loft where he'd been left to die. Brother Hugh looked around him in contempt and then rounded so furiously on the innkeeper, who hovered nervously behind them, telling him that Guy of Rivaux himself would seek vengeance for the insult offered his son.

"Rivaux's son? Nay, but the wench did not tell me! I swear she did not—I swear it!" the man protested piteously, his hands outstretched to the monk. "Nay, but—"

"I am not Count Guy," Brother Hugh muttered tersely. "Nay, save your pleas for him."

"Tell him, I beg you . . . tell him—"

"That you would rob his only son? That you would have let him die?"

"But I knew not who he was!"

The monk turned away in disgust, leaving the man to quake at the thought of Guy of Rivaux's vengeance. While they waited for the men to wrap and bundle Richard's nearly dead weight into the litter, the innkeeper's wife miraculously produced his cloak and clothing. "My s-sword," Richard protested feebly, showing he was still conscious. Ignoring her husband's protests that he'd never seen it, the woman left silently and returned carrying sword belt and scabbard. Gilliane received it curiously, remembering that Richard had said it would be recognized by Warenne. Aside from the fact that it felt heavier than those of her brothers, she could see no difference in the hilt. In fact, it was plain in comparison to some she'd seen. She withdrew it partially from the scabbard, sliding her fingers beneath the quillon, and as the gleaming blade came into view, she could see how Warenne would not be fooled. Along either side of the polished metal were strange engravings, neither Latin nor French, but rather some peculiar symbols. The monk looked over her shoulder and nodded.

"Viking runes," he offered in explanation. "I have heard of this sword—'twas taken from Count Robert of Belesme."

She nearly dropped it then, recoiling from the cold metal in her hand. "God aid me," she gasped involuntarily, shuddering at the thought that she held that which had once been held by someone like Belesme. Then, noting the monk's faintly amused expression, she hastily sheathed the sword, laying it aside as gingerly as if it had been made of eggshells. Averting her head, she surreptitiously signed the Cross over her breast against any curse Belesme might have given it. " 'Tis heavy," she offered lamely, repelled by it.

"Aye." With the barest hint of a smile, the monk reached to take the sword and scabbard. Balancing the weight of it with the air of a man who knew of such things, he nodded. "The bards call it Hellbringer, but 'tis naught but well-fired steel. When it met Roger de Brione's Avenger or Guy of Rivaux's Doomslayer, its spell was broken."

She eyed it doubtfully, still unwilling to touch it again. To her relief, they were ready to leave. Brother Hugh tucked it beneath his arm and carried it after the litter bearing Richard. She pulled her cloak closer as the cold wind hit her again in the courtyard.

"Will he . . . ? Can you . . . ?" She walked quickly beside the monk and attempted to put her fears into words.

"I have tended worse, Demoiselle."

"But his fever—"

"I'd not let it be said I let Guy of Rivaux's son die," he responded simply, bending against the wind. "If God will direct these hands, he will live."

The distance was greater than that which she'd run earlier, and the cold gnawed at her bones. She feared that Richard of Rivaux would not be able to stand it. "Please—I pray you—please hurry," she urged the men who carried him.

By the time they'd reached the abbey, Gilliane had lost the feeling in her face and her feet. Numbly she stepped through the doorway of the abbey house and looked gratefully to the fire that burned in the abbot's center brazier.

" 'Tis indeed his son?" he asked without preamble.

"Aye."

"Then we'd best send to him—I'd not have it said that aught ill befell his heir here."

"Nay!" Richard croaked, rousing again from a near-stupor.

"I have al-already s-sent for him," Gilliane managed through chattering teeth. "G-Garth went."

The abbot turned curious eyes on her, suddenly realizing her presence. "And who is this?" he inquired to the monk.

"I have t-tended h-him," Gilliane tried to explain.

"Warm yourself, child, ere you sicken also." The brother who'd accompanied her set aside Richard's sword and turned to his patient. Another monk handed her a steaming cup of spiced wine, one even hotter than that she'd had of the priest, while asking him, "How fares he?"

Gilliane held her breath for his answer and was rewarded when Brother Hugh answered, "If he takes no harm from being robbed of his clothes in this weather, he will mend, I think. The wound is deep from what I have seen of it, but the arrow struck neither bone nor sinew. Nay, but if 'tis cauterized and packed, 'twill heal." For a moment Brother Hugh's eyes met Gilliane's. "Brother Lymas will aid me, Demoiselle, and you may wait with our abbot, Brother Strigall."

Gillian looked to where the abbot stood studying

Richard, and shook her head. "Nay—I fear not for what I cannot feel."

Abbot Strigall appeared not to hear her as he stared down at Rivaux's dark hair and his closed eyes. "Aye, he has the look of his blood to him, does he not? There is much of his father in his face."

Brother Lymas followed his gaze and sighed. "Aye, none could deny he is Rivaux—I fear our poor rooms will be mean to one such as he."

"Not so poor as your own cell," Brother Hugh reminded him. "Nay, but life will seem sweet wherever he is when he wakes." Turning again to Gilliane, he asked gently, "What is my lord of Rivaux to you, child?"

She colored, wondering what he would think no matter how she answered, but she managed to meet his gaze over the steaming cup. "I am his ward."

"Aye," was all he said.

"You may put him in the bed prepared for him," Brother Lymas instructed the litter-bearers. "Or would you tend his wound first, Hugh? I'd not have a feather mattress burned with the iron."

"I'd lay him on the trestle table."

They lifted Richard again and carried him into the narrow passage between the abbot's room and the kitchens. Gilliane started to follow them, but another monk barred her way. "Warm yourself, Demoiselle, that you may tend him later. What we do is not for your sight."

Dispirited, she let the one called Lymas refill her cup and she carried it to the brazier. Huddling on a small bench before the fire, she could hear low voices and the scraping of feet against the hard floor in another room. It seemed like an eternity as she waited, her hands clasped around the warmth of the cup. He must've wakened, she decided, for she could hear his croaked protest, and then he cried out. She knocked over the bench as she rose anxiously and strode to the hall where they held Richard of Rivaux down.

None of them noted her, so intent were they on keeping him still as Brother Hugh lifted the heated poker yet again. This time Richard did not cry out, but Gilliane could see his body jump on the table. The sickening smell of burning flesh brought back the hideous memories of how Aubery had died. For a moment she clutched the doorway and tried to fight the waves of nausea that swept over her. A long, low moan emanated from Richard of Rivaux, drawing her from her own agony. She forced herself to walk to where he lay.

This time no one stopped her. Two men held his feet and one leaned his weight to hold the wounded shoulder against the hard table. The monk heated the iron again. Gilliane could see the beads of sweat on Richard of Rivaux's head and she wondered if his fever had broken or if they came from the pain. Blood trickled from a puncture wound where he'd bitten his lip. Without thinking, she reached to touch the dampness, smoothing the black hair over his wet brow. He appeared to have swooned, but when the monk brought the poker back and touched the edge of the ugly, gaping hole, his body went rigid. The flesh sizzled much like meat on a kitchen spit. Gilliane's hand convulsed in his hair, gripping it tightly for a moment, and then relaxed with relief when the poker was withdrawn.

She began stroking the damp black fringe ceaselessly, as though somehow it might ease him as the process of cauterizing the wound was repeated several times. The edges of flesh where the arrow tip had been removed were smoothed and shiny now, bearing the seal of a burn just above the swell of a chest muscle. The thought crossed her mind that he would bear the scars forever.

Rivaux lifted his hand weakly, as though he would brush her fingers away, and then let it drop. His eyes were still closed, but his breath was easier as he whispered through cracked and parched lips, "I'd not have you leave me, Gilliane."

Relief flooded her, descending like a torrent of emotion that threatened her composure. Tears welled in her eyes and were brushed away before she reached to stroke his hand also.

Another monk approached and pressed a thick, smelly poultice over the hole in Richard's shoulder. Then Brother Hugh bound Richard's arm to his side and wrapped shoulder and chest with strips of linen over it. Stepping back to admire his work, he exhaled deeply and nodded his satisfaction. "Aye, he will mend, but I'd have him watched this night. On the morrow, I will gather cobwebs to pack the wound better."

"I will watch him," Gilliane heard herself say.

"Nay—'tis not seemly, Demoiselle," Brother Lymas protested. "Art a maid, and—"

"And will be a maid on the morrow still," she interrupted him.

"E'en so—"

"Let her stay—she will have a gentler hand than yours or mine." Brother Hugh eyed Gilliane with a greater respect now. "Art a strong maid to watch this, Demoiselle."

"Gilliane?"

Richard whispered so low that she had to bend close to hear him. Her fingers tightened on his as she put her ear almost to his mouth. "Aye, my lord?"

"I thought you had left me to die."

"Sweet Mary—nay," she whispered back. "I did but seek aid for you."

"Aye." His eyes moved beneath purplish lids and then fluttered open, focusing with an effort on her. The black pupils were circled with gold flecks that seemed to mirror pain. "I can never repay you for this day."

"Follow us, Demoiselle." Brother Hugh laid a gentle hand on her shoulder and nodded to those who'd carried him before. " 'Tis rest that will restore him."

She released his hands and stepped back to allow them to lift him. His eyes met hers in silent appeal, as though he'd not be left again. He winced visibly when they struggled to take him from the table, bringing tears that stung and overflowed onto her face as she felt for him.

They carried him down the long, arched corridor past the dormitories of the monks and to the rooms kept for travelers, sparse rooms with naught but cots and mattresses beneath carved crucifixes showing the Lord's final agony. Laying him upon the cot with as much care as three men could manage, they murmured hopes for his recovery and withdrew. Brother Hugh brought her a small bench.

A timid fire burned in a low brazier, the only source of heat in the room. A draft blew from the high, shuttered window near the ceiling, bending the tentative flames that licked at the logs. One of the monks reached a pole hook to push the shutters tighter, and then they left her alone with Richard. She drew the bench close to the cot and prepared for a solitary vigil.

Only once was she interrupted by someone bringing him a cup of bitter herbs for his pain, something that sent him into a deep sleep. Otherwise, she spent much of the night listening—listening to the low chants of monks at compline, listening to the sound of a man's breathing, sometimes heavy, sometimes almost silent. It was the latter that frightened her, and often she would stir from her own thoughts to lay her head against his bandaged breast to reassure herself that he still lived.

The night passed slowly, creeping like a thief amongst the vigilant, until she thought she could stay awake no longer. She moved closer to the wall, scraping the bench on the cold floor, and leaned her head against the hard stones.

"Gilliane?" he murmured somewhere in her dreams. She snapped awake, nearly losing her balance, and bent over him.

"Aye, my lord?" she asked anxiously.

"You have beautiful hair."

Clearly, his mind wandered. She touched the blunted ends of what had once been her greatest source of pride, and felt a renewed sense of loss. In his confusion, he'd dreamed of someone else. She smoothed back the thick black fringe from his dry, warm forehead soothingly, not daring to speak.

" 'Twas like a mass of copper at my breast," he murmured again. "Amid the stinking of the ship's hold, even the scant light made it shine."

" 'Tis all but gone, my lord," she managed sorrowfully.

"Nay—'twill grow." He half-turned his head to look at her, and his free arm lifted to allow his fingers to brush at the hair against her temple. " 'Twill be even more beautiful—I mean to see it then."

" 'Tis the herbs," she decided aloud, unwilling to admit that this great lord could find any beauty in her.

"Nay." He dropped his hand heavily and sighed. "My protection must seem worthless to you."

"You saved my life at Beaumaule, my lord—how could I think it worthless?"

"And then you saved mine." He lifted his hand again and gestured to the ewer beside the bed. "I thirst yet." He tried to rise on an elbow and fell back, muttering, "Jesu, but I am as helpless as a babe in swaddling."

She poured a cup of the now-cooled wine from the ewer and lifted his head, holding the cup to his lips. He drank thirstily before leaning back. Having no cloth, she wiped his mouth with her palm, and then dried her hand on the skirt of her gown. When she turned back again, he appeared to have slipped back into sleep, and it was almost as though she'd dreamed he'd spoken to her, as though her mind tricked her. And then he whispered again, "You deserve a husband to value you, Gilliane."

"Nay, I—"

"I'd find one for you."

"But I—" She bit back a protest, telling herself that he could not understand that she had no wish to go a beggar into some knight's keeping, that she had no wish to bear sons with no chance of advancement. Instead, she returned to her bench and drew up her knees, hugging them for warmth and comfort, and hoped he would speak no more on the matter. He too fell silent, and then eventually slept again. She leaned her head forward to rest it on her knees, and when she reached that strange netherworld between wakefulness and sleep, the last thought that crossed her conscious mind was that he'd liked her hair.

12

Within four days Richard of Rivaux showed signs of improvement. His fever, which had been constant at first, abated to the point where it rose only between vespers and prime, those hours of darkness. And once he could struggle to sit unaided, it was determined that Gilliane should no longer attend him alone. Strangely, as tired as she was, she experienced a sense of loss as she watched the brothers go and come from his tiny chamber while she stood by, unnecessary and unwanted.

A woman residing in a monastery had no function, for all the useful tasks were already divided between the men. Moreover, having withdrawn from the secular life, those men were disinclined to female company to the extent that some of them regarded the girl among them much like the temptation of Eve. With the exception of Brothers Hugh and Lymas and the abbot himself, none of the monks even spoke with her. Her meals were delivered silently to the small cell she'd been given, and she was expected to stay out of the way except when summoned.

She caught Brother Lymas as he crossed the yard between cloisters and hall, stopping him. "I know 'tis Brother Hugh who ministers to the sick, but what is your task here?"

He held out ink-stained hands, turning them over for her to see. "God has blessed these to His service, Lady Gilliane—He lets me copy His precious word."

"You are a scribe then."

"Aye—and I draw the letters making them pleasing to the eye."

"I would that I could see them," she offered wistfully.

He eyed her doubtfully and then relented. "I see no harm if you do not touch my colors, Demoiselle. Indeed, as I have heard of your plight, I cannot think but that the Church is the place for you also."

"Nay—I have not the piety."

"Piety comes from inner discipline, little Gilliane—few are born with any thought to God or His works."

She fell in beside him and listened to him warm to the telling of his chosen vocation. As they walked, he spoke of his great love of all things written, and when they drew near the room where he worked, he finished with, "Aye, as son to a poor knight with four daughters to marry and two sons to provide for, I was sent here to learn my skill. And I have discovered God's blessing in reading and keeping His Scriptures." He stopped to hold the door open for her, letting her pass in before him.

She moved to the table placed to catch whatever light came from the window and read aloud the Latin words, stumbling over some of them, and then translating imperfectly, "The destroyer of nations comes."

"Aye, and comes still, Demoiselle, for the destroyer of what he has is always man, and 'twill not change until we learn to live God's words. Greed and lust take their toll still, catching poor men in the schemes of the powerful." He came up behind her to look over her shoulder. "'Tis rare to find a demoiselle who can read above her birthname."

"My father could afford to send but one of my brothers away, and I sat with the others at the priest's knee. I know only a little Latin, although I can read and write in French."

"You were fortunate in your priest then, for many cannot read themselves and must rely on memory to say their prayers."

Without actually touching the parchment, Gilliane traced her finger over the richly illustrated capital. " 'Tis so beautiful—the red and gold light the page."

"I pray 'tis as pleasing to God as it is to you," he responded, pleased by her praise.

But her attention was suddenly distracted by the sound of many horses clattering into the courtyard amid shouts from what could only be armed men. Once again she felt a momentary stab of fear as she stood on tiptoe to reach the small window. She watched an impressive retinue of nearly fifty men dismount. "Sweet Mary," she breathed. "Who comes?"

Brother Lymas looked out. "By the looks of it, 'tis my lord of Rivaux come for his son."

"Oh—aye." Her spirits, which had been lowering since she'd been barred from the sickroom, plummeted now. Somehow, she'd not expected him to come so soon—she'd thought she had more time. Richard would be restored to his family, and she . . . well, she would be naught to any of them. With a pang of guilt for wishing Guy of Rivaux had not come, she drew away from the window and turned to hide her fears from the monk. "I . . . I'd seek my chamber now," she managed before she fled.

She sat alone, waiting to be summoned, worrying that she'd not be welcomed by the elder Rivaux. As the time passed with almost unbearable slowness, she turned her attention to the meanness of what little she had. Her meager clothing had gone with Alwina to Warenne's keep, and there was naught but the dress she wore now. Her hands smoothed the wrinkles in the blue wool. A spot caught her attention, prompting her to spit on a fingertip and rub at the stain.

"Demoiselle?"

She looked up, and her heart and stomach knotted fearfully at the sight of the big man in the doorway. He loomed tall, blocking escape, and his green-and-gold eyes took measure of her. She did not need to ask his name. Her breath caught for a moment as she

stared back at a man she'd heard of all her life. The
only rational thought that came to mind was that he
looked so much like his son. Tongue-tied, she dropped
to her knees before Guy of Rivaux.

"Nay, Demoiselle, do not kneel to me." He reached
a strong hand down to her, drawing her up. "My son
tells me I owe you for his life."

"Nay, but—"

A black eyebrow divided by a fine scar rose above
those strange flecked eyes. "Art not the maid of
Beaumaule?"

"I am Gilliane de Lacey, my lord," she acknowledged, feeling very much the fool in his presence.

"I regret the loss of your home and family, Demoiselle, for that I cannot change. But I can offer you
another home at Rivaux so long as you have need of
it." His hand, which had cupped her elbow, released
her, and he stepped back.

"Nay, but I cannot—"

Again the eyebrow lifted quizzically. "Nay? You
mistake the matter, Demoiselle—I offered not out of
pity, but rather from gratitude. My son cannot be
replaced to me."

She stared up, still nonplussed beneath his gaze,
realizing she was in the presence of the man who'd
ended Robert of Belesme almost a quarter of a cen-
tury earlier. He did not look old—nay, he looked
commanding—and almost everything about him except for the green in his eyes and the sprinkling of
silver in his black hair reminded her of his son.
Somehow, she managed to speak finally.

" 'Twas Lord Richard who saved my life, my lord—
'tis I who must be forever grateful."

A smile crinkled the corners of his mouth and
warmed his strange eyes. "Then you may be in-
debted to him as I am to you. 'Tis settled—as soon as
he can make the journey without breaking open his
wound, we leave for Rivaux." He lifted a hand to
touch the hair that framed her face, brushing it back
in a gesture that reminded her of her own father. A

lump formed inexplicably in her throat. "Aye," he agreed, smiling at her, " 'tis as Richard said—'tis a rare color, Demoiselle."

"I am unused to serving great ladies," she blurted out for want of anything else to say to him. "I do not know—"

"Cat would not ask it. When she welcomes you, 'twill be as a daughter." He stepped back abruptly and turned to leave. "My son asks for you, Gilliane."

"Wait—did he tell you I am undowered?"

He stopped and appeared to consider her. His smile broadened, lightening the flecks in his eyes to pure gold. "As my son is already betrothed, that is no concern to me, Demoiselle."

Richard lay abed, his tall frame filling the narrow cot, and his temper was not good. It had galled him to have to turn to his father, to have his father know what a fool he'd been. None had ever dared to ambush the great Guy of Rivaux—and none ever would. He could not imagine his father riding into a trap as he had done. Even his physical weakness now served once again to put him at a disadvantage. And if his father knew that he'd gone to England to promote Gloucester's cause over the Empress's . . . His thoughts trailed off in unwillingness to think on his sire's certain anger.

Gloucester. Robert of Gloucester had to be warned of Stephen's treachery. Richard lurched upward to sit on the edge of the narrow cot and ran his fingers through his thick, disordered hair. He had to find the means to warn Gloucester.

He heard the muffled sound of soft slippers on the hard floor, and when he looked up, he saw Gilliane. She stood, poised tentatively in the open doorway, her bright hair haloed by the stream of winter sunlight from above, and he wondered how he could have ever thought her plain.

"Sweet Mary, but you warm a man's heart on a cold day, Demoiselle." He smiled at the faint blush that rose in her cheeks, and gestured to the seat beside the cot. "Come take your bench and tell me how 'tis that you have deserted me these two days past."

" 'Tis only one—and they would not let me near you when you improved, my lord," she answered almost saucily, her own heart warming at his greeting. " 'Twas your lord father that bade me come."

His smile faded abruptly, replaced by a troubled frown. "Aye—he means to take me to Rivaux, Gilliane, and I'd not go."

"But you yourself said—"

" 'Twas when I thought my life's blood ebbed, and I'd have you safe there," he retorted. "But now I mend here, and I'd return to mine own lands." With an effort he rose, wincing from the stiffness and the pain, and walked to the high window. His back to her, he stared briefly into the open courtyard.

"What day is this, Demoiselle?"

She calculated briefly and guessed. " 'Tis the twenty-first, I think."

"Jesu!" he exploded. "It cannot be. Nay, but—"

"Well, 'twas the seventeenth of the month when you were brought here, and as 'tis the third—nay the *fourth* day—'tis the twenty-first of December."

The twenty-first. And they would crown Stephen king on the twenty-second. Henry of Winchester had delayed him as surely as if Warenne had taken him prisoner. It was too late for Gloucester to take action now, even if he were so inclined. Richard's voice was strained when he spoke again.

"I'd send word to Robert of Gloucester."

"Your father—"

"My father must not know of it," he cut in harshly. "Nay, but Gloucester must be warned that Stephen is king."

" 'Tis settled then?" she asked, swallowing at the unwelcome news. She'd expected it to happen since Geoffrey had first ridden out for Winchester, but to hear it as fact was a blow to her. Both she and

Beaumaule would be bestowed by King Stephen's whim.

Her silence turned him around. "Aye," he answered bitterly. "For now."

"Will Gloucester challenge him?"

"I know not what Robert will do now, Gilliane, but I have hope that he will."

"Does Count Guy . . . does your father know?"

"Nay, but he will raise his standard when he does—of that I am certain."

Her eyes widened in consternation. "But you cannot . . . that is, you are so lately wounded, my lord—you cannot take the field—"

"My father and I will not be on the same side, Demoiselle, for he is sworn to the Empress."

"Jesu! And you would quarrel with him—you would fight against him?"

"I'd fight for Gloucester." He walked to where she still stood. Raising his unbound arm, he reached to lift her chin, and searched her blue eyes intently. "Would it pain you, Gilliane? Would you care if I fell?" he asked suddenly.

"Aye." She tried to look away, unwilling to let him look into her heart. "Aye, for I'd have no guardian—there'd be none to protect Beaumaule from Brevise."

His gaze never wavered as he held her chin with still-strong fingers, holding it steady. "And what of you, Gilliane?" he asked softly. "Would you have a care for me?"

There was a subtle difference in what he asked, and she was afraid to answer him, afraid of what that answer would bring her, afraid to guess the meaning of this quicksilver change in him. Still trying to avoid the warmth in his gold-flecked brown eyes, she fixed her gaze at his mouth, and her own went dry. "If you fell," she answered carefully, "who would kill Brevise?"

"Nay—'tis not what I would hear, Gilliane."

His voice was barely above a whisper now, and his hand forced her chin higher. His head bent closer, until she could feel the softness of his breath against her cheek as her eyes closed. Her fingers clenched into fists and her body stiffened until his lips met hers almost gently, touching softly at first. She gasped in shocked surprise at the feel of his arm as it slid around her, pinning her against the tall litheness of his body, bending her. And the touch of his mouth, light as it was, sent first a shiver and then a burst of liquid fire coursing through her veins. Her hands, which had been at her side, caught at him now for balance, as his arm tightened, and then returned his embrace.

His mouth played on hers, his tongue teased her lips and then her teeth. Somewhere in her mind she knew it was wrong to like what he did to her, knew she could never call him her own, and she made a feeble attempt to protest, turning her head away. His breath was warm and alive against her ear, sending a shiver down her spine. She clutched at his arm for support, bracing herself against the unaccustomed weakness she felt. His good arm held her so close that she could feel his body stir against hers, could feel the rapidness of his breath as his chest rose and fell in rhythm with hers.

"Nay, but I'd not . . . Sweet Mary, but I dare not . . ." she whispered helplessly.

Heavy bootsteps accompanied by the jingle of a knight's spurs came down the hallway and paused outside the small cell, bringing Richard once again to his senses. Cursing himself for a fool, he thrust her away so quickly that she nearly stumbled, and his hand grasped her shoulder as though he would shake her to vent his own anger. Bewildered by the sudden change, she blinked back tears and stared up at him with widened eyes.

"The fault is mine, Gilliane—'tis poor payment for the service you have given me," he muttered harshly, denying the rush of desire that had flooded over him.

It was as though he'd struck her. Not daring to let

him see her tears, she turned and ran blindly from
the cell. Outside, she collided with Guy of Rivaux,
who steadied her. Mumbling almost incoherently,
she begged his pardon and fled.

Guy's flecked eyes hardened as he faced his son.
"Is this how you would repay her kindness?" he
demanded brutally, kicking the door shut behind
him. "God's blood, but if you are able to attempt a
maid, you are able to ride."

"Nay—you mistake the matter."

The divided eyebrow shot upward in disbelief.
"Nay? Look at you—art heaving like a stallion ready
to mount!" he countered in disgust. "And I just saw
the demoiselle flee as though hell pursued her."

Richard ran his fingers through his hair, combing
it away from his forehead. "What passes between
Gilliane de Lacey and myself is on my conscience
alone, Papa," he answered stiffly. "I mean her no
dishonor."

Guy moved closer, searching his only son's face as
though he would see another there. A silent anger
burned within those dark eyes, reminding him too
much of his own sire. Guy raised his hand as though
to strike him, and then let it fall when Richard did
not flinch. It had long been thus between them, a
tenuous truce so fragile that it threatened to break
with mere words. There was far too much of the
blood he'd given him in the boy, and he feared it.

"Then let your acts be tempered by your inten-
tions," he said finally.

"I cannot be what you are, Papa—there is but one
Guy of Rivaux for the bards to praise."

"You bear my blood."

"And naught else!"

"Nay, you have the look of—" He halted and stepped
back, muttering, "Your mother would not have me
quarrel with you, Richard."

"Aye." Richard exhaled sharply, as though he would
expel his anger, and then nodded. "I mean to protect the demoiselle—she has no other to stand for her."

"You have not said why you were in England."

"You did not ask."

Guy sighed. Speech with his firstborn was too often like the beginning of a sword fight—tentative and testing. "I surmised 'twas because King Henry died in the forest of Lyons." His green-and-gold eyes met Richard's and held, and his voice was even. "Aye, I am not the fool you would think me."

"I have never thought you a fool—except in this, Papa."

"I swore to the Empress, Richard—twice I gave my oath to Henry's daughter. All that you are—all that you have—is owed to King Henry. I'd not have you forget that."

"But I did not swear to her."

"Aye, but I did, and you are my son. Sweet Jesu, Richard, but you would try a man! Robert of Gloucester will never be king! The man is bastard-born! Bastard-born!"

"As was the old Conqueror!"

"Aye, but the time is different—Holy Church would hold against Robert now. The time is past for a bastard to inherit—and I do not believe Robert would attempt to usurp his sister's right."

"He knows she cannot rule, Papa."

"Does he? Or is it that you want him in her stead? Nay, my son, but he has too much honor to break his oath to her."

"Unless you wish to swear to Stephen, you'll support Gloucester," Richard shot back defiantly.

"Stephen has no claim—if the Empress were dead, 'twould be his brother," Guy retorted. "And well I know full half the baronage would rather have Count Theobald than her."

"The Curia crowns Stephen, Papa—on the morrow." For once he had the satisfaction of knowing he'd caught the all-knowing Guy of Rivaux by surprise, for his father breathed an oath under his breath. "Aye—I had it of Bishop Henry's own lips."

"Winchester?"

"Winchester. And while I cannot prove 'tis so, I think I owe the arrow I took to him. 'Twas Warenne that would have stopped me, and he is Stephen's man. My folly was in seeking out the good bishop ere I appealed to the Curia itself," Richard added bitterly. "Stephen has taken the seal and the treasury, and Bigod has perjured himself to gain us an amiable king."

"Does Gloucester know?"

"Nay—I had not the chance to warn him of it."

A low whistle escaped Guy. "As they are rivals, he'll not stomach the news well, I fear."

"Nay, he will fight."

"For his sister." Guy paced over to the high window and looked out, staring for a time at the leafless trees beyond the courtyard. "This changes nothing, Richard—Gloucester will raise the Empress's standard, and I will raise mine also in her cause."

"She is wed to Anjou! You cannot want Anjou over Normandy and England!"

"I gave my oath to her."

Guy turned from the window and started for the door. "There is no reasoning with you—honor means naught to you, my son. You are too like—" He caught himself and shook his head. "Nay, I'd not discuss this with you. As my son, you will support Henry's daughter."

Despite the almost continuous quarrel between them, Richard had to know what he meant to do now. "Wait—do you send to the Empress and Geoffrey of Anjou?"

"Aye, and to Gloucester also." Guy paused on the threshold, turning back to his son. "Unlike you, I believe him an honorable man." And then, almost as an afterthought, he added stiffly, "As for Gilliane de Lacey, I'd remind you that she is a gentlewoman—and you are not free to wed. There is the matter of Lincoln's whey-faced daughter—the one you chose for wife."

After he left, Richard sat again on the bed. He

had not a doubt that his father would apprise Robert of Gloucester of Stephen's treachery in such a way that Gloucester would support the Empress. If naught else could be said of Guy of Rivaux, he had the ability to shame a man into doing his bidding.

Defeated, Richard turned his thoughts to Cicely of Lincoln and tried to remember how she looked. It was difficult—he'd not seen her since she was a small, pale child. And then the image of Gilliane de Lacey floated before him. Her bright coppery hair shone in the dim light of Beaumaule's chapel as she urged him to kill William of Brevise for her. Aye, he was caught in a coil of his own making in that matter also—he'd promised his name to Lincoln's daughter and he feared he'd given his heart to the fiery-haired Gilliane. He looked down to where Brother Hugh's bandages bulged across his chest and remembered the feel of her head there. An acute loneliness stole over him with the realization that he could not in honor have her.

13

Gilliane had never seen a place to compare with Rivaux. She stared in wide-eyed awe at the tall, forbidding walls that loomed ahead of them, and wondered what Richard of Rivaux's mother would think of one who came from the likes of Beaumaule. Involuntarily her eyes stole to the man in the litter beside her, and she was surprised by the set look on his face. His very glumness reminded her of the prisoners he'd taken at Beaumaule.

They'd spoken little beyond the commonplace in those last two days at the abbey, constrained by what had passed between them in his cell. She'd played the harlot by letting him kiss her, she was certain, and he'd taken a disgust of her, scarce looking at her since. And now he lay back amid the cushions in the litter, silent and sullen.

His black hair fell forward over his forehead, shadowing skin made pale by his wound, and his dark eyes stared ahead as though they could see something she could not in the space before him. She could stand his silence no longer, and after a furtive look to where Guy of Rivaux rode ahead of them, Gilliane edged her horse closer to his litter.

"My lord," she hissed low for his ears alone, "I would that we could cry peace ere we reach Rivaux."

It was as though he were reluctant to look at her, but he finally turned toward her. "There is no peace to cry, Demoiselle, for there has been no war."

The thin, fragile thread that held her own temper

in check broke, and she no longer cared if any heard her. "Nay, but you wrong me, Richard of Rivaux!" she snapped. "You had no right to force me from my home, to . . . to bring me here amongst strangers when I would not come! And you had no right to touch me, to . . . to . . ." She sputtered, seeking to put her hurt into words, and then finished hotly, "I'd not be punished for what I did not want!"

"Aye," he cut in abruptly, "the fault was mine, and I acknowledge it. I am heartily sorry for what passed between us, Demoiselle."

Somehow the apology did not assuage her anger in the least. He was sorry for having held her, for having kissed her, and her woman's mind had no wish to hear that. That it was illogical to be angered on the one hand because he'd dared to touch her, and on the other because he'd apologized for doing so was irrelevant. It was his manner, she told herself, still seething. He'd pushed her away as though she disgusted him then, and now he admitted he regretted the kiss itself.

"You had not the right—"

"I had not the right. Aye, I swore to protect you."

"I am not a kitchen wench that you may—"

"You are not a wench to be tumbled," he agreed, interrupting her. "And I'd not speak of it longer, Demoiselle, for I have said I am sorry for the lapse. You need not fear it will happen again."

"Jesu!"

She threw up her hands in frustration and then realized he was not attending her. Instead, he'd sunk back against his pillows and closed his eyes, ending any discourse between them. He still looked ill from his wound, and his bandage still bulged even beneath the blanket that covered him. His black lashes lay against almost alabaster skin, and his lids were bluish above, forming circles with the hollows below. Aye, he'd not recovered from the arrow he'd taken as he'd fled to save her. Her anger faded, dissipating abruptly as she recalled what she owed him.

The terror of that last day at Beaumaule came home to her again, much as it had haunted her nightmares, and she could see again the fires burning around her, could hear the screams of the wounded and dying, could smell the breath of the man she'd killed in the kitchen, and her stomach knotted with remembered fear. And 'twas Richard of Rivaux who'd saved her—Richard of Rivaux who'd found her in that dark storeroom, who'd crawled and pulled her to safety amid the fiery rubble of what had been Beaumaule. She hunched closer over her saddle and felt again the safety of his arms about her. And felt again the sensation of his lips on hers as he'd held her in the abbey. Blood heightened the color in her cheeks, and she turned away as she remembered she'd not wanted the kiss to end.

"You will not find Rivaux inhospitable, Demoiselle."

Gilliane looked up into the strange green-and-gold eyes of Richard's father, and her color deepened. He'd reined in and waited for them, and she wondered what he'd heard. She turned away hastily and busied herself with smoothing her cloak over her gown, not daring to discover what he must surely think of her.

" 'Tis so very large, my lord," she mumbled, keeping her gaze on the saddle pommel before her.

"Aye, but 'tis not so fine a place as either the Condes or Harlowe, Demoiselle, and you must not think we are overgiven to ceremony here. You will soon meet my lady Catherine of the Condes, and she will bid you most welcome."

The Cat—the proud Cat of whom Richard had spoken. Gilliane doubted one such as that would even acknowledge her existence, but she dared not dispute the count's words. Instead she nodded. "Aye—I hope I am pleasing to her."

"You will be." To her further discomfiture, he kneed his horse even closer, leaning almost across her to address his son. "Did you not tell her that we have daughters in our house?"

"Aye." It was a monosyllabic reply uttered through nearly clenched teeth.

Guy turned back to Gilliane, favoring her with a wry smile. "You must forgive my son, Demoiselle, for his wound seems to have affected his tongue. Nay, but 'twill be as yet another daughter comes to us."

She knew not how to answer such graciousness. Casting a quick look to see if he amused himself at her expense, she found his gaze pleasant enough, but she felt tongue-tied in his presence. Finally, for want of anything else to say, she blurted out, "How many girls do you have?" and then wondered if he thought her an ungrateful fool. She bit her lips and flushed anew.

"Four. There is Elizabeth, the eldest, once our Demoiselle, and then there are Isabella, Joanna, and Eleanor, the last so named for her grandmother of Nantes. You are probably of an age with Bella for she is seventeen."

"I am nineteen, my lord."

"Liza is twenty."

"And has a temper to match the Empress." Richard broke his silence. "When her husband died without an heir, she came back to Rivaux to make life miserable for the rest of her family."

"You mistake the matter," Guy snapped. "She does but mourn him."

"She wraps herself in widow's weeds that she may live with Maman forever. Nay, but you do her no service, letting her stay at Rivaux when 'tis another husband she needs. Her tongue lashes out with impunity, making hell on earth for the younger girls." Richard pushed himself up awkwardly, shifting the balance of the litter between the two horses precariously. "Have a care, Demoiselle, that you do not draw Elizabeth's ire, for she will make you pay. You are better served to become friends with Bella."

"Pay him no heed, Demoiselle, for 'tis that they have always quarreled since her birth. A brother is last to value his sister, I fear." Turning to Richard, he sighed. "Aye, 'twas always thus between you, was it not? One would think you had never loved her, and yet you were the first to argue against her marriage."

"Because I'd not see her given to a weakling!"

"There was naught weak about Ivo," Guy muttered irritably. "He was son to the Count of Eu, and had he not fallen in a quarrel, he'd have made a good husband."

"Jesu! He was a handsome fool, Papa."

"She had a choice in the matter."

"Aye, and was much struck by his looks, I'll warrant, but you did not see them after. I did, and had he not fallen in battle, I'd think she'd poisoned him, for his tastes ran not to women."

Guy fell silent, unwilling to yield that there'd been anything wrong with his daughter's marriage. Certainly she'd been glad enough to return home to Rivaux, but he believed that to be because she'd borne no children to the union. Still, it was strange that she showed no inclination to take another husband.

"There was naught wrong with Ivo," he repeated finally, spurring his horse forward and returning to his place at the head of the column.

"You should not vex him so," Gilliane murmured.

"Aye, I suppose not." Richard stared unseeing for a moment and then shrugged against his pillows. "But you cannot know how it is to be his son. He would have me in his own image in both spirit and deed, Demoiselle."

"Do you really dislike your sister?"

"Nay, but I'd see her wed again ere she withers like an old woman, content to stay at Rivaux with Maman." He looked again to the gates of the castle ahead, and suddenly ordered the riders who led the litter to halt.

"We are nearly there, my lord," one of them protested.

"Aye, and I'd ride in unaided. I'd not be cosseted and wept over by Maman," Richard retorted.

"Lord Guy—"

"I can ride."

"He'll be angered if your wound breaks open, my lord. Nay, but I'd ask if—"

"My lord, I'd not—" Gilliane started to reason with him, but her words died under his quelling look. "Garth, tell Lord Guy that he wishes to ride."

"Nay."

"Nay that you no longer wish to sit astride your horse?" she asked with feigned innocence.

"You take too much on yourself, Demoiselle! I'd have my horse."

"Garth."

"Aye, lady." With a great deal of reluctance, the boy nudged his horse forward, ignoring Richard of Rivaux's dark scowl.

"You have not the right—"

"And you have an excess of pride, my lord. Would you rather heal, that you may leave Rivaux as soon as may be, or would you rather risk falling at your mother's feet?"

"Demoiselle, 'tis naught to you—" He stopped, well aware of what he owed her, and shook his head.

"Aye?"

"I'd have you draw closer, that I might buffet your ears, if the truth were known." The corners of his mouth lifted in a faint smile. "There is much of my mother in you."

"I shall choose to take that as a compliment, my lord," she responded sweetly.

" 'Twas meant as one."

"So you would ride rather than be carried?"

For a moment Gilliane feared that the quarrel between Richard and his father was about to begin anew, but then she saw Guy of Rivaux rein in and dismount. "Get him his horse," he ordered curtly to the man who still led the pack animals. He walked to the side of the litter and thrust back the hangings, peering intently into his son's pale face. "Aye," he said with surprising softness, "I'd not be carried either. Lean into me."

"My lord, you must not—"

Before the words were scarce out of the man's mouth, Guy had slid his arms beneath Richard's shoulders. "I carried him when he was a babe, and I can do so now." With an effort, he lifted the son who was as tall as he was, easing him out of the litter and letting him slide gently to the ground. "Can you stand? Or have your limbs grown too accustomed to the motion?"

"I can stand."

Despite the cold, small beads of perspiration moistened Richard's brow, and for a moment he swayed. But then he gained his balance and stepped from his father's embrace. "My thanks, Papa."

"Nay, I understand pride," Guy told him gruffly. "Mount him," he ordered the ostler who led Everard's bay forward. "And ride close to him." He turned to Gilliane, his strange gold-and-green-flecked eyes betraying a flash of humor. " 'Tis no small feat for a man in his forty-eighth year—eh, Demoiselle?"

"Jesu, but he is strong," Garth breathed after him.

"Aye." Richard nodded, still watching him. "He is that," he conceded. "But make no mistake—he did it for the love of my mother. He'd not frighten her with the litter."

"Sweet Mary, but you wrong him, I think," Gilliane murmured without thinking.

He shook his head, his face betraying his bitterness. "You know not what is between us."

"You are his son."

"Aye, but he did not want a son—for some reason, Demoiselle, he never wanted a son." Richard grasped the pommel and heaved himself up into Everard's worn saddle with an effort. Wincing against the stiffness and the pain, he reached for the reins.

"Every man wants a son, my lord."

His eyebrow lifted, much as Guy of Rivaux's had

earlier. "Not my father. Four times in my memory I have seen my mother bring forth a daughter and each time, the babe has been greeted with relief by him."

" 'Tis unnatural what you say."

"Mayhap, but I once asked Old William, who was with him from birth, and ere he died, the old man even admitted 'twas so."

"But *why*?"

"Now that he never told me." He reached to pat the saddle sheath that held his sword. "See this? 'Tis Hellbringer, Belesme's sword, and had it not been for Old William, it would have been melted like old mail at the forge. 'Twas he who saved it for me—despite my sire's ire."

"Mayhap he wished to destroy its evil," she offered, understanding how that could be.

"Nay. He did not wish me to have it."

There was no use disputing something that she had no real knowledge of. Gilliane fell silent again, watching the horses ahead of them pick their way along the rock road that led to Rivaux's gate. When they crossed into the fortress itself, she would know none but Richard and Garth, for despite Guy of Rivaux's encouraging words at Dieppe, she was going among strangers.

They were almost there now. The first of the horses had already clattered onto the lowered bridge. Gilliane reined in, uncertain of where she should ride, for there were no others of her rank with them. She stole a look at Richard and saw him straighten to sit tall in his saddle.

"I'd have you ride in with me," he managed through teeth clenched against the throbbing pain in his shoulder.

"Jesu, mayhap you should—"

"Nay, 'tis not so bad when I favor it. But I'd have you draw closer. Garth, stay near on the other side." He winced again as he lifted the reins with his left hand. "I hate weakness," he muttered.

With great misgiving, Gilliane looked about her
uneasily, taking in the high, thick stone walls of the
outer curtain and then the broad expanse of winter-
browned meadow that lay between it and the inner
walls. Four tall towers dominated the curtain, standing sentinel over a small town that clustered in
Rivaux's shadow, and four others marked the corners of the four-story keep itself. And an extraordinary number of arrow slits cut into the thick stone
gave the fortress dominance over the surrounding
countryside.

"Aye—'tis a thing of beauty, is it not? 'Twas raised
from a motte and bailey not much greater than that
of Beaumaule," Richard cut into her thoughts again.
"Mine own keep at Celesin has little to compare with
Rivaux, save that its walls are stone also."

Passing through the second gatehouse, they were
instantly surrounded by ostlers ready to divest and
stable the horses. And waiting on the steps of the tall
keep that filled much of the inner yard were a woman
and four girls, all of whom hastened forward in
greeting. The woman stopped first at Guy of Rivaux's
side, and he slid down to embrace her, affording
Gilliane her first look at Catherine of the Condes.
Small, dark-haired, and beautiful still, the woman
looked up into her lord's face with such love that it
gave Gilliane a pang of envy to watch them.

"Richard! Richard! Sweet Mary, brother, but we'd
thought you nigh dead!"

The clamor of voices drew Gilliane back to Richard of Rivaux, who'd been pulled from his saddle
and stood now in the midst of three clamoring girls,
all younger than herself. He bent to kiss each of
them in turn and then looked up to where Gilliane
still sat astride. "Garth!" he called out to the boy
who'd ridden at the back of the train, "Come dismount your mistress! Your pardon, Demoiselle—I'd
do it myself if I thought I could." Herding the girls
toward her, he introduced them in turn. "Nell, make
your obeisance to the Lady Gilliane de Lacey—Dem-

oiselle, 'tis my littlest sister, Eleanor of Rivaux; Gilliane—Isabella, called Bella; and Joanna, who thinks me invincible. Ouch! You little vixen—'tis my sore side you would press!" He scolded the one he'd called Joanna. "Have a care before I cuff your ears!"

She looked from one girl to another and was struck by all of them. Every one had eyes darker than Richard's and hair that was lighter, more brown than his, with small, delicately formed features like Catherine of the Condes'.

"So you are come home at last, brother."

It was then that she noted the tall girl who stood apart slightly, her hands on her hips, surveying him with the faintest of smiles. She was uncloaked against the cold, and her rich blue samite gown was laced under her arms to pull it smooth over high, firm breasts. But it was her face that men would remember, Gilliane decided as she stared openly at the beautiful girl. Defying tradition, she wore her thick, glossy black hair unbound like a maiden, and it whipped around her face, framing skin as translucent as the best parchment, setting off fine, even features that mirrored her brother's. Only the eyes were different—where as his were brown flecked with gold, hers were a clear, deep green.

"Liza."

There was a slight hesitation between them, an awkwardness born of too many quarrels. And then he opened his good arm to her and she stepped into his embrace, leaning her head against his shoulder.

"Well, I am glad enough you survived, brother, else I'd have had to do penance for all I've said to you these twenty years past."

" 'Twould almost have been worth the dying to have witnessed that." Richard looked over a shoulder nearly as tall as his own. "Demoiselle, come closer that I may present you to the termagant."

Elizabeth of Rivaux turned to her then, and Gilliane was suddenly self-conscious of her own dowdiness as the older girl's green eyes assessed her openly. But then she smiled warmly, tossing back at Richard, "You have brought us something we have need of, brother—another girl to this house. Come, Demoiselle, despite what he may have said, I will not devour you."

"Elizabeth, 'tis Gilliane de Lacey. She—"

"Saved your life. Aye, we had the tale of the boy," Elizabeth said dismissively. "How old are you, Demoiselle?"

"You did not let me finish, Liza," he complained.

"Well, she knows I am Elizabeth, and since I am born of this house, I am Rivaux, so there was naught more to be said, was there? Nay, get you to bed, Richard, and leave the greetings to Gilliane and me— you look tired unto death, anyway."

"Richard."

The woman spoke low, but they all turned to her. For a moment Gilliane thought she ought to kneel at the countess's feet, but then decided to wait until she was presented. It made no difference, for Catherine of the Condes now had eyes for none but her tall son.

"Sweet Mary, but you gave me a fright, Richard."

"Nay, Maman. As you can see, I am all right."

"I can see you are half-dead," she retorted, but incredibly she was smiling mistily at him. "Aye, Elizabeth has the right of it—you should be abed. Arnulf, see Lord Richard to the solar—I'd tend him myself."

"Maman—"

"Nay. You may bully this demoiselle into doing your bidding, my son, but in this house 'tis my will that will be done," she told him firmly. "Arnulf, take Gervais with you, that he does not fall."

Ignoring his protests, Catherine turned her attention to Gilliane. "You must be the maid of Beaumaule, Demoiselle," she murmured, moving forward to catch her before she could make a proper obeisance. "Nay, 'tis I who should kneel to you for my son's life." Like her eldest daughter, she too seemed to inspect Gilliane's poor cloak and the woolen gown that could be seen where it parted. "Come—you must tell me all that has happened since you were met with him."

Gilliane glanced helplessly to where two men already walked Richard toward the tower stairs. Catherine followed her gaze, frowning slightly. "Nay, but I have had enough of the tale to know you are welcome in this house, Demoiselle. Elizabeth, see if there's aught of yours that she can wear ere we sew for her," she directed. "And Isabella, tell Hawise I'd have something hot for the demoiselle to drink. You must be nigh frozen, Gilliane, and wonder at my hospitality already."

"Do I get to sleep with her?" the youngest girl asked, trotting alongside as Catherine shepherded Gilliane inside.

"You have Joanna and Isabella," her mother reminded her.

"Nay, but a pallet is all—"

"Nonsense. Only serving women sleep on pallets here."

Following the men, they climbed up the winding stairs cut into the thick tower walls, past the landings that opened to the main hall, and on up to the third floor. Catherine waited for a manservant to hold the door for them and then stepped inside a room, the likes of which Gilliane had never imagined existed. The roof was cross-timbered above whitewashed walls, and the floors were swept bare, while tall windows provided light to the low, cushioned benches beneath them. Richly carved and hasped cabinets lined the outer walls, while a great curtained bed rested on a raised platform at one end. This then must be the lord's bedchamber.

"We sleep here," Catherine confirmed the obvious for her.

" 'Tis quite fine," Gilliane murmured, awestruck.

"And there are other chambers beyond. My younger daughters share a bed in one, with the women taking pallets beside, and then there is a room for Elizabeth as Demoiselle of the house. Over there . . ."

She pointed to a heavy door. "Over there is my solar. Unlike that in most keeps, 'tis not shared with my bedchamber, so that my women will not disturb my lord when they waken to work. The looms are there also, but for now, 'tis where we put Richard. I have had a bed set that he may be tended closely, so I fear Guy will have to have us underfoot in here."

"You will share my bed, Demoiselle," Elizabeth spoke up. " 'Twas decided that since we are of an age, 'tis more fitting."

An old woman came forward to thrust a steaming cup at Gilliane, favoring her with a toothless smile as she did so, and ten-year-old Eleanor of Rivaux piped up, " 'Tis spiced and sweet—Hawise makes it herself."

Through an open door Gilliane could hear Richard complaining as he was undressed, and the countess hurriedly excused herself to tend to him. Gilliane stared around her, still not comprehending either the wealth or the welcome. She was now among one of the truly great and powerful families of Normandy, and it ought to gratify her that they meant to treat her kindly, but she felt terribly alone, more so than at any time she could remember. Although Richard of Rivaux was now among those who loved him, she was among strangers.

"I asked if you had any clothes to put away," Elizabeth repeated, breaking into her thoughts.

"Nay—what you see is all I have."

"No matter then, I am taller than you, but Hawise can hem."

"Nay, but I—"

"Maman will not let you look like a beggar here, Demoiselle." Elizabeth surveyed her with a mixture of exasperation and concern. "And do you mind if I use your name? I'd call you Gilliane if 'twill not offend you. You may address me as Elizabeth or Liza, as Richard does—it matters to me not."

"Aye."

Gilliane closed her eyes momentarily, straining to hear the sounds that came from Catherine's solar, straining to hear him. She'd heard from Geoffrey that there was little discourse between unmarried men and girls in a great house, so that she wondered if she would see Richard much again.

"Gilliane!" This time Elizabeth spoke sharply, and then when Gilliane flushed guiltily, she relented. "Had I not heard of what has befallen you, I'd think your wits had gone with your hair, but I know you are but tired." Then, looking toward the open door herself, she added, "I hope he leaves you with us when he goes, for I will be glad of the company."

14

The chair teetered precariously, balanced unevenly by the thrust of seven pairs of hands actually on it and a dozen more pressing close by. Guy of Rivaux grinned good-naturedly and tried to maintain his seat whilst the women clamored beneath, holding him hostage in the traditional Christmas chairing.

"Have done, good ladies, have done," he protested, pretending to fear falling. "Nay, but I cannot reward you from here."

"A ransom! A ransom!" the younger girls chanted, while Catherine watched him, giggling like a maid. Little Eleanor reached out, begging, "My gift, Papa —my gift!"

Catherine caught Gilliane's sleeve and thrust her forward. "Get you a hand on the chair, that you may have something also," she urged.

"Nay, I—"

"Hush—he expects it."

"What? Another one? Sweet Mary, but you will beggar me, the lot of you!" Guy's face was flushed from the exertion of the resistance required—it was accepted that they would push and pull until they'd gotten him into his chair, and then they'd hoist it, keeping him off the ground until he gave in and ordered the distribution of Christmas gifts to the women of the household.

Reluctantly Gilliane reached across the younger girls to grasp the leg of the chair, and he immediately capitulated. "Aye, you'd make my stomach queasy, all of you," he teased. "I vow I have had a better ride on a sorry nag than on this. All right—have done, I say."

"Nay, hold him longer," Joanna urged. " 'Tis the only time we have the better of Papa in the whole year."

"Cat, get the gifts—you'll have to ransom me, I fear."

"Oh? And what if I will not?" she asked saucily.

"Vixen!"

He was a big man, tall rather than given to fat, but heavy, and the chair pitched as they tried to lower him carefully. He lost his balance at the last and would have fallen had Gilliane not been in the way. He grasped her shoulder to right himself, and laughed.

" 'Tis two men of Rivaux you have saved, Demoiselle."

Catherine and two of her tiring women carried armloads of garments forward to lay them across the bed. "Come see what my lord's largess brings you—all of you."

"Demoiselle, you do not join the rest," Count Guy chided Gilliane.

"Nay, but I am just arrived."

"Go on."

The Christmas chairing at Rivaux was so unlike that of Beaumaule. Geoffrey and his father before him had merely passed out a new set of clothes to each of the few retainers and been done. But here—here there was much laughing and teasing and many gifts for everyone. Gilliane would have hung back despite Guy of Rivaux's urging had Richard not come up behind her. He laid his hand on her shoulder and turned her toward the bed. She closed her eyes at the feel of his strong fingers against her flesh, afraid to let any see the effect he had on her.

"Aye," he murmured above her ear, "there is a gift from me there also."

"Gilly! Gilly! Come see!" Eleanor shouted excitedly. With the exuberance of a child, she'd given up any pretense to propriety and had immediately taken to Gilliane's childhood name.

Richard released her shoulder and moved to the bed, while Gilliane still stood rooted to the floor, unable to believe their kindness. After a quick conferring with Elizabeth, he lifted up a gown of purple and gold-shot samite. The sleeves were banded with intricate embroidery, and so was the hem.

"Well," he asked, holding it before him, "what say you—do you think it will fit?"

"I think it too short for you," Elizabeth retorted. "You'd best give it to someone else."

His eyes meet Gilliane's, warming until the gold flecks could be seen plainly. "What say you, Gilly?" he asked softly, "Would you like it?"

She stared from one to the other of them, knowing full well that nothing could have been made for her in one short day. "Aye," was all that she could manage.

Impatient of the delay between them, Elizabeth took the gown from him and carried it to Gilliane, holding it to her shoulders to check the length. "You have Hawise to thank that it fits," she murmured. "She measured what you came in whilst you slept."

" 'Tis beautiful."

"And there is more." Grinning broadly at her pleasure in her new finery, Richard ordered another sister, "Bella, get me the girdle, I pray you."

Isabella rummaged in an open chest and drew out a thick golden chain weighted at either end with jeweled medallions. "Is this it?" she asked, lifting it for him to see.

"Aye."

"But I thought 'twas Liza's!" Joanna exclaimed.

"Dolt!" Elizabeth hissed at her. "I sold it to him for ten marks."

"And 'tis your gown also!"

"I sold that to him also." She faced Gilliane apologetically. "Forgive her manners, demoiselle. We had not the time to make you anything, and Richard would have . . . indeed, all of us would give you something. And the purple becomes you better than me."

"Not to mention that I bought it," Richard added dryly. "Sometimes, Joanna, I think Maman ought to have given you to the Church."

"Nay, I am unsuited," the girl answered blithely. "And I do not see how—"

"Demoiselle—Gilliane . . ." Catherine held out a jeweled crucifix. " 'Tis from my lord and me."

As Gilliane turned the small golden cross over in her palm, the others returned to examining their Christmas robes and jewels, and to passing out amongst the serving women their tokens of appreciation for the year's service. Even Guy of Rivaux seemed to be taken with the spirit of the day, moving around the room, passing out small silver coins to everyone. Gillian took the opportunity to slip from the chamber into the passageway behind, where she leaned her head against the whitened wall and cried.

"You did not try—" Richard stopped mid-sentence. He'd seen her leave, but he'd not expected tears. In a few swift strides he caught up to her and turned her into his arms. His left hand slid around her, and the pain in his shoulder made him stiffen for a moment, and then his right hand came up to clasp the back of her head, smoothing her short hair against her neck. "Gilly . . . Gilly, what ails you, sweeting? Nay, but the bad in your life is over. Maman . . ." He could feel her sobs increase rather than lessen. "Sweet Jesu, Gilliane, but . . ."

She clung to him, unable to answer, and he had to content himself with rubbing soothingly between her shoulders while he waited. Elizabeth had said she would be too proud to take much from them, but he'd wanted to give her what she'd lacked. Mayhap he should have waited—it had not been yet a fortnight since her brothers had died. Mayhap she could not rejoice in anything yet.

"Gilliane."

He spoke low, but somehow his voice brought her to her senses. She choked back a sob and tried to master herself, feeling very much the fool. "Your p-pardon," she hiccuped finally.

"I did but think you would like the dress, and Maman said they'd made more than one for Liza," he told her quietly. "But if you cannot—"

"Oh, no! 'Tis beautiful, my lord . . . as is the girdle, and the cross also."

"Then what in the name of Mary ails you?"

"I have nothing for anyone!"

"Jesu! Gilliane, nothing was expected of you. You saved my life—there's naught that could ever repay you for that." He set her back so he could see her face. "I am a wealthy man, Demoiselle. If I cannot give what I would to you—"

"What would you give to me?" she asked suddenly.

"Oh, God, Gilliane. I'd not have you ask me that," he groaned. "I owe you much—there's naught I would not give to you if I could." He brushed her wet cheeks with his fingers and then lifted her chin with a bent knuckle, forcing her to look into his eyes. "I'd dower you so that you may wed, I'd have my father seek a husband for you . . ." Even as he looked at her, pools of tears welled anew, spilling again. "Sweet Mary, but I'd . . . Gilly . . ."

He'd not meant to kiss her again, he had not the right, and yet he could not help himself. And as he tasted the salt of her tears, he was lost. His hand twined again in the copper silk of her hair as his lips met hers.

Guy of Rivaux watched in the doorway, saw his son crush the girl against his body, and knew he had to stop what could only bring shame and dishonor to them both. "Richard!" he called out sternly.

Gilliane felt Richard's body tauten as he drew away. She grasped his arm and stepped back shakily, her face flaming. Glancing from one to the other as they faced each other, she felt beneath contempt.

"The fault was mine," she heard Richard say.

"Aye. Demoiselle, I'd speak with you later," Count Guy told her. "If you would not join the others, perhaps the chapel . . ." He let his voice trail off as he waited for her to leave them.

"Nay." Despite her thudding heart, she managed to face him. "The fault was mine, my lord, for he did but seek to comfort me."

"I am well aware of what he seeks, Demoiselle," he cut in harshly. "I'd speak to you in the chapel."

He did not bear defying. She sucked in her breath and let it out slowly before she dared meet his gaze. "Aye, my lord."

He held the door for her, waiting for her to pass, and then he shut it after her, turning again to his son. "You cannot have her, and well you know it."

"Aye."

"You can bring her naught but ill."

"Aye." Richard turned away to lean against the cold wall. "Think you I have not said such to myself?"

"Then you have not listened, have you? For you are scarce able to stand, and still you are after her like a rutting boar."

" 'Tis not like that at all!"

Guy crossed his arms and leaned back also. "Nay? Then how is it that you would take her? Had I not come upon you, what would you have done with her?"

"Nothing! I'd have done naught! Jesu, Papa! Do you not think I know I owe her more than that?"

"She's a comely maid. If she had hair, she'd be a beauty. 'Tis a pity you contracted yourself to Lincoln's daughter, isn't it?"

"Leave me be!" Richard spun around, goaded. "Aye, 'tis what rankles you, is it not? Not whether I would have Gilliane de Lacey, but rather that I chose Cecily of Lincoln without your blessing!"

"Nay! But you did choose her, Richard, and you will have to live with that. Just last month I had another letter of Lincoln, reminding me that the girl is of an age to bed now." He straightened up and walked closer. "If you burn, Richard, I'd say the time is now to wed her—before you harm an innocent maid."

"Whether I burn or not is none of your affair!"

"It is when you bring Gilliane de Lacey to Rivaux. I'd protect the girl."

"Think you I would not? She kept me alive . . . she held me on my horse . . . she warmed me—"

"Then what would you do with her?"

It was a question he'd asked himself a hundred times in the week, and it had but one honorable answer. He exhaled, forcing all the air from his lungs in capitulation. "What I would do, Papa," he answered finally, "is dower her. Aye, that surprises you, does it not?" he asked bitterly. "And I'd have you seek a husband for her—someone strong enough to hold Beaumaule against Brevise for her, someone wealthy enough to rebuild her home."

"How much dowry?"

"How much is my life worth?" Richard countered. "I have seven castles in England. I'd give one hundred marks and one of them—Ardwick, mayhap."

"And I name the husband?"

"Aye—with her consent."

It was a substantial offer, one that he did not have to make. Nodding, Guy reached out to his son. "I am sorry, Richard—truly I am."

"Nay, save your sorrow for yourself." Richard ducked beneath his father's arm and pushed past him. " 'Tis a heavy burden to always have the right of the matter, I'll warrant."

Guy stood alone for a long time, remembering the years of fear he'd had for his only son. It had been a long struggle to master the temper the boy had been born with, and an even harder one to suppress his own. They were much alike, Cat said, but it was not so. Nay, Guy had fought the demons of his blood that his son could live unafraid. A deep ache gnawed at his breastbone as he thought once again of William de Comminges, and he wished fervently that he were yet alive to guide him.

"You'd think he'd been born with hooves rather than toes," he could hear William say. " 'Tis the man who makes the blood rather than the blood that makes the man." Aye, and any who learned the secret Guy of Rivaux himself bore would turn away in fear and loathing, despite what William had said.

Resolutely he pushed away from the wall to make the long walk to the chapel. Snow fell, blanketing the courtyard softly with its beauty as he crossed it. He stopped to brush the melting flakes from his black hair and composed what he would say to the girl inside. Although he had not met her before Dieppe, he instinctively liked her, not only because she'd saved his son but also because she had a courage and resourcefulness not unlike Cat's. And her lack of a dowry did not bother him, for between what he'd inherited and stood yet to inherit, he was wealthy beyond belief. But his son was betrothed. No matter what passed between Richard and the little demoiselle, there could be but dishonor in the end.

Gilliane knelt before the flickering candles at the side of the altar and tried to pray yet again. The death and destruction at Beaumaule seemed far away, a part of a distant past, and her prayers for the souls of the brothers who'd left her had been said quickly, replaced by an earnest plea to God to deliver her from what she felt for Richard of Rivaux. The latter prayer died on her lips at the sound of footsteps at the back of the chapel. Her heart pounded with dread at what Count Guy would say to her, for she knew full well that he must think her little less than a harlot.

But he did not speak at first. Instead, he knelt beside her to pray also, and she was reminded of that first day she'd met his son. For a time there was naught but silence in the chapel, and then he rose, offering her his hand.

" 'Tis Christmas," he began suddenly. "Aye, this

day we celebrate the birth of God and mayhap the birth of a new life for you, Demoiselle."

"My lord—"

"Nay, hear me first. You have borne much lately, and I'd not overset you further, but there is that which must be said. I offer you this better life in the hope that you will take it." He paused to look at her, to see if she were truly listening to him. "My son will dower you that you may wed, and I am prepared to seek a good husband for you."

"Nay!"

Ignoring her outburst, he went on, "But if 'tis not your will to take a husband, then you are welcome to remain here as daughter to me and Cat so long as you would—unless, of course, 'tis the convent you desire."

"I do not want a husband, my lord," she whispered hollowly. "And I cannot stay here when I am nothing to you. Nay, but Lord Richard took me for ward, and I—"

"Gilliane, 'tis for you that I do this," Guy told her gently. "I have seen how my son looks at you, and I'd not have you dishonored."

She swallowed hard and looked away, shamed. "And 'tis what you think I want also."

"He is not free to wed."

"Did he ask you to speak with me?" She had to know.

"He acknowledges the truth of what I have said."

"And thus I am given the choice but whether to go to a husband asked to take me, to a family who could not truly want me, or to the Church. Nay, my lord, but I'd return to Beaumaule."

" 'Tis not safe. Hearken to me, little Gilliane—a war comes, whether we will it or not, and—"

"And there's none to care what happens to Gilliane de Lacey, my lord," she finished for him. "Aye, I can accept that."

"Demoiselle, you have but lost two brothers— mayhap I speak too soon." He reached to lift her chin as Richard had done. "Think on what I have said—'tis all I ask."

"Aye."

For a moment his flecked eyes were more gold than green. "I would that he had not taken Lincoln's daughter, Demoiselle," he murmured, holding her with his gaze. "Cat and I do not offer lightly—Rivaux's gates are open to you, whether 'tis now or later."

He released her chin and turned to leave. "Pray on it, if you will, and take God's guidance."

She stared after him, unable to believe what he'd offered her. She could live at Rivaux, protected by a lord more legend than man, treated as a daughter in his house, and want for nothing. But she had not the right to be there—she had but done what had to be done. And she did not want to stay at Rivaux, she admitted to herself. She wanted to go with Lord Richard when he left. But to what end? She closed her eyes and tried to blot out the thought that came to mind: even if he were free to wed, she was too lowborn for his wife and too highborn for his leman.

15

Days passed quickly at Rivaux—the Christmas feasts, the New Year, Epiphany, and Candlemas. Gilliane plied her needle in solitude, shutting out the sounds of those around her, lost in her own melancholy thoughts. Despite the bustle of life in a great castle, despite the kindness of those around her, she still felt alone, isolated from both the past and the present, unwilling to dwell on what the future held for her.

She smoothed the soft wool of yet another new gown over her lap and studied the embroidered bright-colored band that decorated her wide sleeve. Aye, she had clothes now, pretty ones, but to what end? As Richard of Rivaux had mended, she'd seen less and less of him, catching but glances of him as he sat at the table above her during meals, watching him from a distance as he passed about his business. The rest of his time, as far as she could glean from Elizabeth, was spent in strengthening his shoulder, practicing with the squires, and biding his time until he could leave.

She wished fervently that he had never kissed her, for it had changed things between them greatly. It had made her dream of him constantly, a foolish maiden's dream that could give her naught but pain. Even in the bed she shared with Elizabeth at night, she could not rid herself of thoughts of him, she could not help reliving the feel of his lips against hers, tossing and turning until his sister had complained. And while she chided herself for a fool, the memory of that one kiss nurtured a hopeless love for him.

It had come as a revelation, this love she bore him, brought about by the loss of his company at Rivaux. The less she saw of him, the more her thoughts dwelled on him. And when she was fortunate enough to cross his path, he was almost always surrounded by servants and men-at-arms, and she had not the chance to speak with him alone. It began to seem that even God conspired to keep her from his thoughts.

She laid aside the altar cloth she was working, and leaned to hug her knees. But last night had been different, she remembered, savoring the reliving of each glance. Last night, the countess had bidden her tall son to her solar, saying that if his wound had healed enough that he could wield sword and shield, then he could entertain them with his lute. And Gilliane had sat with the women of the household, listening at his feet. He was a good singer, one of those blessed not only with a good voice but also with a sense of story. He'd sung the old song about his grandsire Roger de Brione vanquishing Robert of Belesme in single combat. And if Catherine of the Condes thought it strange that he sang of her father rather than of his own, she gave no sign of it.

They were a strange family, Gilliane reflected, for apart it appeared that the father loved his son and the son loved his father, but together . . . well, neither spared the other. It was perhaps that they were too alike, Count Guy and Richard, both of whom quarreled over the smallest things. It was as though Guy of Rivaux despised any sign of his own temper in his son.

Even last night there had been an encounter of sorts over Richard's choice of song, with the count snapping that he'd very much rather hear of something else—that Robert of Belesme had been dead twenty-three years, and 'twas time to let tales of him die. But Richard had persisted, and Elizabeth had murmured low for Gilliane's ears alone, "Alas, but my brother cannot understand that my father hated Count Robert so. To Richard, 'tis enough that the devil's spawn gave him breath."

"Aye—I heard the tale," Gilliane hissed back. "But do you not think that the greater he makes Belesme, the greater his father's feat?"

"Mayhap." The older girl shrugged and turned her attention back to the song. "But Papa likes not to be reminded of him."

But when Richard reached the place in the song where he described his grandmother, Eleanor of Nantes, singing, "Her beauty was as the sparkling sky, her eyes like shining stars, and her lips as red as roses," Gilliane became aware that he was watching her. And she had shivered with excitement at the expression in his dark eyes.

She laid aside her embroidery and rose, stretching her muscles. It was so foolish of her to indulge in such hopeless fancies, she chided herself. What she'd seen was but the mirror of his song. Aye, 'twas no more than that, for when he'd risen to seek his bed, he'd passed her, brushing against her, stopping but to ask her pardon. But he'd sung to her, she was certain of it, another part of her mind argued—'twas not fancy.

Jesu, but she was beginning to lose her good sense. Resolutely she picked up her cloth and began to stitch again. 'Twas that she refined too much on kisses that meant far more to her than to him, she told herself severely, bending closer to examine the intricate pattern she made.

" 'Tis beautiful, Gilly," Isabella breathed. "Wherever did you learn to do that? Maman has paid dearly for work not so fine as yours, I swear to you."

"Well, when there's naught to do but sew, one becomes skilled, I suppose," Gilliane answered, grateful to be drawn to safer thoughts.

"Aye, our poor efforts look as though we had not

but thumbs on our hands," Elizabeth agreed readily. "Not even Maman can do what you can with a needle. If I thought it possible, I'd ask to learn of you."

"Nay, with your beauty, you've no need of sewing skill," Gilliane answered.

Elizabeth stopped mid-stitch and lifted her brow much as her brother was wont to do. "Nay, Gilly, 'tis not beauty that holds a man in thrall—I can attest to that. Nor housewifely skills either," she added judiciously.

Her curiosity aroused, Gilliane longed to ask of Elizabeth's husband. Having once been mistress of a great keep, surely the girl could not like being but a daughter in her mother's house. But Richard had said she had no wish to remarry—she who had dowry enough for ten husbands. Sometimes it was difficult to see God's justice in such matters.

"Can you work the new French style?" Bella asked.

Gilliane shook her head, no longer truly attending. Even as the girl spoke to her, she could hear his voice at the other end of the solar, and she was instantly alert. Every fiber of her being strained to hear as he addressed his mother. Drawn by his presence, she tried to watch covertly from where she sat. He stood straight, no longer favoring his shoulder, and he was magnificent in a red samite tunic that gleamed as the light caught the golden embroidery across his chest.

"So soon?" She heard the consternation in Catherine of the Condes' voice, and her own chest tightened painfully. "Nay, but you are not healed—'tis but a month, my son."

"Last night you told me I was well," he teased.

"But singing is different from riding mailed and armed," Catherine retorted. "Richard, you are but come home—nay, I'd not have you leave yet."

The awful knot in Gilliane's stomach nearly made her sick. She stared across the length of the solar, willing him to look at her. Nay, but he could not leave her.

"And Gilliane?" Cat demanded. "What of her? Richard, I'd have her here, if it pleases you that she should stay."

"Aye. I'd provide for her—I have already spoken to my sire in the matter."

There was a trace of bitterness in his voice that was not lost on his mother. "My son—"

"Nay," he cut her short. "Spare me the telling of how 'tis he loves me. Just let it be said that once again I do his bidding in this."

"Well, she seems content here," Catherine countered, "and we are glad enough to have her."

Nay! Nay! A thousand times nay! Gilliane wanted to cry out, to tell them she had no wish to stay. Instead, she sat still as stone, unable to move. He was in truth leaving her without so much as a backward glance.

"I mean to seek out Gloucester," he continued. "It has been over a month since Stephen's crowning, and I've still not heard what he'd do in the matter. Papa says we are summoned to Easter court for our oaths of fealty, and I'd not go if Gloucester means to fight."

"He keeps his own counsel," Cat sighed. "Guy does not think he has decided."

"Aye—Stephen's treachery caught him unaware."

Gilliane glanced about her wildly, her heart thudding in her chest. Content at Rivaux? Sweet Mary, but she would not stay, a pauper amongst them, no matter how great their kindness. She bit off her thread, bending her head low so that neither Elizabeth nor Isabella would see her pain.

"When will you ride?"

"On the morrow."

"Does Guy know?"

"Aye."

"And gives his blessing to your going to Gloucester?"

Richard ran his fingers through his hair in the distracted manner Gilliane had come to recognize. She willed her heart to silence, that she might hear.

"Nay—when has he ever? He would have me rot

at Celesin whilst he makes up his own mind what he would do."

"He is decided. Surely you who are his son cannot think he would break his oath to the Empress? He means to fight for her, Richard, and does but wait for her to move."

"I accept he swore to her, but I did not."

"He thinks Robert of Gloucester will follow her also," Cat told him quietly. "He also swore, as you recall."

He had no answer for her. Already his wound had delayed him far too long, and it was time that he discovered whether Gloucester would be king. If not, then he was for his own lands, and the others could fight it out between them. There was but one whose rule could benefit him.

"I suppose you have heard that Lincoln comes to press Guy to declare for Stephen?"

"Aye."

"And for your marriage also."

For some reason, any mention of his impending marriage to the Maid of Lincoln made him uneasy now. "I'd not wed in troubled times, Maman," he said evasively, looking away. "What if Papa declares for the Empress and Lincoln for Stephen? Nay, but I'd have a bond of blood with them both and would have to choose between them."

"It has been six years—the girl is fifteen, I think. There will come a time soon when you can delay no longer and maintain your faith in the matter."

"Aye—but not now."

Catherine appeared to consider her words carefully, knowing she trod on dangerous ground. On the one hand, it had been Richard who had first asked for the marriage, had contracted himself almost without Guy's grudging consent; and on the other, she knew that Guy still opposed the alliance on the grounds that no matter how wealthy the Earl of Lincoln, he was still a faithless fool. But he would see that Richard honored his pledge to the girl, even if he had to shame him into doing it. There was no middle ground with Guy of Rivaux—a man's given word was his honor. He owed that to Belesme, she supposed, for he was determined to be as different from him as night to day.

"Seek his blessing, my son," she urged finally, still torn by his leaving. "I'd not have you go angered with him."

"Nay—'tis he who is always angered with me."

"He loves you."

"He loves his blood—not me," he retorted. Then seeing the troubled expression on Cat's face, he relented. "Nay, Maman, but I'd not quarrel with you. I know you cannot help loving him."

He had the wrong of it, she knew, and yet she was powerless to make peace between the two men she loved most. She rose and stood on tiptoe to brush a kiss against her son's face. "Sweet Mary, but I will worry about you, Richard," she whispered. "When will you leave?"

"On the morrow."

Gilliane felt chilled in the depth of her bones. He would leave her on the morrow without so much as another thought. He'd think her safe and count that he had done honorably by her. Jesu, but he could not go—he must not. She closed her eyes and gripped the edge of her bench.

"You are my most precious son," Catherine whispered through her own aching throat.

"Nay, I am your only son." He strove for a lightness, a teasing that he did not feel. Parting from his mother was always painful, made doubly so because he knew how he tested her loyalty to his father. "Come, let us not weep over this, Maman. If Gloucester needs me not, I swear I will come again before St. John's Day in June."

"Aye." With an effort, Cat drew back and managed to smile up at him. "Nay, if you must go, I'd bless you and wish you Godspeed."

Her own heart sore, her stomach sick, Gilliane

silently laid aside the embroidery and slipped out to wait for him. When Isabella thought to follow her, Elizabeth put out a slippered foot to stop her. "Nay," she murmured, " 'tis no concern of yours."

Lying in wait for him, Gilliane practiced in her mind what she would say to him, but when he did emerge, words deserted her. He stopped abruptly when he saw her.

"You heard?"

"Aye." Her mouth had gone suddenly parched, too dry for speech.

"Gilliane—" he began gently.

"Nay! I'd not stay—I'd not! Sweet Mary, but I am not a horse to be stabled just anywhere!" The words, when they came, where nothing like the conciliatory plea she'd planned. Instead, they tumbled out. "Did you think not to bid me farewell even? Am I as naught to you?"

" 'Tis not as you think. I—"

" 'Twas not I who made myself your ward, my lord—nay, I protested it! But you swore to protect me, to . . . to take revenge against Brevise! To rebuild Beaumaule! Have you forgotten your fine words so soon, my lord? When I held you on your horse, when I warmed you in that ship's hold, when I found aid for you—'twas not for this!" She choked, unable to find the means to convey her hurt to him.

"Gilliane—"

"Nay! I did not care for you that I may be left among strangers!" Tears welled in her blue eyes, blinding them. She blinked and brushed angrily at the wetness on her cheeks.

It was a gesture far more moving than the tears themselves. He'd not meant to hurt her—quite the opposite, in fact. He'd meant to save her from himself, from what he would make of her. But as he stared into her upturned face, he felt totally helpless.

"You swore to me!" she reminded him. "You swore on Belesme's sword!"

He ought to turn away, he ought to be harsh for

her sake, but he could not. He reached his hand to lift an errant lock that fell over her face and brushed it back with his fingertips. Even the feel of the coppery silk that was her hair burned him. There was not a night that he had not imagined it spilling onto a pillow beside him.

"Gilliane," he began again softly, " 'tis because I swore to keep you safe that I would not take you with me. You are a maid. 'Twill be said . . . Jesu!" The quivering of her chin and the welling tears were making it impossible for him.

"Please, my lord, I pray you—"

She got no further. His arms slid around her, pulling her close, and she leaned into him, smelling the clean scent of Hawise's harsh soap. "Gilly, 'tis impossible," he whispered into the crown of her hair. "I have other . . . There is that which I must do." She was so near he could feel the swell of her firm breasts pressed against his body, and his resolve almost deserted him. For a moment he allowed himself the forbidden pleasure of rubbing his cheek against her shining hair, savoring the warm, sweet scent of roses that lingered there. He could feel the suppressed sob that shuddered through her. His hand came up to smooth the silken mass, stroking it where it lay against the back of her head.

"Were it not for Lincoln's daughter . . ." he murmured, daring to voice what was in his heart. But his voice trailed off before he betrayed both of them to his desire for her. Cicely of Lincoln was in truth his betrothed wife, and he would have to honor his pledge to marry her.

"Aye?" she whispered, holding her breath for his answer.

Abruptly he thrust her from him and looked away. "I have to take her, Gilliane—there is no choice for me."

"But I—"

"And I'd not make you into a whore for me."

"Richard, I pray you . . . you said I could go to Celesin with you, and—"

"Jesu! You cannot ease this for me, can you?" he asked. "You would tear at me for what I cannot help, Gilliane! Leave me be ere we regret this!" He turned his back to her as though he meant to leave. "You are far safer in my father's care than mine, Demoiselle."

"I'll not wed any paid to take me!" she blurted out.

"That is between you and my father."

She had not the means to stop him. She'd appealed, nearly baring her heart, and he'd denied her. She stood like stone while he walked away, and then she fled to the empty chamber she shared with Elizabeth, too mortified to cry even. Flinging herself to lie on the bedcovers, she stared unseeing at the richly embroidered canopy overhead. She'd made a fool of herself in his eyes.

"Gilly?"

It was Elizabeth, come after her, something that Gilliane did not think she could bear. "What?" she responded sullenly.

"Ah, Gilly . . . Gilly," Elizabeth clucked soothingly, sitting beside her on the bed. "You love him, do you not?" she asked softly. When the younger girl did not answer, she reached to pat her. "Well, if it means aught to you, I think he loves you also."

" 'Tis impossible," Gilliane whispered hollowly.

"Nay, naught's impossible whilst you live and breathe—or so my father has told me." Leaning closer, she smoothed the copper hair back from Gilliane's face. "If I share no man's bed, Gilly, 'tis because there's none I would have, but if there were, I'd let naught stand in my way."

"What if you could not in honor have him?" Gilliane managed to ask, turning on her side to face her.

"Well, I was once wed to a handsome man, one whose wealth was matched by his face, one who appeared to be all my father could want for me,"

Elizabeth recalled bitterly. "And he was naught that we thought of him. I was glad enough that he died."

"And yet—"

"He loved neither man nor woman, Gilly—'twas himself that he admired beyond all. Look at me—I am not a plain woman, and yet he turned from me from the beginning."

"Nay, but he could not—you are beautiful," Gilliane protested loyally.

"Aye, but it gained me naught. For five years I was wed to him without the comfort of his love or his babe." The green eyes met Gilliane's squarely. "My husband was as different from my brother as night unto day."

"Why do you tell me this?"

"That you will know that happiness does not always come in the marriage bed. It comes, I think, from loving the man himself."

"But he weds Cicely of Lincoln!"

"Because he must, Gilly, but that's naught to you."

Gilliane stared at the beautiful girl beside her, scarce able to believe what she'd heard. Was Elizabeth seriously suggesting she become Richard of Rivaux's leman? As if the other girl knew her mind, she nodded.

"Given the choice between a husband I could not love and a love I could not wed, I'd take the latter, I swear to you."

"But your family would condemn you."

Elizabeth appeared to consider for a moment, and her green eyes grew distant with thought. "Aye, but 'tis not they who lived with my husband, was it? They would mayhap condemn me, but they would love me still."

"He leaves me here."

"Aye. Now, there is your problem—you can scarce win him if he is gone and you are here." Elizabeth rose and smoothed her sleek black braids against her breasts, straightening the ornate gold bands that bound them until they hung even with the jeweled pendant she wore. "But however you decide, Gilliane, I am for you in this."

Gilliane lay for a long time after Richard's sister left, her confused thoughts tumbling despite her best efforts to sort them out. It was easy for Elizabeth of Rivaux to speak thus—she was the pampered daughter of a great house. Gilliane, on the other hand, was a nobody. Aye, if the beautiful Elizabeth sinned with a man, Guy of Rivaux would see them wed to cover his honor, but there was none to stand for Gilliane de Lacey. Besides, she had not the means to stop Richard from leaving her. She could scarce throw herself at his feet and offer to lie with him, could she? Her humiliation would know no bounds if he refused her even that. And neither could she stay at Rivaux forever—she'd not hang on Count Guy's charity. After much thinking, she concluded that her only answer was to leave Rivaux. But for where? Beaumaule had burned to the ground, and she had no claim to anything else. Mayhap she would have to throw herself on the mercy of an abbess. With that unhappy thought, she dragged herself from the bed and returned to work.

Inside the solar, Gilliane again took up her seat beneath the window and looked out into the courtyard. As she watched, Richard emerged from the armorer's shed carrying a practice lance. He'd exchanged his fancy tunic for a plain woolen one that hung only to his knees. Behind him, Walter of Thibeaux bore his heavy leather *cuir bouilli*, and still another man held the quilted felt gambeson. The cold February air whitened with their breaths. For a moment she wished he might somehow fall—and then hastily begged God's forgiveness for the thought. A bruise would not keep him there, and she'd not have him hurt.

Catherine of the Condes looked to where Gilliane sat intently watching out the tall, narrow window. The girl's profile, outlined by the winter sunlight, betrayed her anguish, and Catherine's heart went out to her. If only Richard had not chosen the maid of Lincoln, she sighed. But he had. She pulled herself up by a cabinet edge, and several of her women hastened forward, anxious to do her bidding.

"Nay, I'd speak with the Demoiselle only."

At first Gilliane did not hear her come up, but Catherine's hand on her shoulder made her start guiltily. She flushed, afraid her thoughts were betrayed on her face.

"Nay, do not rise, child," Catherine told her. Looking past Gilliane into the yard below, she saw her son slip the gambeson and stiffened leather on. Turning back to the girl, she shook her head. "I thank God that I am not a man—I'd not live in my saddle, weighted down with all that."

"I was always sorry that I was not a son," Gilliane admitted, smiling grudgingly. "Aye, I thought my brothers had the better life."

"My father was wont to say that he baked in summer, froze in winter, and had naught but salt meat and cold bread to eat when he rode to war."

"Earl Roger?"

"Aye." Catherine plumped a cushion and sat down beside Gilliane. "But we are women and care not about war, I think, unless 'tis our men who fight." She reached for the altar cloth on the girl's lap and lifted it to the light. " 'Tis as fine work as I have ever seen, Demoiselle—you have uncommon skill."

"Nay, 'tis but that I have practiced."

"So have I, and yet I dare not offer anything of mine to Christ's altar. What say you—if I would purchase for you a goodly piece of cloth for a new gown, would you embroider new hangings for my bed?"

"There is no need—I should be pleased to work it without the cloth for me."

"Nay." Cat's eyes twinkled, pleased that she'd found something to divert the girl's attention from her son. "You will earn the gown, I promise you. Your stitches are nearly as fine as the French *orfrois* that we prize so highly."

"I had once thought to learn it, but there was none to teach me."

"Mayhap Master Ollo will know of one who can instruct us," Catherine offered. "He is supposed to come today, and I am told he carries some pieces worked in the French style. Aye, I should like to see it done also, and 'twill give us the excuse of examining all his wares."

Gilliane sat, to all appearances listening to the countess, but her mind raced ahead. If there were indeed a cloth merchant coming who dealt in fabric worked with gold and silver, then mayhap he would have need of one skilled with a needle. An impossible scheme formed in her head and grew. She would leave Rivaux, freeing all of them from any obligation to her.

"What say you, Demoiselle—would you see what he has?"

"Oh, aye." A pang of momentary guilt stabbed at her, but Gilliane was certain that once she was gone, they'd be relieved not to have to provide for her.

16

Gilliane paused to suck on her sore fingertips, wondering if they would ever become callused enough that they would not hurt from pushing the needle through the stiff silk. Master Ollo praised her work, saying she showed great promise, but she wondered if she would ever truly learn the small, intricate stitches that made *orfrois* so highly prized. She lifted the end of the piece she worked to examine it and sighed. While it was far above that done in any castle solar, it could not compete in trade with the sample Master Ollo had provided her.

Master Ollo. The old merchant had taken an instant liking to her at Rivaux when she'd questioned him about his cloth, praising this one and that until the others had left. Then she'd shown her own needlework, producing the fine altar cloth she'd made, and he'd admired it. She was but a freewoman of Caen, she'd told him, and she wished to learn the French art, but she had not the means to reach Flanders on her own. Aye, and he'd believed her—believed even that her hair had been shorn during a fever, believed that the countess would not wish her to go because of her skill. And together they had plotted her escape. She'd left Rivaux beneath the noses of Count Guy's sentries, disguised as a boy, riding in the back of the cloth wagon.

She rose and stretched aching shoulder muscles, flexing her spine to ease it. Looking out into the yard from the tall casement window, she could see

the length of the merchant's great warehouse, and
she could smell the sorting house, where workers in
wooden shoes sorted, washed, and beat the raw wool
before it was dried and carded. The scent of oil used
to smooth it seeped through a crack in the casement,
reminding her of a different oil, the kind used on
mail, and a terrible longing gnawed at her heart.

She'd never again arm a man to fight, nor wait for
him to come home to her. Nor would she bear her
lord's babes and tend his castle. Already she felt as
one of those sere, dried old women who, maidens
still, sat in drafty corners and did naught but spin
and sew. But it was not her lot to be a wife, she
reminded herself, for she would not wed the sort
who would wed with her. Nay, she'd not have an
errant, nearly landless knight, who'd use her, get an
endless number of children of her, and drag her
from keep to keep. She paused, remembering Beaumaule. She did, after all, possess Beaumaule. A self-
derisive snort escaped her. Beaumaule was naught
but rubble now.

Nearly overwhelmed by her self-pity, she turned
her attention again to the long building that abutted
the merchant's fine house, and wondered at the lot
of those who labored as warpers, spoolers, weavers,
fullers, and tenters. They worked hard to weave,
shrink, and stretch woolen cloth that was prized
throughout Christendom. A teasel-boy passed the
window, carrying the brush he used to raise the nap
to a fine sheen. Nay, but she had the easier task, she
told herself resolutely. She would always work in the
warmth and comfort of the house, and she could
admire the fine silks the others never touched.

Seating herself again, she lifted the bright blue
sendal and pulled the needle from the seam where
she'd stuck it. This piece was for Master Ollo himself, he'd told her, and it needn't be so fine as that
she'd work for the lords who patronized him. She
pulled the gold thread through the stiff silk and
thought of Richard of Rivaux. He had many rich

garments embroidered in gold, and he probably never gave a thought to the nameless women who'd stitched the intricate designs that blazoned across his chest. It was a lowering reflection, one better forgotten. He was far away—in Caen, or Rouen, or wherever it was that he sought Gloucester—whilst she was now in Flanders. And she wondered what he'd thought when they discovered her missing. Nay, but he'd probably already forgotten her—his fine words and his kisses were most likely but a pleasant dalliance to him.

She tightened the last stitch and knotted the fine thread, breaking off the remainder with her teeth. Aye, if the truth were admitted, he probably considered himself well rid of her, for she would not but be an encumbrance to him. 'Twas why he'd sought to leave her at Rivaux with his family. The familiar pang of guilt assailed her at the thought of them—she'd not so much as left a word of thanks for all they'd given her.

"Alys?"

For a moment the address meant nothing to her, and then she remembered she'd even lied to Master Ollo about that also. "Aye?"

"I would see that which you have done." He spoke kindly enough, reaching to take the cloth from her lap and holding it to the window light. "Aye, 'tis good," he approved.

But he did not move away. Instead, he studied her soberly, assessing her almost as he had the cloth. She kept her eyes demurely averted, fixing her gaze on his knee. He cleared his throat as though he would have her attention.

"Alys, I know it has been scarce a fortnight . . ." His voice trailed off while he waited for her to look up at him. "Aye, but I have watched you these days past, and there is a pleasing gentility about you not often found in townswomen. You have skill with your needle, but you also show promise in other things. I have seen you direct the others, offering advice to lessen waste."

She looked up briefly to see warmth in his eyes, and she wondered where his words led him. She did not have long to wait. He laid aside the cloth and moved closer to touch the crown of her hair.

"My wife departed this earth two summers past, Alys, and there's been none since."

She sat very still, afraid to hear the rest, certain he meant to ask her to his bed. And if he did, she would have to leave his employ.

But he stroked her hair awkwardly, murmuring, " 'Tis such pretty hair you have, Alys—I have never seen the like. 'Tis a pity that it had to be cut for your illness."

She felt another stab of guilt for lying to him about so much. "It will grow," she mumbled, embarrassed.

"Alys . . ." Again he hesitated, and then he dropped to the bench beside her, reaching to possess her hands, turning them over in his own. Irrationally, she noted that the veins stood out like blue cords on his wrists, and that the dark spots on his skin showed his age. "I am not a young man," he added almost as if he knew her thoughts. "But I am wealthy, child, and you would want for naught. As wife to a merchant, you would have some standing beyond freewoman."

Holy Jesu, but he was asking her to wed. She looked up then, taking in the thin hair he combed over the top to hide his baldness, the sunken dark eyes that watched her, and his stooped shoulders. The thought that he could not live long flew to mind and was dismissed. He was kind, but he was not Richard. She groped in her heart for the means to refuse him.

"Nay, I cannot. 'Tis an honor you offer me, but—"

They were interrupted by the loud clatter of armed men riding into the small yard in front of the house. The old man whitened, his sallow complexion making his eyes black, and he dropped her hands quickly. "Hide the piece, good maid, that they rob me not of it. I know not why they are come, but I can hear the sound of mail and spurs."

Gilliane quickly folded the rich cloth she'd been stitching and sought the means to hide it. Moving to a box bench beside the door, she opened it and hastily thrust the sendal beneath the lid. She could hear Master Ollo plead with someone that he'd done naught to cause offense.

"Nay," she heard a familiar voice answer him. "I have but come for the girl you took from Rivaux."

"She is a freewoman, good sir," the merchant protested feebly.

Gilliane crouched low before the box bench and hoped he would not see her. Her heart was in her throat, beating wildly as she heard his heavy boots cross the wooden floor. His mantle brushed over her as he lifted his hand above her, and she felt his strong grip beneath her arm, raising her roughly. For a moment, she thought he meant to shake her as she looked up in horror at the eyes that glittered beneath the shadow of the helmet nasal.

"You have your wish, Gilliane de Lacey—you are going to Celesin with me."

There was such cold anger in the tone of his voice that it frightened her. "You have not the right to come for me! Nay, but I . . ." Her protest, begun strongly, ended feebly.

He did shake her then, so hard that she felt her bones would rattle within her skin. "I take the right," he answered curtly, his grip painful on her shoulder.

"But she is a freewoman," Master Ollo tried again, this time more timidly. "She is Alys, a freewoman of Caen."

"She is Gilliane de Lacey, mistress of Beaumaule," Richard snapped, still holding her. "She ran away from my father's keep." The gold flecks in his eyes spread out from the black pupils as he continued to stare at her. " 'Twas poor payment for my parents' kindness to you."

"They pitied me!"

"Nay—they liked you right well."

"I would not stay there!"

He released her and dropped his hand. "Aye." He nodded grimly, his eyes still cold on her face. "You wished to go to Celesin, did you not? Well, you behold before you one who leaves his duty to come for you, Gilliane de Lacey. I pray you do not regret the choice you have made."

"I chose to come here!"

His gaze raked the room almost contemptuously before settling again on her. "Nay, but I can offer you better than this," he told her harshly. "You will not have to sit and sew in my keep."

Despite all of her girl's dreams of him, the man before her was neither kind nor gentle. She bit her lip to still the shiver that his coldness gave her. "I am to wed Master Ollo," she announced baldly.

"Nay. For good or ill, you are tied to me—'tis I who will kill Brevise for you."

The merchant looked from one to the other and then looked away. He'd not lived fifty years and more by tempting the tempers of great lords. "If you say she is yours, take her," he offered to conciliate the towering knight before him.

"Do you come willing or not?" Richard demanded of her.

"Nay." Sweet Mary, but she could not go with him like that.

She had not the time to back away. His jaw tightened visibly and the gold faded completely from his eyes. In one swift move his mailed arm snaked out, encircling her roughly and lifting her over his good shoulder. She cried out as the steel links cut into her flesh, but he ignored her, carrying her like she was but a sack of grain past the bemused stares of Master Ollo's embroiderers and into the crowded yard. Without a word, he flung her over his saddle and prepared to mount behind her.

"Wait." She licked her lips at the expression on his face. "Please, my lord—I would ride."

"In my haste, I brought no other horse. Aye, Gilliane de Lacey, I have searched full half of Normandy for you, sitting my saddle until my legs pain me, freezing these two weeks past—and all the while you were warm in Flanders."

"I did not ask you for the service," she retorted. "You refused what I asked."

"My wound chafes beneath the weight of my mail, my backside is saddle-sore, and my goodwill is gone," he continued, swinging his tall frame up behind her. "But I give you your wish and pray you do not rue the day you made it. Now, be still and make me room." Almost by afterthought, he wrapped the cloak she'd made him around them both, drawing her closer, pressing her against the steel links that were like ice beneath his crimson surcoat.

"You have the cloak," she observed foolishly. "Where is Alwina?"

"They came to Rivaux the day I left it—I sent her on to Celesin to await you there."

The arms that she'd dreamed of held her prisoner now, surrounding her as he grasped the reins. She tried to crane her neck, to look up into his stranger's face, but all she saw were his chin and the helmet. "But what of Gloucester?" she asked.

"I know not," he answered tersely. "I sent to him, but I have been sitting my horse in search of you, and I have not heard."

"I will go back to Rivaux," she sighed. "I'd not keep you from your duty to him."

"Nay." His arm tightened around her. "We go to Celesin together."

"You punish me for not wishing to stay at Rivaux!" she cried out, goaded by his harshness.

"Punish you?" he snorted derisively. "I do but give you what you ask."

"I never asked for your anger!"

"Nay? Then how is it that we awoke to find you gone, gone without so much as a word to my lady mother, who showed great kindness to you—or to my sister Elizabeth, who had a care for you? Or my father even? He would have kept you as a daughter in his house, finding you a husband, Gilliane de Lacey. But nay—you stole away in the night, leaving all of us to worry that you were cold, or hungry, or mayhap dead."

"I am sorry for the trouble I caused them," she managed low, shamed by the truth of his words.

"Aye, and you have a hard three days' ride to Celesin to regret what you have done."

She shivered, as much from his coldness as from the weather, and pulled the fur-lined mantle closer over her chest. His heavy gauntlet held the reins tight beneath her breast, scarce giving her room to breathe. A sideways glance at Everard of Meulan yielded nothing—his face was as set as his lord's.

They rode until she was numb and her lower limbs ceased aching. Her whole body cried out from its fatigue before the man who held her reined in at last. Thinking they stopped for the night, she looked around and saw nothing. He threw the reins to Garth and dismounted, reaching up to her almost as soon as his feet were planted on the ground. She slid down into his arms and found she could not stand at first. Clutching at his arms for balance, she leaned into him. He steadied her and gestured to Everard.

"Walk her about until I relieve myself."

The captain slid an arm beneath hers and steadied her. "Can you step, or are your limbs too stiff?"

"They pain me," she muttered through clenched teeth as she tried to walk.

"Aye, as do mine, Demoiselle."

Inexplicable angry tears scalded her eyes, threatening to humiliate her further. "He has not the right! He has not the right to treat me so!"

The captain stopped. "Nay, I'd not tempt his temper further, lady. He quarrels with Count Guy over you."

"I did not ask him to!"

"You fled." He spat on the ground in disgust.

"Aye, and kept all of us in our saddles this fortnight past."

"I'd go back to Beaumaule."

"Nay, but he'll not give you the choice now."

Richard returned to stand before her. "If you have the need to relieve yourself also, there are those trees for privacy, Gilliane. Otherwise, we'll ride on."

"Ride on? Holy Jesu, but . . ." She gaped in consternation. "I thought . . ."

"That we would eat and rest?" he gibed. "Nay, but I'd have you see how it has been for me these two weeks past. Garth, cut her a piece of the meat and some bread ere she mounts."

She looked around her in mute appeal to the men who stood about, and she was surprised by their hostility. These were the same men who'd ridden with them from Beaumaule. Garth fumbled in the food bag, drawing forth a chunk of hard cheese. She started to protest that she'd rather starve, and then thought better of it. Given the way they looked at her, they just might let her. Instead, she took it and began to gnaw at it, hoping that the meat was better.

"Put your foot in my hand," Richard ordered her as he walked to stand beside the big black horse.

Still clutching the cheese, she moved closer, muttering, "You have the devil's own temper, if you would but admit it."

"Admit it? Aye, I have it of my sire." He cupped his hands to boost her up, and smiled faintly. "And you tempt it sorely."

17

Her bones still aching from the three-day ride, her skin chafing from the rubbing of his rough mail through her gown, Gilliane welcomed the sight of Celesin. The man behind her eased off his helmet and set it over the pommel before her, speaking finally.

"Behold that which you wanted to see so badly."

For some reason, he was still angry with her—indeed, he'd been angry the whole journey, scarce speaking to her, keeping his own counsel, ignoring her despite the fact that he held her against his body. And her stung pride would not allow her to beg his attention. Instead, she'd ridden before him as stiff and silent as he.

"You are displeased? Do you wish you'd not fled Rivaux?" he gibed at her back.

It was an ancient keep, one whose old walls intermingled with the new, giving the stones different hues of yellow and gray. But it was now large and well-secured, sitting perched atop solid rock and overlooking a bend in a river. Above it flew the red flag of Rivaux—with an exception. The black hawk did not swoop, but rather sat like a bird waiting in its aerie.

He nodded. "Aye—'tis the lot of firstborn sons to wait, ready to fall upon the carrion when their sires die."

" 'Tis an evil thought."

"There is evil in us all, Gilliane." His knee directed

the horse they rode up the narrow path. "But it pleases me that you have found your tongue. I'd thought you'd gone dumb these three days past."

"And I thought you merely ill-tempered." She tried to turn against him, looking up at his shadowed face, trying to read his expression. What she could see was unfathomable, but she gambled anyway. "Aye, but there was a time I thought you kind."

She could feel him tense at her back, and then he shrugged, "There is kindness also, but kindness gained me naught. I sought to protect you, Demoiselle, and you fled."

"Sweet Mary!" she exploded, having had enough of his coldness. "Protect me? You sought to leave me amongst strangers who did not want me!"

"Hold your tongue," he ordered sternly. "I'd not have you carp before my men. If you've aught to say on the matter, you may say it when we are alone."

"Nay! I'll not hold my tongue!" She tried to twist her body again, but his arm across her ribs was like a vise. "Jesu, but it is as though Richard of Rivaux is two men! First you come to Beaumaule and threaten me, then you return to save me, and now you would threaten me again. Nay, but there is no sense to be made of you!" This time, he eased his arm, and she was again able to look up at him.

"I recall a few things also, Gilliane." His dark eyes met hers, challenging her, bright beneath the shadow of his nasal. "Aye, I remember all that has befallen me since I met you. There are those who would count us more than even."

"Then why did you come for me?"

He did not want to tell her that she'd become almost an obsession with him, that she had such power over him that he'd forgotten Gloucester when he'd discovered her gone from Rivaux. Aye, he'd struggled within himself, torn between desire and honor, between desire and duty, and desire had won.

She waited, disappointed that he did not answer. The horse picked its way up the rocky road, swaying her tired body. She bit back a dozen questions rather than ask anything of him again. The man who held her was not the man of her girlish dreams, and she was suddenly afraid of what her pleas at Rivaux had gained her. She felt him flex his left arm, transferring his reins to the right, and she was intensely conscious of his strength. And then she felt him wince as he drew her back.

"Your shoulder—does it pain you still?" she asked involuntarily.

"Aye, but it mends." To demonstrate, he lifted the arm again. " 'Tis tender, but it drains no more, and the scar fills it in. If I have aught to be thankful for, 'tis that 'twas only flesh that the arrow took."

"You should not have come for me."

"Seventeen days I have spent in my saddle for you, Gilliane, seventeen days in cold and pain—nay, if you'd not wanted me to come, you'd not have fled."

"I'd not have stayed at Rivaux as naught but a pensioner to your family."

"If you tell me that you would wed the old burgher, I'll know you for a liar."

"Nay."

He glanced down to where the hood of her cloak fell back beneath his own, and he could see the bright crown of her head against his breast. "I think 'tis your hair that draws me," he decided dispassionately. "When first I saw it, 'twas like none other of my memory. I remember picking it out of the brazier and wondering at it."

"My *hair*? Sweet Jesu, but you have plagued me for my hair?" she demanded incredulously. "I have never heard the like of that. You must be daft. 'Twas not your shoulder that the arrow took—'twas your wits."

"It made me decide that I favored red-haired women."

It was the first time since they'd left Master Ollo's house that he'd said anything pleasing to her, but his meaning was not lost on her. For three days she'd argued within herself as to why he had come for her, first saying that 'twas anger, then that it offended his honor for her to flee his protection, and finally that he came to take her for leman. She'd be a fool, she knew, but somehow it gratified her that it was the latter.

"Even in the darkness of the ship, I could see it," he went on. "It caught and held what there was of the light. And when I awoke among the monks, 'twas the first thing mine eyes could see."

"Now I know you mock me," she managed despite the thudding of her heart, "for there's scarce any of it left."

"Nay?" He raised his heavy glove at her crown and tugged. "Then what is this?"

"But it will not plait."

"I can wait for it to grow."

The fire burned brightly in the large brazier in the center of the room, heating it. Gilliane leaned back in the huge oaken tub, sliding down further than the small seat on the side, letting her tired, aching body luxuriate in the warm water. A thin film of scented oil from the East floated on the top, making a swirling pattern with the soap. Two women scrubbed her body, relieving her of even the trouble of lifting her arms unaided, something she'd never experienced before, while Alwina waited, her arms crossed in disapproval.

"Would you have your hair washed, Demoiselle?" the woman called Neste asked politely.

It was an inviting thought, but she was too sleepy to wait for it to dry. "Nay, 'twas clean the day I left Douai."

" 'Twas a pity to cut it."

She dodged her head beneath the woman's hand and twisted away. Sweet Mary, but she tired of hearing of her loss. " 'Twas most necessary at the time," she muttered ungraciously.

"Aye, I have heard of when 'twas done for Count Alan of Brittany's wife to keep it from sapping her strength ere she died."

" 'Tis less for you to do, so I'd not complain of the lack."

The other woman, one Grisel by name, picked up a bucket of steaming water and asked Gilliane to stand. Somewhat self-consciously, she complied, feeling very much as though they inspected her. Beads of oil mingled with soap scum where the water line had been. Grisel waited until she straightened up and then threw the full contents of the bucket over her, while Neste readied the soft woolen sheet. As Gilliane stepped over the side of the tub, she was enfolded in it and rubbed dry until her body shone.

A serving girl brought a cup of mulled wine, and Gilliane sipped the spicy sweetness of it, wondering if Richard meant to come for her. Neste dragged a comb through the tangles in her hair, exclaiming again about the beauty of it, and then they all withdrew, leaving her alone with Alwina and ready for bed.

Still carrying the wine with her, she surveyed with satisfaction the chamber she'd been given. Rivaux might be angered with her, but he'd spared nothing for her comfort. The room was well-furnished, with tall cabinets of carved wood at either side of a curtained bed, several large lacquered clothing boxes, a table, and two narrow benches. Curious, she opened a cabinet and saw neatly folded chausses of soft wool, snowy cambric undertunics, and a row of brightly dyed leather slippers. A crimson tunic, ornately embroidered with gold and gemstones, lay at the top. Everywhere she looked, she saw his things—his boots, the cloak she'd made him, Belesme's sword standing near the bed.

"Aye, 'tis to his chamber he's brought you," Alwina said finally. " 'Tis what you have wanted since first he came to Beaumaule, Demoiselle."

A denial sprang to her lips and died, for Gilliane

knew 'twas the truth. "I'd have you leave me, old woman."

"I pray he makes no babe within you," Alwina muttered, passing her. "I'd not have all know your shame."

The door closed, leaving her alone, and Alwina's words brought home the enormity of what she'd done. From the beginning, she'd tried to gain his notice, telling herself she made the cloak for her honor, that she'd fought to save him out of fear, that she'd begged to come to Celesin with him out of loneliness. She'd set herself a path of dishonor and trodden it willingly, despite all her fine denials to Simon of Woodstock and the others who'd warned her.

She could hear steps on the stone stairs, muffled steps that drew nearer as they reached the third landing, and then she heard him telling someone below that he'd not be disturbed. Her heart pounded apprehensively and a knot of fear formed in the pit of her stomach. Still wrapped in the woolen blanket, she passed her tongue over suddenly parched lips and waited.

He seemed to fill the room as he came through the door, kicking it shut after him. As he turned back to drop the bar in the cross-latch, her body went numb, and her limbs seemed to have taken root in the floor.

Her eyes were enormous in her face, betraying her fear, but it gratified him that she did not back away. After arguing with himself for two weeks and more that he had no right to take her, he knew he could not stand it if she turned from him now. It would not take much to make him leave her—already the guilt for what he was doing to her gnawed at him. She deserved to be wife to a man, and that he could not make her. His eyes dropped to where she held the woolen sheet wrapped against her breasts, and his mouth went dry with his desire for her. With the sputtering pitch torch he'd used to light his way still in his hand, he walked to the brazier, tossing it into the fire, speaking casually to hide the eagerness he felt.

"I'd have you pour me some of the wine."

When she did not move, he walked closer, standing over her, and reached to lift her chin with his knuckle. The gold flecks warmed his eyes despite the seriousness of his expression. His still-wet hair appeared even blacker, gleaming in the firelight, and he was already half-undressed, with his creamy cambric undertunic spotted with water where it lay against his skin, and his chausses clinging ungartered to the curve of his calves. The irrational thought crossed her mind that he'd bathed for her.

"Gilly, you know I'd lie with you."

She nodded, unable to speak.

"And you?"

"Aye," she choked, trying to look away from his strange eyes.

"Art afraid?" he asked softly, knowing she would be.

"Aye."

"I'd wed with you if I could—you know that, do you not?"

Her throat ached and her chest tightened, threatening to stifle her breath, but his hand forced her to look up at him. She closed her eyes, unable to meet his. "Nay."

"Gilliane, I swear to you that although I cannot give you the protection of my name, I am yours in truth—that I will love and protect you, giving you whatsoever else you desire of me." Abruptly he released her and moved to get the pitcher of warmed, sweetened wine, pouring its contents into two silver cups. "Take some—'twill ease you."

Her hands shook as she tried to drink, but she was glad of the time he gave her. The room was acutely still save for the sounds of the pitch torch popping in the fire, and the tension grew as fear and excitement vied within her. Too nervous for words, she turned away from him, unable to let him see what his very presence did to her. He set down his cup and walked slowly, deliberately, each footfall seeming louder than the last, until he came up behind her and lifted a strand of her hair, bending to brush his lips there, letting his warm breath caress the back of her neck. A shiver sliced through her as the cup slipped from her nerveless fingers, clattering to the floor.

"I'd see you, Gilliane." His voice was soft and low, almost a whisper, as his hands slid around her to loosen the soft sheet she wore.

"I . . . I cannot," she gasped, clutching at his hands, holding them still against her breasts.

His lips found her neck again at the back of her bent head where her hair parted, falling forward, and he nuzzled the smooth skin softly, kissing lightly down to her bared shoulder, sending waves of excitement coursing inward. She held his hands so tightly that her knuckles whitened, and she stood still as stone within his embrace. This time, when he asked, his breath rushed against her ear. She squeezed her eyes shut to still the raging need that threatened to engulf her.

"Let me look on you, Gilly."

Holding both her hands with one of his, he managed to free the other and slide it beneath the overlap of the woolen sheet, brushing it lightly over the curve of her breast, over the suddenly tautened peak. She sucked in her breath very much like a sob, and let him loosen her hands. The sheet fell away, sliding over her bare skin to land in folds at her feet. For a moment he stood very still himself, and then his palms moved over her breasts, cupping them, as his thumbs massaged her nipples until they strained against his hands.

Agony . . . ecstasy—she knew not what she felt, but it seemed that the center of her being lay beneath his fingers. And when she thought she could stand no more, his hands slid lower, tracing the line of her rib cage to her waist, pulling her back against the warmth of him, molding her into his hard abdomen until she could feel the rise of his body against hers. His palms moved over her flat belly, drawing fire in their wake, until his fingers found the wetness below.

"Nay, I'd not . . . Ohhhhh . . ." Her protest turned to a moan as the urgency of his fingers elicited a need she no longer wanted to deny.

He could feel her sag against him, giving in to her desire, feeding his. He lifted her from behind, half-turning her to carry her against him. She buried her head in his shoulder, and heard his beating heart beneath. The drawn bed curtains brushed over his back as he bent to lay her within, and then he followed her down, crouching over her. Pulling off his undertunic, he flung it to the foot of the bed, and began untying his chausses.

His eyes glittered strangely in the darkness as he eased his freed body down to hers, and she stiffened beneath him with fear. Cursing himself for his eagerness, he rolled to lie beside her and took her in his arms. He wanted her body freely given, even if he had to wait. He held her very quietly, letting his own urgency abate, and then slowly, carefully began the task of arousing her again.

He smoothed her bright hair back from her temples with his hands, cradling her face between them, and bent his head to taste of her lips. Her eyes widened, then closed as her lips softened, parting to receive his teasing tongue. He'd meant to explore her mouth leisurely, but her answering kiss ignited the fire in his body anew, and he plundered instead, taking full measure of her. While one hand held her head, cradling it for his kiss, the other caressed lightly from her cheek to her neck to her throat and lower to her breast, brushing again at the peak until it hardened. She stiffened again, this time not from fright, as his thumb and forefinger rolled her nipple, and then she relaxed, giving herself over to the pleasure of his touch.

"Sweet," he murmured, releasing her mouth to

trace quick warm kisses in the path his hand had taken. Her eyes were closed, purpling beneath their lids in the faint light, and her breath was rapid, raising her breasts with each quick, shallow intake until he curled his tongue to lick at one hardened nob. Her hands, which had been clenched, groped for and clasped his head as her fingers massaged his thick hair, holding him to her breast.

He sucked, savoring the sensations he was creating in her while she moaned the low animal noises he knew for a woman's desire. His hand splayed over her flat belly, feeling the quivering need within, and then slid to the smooth, silky curve of her hip, moving his palm over her.

Gilliane felt as though there was no part of her that did not desire his touch. Her fingers worked ceaselessly, opening and closing over the thick strands of his hair, as her body grew hot with wanting more of what he would do with her. And then she felt him touch her, touch the softness between her legs, stroking her until the center of her being seemed to be there, and she arched her back, straining for more.

He had what he wanted—he had her willing. His mouth left her breast, returning to kiss her again, and this time when his tongue parted her swollen lips, he eased his aching body over hers, striving for his release as well as hers. As his knee slid between hers, her legs opened to receive him. She went rigid at the insistent feel of him against her maidenhead, her moan intensifying as it gave way, and he willed himself to hold back, to soothe, until she relaxed. As he left her mouth to whisper almost incoherent words of love and encouragement into the shell of her ear, her arms clasped him tighter. Slowly he began to move within her, ready to ease off if she cried out again, but her hands began stroking his back, and the fire returned with an intensity that threatened to consume him.

She'd expected him to hurt her, had heard whisperings of that even in the seclusion of Beaumaule, but she was unprepared for the greater need that came after. As he moved, what had gone before seemed as child's play. She was alive to the feel of him within, straining for some greater promise, unable to restrain her own need of him. Her hands moved ceaselessly, goading him on, begging more, and her body rocked and bucked against his, taking until she thought she could take no more. Conscious will ended, obliterated by the fire that engulfed them, until his hard, almost anguished breathing turned to an animal cry of his own, and she felt the flood of his seed before he collapsed, breathless and spent, over her.

Then she floated. Despite his weight on her, she floated, feeling a peace like the calm after a storm. Reluctantly she opened her eyes to find him watching her, and the peace was gone. She'd had what she'd asked for—she'd given herself to Richard of Rivaux—and she was suddenly shamed. Still beneath his heaving body, she tried to turn her head away and hide from him.

He'd watched the emotions cross her damp brow, one after the other, seeing first the ecstasy of union, the contentment, and then the shame. "Nay," he whispered gently as he eased his body off hers, " 'tis love I feel for you." He smoothed her wet hair with the back of his hand, feeling the dampness of tears on her cheeks.

"That does not make it right," she answered dully. "No matter what words we use to couch what I am to you, the truth is that I am but your willing whore."

"I love you, Gilly. Stay with me, and you'll want for naught, I swear it." Even as he spoke, he saw her tense. "I can give you—"

"Can you give me sons of your name? Can you give me sons who can stand tall beneath the banner of Rivaux?" she blazed suddenly. "Nay, you cannot!"

"Gilly . . . Gilly . . ." He sought to take her rigid body into his arms, but she pulled away.

"God aid me, Richard of Rivaux, but I love you

also," she whispered through the ache in her throat, "and still 'tis not right what we have done. 'Tis sin."

"Then God forgive me, but I mean to sin and sin again," he admitted. "Nay, Gilly, but 'tis not wrong to take what happiness we can."

"You will wed another."

"Not willingly."

"You will get your sons of her."

Realizing she was serious, he propped himself up on his elbow and reached to stroke the tangled mass of copper at the back of her head. "I would that I could break my oath to Lincoln's daughter, Gilly—I swear to you—but I cannot. Aye, and I'd promise not to lie with her also, but I owe too much to my sire and grandsire to let my name die."

"You'll love her."

"Jesu! I cannot even remember what she looks like," he sighed. "But even if she were the most beautiful girl in Christendom, I'd not love her." He laid a hand on her shoulder and tried to turn her back. "For good or ill, 'tis only you I'd love."

She wanted to believe him, to think that to him she was more than just a wench to be tumbled. Reluctantly she allowed him to turn her over.

"Do you think I'd have ridden all the way to Douai in Flanders for you if you were naught to me?" he reasoned. "Do you think I would have risked my father's certain wrath for you if you were but another wench to me?" He waited for his words to sink in, and then he added, "Aye, and do you think I'd have come for you rather than seek Gloucester when there is a crown to be fought for? Sweet Mary, if you cannot know it—"

"Aye."

It was more a sigh than a word. He leaned closer to brush a soft kiss at her temple. "Then let us speak no more nonsense, Gilly."

"I just do not know how I can bear it when you go to a wife."

"When that time comes, I'll be an unwilling husband." He glanced out of the bed to where Hellbringer stood balanced against the wall. "Would you have me swear that on Holy Rood also?"

It was enough that he would. She turned against him, burying her head against the healing scar on his shoulder. "Nay," she murmured, holding him close, " 'tis enough that you have sworn to kill Brevise for me."

They lay, locked for a time in a close embrace, each savoring the nearness of the other. After a time, she thought he'd drowsed off, and she started to ease away to give him room in the bed.

"Nay."

Even in the darkness, she thought she could see the slight curve of his mouth as he smiled at her. His eyes, which had been closed, caught the faint firelight as his arms pulled her even nearer. His hand moved over the curve of her hip possessively, renewing desire.

"My only regret," he whispered as his mouth nibbled again at hers, "is that 'twill take your hair a full year and more to grow."

18

" 'Tis dear, my lord," the merchant warned him.

Richard turned the golden filigree heart over in his palm and studied it, letting the light from the narrow window catch in the pearls and tiny cabochon rubies that winked among the openwork. It was as lovely as she was. He lifted the fine square-linked chain to let the light filter through the heart, and nodded.

"I would have it."

"It comes from the East, and cost me a full fifty marks. I'd have at least sixty for it."

"I said I would buy it." Richard gestured to his chamberlain to bring forth the casket where he kept the money. "Count out sixty marks and gain a receipt for this," he ordered. "Aye, and I'd have the small mirror also."

"Your lady is most fortunate, my lord," the merchant murmured in appreciation.

"Nay, 'tis I who am the fortunate one," Richard answered, slipping the locket into the purse that hung at his belt. And it was true. The month he'd had Gilliane de Lacey in his house and his bed had been the best of his life. A slow smile of remembering spread across his face as he thought of her as last he'd seen her, her sleepy eyes awakening to his passion, her body coming alive to his touch. There was still as much fire between them as at the beginning, more mayhap, for each new lover's discovery brought greater delight than the last. He was besotted, he knew it, and yet he fervently prayed that 'twould always be so.

"Would your lordship see anything else?"

For a moment Richard stared blankly, reluctant to leave his thoughts of her, and then he shook his head. "Nay, but you may see of either my chamberlain or my steward if there's aught else we need."

The fellow drew back, bowing as he left, and Richard looked about his busy hall. From his carved chair on the dais he could see his steward look up impatiently from where he directed a clerk at accounts, dismiss the Italian merchant with a wave, and turn again to his work. And across the room, his marshal and his captain disputed with his seneschal out of his hearing. There was so much to running Celesin that sometimes he chafed at the task, almost wishing he'd not been quite so prosperous, for in the two years since his knighting, his household had grown from but the fifteen he'd had at Rivaux as son in his father's house to nearly ten times that in his own. Poor Gilly—she strove so to acquaint herself with the workings of the place, but 'twas so very different from what she'd had at Beaumaule.

A messenger caught his eye as the fellow slipped in the side door and conferred with Everard briefly. Richard tapped his heavy signet ring against the table before him, curious now that his captain pointed toward him. The messenger, still carrying his round parchment case, made his way forward, stopping on bended knee before Richard, holding out the cylinder, its seal affixed at one end.

"Greetings from my lord, Earl Robert of Gloucester, to his liegeman Richard of Rivaux, lord of Celesin and Ancennes, and warden of sundry English castles."

"Aye."

A page rushed to take the parchment case and carry it to Richard, who examined the wax seal before breaking it with his thumbnail. It had been weeks since he'd heard of Gloucester, and there'd not been a word regarding England's crown or the usurper who wore it.

"My lord?" Everard crossed the room to hover while Richard read the earl's letter, waiting impatiently for the news that could change their lives.

But Richard was not attending, choosing to reread the curious message instead, his brow furrowed in concentration, and then his face cleared. "Aye," he addressed Gloucester's man, "tell Earl Robert he is most welcome at Celesin."

"He comes here?" Everard asked, betraying his surprise.

"Aye, on his way to England."

"God's bones! What says he?"

"Not enough." Richard sighed heavily, uncertain whether to be disappointed or relieved. From the sound of it, Gloucester did not mean to fight Stephen now, and that gave Richard more time to spend loving Gilliane de Lacey rather than going to war. But it also forced him to consider the unthinkable: Stephen would expect him to do homage for his English possessions ere long. And lurking in the background was the thought that either way, Guy of Rivaux would not be pleased with him.

He heaved himself up from the heavy chair, murmuring low for Everard alone, "Walk apart with me."

"But, my lord, 'tis court day," his estates steward, Drogo de Montfort, protested feebly.

"I leave it to you to give justice as you do when I am gone," Richard retorted, stepping down from the dais. "Aye, I have heard no complaint of your wisdom."

It was an honor to sit in judgment when the lord was in residence, for it signified a great trust. Drogo bowed respectfully to hide his pleasure, and turned back to those who waited for their lord's will. "The clerks of Celesin will present the petitions for me," he called out clearly, "and all cases save those of bodily harm will be heard this day."

"It does not appear that Gloucester means to challenge Stephen," Richard mused aloud to his captain as they reached the outer chamber.

"Jesu! 'Tis King Stephen, then!"

"He says he comes to discuss matters of import to both of us—that he'd have me go to England with him."

"Then . . . ?"

"Nay." Richard shook his head and sighed. "There is no mention of raising mine levies for him."

"He'd dare not write of it—e'en if it were his intent," Everard reminded him. "Too many wait to know of his plans."

"I know, but I know Gloucester also. For some reason, he chooses not to fight."

"When does he come?"

"Tonight—he lies a scant twenty furlongs from here." Richard fingered the hard bulge in his purse pensively, wondering how Gilliane would react to the news that Gloucester wished him to go to England.

Apparently she was in Everard's thoughts also, for he appeared to consider before he asked, "And what of the Demoiselle? There will be those who say you had not the right to take her from Beaumaule."

It was a question Richard had asked himself a hundred times and more, knowing sooner or later he would have to face it from whoever wore England's crown. He'd made himself her guardian, had left his pennon over Beaumaule's ruins, a warning to any who would gainsay him, but there was no guarantee that a King Stephen would confirm his authority there. He could perhaps claim the small keep by right of having taken it under fire, but that still did not mean that he could enforce his wardship over Gilliane.

"If we go to England, I'd leave her here," Everard advised.

But Richard was loath to leave her anywhere. "Nay," he decided abruptly, "if I go, I take her with me. If

Stephen would have mine oath, he will have to confirm the wardship of Beaumaule to me."

"You swear to him then?"

"I do whatever Gloucester does."

"Count Guy still stands for the Empress."

"Art always ready with reason, Everard," Richard
chided him. "Aye, I know where my father stands—
was there ever one to doubt him? And I know I hold
the greater part of my lands of him, but I am vassal
to Gloucester also, lest you forget that. If my father
raises his standard and takes the field for her, I will
send him the troops I owe of Celesin and Ancennes,
but I will not fight against Earl Robert in any case."

"He could hold your lands forfeit," Everard reminded him.

"For a time mayhap, but he cannot deny me my
patrimony when all is done. These lands, Harlowe,
Rivaux itself—all will come to me, whether he wills it
or not."

"And you could starve whilst you wait."

"Ah, Everard, art always my father's advocate, are
you not?" Richard's dark eyes warmed and his mouth
twisted in a rueful smile. "Sometimes I wonder
whether 'tis I you serve—or whether my father set
you to watch over me. But you worry for naught.
Nay, but so long as I do not meet him in battle, my
sire to too honorable to take back that which he has
given." He reached to clasp the older man's shoulder
affectionately. "You worry too much."

"Aye."

"For now, I'd have you seek out both stewards and
have them prepare for Gloucester's arrival."

"And you, my lord?"

Richard exhaled heavily and squared his shoulders, wondering how Gilliane would take his news.
"I go to tell her there will be company."

Gilliane's fingers worked ceaselessly, making the
quick, tiny gold stitches on the crimson sendal tunic.
While it was not quite *orfrois*, it was the closest she

ould make it, and she hoped he would be pleased.
ven as fine as it was, it seemed small payment, for
here was no gift to compare with the rich samite
nd sendal and velvet gowns, the jewels, and the ease
f life he'd given her. The harshness of Beaumaule,
he horrors of the past, seemed so very distant now
s she basked in the warmth and security of Richard
f Rivaux's love.

She'd not known such luxury existed before she'd
een Rivaux, and even Celesin still was a marvel to
er. Whereas the inner walls of the hall at Beaumaule
ad been but rough stone, those at Celesin were
lastered and whitewashed, and the solar in which
he worked had clean-swept floors covered with woven
nats and walls hung with brightly patterned carpets
mported from the Moors in Spain. Above her, on a
aised platform, his bed was cushioned with three
eather mattresses, sheeted in softest wool, and veiled
vith curtains of gold-shot silk baudequin beneath
eavily emboidered hangings of sendal. And thick
nulticolored silk cushions abounded, adding to the
ppearance of overwhelming wealth. Aye, and even
hough this day she was alone save for Alwina, she
new that she had but to clap her hands loudly for a
age to scurry forward, eager to run her errands.
ndeed, the place was overrun by those who ran his
ousehold, managed his estates, and executed his
very wish as though it were by writ of law. And,
nce they understood that she was more than whore
o him, they treated her with courtesy and deference.

It had not been so at the beginning. There had
een sniffs and sneers and whispers behind her back,
whispers that somehow carried just enough for her
ars to hear. But one of his knights had gone too far,
peculating on who would have her when he was
one, and Richard had heard. His wrath was swift,
is punishment so harsh that the fellow had been
ortunate to remain alive. And since then, there'd
ot been another to speak ill of her. Except Alwina.
Aye, Alwina muttered her disapproval in a dozen

ways, predicting direly that Gilliane would bear hi
bastards and then go to the convent in disgrace
Noble bastards, she'd remarked pointedly, did no
enjoy quite the status of those with royal blood.

A pang of conscience assailed her. She had not th
right to love him; the union that gave her so muc
pleasure was more like to be cursed than blessed
And yet she could not help loving him—she coul
not. Even when he wed Lincoln's daughter, she'
still want him in her bed. Lincoln's daughter. Sh
could not bring herself to use the girl's name, fo
then his betrothed bride became a person, anothe
woman to vie for his love. And that troubled her
She could not imagine that any could lie with hin
and not love him. But what if in doing his duty h
came to love Lincoln's daughter also? Nay, that woul
be more than she could bear.

Resolutely she pushed back the jeweled cap tha
slid forward on her head, his gift to cover the crow
of her hair. She was neither wife nor maid now, an
while a wife would bind her hair, Gilliane could no
for lack of enough to braid anyway, and yet Richar
tried to give her a wife's status by providing shim
mering veils and caps. Well, there was naught to b
gained but a sore heart if she did not accept her tru
lot and take what love he offered whilst she could
She held the tunic closer and bent to take anothe
careful stitch.

He stood and watched her, spellbound by the sigh
of her, her copper head framed in the early-sprin
sunlight much like the paintings of the saints. Th
deep green samite of her gown shimmered as he
hand moved, and the undersleeve of gold reflecte
the sun itself. Gone were the serviceable wools sh
once wore, replaced at his insistence by silks—if h
could not make her his wife, he could at least dres
her as befitted a queen.

And the transformation had been worth ever
mark, for whereas he'd once thought her pretty, h
now knew her beautiful. Aye, there could not be a

man to look on that bright hair who would not envy him. But she was so solemn now, as though pained, mayhap by thoughts of the past, by memories of the horror of those last days at Beaumaule—and he wished he had the means to ease her.

Alwina saw him first, rising silently as she did so. The old crone did not like him, he knew, and disapproved of what he'd made of her mistress. He ought to send her away, but she'd been with Gilliane since her birth, and if Gilliane would tolerate the woman's insolence, then he'd not interfere. But still it rankled him that Alwina could not see that what he did, he did for love as much as lust.

Gilliane looked up as the old woman picked up her sewing and prepared to leave the solar. "Nay, but—" She stopped when she saw him and nodded. "Aye." The open desire in his face as his eyes met hers sent an answering shiver coursing through her. To hide her own racing pulses, she folded the tunic neatly, laying it aside, and smoothed the green samite in her lap. Out of the corner of her eye she could see Alwina march past him.

"I worry for your eyes," he murmured, barring the door behind her woman. "You stitch too much."

"There's naught much else for a woman to do in a well-run keep." A thrill of anticipation made every fiber of her being seem to come alive in his presence.

He walked behind her and lifted the jeweled cap from her hair, brushing lightly over its silkiness to smooth it. "There's always something else for a woman to do if she wishes."

She thought that he was going to kiss her neck, as he was so often wont to do, but then she felt the cold metal slide around it as he fastened the chain. The golden heart slipped forward, its weight seeking the bottom of the loop. She looked down and gasped as the rubies and pearls seemed to wink back at her.

"Sweet Mary—'tis lovely! Nay, but I—"

"Aye, you can," he whispered, kissing the place

where his hand held back her hair. " 'Tis but a small token of what you have given me, Gilly."

She knew not what was wrong with her, but even the softness of his voice sent waves of desire flooding over her, and the feel of his lips on her skin made her ache with the wanting of him. She fingered the pendant and closed her eyes to keep him from knowing how his very presence affected her.

As if to echo her own thoughts, he bent low to nuzzle her ear, sending his warm breath into it. " 'Tis not possible to get enough of you, Gilly." And as he spoke, his fingers slid beneath the layers of gown and undergown, moving downward over suddenly hot skin to cup a breast.

He could feel her tremble and heard her sharp intake of breath. He'd not meant to lie with her, he'd come to tell her of Gloucester, but the temptation was great. With an effort, he started to draw his hand back, to focus again on why he'd sought her. But her hand caught his arm, holding it there, and she rubbed her cheek against the hair on his forearm.

"I like what you do to me, Richard," she whispered.

He needed no further urging. With one hand still inside her gown, he slid the other beneath her arm and lifted her, holding her back against him, and leaned to explore the softness of her skin with his lips and his hands. She was so often pliable, gentle, and yielding, but this time she was almost rigid in his arms.

She stood, holding her body taut, tense with near-agony as his fingers rolled her nipples, hardening them, until she thought she would shatter into pieces. The tension built until she could stand it no longer, and she caught at his hands, pulling them away, and turned into his arms. Reaching for his neck, she pulled his head down to hers. There was no gentleness in the kiss between them, only urgent, mindless need. She clung to him, taking as much as she gave, until at last he set her back, his chest heaving, and gasped, "Art like fire that burns me, Gilly!"

"Aye." Despite the heat in her own blood, she managed to smile up at him, and her fingers began loosing the laces that gave her gown its fit beneath the arms. He watched, mesmerized, while she drew off the silk overgown, then unlaced the sleeves of the golden undergown. His pulse pounded in his temples like thunder and the heat in his loins was unbearable, and yet she moved slowly now, revealing the soft cambric undershift that outlined her body against the light from the window. For answer, he pulled his overtunic and tunic off and flung them to the floor. His eyes still on her, he slipped off his shoes and bent to unwrap the leather cross-garters that held his chausses smooth against his leg. She grasped the undershift at her hips and began easing it upward, revealing the whiteness of her legs and thighs. His mouth went so dry he could not speak. In one quick stride he caught the undershift from her hands and pulled it off, flinging it to land in the pile of his clothes. His eager fingers found the ties of his chausses, loosened them, and pushed them down.

She stared at his aroused body, unable to think for the pounding in her head and chest. "Well?"

She was naked save for the locket that hung between her firm, rounded breasts, her bare skin gleaming like alabaster, and she waited eagerly for him. An unholy gleam crept into his eyes as he advanced on her, backing her into the thick carpet that hung on the wall. Her eyes grew wider with the realization that he was not going to take her quickly despite his obvious desire. Instead, he leaned into her, a hand at either side, pinning her against the thick carpet, and slowly, deliberately, kissed her again.

She wanted him to take her, to carry her to bed and lie with her. She wanted the feel of his weight over hers, the feel of his body within hers, and yet he was denying her the quick slaking of her desire. Could he not see that she would not wait?

He tasted and teased, playing about the corners of her mouth with soft nibbles, and brushed his body

against hers, feeling the fire within her, prolongin
his own exquisite ache. Her arm came up to clas
him, to pull him closer, and her mouth opened ea
gerly beneath his.

" 'Tis not as though we are groping in the hay
loft," he whispered, still delaying. "Aye, we have a
the time we need."

He was so close and yet so far from giving he
ease. She arched her body against his, tantalizin
him with her eagerness, and when he raised his arm
she edged along the wall closer to the bed, backin
against the small step that led to the bed. To he
relief, he lifted her, holding her waist.

"Please," she moaned.

"Aye." He drew her arms around his neck an
held her, letting her slide against him, holding he
still against the wall, and then his hands moved ove
her, trailing fire from her shoulders to her arms an
down to her hips, cupping them against him. His lip
sought hers, this time with an eagerness to matcl
her own, and as his tongue possessed her mouth, h
possessed her body and felt her shudder of ecstas
as he entered her. And then he began to move
tentatively at first, afraid to hurt her, but her hand
clutched convulsively at his back, raking him witl
her nails, as she writhed and moaned against him.

It did not take long—her breath came in gulps a
she gave herself up to what he did with her, and he
low moans and small animal cries grew in intensit
until she cried out in great gasps as wave after wav
of pleasure carried her higher and higher until he
joined her, his groan of release matching hers.

She kept her eyes closed when it was over, scarc
able to believe what she'd experienced. His body stil
pinned her to the wall, still penetrated hers, and ye
the intense heat between them had faded to a warn
glow. His hard, flat belly heaved as he let out hi
breath in an attempt to master it. She could feel hi
hand smooth her damp hair back from her temple

stroking it with a gentleness that belied what had just passed between them.

"I have played the whore again," she whispered finally.

"Nay, you have loved me."

When she would have spoken again, he silenced her with a finger to her lips. Reluctantly he eased away from her, separating their bodies. His hand groped at the bedside cabinet for a cloth while his arm circled her.

"I was like a hound bitch in her season."

It pained him to hear her condemn herself for giving her body to him. Cloth in hand, he met her eyes soberly. "Gilly, there is naught about you that displeases me—save that you are ashamed of loving me." He reached the cloth between her legs and felt her stiffen in embarrassment. "Nay, let me aid you. Look at me, Gilly," he commanded. "What we have done is done of love, and despite all the Church's fine words, I do not believe God thinks it wrong for me to love you."

"You do not think me wanton?"

"I do not. I think you a woman with the appetites God gave you. It pleases me that you would lie willingly with me."

It was wrong of her to tear at him for what he could not give her, and she knew it. When she'd asked to come to Celesin, she'd known what it meant— she'd made her choice then. He stepped back and dropped the cloth into a basin. "But . . ." His flecked brown eyes met hers again, and this time there was a glint of rueful humor in them. " 'Twas not for this I sought your company anyway." Reaching for her undershift where she'd dropped it, he straightened and handed it to her. "Alas, 'tis easier to speak when you are covered."

She took the garment and shrugged it over her head, settling it over her hips. Then she turned to watch him dress, waiting for him to tell her why he'd come. His black hair was damp and rumpled from his earlier passion, and his back was red where she'd scratched it, but she was again struck by the thought there could be no handsomer man—not in Normandy, not anywhere. He sat on a low bench and crossed his garters over his chausses, smoothing them, his head bent down to the task.

"Gloucester comes."

Sudden fear gnawed at her insides, holding her breath in abeyance. In the month since she'd been at Celesin, they had been away from the rest of the world, away from the politics and threats of war. She willed herself to hide her fear.

"I but had his message this morning," he continued. He leaned back, his shoulders against the wall, and watched her carefully. "I do not know what he means to do, but he'd have me go to England with him, Gilly."

"Nay!" she cried out involuntarily, and then tried to calm the rising panic she felt. "Why? Why must you go?" she asked in a calmer voice, turning away.

"Gilly . . . Gilly . . ." He heaved himself up from the bench and moved behind her to grasp her shoulders and turn her back to him. "Sweeting, do you not know that whither I go, you go also?"

"But England! Sweet Mary, what if Brevise . . . what if King Stephen . . . ?" She choked, unable to put her worst fears into words.

"They will not," he answered grimly, taking her again into his arms and cradling her against him. "If I find I have to swear to Stephen, I'll get wardship of Beaumaule in the bargain."

"And if you cannot?" she whispered into his shoulder.

"I'll fight to keep you."

19

Gilliane watched from the tall tower window, awaiting the nearing mesnie with some trepidation, while Richard stood on the courtyard steps with almost boyish eagerness. An approaching herald sounded the trumpet call, and then the bridge began to lower. Despite the chill of an early-spring mist, Gilliane leaned forward through the open window for a better look at Robert of Gloucester as he led his men into Celesin. And she was more than a little disappointed by her first glimpse of him, thinking this then was the great earl, the man who inspired such loyalty and trust.

But though he was neither particularly tall nor very handsome, Robert of Gloucester nonetheless drew people to him, and it was oft remarked for a pity that this best son of the old king had been born a bastard. Nearing forty-six years of age, he was the undisputed landholder of such vast lands that only he could rival Stephen of Blois for wealth, power, and popularity in England. And although three months had passed since Stephen had usurped the throne, all Normandy and England still waited and watched to see what, if anything, Earl Robert intended to do about it.

She stared downward, thinking that all of her life she'd heard her father and brothers speak of him with awe—"Robert, the king's son, the one who helped defeat the French king at Bremule"—the great military leader, the man everyone respected. And yet when she saw him, he looked like any mortal lord. Nay, but if looks made a hero, then Guy of Rivaux was the greater man.

He dismounted, handing his reins to one of Richard's ostlers, and removed his helm, exposing softly curling brown hair well-tinged with gray, and strong, regular features. His helmet still tucked beneath his arm, he exchanged the kiss of peace with his taller host, stretching to reach first one cheek and then the other, then waiting for Richard to do the same.

Richard had said she could greet him, but she'd found an excuse, not ready to face a stranger's disdain. Nay, but her love was too new, too precious to tarnish just yet. But there was a pang of regret—had she been the lady of the house, she'd have been honored with Gloucester's kiss also.

She heard Richard speak low to him and direct his gaze upward, and she saw the earl frown for a moment before he raised his hand in salute to her. She lifted her hand to acknowledge the honor and drew back inside. Sweet Mary, but what had Richard said?

"So Gloucester comes," Alwina muttered in disgust, plying her needle forcefully behind her. "Aye, and what of it? If he'd meant to wrest Stephen's crown, he'd have raised an army instead of lingering, and he would have moved ere now."

"I pray you are right." Gilliane closed her eyes tightly and whispered a fervent plea to God that he'd not come to ask Richard to fight.

The old woman looked up and her expression softened at the intensity of Gilliane's prayer. Given everything that had happened to her, the girl could not be entirely faulted for falling under Richard of Rivaux's spell, for taking what he offered. And as much as she hated to admit it, she believed he did in truth love her mistress.

Running footsteps sounded on the stairs and one of the pages burst in eagerly, his face flushed with excitement. "My lord of Gloucester comes!" And then, remembering himself, he dropped on bended knee to add, "And Lord Richard bids you come to meet him."

Not knowing what Richard had told the earl of her, Gilliane was at once both glad that he took pride in her and afraid that Gloucester would think her little more than a whore. The thing that never ceased to amaze her was that Richard alone seemed unconscious of the difference in their stations, seating her to sup on the dais beside him when she belonged far below. But surely he did not mean to bring her into the earl's company at dinner—as daughter to a lesser lord, she had not the right.

"You'd best cover your hair," Alwina reminded her pointedly.

"But what if Richard has not told him—what if he thinks me but a ward?"

"There are those to tell him differently."

"Aye." Gilliane's mouth went dry at the thought of facing Gloucester, and yet she'd do Richard's bidding. Her hands shaking, she picked up a blue-and-gold baudequin scarf and draped it over her head, pulling the ends back over her shoulders.

At the last landing, she stopped to nervously smooth the deep blue sendal of her gown with her damp palms, hoping that Gloucester would offer her no insult for what she had become. Her soft kid slippers, particolored in red and blue, peeped beneath the skirt of the overgown, while her long, full-cut sleeves folded back to reveal red silk beneath. The filigree heart nestled between her breasts, reassuring her. She walked down slowly, the jeweled medallions of her golden girdle swinging against her skirt.

Owing to the damp cold, they'd moved inside to the main hall, where Gloucester's retainers mingled with the men of Celesin while their lords shared cups of mulled wine. There was an almost festive air to the place despite the fact that the visitors were travel-stained and mud-splattered from their ride. Gloucester himself, plainly dressed in a brown woolen

tunic, sat with his head cocked, listening to Richard
tell of what had happened at Winchester.

Richard stopped mid-sentence, aware that Gilliane
had entered the room, and rising, he murmured his
apology to the earl. His eyes feasted on her, taking
in the pale, nearly translucent skin, the eyes made
even bluer by the deep color of her gown, and the
few strands of copper hair that escaped the lovely
veil. His mouth was almost too dry for words when
he turned back to announce to Gloucester with pride,
"I make known to you the Demoiselle of Beaumaule,
my lord."

If Gloucester thought it odd to find her thus,
dressed as fine as a royal princess in a young lord's
house, he gave no sign of it. Instead, he surveyed
her with little curiosity, smiling as she sank in low
obeisance before him.

"Geoffrey de Lacey's sister then?" he murmured,
raising her before Richard could offer his hand.

"Aye."

"I am sorry to hear of your loss, Demoiselle," he
continued politely. "Geoffrey was good and fair."

"Robert, I have taken the Lady Gilliane for ward
as there was none to hold for her," Richard explained smoothly. "Alas, her younger brother is dead
also."

"Aye. She could have turned to me as liege to
Beaumaule, but I recognize there was not the time."

Gilliane's heart paused with dread. Did Gloucester
think to take wardship of her as her brother's nomi-
nal overlord? Her fingers grasped the heavy silk of
her gown almost convulsively as she looked from one
man to the other. But the earl turned instead to
address Richard.

"There are scarce the rents or fees to interest any
in her wardship, but if you are willing and able, I'd
support your claim. I have heard that little is left of
Beaumaule but burnt wood and a few stones."

"I have set my men to rebuilding it," Richard
admitted. "While the land is not so much, the keep

commands the old roads, should we have need of it later."

"Aye." Gloucester glanced back at Gilliane for a moment, his brow creasing. "If you would have aid in dowering her, I'd aid you." Addressing her, he added, "How old are you, Demoiselle?"

"Nineteen."

"And Geoffrey did not seek a husband for you?" he demanded, surprised. "God's bones, but I'd not thought him so lax!"

"Nay, but he had not the money. The lord king fined him heavily for my sister's wedding."

"Your pardon, Demoiselle, but 'twould seem your right to be given first—you are the eldest girl, are you not?"

She sighed, hating to explain yet again. Keeping her eyes downcast demurely, she nodded. "But I was the plainest one, my lord, and Geoffrey was pleased to have me order his keep."

"Whoever said you were plain was half-blind," Gloucester observed dryly.

"Alas, but you have not seen my sisters."

"Nonetheless, I trust Rivaux will remedy your lack."

"Nay, but I'd not wed," she managed, afraid that he would have her given to another. There were, after all, dozens of men and boys in his wardship, and it was not impossible that one would take even a knight's daughter if Gloucester provided the dowry.

"You wish the veil then?"

"Nay."

Richard poured him another cup of the spiced wine and pushed it toward him, diverting the earl from his questioning of her. "She has but lost her home and her brothers, and has not had time to consider wedding."

Taking the cup, Gloucester nodded and passed on to more pressing matters. "I leave her marriage to you then. 'Tis not as though I do not have aught else to do. Stephen summons me to Easter court to do homage for mine English lands."

Despite the earl's frown, Richard held a bench back for her to sit, indicating that he'd have her stay. "There's not much for a maid to do in Celesin, my lord, and I thought she would be glad of the company." He pushed the bench closer as she sat, squeezing her shoulder for reassurance. "But 'tis nearly Easter now. Do you go?"

"Aye. I have already instructed Mabel to tell him I will come as soon as may be—within the fortnight, I expect." Gloucester looked away as he spoke, unwilling to meet the younger man's eyes. "He caught me unprepared."

"Jesu! You'll recognize his right to rule? Nay, but . . ." Richard did not want to believe what he'd heard. "He usurped the throne, Robert!"

Gloucester cast a quick glance at Gilliane. "The Demoiselle—perhaps she'd not wish to hear of this," he murmured in warning.

"Nay, she has no love for Stephen herself," Richard retorted, brushing the objection aside. " 'Twas Brevise who killed her brothers, and he is Stephen's man."

"Aye." The earl put his elbows on the table before him and peered into his cup of wine, swirling it, and weighed his words. "I have little choice in the matter just now."

"He had not the right!" Richard exploded. "God's bones, but he claims his crown through his mother! If we are to accept that, then 'tis Mathilda who should rule! At least the baronage swore to her, after all!"

"Aye. And Stephen and I disputed who should be the first to take the oath to her—so eager was he to swear," Robert of Gloucester recalled.

"And neither is fit to rule! If there would be any justice—"

"Nay, do not say it. There was a time perhaps—"

"Your grandsire was bastard-born, and yet Normandy called him duke and England called him king!" Richard argued hotly, knowing what Robert would tell him.

" 'Twas a long time ago, Richard." The older man lifted his cup and drained it. "Aye, but William the Conqueror was no ordinary man—and even he had difficulty holding Normandy at first. As for England, though he claimed it by right of blood, it could not be disputed that he'd won it by right of arms."

"As can you!"

"Nay." Gloucester turned light brown eyes on Richard and shook his head. "Holy Church recognizes no claims of bastards—it takes a dispensation now to go into the clergy. But even if it did not, I'd not break faith with my father."

"Jesu." It was not what Richard had wanted him to say, not what he wished to hear.

"All I am—all I hold—came from my father, Richard," the earl reasoned carefully. "You behold before you a man bastard-born of but a common woman of Caen, and yet my father raised me high, giving me an heiress, making me Earl of Gloucester—that I would support my sister. I'd not break his faith in me," he repeated softly.

"But Stephen—'tis to Stephen you would swear."

"Conditionally." Gloucester's eyes met Richard's and held. "Aye, he is fool enough to think he can buy my loyalty with mine own lands."

"But if you swear—"

"He sends to the Holy Father, asking recognition of his claim on the grounds that my sister is a bastard also—he would say that her mother was a nun ere she wed. I mean to use his appeal to justify my oath. But I have said to him that I will swear if he confirms the honor of Gloucester and my lands to me."

"Nay, but I fail to see how you can do it."

"If there is any justice, the pope will find the oaths we took to Mathilda binding when all is said and done. And if the Holy Father refuses to bastardize her, or if Bigod recants his perjury, then I am absolved." He leaned closer and his light brown eyes were sober as they held Richard's. "And already Bigod thinks his reward from Stephen was not enough."

"Holy Jesu!"

"Aye. 'Tis but a matter of some time before Cousin Stephen will prove it takes more than a pleasant face to rule those who know in their hearts that he has not the right. To show the truth of that, he is such a fool that he believes he can have me for friend rather than enemy now."

"Nay, but I'd not swear to him."

"That choice is yours, but I advise you to think on it. You also have English lands, and your grandsire of Harlowe grows old."

"But his treachery—"

"His treachery came when I was still in Normandy, still attending to my father's burial wishes. Had I rebelled then, I would have had no access to my English levies—nor to my lands. He had but to take my countess hostage and dispossess me. Nay, 'tis better to bide our time and wait for his mistake, Richard. But were I you, I'd swear to him also, for 'tis known your father will not. Think on it," he urged. "Think that Stephen will be disinclined to take Harlowe if one of you appears to side with him."

"I'd be forsworn—I cannot claim to have given my oath to the Empress."

"Then swear with reservations. Say that if it should be proven that Mathilda has the better claim, you are absolved from your oath," Gloucester reasoned. "He is so eager to appear to have support, I'll warrant he'd even accept that."

"And then? What happens then if 'tis ruled for the Empress? God's blood, but I like not the choice."

"And then I keep my oath to my father—I can do no less. But when I move, 'twill be with the full resources of my lands and title at my back."

"And what if the Holy Father bastardizes her?"

"He dares not. She is wed to Geoffrey of Anjou,

and whether her Angevin husband likes her or not, he'll not want it said she is bastard-born."

"*I* like her not."

"Mathilda?" Robert raised a curious eyebrow, and then appeared to think of his half-sister. "Well, I was raised in household with her, and 'twas always understood she took precedence over me, of course. But I do care for her—I think her more man than full half of those that are. I believe you will find she has my father's courage as well as his temper when the time comes."

"You will raise her standard then." It was a statement of grudging fact rather than a question.

"Aye." Gloucester leaned back, his strong fingers still playing with the stem of his empty cup. "For now, I will but renew old alliances and wait."

"My father will be overjoyed to know you support her," Richard muttered bitterly. "He told me you would keep your oath."

"Guy of Rivaux is a wise man—he knows that loyalty that is bought is faithless. I'll count it as an honor to fight with him at my side."

It was hard for Richard to accept that his father had been right in this also—that he'd instinctively known what Gloucester would do. But in some ways, the two of them were more alike than Richard cared to admit. "Aye," he sighed finally, "but full nine-tenths of the baronage support Stephen now, and they are not like to change for a woman."

"Mayhap, but I'd not wager on that. Already Stephen promises more than he can provide—and as those who opposed him also swear fealty to him now, he will have to dispossess those who supported him from the beginning. There is only so much land in England to give. And then, Richard, there will be much unrest."

"King David's invasion from Scotland was turned back."

"My Uncle David turned back because Stephen paid dearly to gain relief from him. How long do you think Scotland will stay out of the fray if Mathilda's standard is raised?"

"Not long," Richard admitted. "He'll take the excuse to raid English lands."

"There'll be many to join us. Aye—I even have hope of Lincoln once you are wed to little Cicely."

Gilliane, who had been listening with mere curiosity, was suddenly intent at the mention of Richard's marriage. Her body stiffened apprehensively, but she managed to appear outwardly calm. It had to be expected, she told herself—there would be many who'd have him honor his contract with Lincoln's daughter.

Richard's hand crept to smooth the baudequin veil at the back of Gilliane's hair, and he felt the tension in her body. "These are troubled times, Robert," he began evasively. "And Lincoln is not noted for his loyalty."

"The girl is fifteen, and your contract with her is of long standing," Gloucester reminded him.

"Aye, but I am not ready to wed."

Richard's finger twined absently in an escaped lock of Gilliane's hair, and the intimacy of the gesture was not lost on the earl. He set down his cup and spoke softly, seeming to address the goblet rather than his host. "I have not been unhappy with Mabel, though she was chosen for me. A good, chaste woman is about all a man has a right to ask."

Abruptly Richard released the hair and sat up straight. "Gilly, we neglect our guests—I'd have you see that all is in readiness for supper."

She flushed, embarrassed that he'd dismissed her so quickly as talk turned to his marriage. In effect, she was being told to leave so that they might discuss a matter of great import to her. Her color heightened, but she managed to rise gracefully, keeping her voice even as she faced Gloucester. "Your pardon, my lord, but I find myself dismissed so that you may speak of Cicely of Lincoln." Her displeasure evident in her carriage, she then walked carefully the length of the hall, her head held high.

"She is a comely lady," the earl observed, watching her thoughtfully.

"Aye, she is that. And she speaks her mind also," Richard muttered dryly, knowing that she was angered with him.

"You are young, and handsome also—and unwed. If you do not seek a husband for her, 'twill be remarked, and there will be those who will suspect she is unchaste."

" 'Tis naught of their affair."

"Ah, but there are enemies who would eagerly dispute your honor in even so small a thing as this."

"I'd not send her away—if 'tis what you ask."

Gloucester's eyebrow lifted again. " 'Tis a dubious favor you would do the demoiselle, Richard of Rivaux. Have you thought that in keeping her, you risk having her called leman to you?"

Richard drew in his breath and looked away. " 'Tis the truth."

For a moment the earl stared, and then he shook his head almost sadly. An upright, truly pious man, whose own illegitimacy had weighed heavily on him, Robert of Gloucester was not inclined to view the debauching of maids lightly. "You have taken the Demoiselle of Beaumaule to your bed?" he asked finally.

"Aye—and to mine heart also. I'd not wed Cicely—at least not yet."

"And she came willing to you?" the earl wished to know.

"Do not fault her for it—the fault is mine alone, Robert. She was but bereaved of her brothers and had no other place to go. And I wanted her."

"You forced her then."

Richard winced under the censure in the older man's voice, but he could not let Gilliane bear Gloucester's wrath. "Aye," he lied.

"Jesu, but I'd thought better of you," the earl

muttered in disgust. "If you burned, you should have taken your lawful wife—you should have wedded Lincoln's daughter."

"I do not want her, Robert."

"You are contracted to her." Robert of Gloucester poured himself another cup of the now-cooled wine and mused aloud, "The most honorable choice now will be for the Demoiselle to take the veil."

"Nay. She is content enough with me."

"And what of Lincoln's daughter—what of Cicely of Lincoln? 'Tis not right what you do, Richard. A wife has the right to expect her husband in her bed alone—think you I cannot remember the pain my father's queen suffered when she was surrounded by myself and a dozen other reminders of his inconstancy?"

"Robert, you have not heard me—I mean to keep Gilliane de Lacey so long as there is breath in my body. Aye, and if I thought 'twas possible to break my betrothal, I would, but failing that, I will take Cicely of Lincoln in my own time." He rose abruptly, towering over the earl. "But you must be tired and in need of bathing after your ride." Clapping his hands loudly, he motioned one of the lurking pages forward. "Show my lord to his bath, I pray you."

The long-awaited reunion with Robert of Gloucester had been a disappointment to both of them, for Richard had no wish to accept Stephen as sovereign, and Gloucester had hoped to urge the politically advantageous marriage on him. Well, he'd delay as long as possible on both counts.

He climbed the steep steps to the solar slowly, wondering how he could tell her that 'twould be better if she supped alone until the earl left Celesin— that Gloucester did not understand. He stopped in the doorway, expecting to see her seated at the window, practicing her interminable needlework, but the room appeared empty.

"Gilly?"

"Aye," came her reply from the depths of the bed.

"Gilly, I am sorry," he murmured, parting the curtains to sit on the edge of the deep mattress. "I did not wish you to be there when I told him what you are to me." He reached to stroke the heavy silk of her gown where it covered her rigid back. She lay unmoving beneath his hand.

"I know you must wed her."

"Gilly . . . Gilly." He spoke softly, easing his body to lie beside her, and tried to take her into his arms. "I will delay as long as possible—and even if I am forced to take her, I cannot be forced to love her." His fingertips traced the line of her shoulder lightly, moving from her arm upward to twist a strand of coppery hair against her ear. "Nay, do you not know, Gilly, that there's not room in my heart for another?" he whispered, turning her to face him. " 'Tis you and only you I would love."

20

Gilliane looked out into the sodden street, thinking how much she hated London. It had rained the two days since their arrival in a driving storm, and the standing water clogged the narrow, cramped lanes, making cleaning impossible. To her, used to the isolation of Beaumaule and Celesin, it seemed that the city teemed not only with people but also with stinking garbage and offal.

They'd come at last, summoned by King Stephen's ultimatum: Count Guy and Richard of Rivaux would do homage for their lands, both English and Norman, or lose them. And after a brief conference between father and son at Celesin, attended by envoys from Anjou and Gloucester, it was decided that they should offer together their conditional homage, much as Robert of Gloucester had done the month before. Faced with the common problem, father and son had not quarreled in this. Indeed, it had been an almost pleasant meeting—until Guy had suggested that they leave Gilliane safe at Celesin. In this Richard was adamant, refusing to part with her even for the month they'd be gone. Guy had shouted at him then, arguing that he risked her for his own selfish passion, that 'twas not certain that Stephen would recognize Richard's wardship over her. And she, afraid to have him leave her, had sided with Richard.

Not that Guy of Rivaux seemed to fault her for what had happened—quite the opposite, in fact. Aye, despite the unblessed love she shared with his son, he continued to treat her as a daughter. Not that she had not been worried when word first came that he arrived at Celesin—she had more than half-expected him to censure her, to call her whore or harlot. But he had not. He'd offered her his kiss instead, making no mention of her flight from Rivaux. Aye, Guy of Rivaux was a good man.

And now she stared through the thick, distorted windowpanes of the merchant's house they'd taken for lodgings, and wondered what would happen now. King Stephen had moved from his Easter court at Oxford to Cotton Hall at Westminster, and Count Guy and Richard had gone there to discuss the terms of their swearing, while all she could do was sit and wait. It seemed that the day dragged, made even drearier by the incessant May rain, and homesickness stole over her.

Disheartened by the silence, she turned back to the richly furnished room, moving to trace the edge of a well-waxed table with her fingertips. 'Twas a Lombard's house, Richard had said, belonging to a wealthy merchant who kept businesses in Italy and Flanders as well. It seemed odd to her that such men were disparaged when they apparently lived better than full half of the nobility. Aye, every single item in the room was better than anything she'd had at Beaumaule.

A cart rolled past, its lone occupant calling out his services from beneath a dripping canopy, and men and dogs scurried about the narrow lane despite the steady downpour. From time to time an occasional rider could be heard, sending her heart thudding until he passed. Gradually she realized that, given the business of a king's court, even a Norman count might have to wait, and she finally drifted to pick up the new undertunic she worked for Count Guy. It would have been for Richard, but he already had more than was godly.

Settling into a leather-slung Italian chair drawn up to the small fire that chased the chill from the room, she began to stitch the narrow neat border at the neck of the garment. It would have leaves and stag heads intertwined with bright-colored vines when she was done. Aye, but she knew not how Countess Catherine managed to keep her wits in her lord's absence, for she had not the solace of her needlework. That at least kept Gilliane occupied and away from thoughts better not considered.

She paid no heed to the riders now, considering that they were but men going about business, until she heard the voices of Count Guy's ostlers. And then the door latch lifted and Richard filled the open doorway. Her heart caught in her throat at the expression on his face.

"Sweet Mary!" she gasped. "It went ill?"

"My father was right—I should not have brought you," he answered bitterly.

"But what—?"

"Brevise." He unclasped his wet cloak and flung it into a heap in the corner before turning to slam the door so viciously that it banged on its heavy hinges. "He seeks wardship of you."

"Nay!"

" 'Twill not happen," he muttered grimly. "God's bones, but the boldness of the man! He kills your family, burns your home, and dares to ask to be your guardian, saying there's none better to care for you! Had I been armed then, I'd have struck him down!"

She rose, clutching the corner of a table against the rising nausea. "And King Stephen—what did he say?" she asked, feeling suddenly afraid.

" 'Tis not Stephen I fear, Gilly—'tis Maud. Stephen, for all his faults, is not given to unkindness. His queen, however, is aware of what he owes those who have supported him."

It was then that he noted her blanched face, and his own fury abated. "Holy Jesu, Gilly, I did not mean to worry you for naught." He crossed the room quickly and drew her against him, cradling her against the stiff embroidery on his chest. "Nay, but 'twill not happen—both my father and Gloucester stood against it." His still-cold hand smoothed her hair, stroking its silkiness over her neck. "If anything, you will but be asked to court."

Her hands flew to the blunt ends of her hair. "Oh, nay! They will mock me for this!"

"It has grown much since first I saw you, Gilly."

"But 'tis overshort still!"

"Gilly . . . Gilly—nay, but there's none to look on you who will not think you beautiful." He held her back from him to study her face. "Hair or no, I think you the loveliest woman I have ever seen."

"Then you are besotted. Richard, all the maids will wear their hair long and unbound, and . . ." She stopped guiltily and looked away. "Aye, but I am not—"

"You are mine."

"I have not the right to be—and they will know it."

They were interrupted by a pounding on the door that brought a manservant from the back room to answer it. Two men stepped inside, dripping a puddle on the flagged stone floor. One of them glanced apologetically at Richard while drawing a parchment case from the folds of his cloak. Bowing quickly, he held it out.

"Art Rivaux of Celesin?"

"Aye."

"We are come with greetings from the Queen, and are bidden to see the Demoiselle of Beaumaule into her presence."

One of Richard's hands closed protectively over Gilliane's arm even as he reached for the letter case with the other. He felt the tremor that passed through her.

"I have but come from Stephen's court myself, and heard no word of this."

"The Queen—"

"Nay." Richard dropped Gilliane's arm and broke the wax coating with his thumbnail, taking care not to damage the parchment. Even as he unrolled and read the letter, he shook his head in denial. His expression darkened as his eyes scanned the page, and then he handed it back. "Tell Maud . . . tell the *Queen*," he amended, "that the Demoiselle Gilliane de Lacey is ill and therefore unable to attend her."

"You refuse her?" the man asked incredulously.

"Aye."

"Nay, but you cannot. 'Tis the Queen who—"

"What goes here?"

The two messengers spun around at the sound of Guy of Rivaux's voice. Coloring, the one who spoke answered, "Queen Maud bids us bring the Demoiselle of Beaumaule into her presence, but my lord of Celesin refuses us."

For a moment Guy's gaze met Richard's, and then he pulled back his cloak to rest his hand on the pommel of his sword, a gesture not lost on Maud's men. "As do I. You may tell Maud that the matter of this demoiselle's wardship is settled between ourselves and the king."

Even as Guy spoke, Richard edged to where Hellbringer rested against the wall. Alarmed, the two men backed toward the door, being careful to give the Count of Rivaux a wide berth. He stepped aside, faintly amused.

"Nay, but we are come in peace, my lords." Grasping the latch, one of them turned it. "Your message will be delivered."

"God's bones, but 'twas well-said," Richard breathed in relief as the door closed after them.

Guy's amusement faded, and his flecked eyes grew cold. "I told you to leave her in Normandy, did I not? For your own comfort, you have gained us an enemy we did not need—unlike Stephen, his queen neither forgives nor forgets."

"You did not have to support me in this then."

"You are my son."

Gilliane watched the two men stare across the sudden chasm between them, and felt a new wave of nausea wash over her. It was Guy that noted it first.

"Art all right, Gilliane?" he asked, his eyes narrowing.

"Aye—'tis the rain," she lied.

"Then you had best rest, for I've not a doubt but what Maud will carry the tale to Stephen and you will have to make your obeisance to her."

"Sweet Mary, but I'd not do it," she almost whispered. "Can I not return to Celesin?"

" 'Tis too late for that," he answered abruptly. "Nay, but we must be forthright now and hope that Stephen confirms Richard's wardship over you."

"But you said—" Again the terrible nausea threatened her, cutting speech short.

"I said 'twas between us and the king." Guy's face softened briefly. "Nay, do not worry for what cannot be helped, child—I mean to tell him that we'd keep you, and as much as he wants our oaths, I doubt he will object. 'Tis not as though you were heiress to much."

"Art sick, Gilly?" Richard moved closer to peer into her pale, sweaty face. Lifting his hand to brush back her hair from her forehead, he felt her brow. "There is no fever," he murmured, relieved.

"I'd lie down, I think," she managed.

"Aye."

She had but reached the feather bed they'd brought when there was much stomping and pounding anew. Lying down, she clung to the edge of the mattress and listened as the room spun around her. Richard closed the door between them, but she could hear the sound of voices yet.

"Jesu! Is this how you would greet an old friend? Nay, put away your swords, my lords—'tis Gloucester who comes."

"I feared you came from Maud," she heard Richard say.

"Nay, I did but wish to tell you that Lincoln is arrived and asks for you."

"Let him find me then."

"He means to press you to honor your contract for

his daughter—I heard him speak to Stephen ere I left."

There was a silence between them, and then it was Guy of Rivaux who spoke. "You cannot delay forever, Richard—you will have to take the girl. There are no grounds to break the oath you gave her."

Richard's answer was so low that Gilliane could not hear it, but in her heart she knew that his father spoke the truth. She drew up her knees and huddled into a ball, sick in both body and spirit. The joy she'd known at Celesin seemed so very far away, and the knowledge she carried within her would be a burden to him now. She closed her eyes and tried not to cry.

In the outer room, the three men huddled over the small fire, drying the chill from their clothing and sharing cups of ale brought by the merchant's housekeeper. Warned by Guy of Rivaux's frown, they had lowered their voices and now spoke in hushed tones.

"Where stands Lincoln on Stephen?" Guy wanted to know.

"Firmly for now. As I told Richard, I believe his marriage could change that."

"Only if he thinks the Empress will win," Richard retorted sourly. "You cannot believe he will change sides without promise of reward."

"That his heirs will have Harlowe and Rivaux is reward enough," Guy muttered dryly. "I told you that at the time you wished to wed the daughter."

"I'd tell him I will take her when the peace is settled."

"Aye, and he will tell you 'tis now. I'd not thought it possible, but Stephen weathers rebellion well."

"You will have to take her," Robert of Gloucester declared finally. "I gave my guaranty to the agreement between you."

" 'Tis a pity you are not a Turk—else you could have them both. As 'tis, I tried to tell you—"

"Aye, and when have you not? Jesu, Papa, but all you have done since my birth is tell me! Aye, I have o wed Cicely! I accept it! Does that please you, Papa—to have been always and in all things right?" Richard rose, kicking his stool violently. "Aye, I'll wed her against my will. Does that please you? 'Tis always your honor, is it not?"

"Richard—"

But his son was too flushed, too angered to listen. "Nay, I'd not hear it! You think because your choices have been clear, that mine must be also! Well, they are not. I will marry Cicely of Lincoln for mine family honor, Papa, that we may both suffer for it! I will have an heiress and she will have a cold husband in her bed!"

Gloucester stared at the man he'd fostered, scarce able to believe what he heard. "Richard of Rivaux, 'tis to your sire you speak," he reproved him. "Nay, but I'd not hear this—not when 'tis your father to whom you owe your very blood!"

Guy of Rivaux winced visibly and turned away. "Nay, leave him be." He spoke low, gesturing wearily. "He cannot help the temper he has of me."

The door behind them banged shut, and they were suddenly alone. "Do you go after him, or would you have me do it?" Robert asked, still stunned by Richard's outburst.

"He has the right to tell her unaided."

The room was dim, owing to the storm, and there was no sound within. Richard moved reluctantly to brush aside the curtains that shrouded the bed. She lay curled and silent, unmoving, and for a moment he thought she slept.

"Gilly?"

"Aye." With an effort she rolled to sit within the deep feather mattress and managed to control the tearing, searing pain that threatened her composure. She faced him, meeting his eyes.

"You heard?"

"Aye."

"Gilly—"

" 'Twas to be expected, was it not?" she cut in

calmly. " 'Tis not as though I did not know it, after all. From the first time I met you at Beaumaule, you told me you were betrothed."

"Gilly, do not—"

" 'Tis all right, my lord."

" 'Twill not change what is between us, I swear."

"Nay." She reached a finger to his lips. "Do not swear that which we cannot know."

"I know. I've no more wish for Cicely of Lincoln in my bed than for Queen Maud herself," he muttered bitterly, reaching to draw her against him.

She rubbed her head against his shoulder, savoring the hard feel of him. "You cannot in all faith refuse to honor that which you have promised, Richard. You will wed her and bed her and get your heirs of her."

"The only sons I want are yours," he whispered softly, holding her close.

The ache in her breast was almost unbearable. "Nay—any sons I'd bear you could not stand beneath the pennon of Rivaux, my lord. Take Cicely of Lincoln and do your duty to her—'tis her right."

" 'Twill change naught between us, Gilly. I will love you still."

She swallowed hard then, not wanting him to know how terribly she hurt. "Love me, then," she choked, turning her head into his chest. "Aye, love me now."

21

"Sweet Mary, but what is that?"

Gilliane turned around from folding back the wide sleeves of her favorite deep blue gown to see what Richard had in his hands. A boyish grin lightened the face that had been so strained since first they'd known Maud would see her, and he held out a roll of silk, pressing it into her palms. She looked down, perplexed.

"Nay, unroll it."

But he could not wait to let her. Instead, he pulled one end of the material and revealed two bright skeins of coppery hair bound in embroidered silk cases. She stared in disbelief for a moment and then looked at him.

" 'Twas no simple thing to find the color, but I'd not have you go to court shorn." He took one of the cases and held it up to her head to compare the hair with her own. "You are but fortunate 'tis the fashion to wear it thus."

"But where . . . ?"

"And while 'tis not perfectly matched, the silk separates it enough that 'twill not be noted."

"Richard, did you cut off some poor maid's hair for this?" she asked, still not quite believing what she saw.

"Nay, I paid a full pound for it, Gilliane de Lacey— and I'll take your thanks now." He caught her at her waist and pulled her close, nuzzling her crown. "Later, we'll have yours twined into it so 'twill be thought to

be your own." His hand moved possessively over the
curve of her hip, smoothing her gown and pressing
her against him. "But for now . . ."

"Richard! I am but just dressed!"

"Aye," he murmured agreeably, leaning to nibble
at the corner of her mouth. "Sweet—art sweet, Gilly."
He took the other piece of hair and dropped both of
them to the floor.

"Would you have me late to see the Queen?"

Both of his hands slid around her, one to stroke
her back lightly, the other to guide her hip against
his. And his breath sent a shiver of anticipation through
her as he whispered against her ear, "Aye."

There was so little time, and neither could know
what would happen once he took her to court to face
Stephen's queen. Aye, and then he'd be wed in Lincoln. With almost a sob, she flung her arms around
his neck and brought his lips to hers. "I'd not have
you hurry overmuch," she answered, giving herself
up to his kiss. Already his hands had moved to tug at
the laces beneath her arms, and liquid fire sped
through her veins at the thought of what he would
do with her. As his mouth left hers to trace light soft
kisses along her jawline to her ear, she closed her
eyes and reveled in what he would do to her. "Oh,
aye," she gasped as his lips found the sensitive hollow
of her throat. "Sweet Mary, but I'd not have you
tarry overlong either."

She felt Guy of Rivaux's reassuring hand on her
shoulder as she entered the long reception room at
Westminster Palace. They paused while Richard whispered their presence to a royal page, and Gilliane
smoothed the brilliant blue silk with her palms, taking care not to unfold the wide gold-trimmed sleeve
where it rolled back to reveal the fitted wrists of her
undersleeve. Then her hand crept to feel the filigreed heart that hung down between her breasts. On
either side, plaits of red hair encased in long tubes of
gold-embroidered blue silk rested against her shoul-

ders, and she felt an overwhelming sense of gratitude and love for the man who'd bought them.

"Make way! Make way!" One of the household guards stepped forward importantly to clear the crowd, calling out, "Guy, Count of Rivaux! Richard, Rivaux of Celesin and Ancennes! The demoiselle of Beaumaule!"

"Holy Jesu," she breathed.

Stephen's queen, Mathilda of Boulogne, known as Maud, leaned out of her high carved chair with interest. "This then is the de Lacey? Come forward, child, that I may look at you."

Gillian moved forward reluctantly, sensing that somehow the woman before her was not her friend, and dropped low in obeisance before the chair, to the approving murmur of those about her. Nearly touching the floor with the jeweled chaplet that held her filmy baudequin veil, she waited for Queen Maud to speak again.

"You may rise, Demoiselle."

Two pages assisted Gilliane to stand, and she faced the queen. Maud's dark eyes narrowed shrewdly, moving over the expensive gown and the jewelry the girl wore. "I'd heard you were not an heiress." She spoke almost reproachfully.

"I am mistress of Beaumaule," Gilliane answered proudly, stung by the queen's tone.

"And unwed, I am told."

"Aye."

"There is some dispute as to your wardship, I believe, with my lord of Brevise claiming the right as one whose land marches with yours, whilst yon Rivaux would say he has it."

The hairs at her neck prickled in warning, but Gilliane forced herself to smile demurely and appear innocent of the quarrel. "Alas, but I am but a woman, Your Grace, and have no knowledge of such things."

"But you have been under Richard of Rivaux's protection?"

"Aye." Out of the corner of her eye she saw a man

standing to one side watching her, and her heart nearly stopped. At his belt he wore the buckle she'd sold the traveling merchant, and instinctively she knew he was William of Brevise. And she could hold her tongue no longer. "Aye, I have been under Richard of Rivaux's protection, Your Grace, as I sought it after my patrimony was burned and my brothers murdered by my lord of Brevise."

The room went still, and even the king turned to look at her. " 'Tis a lie!" the black-visaged Brevise spat at her. "The girl knows not what she says!"

Gilliane faced King Stephen, and before any thought to stop her, she approached him. "My lord king, though I am but a woman, I claim your justice for the deaths of my brothers Geoffrey de Lacey, cruelly murdered by William of Brevise's deceit, and Aubery de Lacey, a boy of but eleven years, burned to death in Brevise's raid against Beaumaule."

" 'Tis a lie! She lies to cover her disgrace!"

"Nay, Your Grace, but he wears my grandsire's belt, and I know how he came by it." Her eyes met Stephen's without wavering. " 'Twas taken from a trader murdered outside Beaumaule's gate."

She'd found the king unprepared for such charges, and he stared, first at her and then at William of Brevise. "The accusations the Demoiselle makes are of a most grave nature, Lord William," he said finally.

"Aye, and she lies, Your Grace." Thinking to sway Maud more easily, he turned to the queen. "Ever have I been my lord Stephen's man, in each and every thing—and I'll not stand charged thus by a girl who seeks to cover her shame," Brevise lashed out, accusing blindly to divert them. "Aye, ask why 'tis that Rivaux would not yield her—ask how 'tis she sought succor of him at Celesin rather than coming to her king."

Richard saw Gilliane go white as the man's barbs hit home, and shaking off his father's warning hand, he stepped forward to face Maud. "When the Demoiselle of Beaumaule turned to me, there was no anointed king," he answered evenly, "and basely accusing her of what he cannot know does not prove him innocent of what she says."

"What know you of this?" Stephen leaned forward to ask.

"When first I came to Beaumaule seeking shelter from the storm, I found Gilliane de Lacey burying her brother, sire, and when I returned, her house was burning and Brevise's men overran her keep. We found Aubery de Lacey's body among the ashes of the stable."

"I was not there!" Brevise spat at him. "Aye, had she turned to me, I'd have punished those who committed the crime!"

"Jesu! And who would punish you?" Gilliane demanded. "Nay, but my man saw you there—saw you lead the charge!" Turning to Richard, she appealed, "Tell them—tell them 'twas Brevise you saw."

Knowing his son trod a dangerous path, Guy of Rivaux nonetheless held his counsel and waited. And every ear in the hall strained to hear what Richard would say. Maud's knuckles whitened as she gripped her chair, and Stephen's gaze was fixed on the young man before him.

"I saw the banner of Brevise, I saw men fight beneath his colors, and I hanged his own captain there."

"But you saw me not!" Lord William crowed triumphantly.

"I think I did." The gold flecks nearly disappeared from Richard's dark eyes, chilling them. "And I am willing to put it to combat to prove who lies."

The stout, florid baron stared upward in dismay, and all the color drained from his face, blanching it. Richard of Rivaux was much taller, outweighing him as much as a stone, and his reach was greater than any but his father's. Already there were those who would say the hawklet could take the hawk if all odds were even. Brevise swallowed, his Adam's apple dipping within his fleshy neck.

But Stephen had not summoned two of his most powerful Norman barons to provoke a quarrel when 'twas peace he needed most to consolidate his power. He raised his hand, silencing the sudden buzz of excitement that was spreading through the room. "Nay. Whilst the demoiselle's charges are serious and must be considered, I'd not have it resolved thus. That she has lost her brothers cannot be denied, but 'tis possible that she is mistaken in claiming 'twas my lord of Brevise."

Lord William relaxed visibly, and his color returned as he nodded gratefully. "Aye," he growled, emboldened. "I'd not meet the whelp over naught."

"Naught!" Gilliane fairly exploded, and then caught herself. Appealing again to Stephen, she managed to speak with a calmness that she did not feel. "My lord king, as I am a woman and cannot redress the matter myself, I'd seek justice for my brothers' souls. If it pleases you, I would ask that my charges be heard in the royal courts."

"I'll not pay *wergild*—nay, I'll not be fined!" Brevise retorted angrily. "The wench lies!"

"You mistake the matter, my lord," Gilliane answered him coldly. "I'd not ask money—'tis your life I would have."

"Demoiselle." This time it was Maud who spoke, and there was surprising gentleness in her voice. "We share your pain in your loss, and would see your grief redressed."

"Aye." Stephen nodded. " 'Tis our will that the matter be considered. If you will but present witnesses before the courts, we will give you justice."

Justice. Gilliane knew in her heart that she would present those who'd survived from Beaumaule to swear, and William of Brevise would seek the perjury of six men, and there'd be naught done. But she'd not risk Richard's incurring royal wrath further. She managed to nod her acquiescence despite the bitterness that nearly choked her.

"There is yet the matter of the Demoiselle of

Beaumaule's wardship, Your Grace." Thomas of Lincoln stepped forward now to speak. "I do not believe that has been addressed."

It was the first time Richard had seen his prospective father-in-law since he had been sixteen years old, and he felt a surge of dislike for the tall, gaunt Lincoln. He opened his mouth to protest, but Robert of Gloucester suddenly spoke up. "As suzerain to Lord Richard's English lands, I support his claim. When there was none else there, the Lady Gilliane turned to Richard of Rivaux, and as there is not above fifty hides of land and a burnt keep for income, I see no harm in his wardship. Nay, but I am overlord to Beaumaule also, and I've no wish for the task."

If there was anyone that Stephen yet feared, 'twas Gloucester, and despite a lifelong rivalry with the man, he had no wish to offend him now—nor did he wish to make an enemy of either Rivaux. "So be it then," he agreed, readily disposing of the matter.

The tenseness passed for all but Gilliane, and she dared not speak further. Queen Maud beckoned her closer, murmuring, "Perhaps you would wish to attend us, Demoiselle. It cannot be comfortable for you among men." And even in Stephen's relaxed court, a royal suggestion was taken to be a command. Again Gilliane felt the hairs at the back of her neck stand.

Richard's jaw tightened and his hands clenched at his sides, but somehow he managed to appear almost pleasant. "I'd seek a private audience with Your Grace this day."

"What tempests you stir, Demoiselle." Maud's eyebrow lifted in surprise at the request, but she did not deny it. "Aye, I will send to you, my lord," she sighed.

Richard drew back, aware that he'd gained all he could for now, and heard his father murmur for his ears alone, "Art fortunate none asked how you came to be in England during that storm."

*   *   *

The Queen's apartments at Cotton Hall were spacious and open, reflecting the late King Henry's second wife's attempt at comfort. But Gilliane saw neither the wealth nor the luxury there, viewing it instead as a prison from which she could not escape. Aye, and if Maud kept her in the royal household, there'd be no way to hide her shame from everyone's eyes. A new wave of nausea swept over her, forcing her to lean her head against the wall.

"Art ill?" one of the other girls who served the Queen asked.

"Nay," Gilliane lied, straightening up and swallowing the gorge that rose in her throat. The girl who watched her curiously had eyes bluer than her own and hair like pure gold. Gilliane tried to smile at her, thinking this could well prove to be her only friend at court. "From whence come you, demoiselle?" she asked as the sickness subsided.

"Lincoln."

The room reeled around her, but Gilliane forced herself to look again. Though the girl was smaller than she, she had claim to true beauty, possessing a clear complexion, delicate features, and a trim, well-molded figure. This then would be the one who would share Richard's marriage bed.

"You are betrothed to Lord Richard?"

The girl colored slightly and nodded. "Aye. 'Tis why I would have speech with you, Lady Gilliane. You know him—and I'd know what he is like."

"You'd ask me what he is like?" Gilliane echoed numbly, feeling as though she surely dreamed this awful circumstance.

"Well, I know him not," the girl responded defensively, "and I thought . . . well, I would discover if he is as harsh as he looks. That is—" She wavered under Gilliane's incredulous expression, and then blurted out, "They say Count Guy is a hard man, and I scarce know his son. Nay, but I have not seen him since I was but nine."

Richard harsh? Guy of Rivaux hard? The older girl fought the urge to laugh hysterically, thinking it beyond belief that she should be asked to describe her lover to his bride. "Nay," she managed finally, "they are both kind."

"I suppose you cannot know him well," Cicely of Lincoln sighed, "and no doubt you would see him differently than I. But Papa says I must bear it, for he can make me a countess twice. Alas, if the old king had not made Earl Roger give up his claim to Nantes, 'twould even have been thrice."

"You do not wish to wed him?" Gilliane choked.

"Well, I shall like being a countess, I suppose, but . . ." She hesitated and reddened. "I should not speak of such things, I know, but he seems so very big that I . . . well, I know not how 'tis done, but—"

"You will survive," the older girl muttered dryly, starting around her.

"Wait. As you and I are but newly arrived, I thought perhaps that we might share a bed—the others here are but filled with overweening pride and self-consequence."

"Nay, I have another bedmate," Gilliane lied, hurrying past her.

Sweet Mary, but how was she doing to bear it? Until the Queen and her ladies found her out, she'd be expected to spend her days with Lincoln's daughter. That the girl did not want Richard was no consolation at all, for once they were wed, once she'd shared his bed, Gilliane was certain she'd love him also. Nay, but she had to think of the means to leave Maud's court, and soon.

She pulled a bench close to one of the long, narrow windows that lined the Queen's hall and stared into the well-tended garden outside. The rain had ended, and the May flowers glistened, their wet petals shining in the sun. On any other day she would have thought them beautiful, but today they were just there. She pressed her fist against her still-flat stomach and held it, wondering what Richard would do if he knew. But nay, she'd not tell him—'twould serve no good to do so—and she'd not tear at him further or make it harder for him to do what must be done. She'd known he was betrothed, known that it could not last forever, and yet she'd taken what she could of his love. Well, she sighed heavily, 'twas now time to pay for what she had done.

"Demoiselle."

Never had she heard such censure, such reproof in one word before. Her head snapped back from her reverie, and she looked up to face the Queen herself, and by the looks of it, Maud was furious. The knot in Gilliane's stomach tightened apprehensively.

"Lord Richard tells me that which I am loath to hear."

Gilliane's mouth went dry as she realized that the others in the room stared curiously at her. For one awful moment she thought she would be truly, utterly sick. The stiff silk of Maud's overgown swished angrily as she strode closer, blocking all else from view.

"I will have no unchaste ladies in my household, Gilliane de Lacey. If you have lain willingly with a man unwed, you will have to leave." There was a pause as Maud surveyed her, and then she demanded, "Have you?"

There was no use denying it to anyone, for before long 'twould be known. Gilliane took in a deep breath and looked up, meeting Maud's icy eyes. "Aye," she answered almost inaudibly, and then repeated clearly, "Aye."

"He comes for you."

As Gilliane looked about her, she could see the disdain and the hostility in the faces of those around them. And what had seemed so wonderful, so very good between her and Richard of Rivaux, was suddenly sordid and wrong. She rose slowly, nodding. "And I'd go with him, Your Grace."

"You will not come again into my household."

"Aye."

She walked past the silent, staring women, expecting to be spat at as she passed, but no one said a word until she reached Cicely of Lincoln, who hissed under her breath, "Filthy whore." She winced slightly, but held her head high, moving slowly until she reached the door.

Richard was waiting, and his face was flushed as though he'd been in an argument. Wordlessly he gripped her elbow and steered her through the antechamber. It was not until they'd reached the outside air that he spoke. His shoulders hunched, his face grim, he walked faster, waiting for the safety of the courtyard to explode.

"I will kill him! Jesu! 'Twould never have been said had he not spoken!"

She walked faster, trying to keep up with his furious stride. And then, realizing they were indeed alone now, he stopped. She bent to pull her slipper over her heel before she lost it.

"I am sorry, Gilly."

" 'Twas to be expected, was it not?"

"Not like this—nay, not like this."

"The fault is as much mine as yours, Richard."

"I'd thought to persuade her to let me take you back to Celesin—or perhaps even Rivaux." He reached to brush back a strand of her hair that escaped from where it had been plaited into the false braid, stroking it against her face lightly with his fingertip. "But Brevise had already accused you—had told her that you were my leman."

"Aye, he said that before King Stephen."

"She asked me if it were true, Gilly. I could have denied it—even should have. But Lincoln had complained also, and she would know, saying she'd discover it."

"As she would have, and 'twould have been worse then."

Thinking she meant that they would have examined her for her maidenhead, he nodded. "Aye, I'd not wish for that. I have heard 'tis done before witnesses."

"They think me a whore."

"Gilly, I told her that I was proud of loving you—my only regret is that it pains you." His finger twisted in the strand of hair, twirling around the tip, as his eyes searched her face. "I am proud of loving you, Gilly."

"Aye."

"It shames you to love me, doesn't it?"

She reached up to clasp his hand against her cheek, and held it close, feeling the strength, the warmth, the vitality of it. "Nay, it does not, Richard. For whatever pain it gives me, I know that I would still make the same choice." A rueful smile twisted the corners of her mouth as she looked up at him. "Aye, and I do not even regret that the queen knows of it, for Cicely of Lincoln wished to be my bedmate had I stayed."

"Better you than me." He grinned, relieved that she could still smile. "Come—as soon as I give the fool my oath, we are for Celesin. I'll tell Thomas of Lincoln to keep his whey-faced daughter another year." He reached to catch her hand and started to walk again.

"She is not truly whey-faced."

"I care not if she is Helen of Troy come back."

She kept pace beside him, grateful for a few more days of his company. He would marry Lincoln's daughter, but for now there was still a little time to love him.

22

She drowsed, unwilling to waken, reluctant to leave the warmth of his arms. She had not much more time for this, and she'd savor every moment, storing every memory for that day when she no longer had him. He stirred, rolling to lie on his back, and pulling her into the crook of his arm.

"I cannot go to Celesin," he admitted, sighing heavily, revealing that he'd been awake thinking for a time. "Were it only for me and you, I'd not take her, Gilly." When she lay very still and made no answer, he sighed again. "Aye, when I was young and foolish, I pushed my sire for the betrothal, demanding an heiress for mine own consequence. And now 'tis a matter of his honor and mine that I take her."

"You do not have to explain to me, Richard." She spoke quietly, drawing closer to lay her head in the small hollow of his shoulder. "I have long known what would happen, that there could be nothing else."

"It does not seem right to wed where I would not love."

"It would seem stranger if you did."

"Aye, I suppose so, but I have seen my mother and my father, and I'd have what is between them. And so it is with my grandsire Roger and Eleanor of Nantes. Through my folly, I will not be like them— I'll be the one to lie where there is no love, seeing Lincoln's daughter where you should be." His hand brushed over her stomach and then rested there. "If

there were any right in the matter, my sons would be
born of your flesh, sweeting."

"Nay," she managed finally, fearing that somehow
he had guessed, "my sons would be but bastards."

"Robert of Gloucester is a bastard, Gilly."

"And his father was a king who dared to set his
bastards high, knowing none could gainsay him."

"Still I'd keep you, seeking your company and
your bed—aye, and I care not if Lincoln knows it."

"And what of Cicely?" She forced herself to use
the girl's name. "What of his daughter? Does she not
have a right to have you alone once you are wed?"

He half-turned to look at her then, and his eyes
were troubled. "One would think you wished me to
wed her, Gilly."

"Of course I do not wish it!"

"Then I'd not hear you say such again." He rubbed
her cheek with the back of his hand and leaned
closer until his face blurred before her and she could
feel his breath on her skin. "There is no way I could
deny what is between us," he murmured softly as his
lips touched hers.

It was always thus with her—he had but to touch
her to send fire through her veins. She closed her
eyes and eased into his embrace, telling herself that
these few last bittersweet days were worth what she
faced. Aye, no more harm could be done in lying
with him now, and he was not wed to Cicely of
Lincoln yet.

"My lord of Rivaux?"

The messenger, wearing the blue and gray of
Harlowe, stood just inside the door. Flecks of foam
from a hard-ridden horse spattered over his short
tunic, attesting to the urgency of his mission.

"I am Richard."

"My lady sends to Count Guy." The fellow wavered, uncertain whether to deliver the father's message to the son. Finally he drew out the parchment

case and extended it, not bothering with the customary obeisance. "I am bidden to wait for a reply."

Curious, Richard broke the seal quickly and drew out his grandmother's letter, whitening as he read. "Sweet Jesu," he breathed, rereading in disbelief. "Aye, I will come." Turning to Gilliane, he ordered almost curtly, "My father is gone to Bristol with Gloucester—send to him, saying that my grandsire of Harlowe dies and my grandmother would have him come in haste."

"Lord Roger?" she echoed, scarce able to believe that a man of his stature could die. For even in her childhood she'd listened to the traveling bards sing of Roger de Brione and his single combat with Robert of Belesme, and somehow he'd seemed more than mortal in the telling of the old song.

"Aye. There's not much time, Gilly—she writes that 'tis grave, and he'd have my father come."

"And you?"

"Aye, he sends for me also." Turning back to the man of Harlowe, he nodded. "If you will but partake of some bread and ale whilst you wait, I'll make myself ready to ride."

Gilliane clasped her hands together tightly and closed her eyes. There was no question of her going, for she had not the right, and it was nearly time to part with him, anyway. But somehow it seemed hard and selfish to strike him two blows at once.

He saw her stricken look and mistook the reason. "Nay, sweeting, 'twill be but for a few days. I mean to leave four knights for guard to keep you safe, Gilly, so you need not fear in my absence."

"Aye."

With a heavy heart she moved about the merchant's house helping Richard's body servant with the hasty packing of his things. As her hands folded the crimson tunic she'd recently worked so carefully, they shook. And the finely stitched undertunic of whitest cambric, bleached and softened that it would be smooth against his skin—that must go also. He would have need of his best if Earl Roger died.

It did not take long to gather things for a hasty ride, and all too soon they were ready. She busied herself about the small sleeping chamber, trying not to realize that this was the last time she would see him. She closed and locked each chest and cabinet carefully, and scanned the room for anything that might be left by mistake.

"Gilly."

He leaned against the doorway, filling it. And for one brief moment she allowed herself to think that that was how she'd remember him, that he'd always be with her, watching from the door.

"Aye."

"I'd have your blessing and a kiss ere I leave."

"Go in peace with God, then." She moved to stand before him and rose up on her toes to brush his lips lightly.

"Nay."

He caught her close, holding her as though she were life to him, and kissed her long, tasting of her, until she broke away, breathless and trembling. "Sweet Mary," she gasped, "but if you would do that, you'll never leave."

" 'Tis how I would have you remember me, Gilly." The flecks in his dark eyes lightened them, and his mouth twisted into the semblance of a grin. "Aye, I'd have your thoughts until I return."

And then he was gone. She stood still in the middle of the room, listening to the sound of the horses growing more distant, taking with them a part of her life. Brushing at a tear of self-pity that trickled down her cheek, she straightened her shoulders and sighed. Aye, she had not the time to feel sorry for herself, she told herself fiercely, for she had to consider the child within her first. No matter what happened, she'd not have his babe share her shame. She pressed her hands against her belly and felt a great sense of protectiveness for that which had been conceived in love, a child whose very being would be a living memory of him.

The fat candle on the spike sputtered as the wick was almost drowned in the melting tallow. Gilliane bent closer over the sheet of parchment, her head casting deep shadows over her careful script. From time to time she leaned back and held the candle closer, taking care not to drip the grease onto the words. It was the most difficult letter she had ever written—and the most important—for her proposal had to be couched in the most careful of terms lest it be rejected.

She finished finally and sat back to wipe the ink from her sharpened pen. Laying it aside, she sifted sand from a leather pouch onto the parchment to dry the ink before it smeared. Aye, her letter did not say exactly what she wished, but then neither would it betray her if it fell into the wrong hands. And what she would say was best left for a meeting.

It was late, too late to send it before the morrow. She carefully rolled the parchment, taking care not to crease it, and inserted it into a waxed cylinder lest there should be yet more rain ere he received it. She placed a small chunk of wax from her writing case into a handled tin vessel and held it over the flame, heating it, and then poured the warm liquid over the flap that closed the end of the cylinder, sealing it. It was done.

Laying everything aside on a low table, she leaned to blow out the candle and undressed in the darkness. As she parted the filmy baudequin curtains and pushed back the heavier sendal hanging to ease her body into the bed, she felt again her loss. The deep feather mattress was strangely cool, unwarmed this time by his body heat, and she fought the urge to allow herself this one bout of tears. Nay, but it would not serve—'twould but upset the babe she carried.

Once she made up her mind, sleep came quickly,

but it did not last. Within but an hour or so her rebellious mind had come almost awake, lingering in that netherworld where fears come forth to be magnified. What if he came after her? What if he hated her for what she did? Aye—what if? She forced herself to consciousness then. Nay, but she could not dwell on such things, else she would go mad.

She rose then and moved to the window, unshuttering it to look outside. There was a full moon—'twas why she had not slept, she told herself—and the narrow, cramped buildings lined the lane like sentinels, standing a silent, approving watch over the dogs that sniffed amongst the garbage and litter in the street. A lone figure crept along, outlined by the moonlight, and disappeared into a creaking door across the way. A faint breeze stirred, bringing with it the intermingled smells of flowers in boxes and the stench of the refuse below. She wrinkled her nose and thought perhaps she detected rain.

Owing to the warmth of the late May air, many of the upper-story windows were unshuttered also, and she heard the insistent wailing of a babe coming from one of the other houses. And she dared think of her own, wondering how much longer before she would feel it quicken. She wanted a son desperately, his son, but she prayed 'twas a daughter she carried. It had to be. Anything else would jeopardize the bargain she meant to make.

It seemed she sat there forever, not wanting to go back to the empty bed, but finally her tired body insisted, and she dared try to sleep again. This time, she rolled into the depths of the mattress and drew up her knees against her, curling around them. And as she finally drifted off, the dreams that came were pleasant. The sun was shining at Celesin, and she stood within his arms, watching the small dark-haired boy that was their son.

"My lady?"

She roused slightly and opened her eyes to peer at the merchant's housekeeper, who'd served them since they came to London. The room was bathed in light from the still-open shutters, and the sun was high in the sky.

"Jesu!" Gilliane sat up and looked about. " 'Tis late."

"Aye. I'd not have wakened you, but I feared you'd slept overlong. So when the bells rang tierce, I thought I'd best see if you were all right."

"I am all right."

She moved too quickly and was assailed by a wave of nausea. Well, it would pass, and before long, she'd not have it at all. She saw the woman peering at her curiously, and she shook her head. "Nay, 'tis naught. Is Garth about?"

"Humph! Aye, he is—two sausages and a full bowl of porridge he's had of me already!"

"He grows."

At least Richard had left her Garth—she'd not relish asking one of his knights to carry her letter. She rose and reached for an undershift to cover her nakedness before padding to one of the cabinets to select a gown. There was no need to dress in silks now, for he had gone. Instead, she chose a plain English wool woven so fine 'twas thin and soft.

"Would you have me aid you?"

"Nay. I'd have you send the boy to me."

She pulled on the overgown and folded back the sleeves to expose the fine bones in her wrists. Picking up the polished steel mirror Richard had given her, she studied her countenance with a frown. At least her hair had grown to where it slipped just past her shoulders now.

"Demoiselle?"

"Aye. Close the door after you, Garth," she directed, reaching for the sealed parchment case. "You once rode for me to Rivaux and found it, did you not? Well, this day I'd have you seek out Clifford's keep in Kent."

He looked up, surprised.

"Aye." She nodded. " 'Tis for Simon of Wood-stock's eyes—and his only."

23

Despite the lateness of his arrival at Harlowe, Richard was escorted immediately into the bedchamber where his grandsire lay. Although a number of retainers grouped about the tapestry-hung bed, the room was strangely silent, and for a moment Richard feared 'twas over—that he'd not come in time. Then, almost in unison, heads turned at the sound of his spurs clinking against the planked floor.

A small, incredibly frail-looking woman leaned back from the bed itself. A quick glance at Richard and she rose, coming forward with her hands outstretched.

"God be praised—I knew but that Stephen had summoned you to London. I feared you would not come."

Despite his sweaty, travel-stained appearance, he opened his arms and enfolded Eleanor of Nantes against him, taking care not to crush her. "Nay, naught but hell could have barred my way, Grandmother."

"Art so tall and strong, Richard." She looked up mistily, her pride in him written on her face. "Aye, but you have the look of your father, and next to Roger, he is the handsomest man of my memory."

Though she was old, she had retained her great beauty with dignity. Instead of wrinkling, her skin had grown thinner, almost translucent, and tighter over her fine, delicate bones. And her hair, once almost as dark as his, was softly silver. Even now, 'twas not difficult to see what had made his grandsire and Robert of Belesme fight over her. He held her close for a moment, and then bent to brush his lips against the smoothness of her cheek.

"How fares he?" he dared to ask, his hand smoothing her hair against her crown.

"He was wont to do that also," she whispered, turning away to hide her tears.

"I am too late then?"

"Nay, but I can almost wish you were, Richard. He suffers greatly where the leg will not heal, and yet he'd not die ere he spoke with you and Guy. He has already sent his love to Cat, knowing that she cannot come."

His throat constricted painfully and he nodded. "I'd see him."

"Aye, but you must not weep—he'd not want it." Choking back a sob, she managed to whisper, "He says he has no regrets in this life, and goes readily save for me. Oh, Sweet Mary, Richard, but I'd not thought I'd be a dowager—I shall not know how to go on when 'tis over." She swallowed and tried to breathe for a moment, and then took his hand. "Come, we tarry too long, and I'd not worry you over an old woman's tears."

" 'Tis all right, Grandmother," he whispered soothingly. "Nay, but you still have the family."

"Aye, but I have had Roger since my birth—through all that has passed, he has always held for me."

"Aye."

"May God in His wisdom make you like him, Richard."

Those around the bed moved back as he approached, and he could see the reddened eyes of his uncle, Brian FitzHenry, and his aunt, Aislinn of the Condes. At least if his mother could not have come, they were there. Brian clasped his shoulder and looked away, unable to check the tears that trickled down his face. Aislinn pressed a quick kiss on his cheek and fled.

He was unprepared for the sight of his grandsire

in bed. All of his life, he'd seen him as a strong man, a man whose stature came as much from his character as from his build. But now Roger de Brione lay still, his blue eyes closed beneath mottled lids. Unlike Eleanor's, his face was lined, etching deeply the handsomeness that had been there. His skin was dry and flushed with fever beneath the shock of pure white hair. But the thing that struck Richard most was that he seemed to have shrunk in size. He knelt beside the bed and reached to grasp Roger's hand.

" 'Tis I, Grandsire—Richard."

"Richard?" The old man's eyes fluttered open to focus on him, and he struggled to sit, falling back exhausted. " 'Tis what bothers me most about this," he muttered. "I cannot rise."

Richard slid his other arm around him and braced him with his shoulder, lifting him. "Aye, you can. Does it pain you much—the leg, I mean?"

"Nay, but it does not heal. The surgeons would have taken it, but I'd not let them. Jesu, but what good would there be in an old one-legged man?"

"He'd be worth more than ten whole if he were Roger de Brione."

"Nay, my time has come—I'd not survive the cutting anyway." His fingers grasped Richard's firmly, belying the fact that he was dying. With his other hand he touched his grandson's face. "Do not weep for me, I pray you—I am shriven and go with but one regret."

Richard's jaw quivered with his effort to control the unmanly flood of tears that threatened. The back of his grandsire's hand brushed at those which brimmed.

"Of all that I would change, 'tis what is between you and Guy," Roger whispered so low that Richard had to lean to hear. "Aye, I'd have you cry peace and cease tearing at your mother's heart." He looked up at Eleanor and murmured, "I'd be alone with him."

"Aye."

"You tire," Richard choked.

"Aye, but there will be an eternity to rest later."
Roger dropped his hand and appeared to wait for
more strength, not speaking until the door closed.
He rallied then, his blue eyes showing some of their
old intensity. "I'd feel your hand in mine, Richard."

" 'Tis there."

"Guy—I'd hoped to see Guy again." For a moment
the young man thought him confused, but he spoke
low again. "There's been no better son to me than
your father—aye, he makes me as proud as if he'd
been born of my own blood."

"No prouder than we are of you."

"Richard . . . Richard. You cannot know what you
mean to him."

"My father—" He started to protest and realized
'twas not the time to vent his feelings about Guy.

"Nay—hearken to me. I had no son—but my daughters gave me the sons I lacked."

"You should not speak, Grandsire. Nay, but let me
hold you."

But Roger ignored him. For a moment his eyes
grew distant and Richard was afraid the end had
come, but the weak voice grew suddenly in intensity,
gaining strength as he talked again. "Given all that
has passed with him, Guy of Rivaux has striven to
make you a good man—I'd have you know that."

"Aye—in his own image." Richard fought the bitterness he felt, knowing it was not right to argue
with a dying man.

"Not in his own image—never that. If there is
anything Guy of Rivaux fears, 'tis that you will be
like him." The blue eyes cleared and fixed on Richard's, burning them with the urgency of what he
would say. "Aye, he fears greatly the blood he has
given you."

"I have heard Eudo of Rivaux was a hard man."

"There's naught of Count Eudo in you."

Richard stared, uncomprehending. "Grandsire—"

"You were born of the blood of Belesme, Richard." Roger's fingers tightened as he spoke, and he

pulled his grandson closer to make no mistake of his words. "Aye, you bear the blood he hates."

"Jesu!"

"For these twenty-three years I have waited for him to tell you of it," the old man rasped, lying back. "But my time ends, and soon there'll be none to tell the tale. Guy would but protect you from what he fears in his blood."

Clearly his grandsire's mind had wandered into the realm of fancy, and his ancient quarrel with Robert of Belesme had somehow intermingled in the final meanderings of his mind. Richard leaned forward and brushed the white hair back from the lined brow. "Hush—do not speak so much."

"You think me daft, but 'tis my leg that rots rather than my mind. Your other grandsire—your father's father—was Robert of Belesme."

A shiver of suppressed fear shook Richard—and denial. "Nay, but Belesme was ... Jesu, 'twould make my father a bastard."

"I'd not tell the tale otherwise, but Guy feels as you do. And he mistakes his temper for the madness he saw in Belesme, Richard. Ever does he seek to control what he fears."

"He's spared me naught—he'd make me what I cannot be."

"You did not know Belesme—we did."

Richard looked down to where the blue lines of his own veins could be seen at his wrists, and he felt a sense of revulsion now for the blood that must flow through them. And so many quarrels he and Guy had had took on new meaning to him. Roger's eyes followed his and he nodded, confirming yet again what he'd said.

" 'Twas why he did not wish me to have Hellbringer then," Richard mused aloud. " 'Twas why it was William that gave it to me."

"Aye—you have the look of Belesme."

"Nay, I look as my father."

"And he also."

"And none knew of it?" Richard asked incredulously, still not wanting to believe. "Surely 'twas noted if—"

"Belesme was disfigured by then, and none remembered." Roger closed his eyes and waited, seeking more wind. " 'Twas too dangerous to tell—as it is now. You dare not speak of this to any but Guy."

Part of Richard believed him then, but part still sought to deny. "Jesu, Grandsire, but there's naught of Belesme in him! Belesme was devil's spawn—mad, vile! Guy of Rivaux brought him to justice."

"To atone for the guilt he felt over what Robert had done, Richard."

He knew Roger had no reason to lie, but every rational feeling rebelled at what he'd heard. Richard closed his eyes as though he could blot out the thoughts that came to mind.

"I tell you what I told Guy then: 'tis not what you are born—nay, 'tis how you live and die." He paused, straining for some resource to sustain him, and sighed deeply. "I'd leave you knowing that Guy of Rivaux has fought and striven against enemies of flesh and mind, that you have not had to fight them. Honor him for that."

The latch lifted at the door and both men fell silent. A page crossed the room, his soft leather slippers scuffing almost noiselessly against the floor. He leaned close to Richard's ear and whispered, "Your father is here."

"Guy is here?" Roger struggled harder to pull himself up, and his face went white with the pain. "Sweet Jesu, but I'd see him." His blue eyes met Richard's for the last time. "Make your peace with him."

"I will try," Richard promised solemnly, leaning closer to kiss the weathered cheek. "Go with God, Grandsire, and know that you have my love."

"And you mine also," Roger whispered, releasing his hand.

Richard passed Guy wordlessly, his head bowed to

keep from meeting his eyes, but his father stopped
him. "Is he awake?" Guy's face was lined with fatigue, but his flecked eyes mirrored a greater pain.
"Your man found me ere I reached Gloucester's
keep, and I turned back in haste, afraid I would be
too late."

"He awaits you."

Richard lifted his hand and dropped it, unable to
speak further. There were so many things he'd know
of his father, so many things to know when this was
past. And so many quarrels to put behind them if
he'd keep his promise. Numbly he turned away, scarce
hearing Guy's hushed greeting at the bed.

In the outer chamber, Eleanor caught him to her
and wept. He stood holding her helplessly, thinking
that a better man than he died. Finally his aunt
moved forward to take her from him, leading her to
sit on a cushioned bench. Brian FitzHenry looked up
and wiped his hand across wet cheeks.

"There will not be another to equal him, I fear."

"Nay, and well we know it," Richard managed
through his own tears.

The outer chamber was quiet save for the soft
weeping of those who kept the death vigil with them.
From time to time the physician rose and paced
anxiously, complaining that they tired Earl Roger
now with so many visitors, but Eleanor merely shook
her head, saying that it was as Roger wanted it—that
not every man had the opportunity to say farewell to
his heirs. "And Guy of Rivaux and Brian are the
sons I could not give him, so I'd not keep them
away."

It seemed an eternity they waited, but finally the
door creaked open, and a dozen pairs of eyes watched
Guy come out. Richard was stunned by the ravaged
expression on his father's face as Guy whispered,
choking, "Brian, he would speak with you also," before he turned his head into the stone wall and wept
openly, his broad shoulders heaving with the great
sobs that racked his body. In all of his nearly twenty-

four years, it was the first time Richard had ever seen his father cry. Nay, but the Guy of Rivaux that he knew was strong and harsh, unable to love any but his wife and daughters, hard and unyielding to all others. With an effort, he forced himself to walk across the room and lay a tentative hand on his father's shoulder.

"Nay, Papa—he would not wish it."

"Aye, but 'tis hard to part with that which one has come to love," Guy answered haltingly, turning into his arms.

For a time they stood, two men grown, holding each other tightly, both weeping. Finally Guy mastered himself, looking into eyes level with his own. "Art like him in many ways, my son, for there is a kindness in you that I did not note until now."

Richard shook his head. "Maman says I am more like you than anyone."

For a moment Guy's face grew wary, and then his mouth twisted into a faint smile and his eyes lightened. "Aye, I could not deny you if I wanted."

" 'Tis my temper as much as my looks, Papa."

It was as though darkness descended. Guy stepped back and turned away. "He told you of what I have given you," he murmured tonelessly. "I would he had not—'twas a curse I'd not have you bear."

"I think it means more to you than to me," Richard told him quietly. "I knew him not and cannot therefore feel as much pain in the knowing. I only know I am proud to be Guy of Rivaux's son." And he did something he'd not thought possible. He leaned closer and kissed first one of Guy's cheeks and then the other in the traditional gesture of peace. "Nay, I am not ashamed of anything I have of you." Then, realizing that the chasm between them would be bridged slowly, that years of pain would not go away in one night, he grinned almost sheepishly. "Nay, do not think me a fool for this, Papa."

"Jesu, but what a maudlin pair we are become,"

Guy murmured gruffly. But he draped his arm about
his son's shoulder and gestured to the stairs. "Come,
let us walk apart. If there is aught you would know, I
will try to tell it."

24

The first time that Gilliane realized something was very wrong, there was an insistent, loud pounding on the heavy outer door, and angry voices could be heard as a crowd milled in the narrow street. The men Richard had left to guard her peered anxiously out the windows, and one shouted to ask their business there.

"Send out the harlot! Send out Rivaux's fancy whore!"

Gilliane whitened, scarce able to believe what she heard. But even as she listened, she heard the chant grow. She ran to the upper story and opened one of the shutters to look on the crowd below. They were crudely armed, some carrying poles and others sticks. A stout woman saw her and pointed, directing the others.

"There's the witch! Burn her!"

A hail of stones hit the house, forcing Gilliane back. She shuttered the window with shaking hands and tried to comprehend. A chill crawled down her spine as she realized they'd called her a witch. Bernard, the knight in charge below, yelled back at them.

"Nay, but she is under my lord of Rivaux's protection also!"

"The witch dried my milk!" someone cried out.

"Aye, and my dog has died since she has come here!" called out another.

"And my babe sickens!"

"Would you anger Rivaux?" Bernard challenged them. "Nay, but he would have her safe!"

"We'd free him from the witch's spell!"

The clamor grew louder, and the crowd pressed forward, pushing against the bar latch, bowing i inward, to no avail. Richard's knights drew sword: while the merchant's housekeeper and servants piled furniture to block the door. A sense of despair stole over Gilliane as she watched their almost frenzied preparations for an assault. They were but four armed men and half a dozen others against a mob crying for her blood.

For several hours the mob milled, gaining strength One of the absent merchant's servants, hoping to spare his master's house, volunteered to escape from the back and seek help. But they caught him before his feet had scarce touched ground, and his cries of terror could be heard as the crowd tore him apart Inside the house, the mood was grim, and it grew grimmer as those outside shouted their triumph a the arrival of a large beam for battering.

Bernard raced to the small stairs, hissing up a her, "Hide yourself as best you can, Demoiselle." I was an impossible task—with her red hair, there was certain to be one to recognize her. For a brief moment she considered shearing it again, and then decided against it—it would make no difference, after all. Knowing the futility of what she did, she lay down and rolled beneath the curtained bed, holding her ears against the relentless thudding of the beam against the thick door.

"We are armed!" Bernard shouted at those who beat the heaving door.

But even as he spoke, the wood bar splintered against the concentrated weight of a dozen men, and Gilliane could hear the clamor as her defenders sought vainly to push ten times their number back. The howls of pain and the moans of agony carried upward while steel weapons and wooden pikes clashed in a murderous frenzy. And she could hear the retreat of Richard's knights backing up the stairs. The room filled with the thunder of bootsteps, the closely confined slashing, and finally the crash of the shutters splintering with the weight of someone being thrown through them. And as some fought, others already looted, pulling down locked cabinets and stripping the sendal and baudequin hangings from the bed. She lay as still as stone, not daring to breathe.

And then she could smell the fetid, sickening breath of the man who crawled beneath the bed, yelling, "I have found the witch!"

She bit the dirty hand that groped for her, tasting the mingled filth and blood, and then there were others pulling at her, some at her feet and others at her hair. Tears of pain welled as she was dragged headfirst from the bed. She kicked loose and tried to roll to a crouch as she cleared the frame. Clawing at her attackers, she was kicked and pummeled and spat on.

" 'Tis the devil that gives her strength!"

"Aye, 'tis the devil's own hair she has!"

Someone held up the terrified cat that belonged to the merchant's housekeeper, shoving it into her face. "Aye, 'tis her familiar!" The poor animal scratched and hissed until the one who had it flung it out the window. It apparently landed on its feet and ran for safety, for above the din Gilliane heard someone shout, "Aye, 'tis the devil, all right—the beast is unharmed from the fall!"

"I am but the demoiselle of Beaumaule!" she cried, trying to rise. "Have done, good people!"

She was kicked from behind and sprawled forward, doubling over to protect the babe within her as she fell. All around her, they were tearing open chests and cabinets, splintering them at the locks, and dragging forth Richard's rich tunics and her clothes. Dirt-caked women held up samite gowns, crowing toothlessly over their finds.

"Burn her! Burn her! Burn Rivaux's harlot!"

Bernard, who lay beaten and severely wounded,

gasped out, "Nay, but you know not what you do. If you would think her a witch, have her tried."

Gilliane grasped at the idea immediately. "If you burn me without trial, I am Norman—there's not one of you who will live when all is done," she promised, hoping against hope they'd listen.

"Nay—burn her!"

But there were those among them who were not now so sure—there were no *wergilds*, no fines if the victim were Norman, only a cruel death, and punishment was swift. Several backed away uncertainly. "Nay, you burn her then—I'd try her first," one of them muttered, suddenly afraid.

"She is a witch!"

"Aye, but—"

"She kills your babes!"

" 'Tis for the Church to decide," the man who'd first found her maintained stubbornly now. "Aye, we'll have her tried and then she will burn."

But it was not over—she'd merely bought time. One of the stouter women, saying they'd take her to the priest, pulled her up by her hair and thrust her toward the stairs, flinging her down them as though she were but a sack of grain. She hit the wall and broke her fall. Those who crowded below caught her roughly and pushed her before them toward the shattered door.

Her dress caught on the broken hinge, tearing, and someone suddenly caught at her sleeve. "Nay, but let us see if she has the devil's mark on her!" And then she was pulled about as her dress was ripped from her and the pieces trampled into the garbage and offal in the street. She struck out and clawed at them to no avail, and then stood before them naked and bleeding.

"I see naught," one man dared to say.

"Fool! 'Tis the red hair!"

A contingent of riders came into the lane, and Gilliane wrenched away from those who held her to fling herself before them, knowing she had the better chance with any knight. The crowd parted, scrambling for safety at the onslaught of hooves, and Gilliane feared to be trampled. At the last moment she rolled clear, putting the riders between herself and those who attacked her.

"What goes here? Jesu—Gilly!"

Richard dropped his reins and dismounted, drawing his sword. "Nay, but block the alleys," he ordered curtly. "I'd have none escape."

Guy sat astride behind him and surveyed those who carried garments of samite and sendal in filthy hands. "Kill any who would flee!" he called out as his men moved to seal the narrow lane. "And go house to house and bring them out."

Richard strode over to where Gilliane lay in a battered heap in the dirty street. Slowly, in full view of everyone, he handed his sword to Everard of Meulan and drew off his own red-and-black tunic. Kneeling beside her, he pulled her up to sit and slipped it over her head. His hand picked at her hair, removing the litter that clung to it, and then he brushed it back from her bruised face. His jaw worked with anger as he stared at the scratches and cuts that oozed with still-clotting blood.

Those who had been clamoring to kill her but moments before were strangely silent now, staring dumbly at the sight of the great lord, shirtless and on his knees in the mud and mire. And then, fearful that they would be punished for harming the girl he held, they turned almost in unison to one who was attempting to lose himself amongst them.

" 'Twas he! He said she was a witch!"

"Fools!" he spat at them. "Hold your tongues—he cannot kill us all!"

"A witch," Guy muttered contemptuously. "If any burns today, 'twill be those who have harmed her."

"My milk dried," a woman said sullenly, looking at the ground. "And Borton's boy sickened and Elbert's dog died. Aye, and all has happened since she came."

"Jesu!" Everard's face mirrored his disgust. "And

how many dogs and babes have died ere she came? Nay, but there are those that die every day! And if your milk dried, old woman, mayhap 'twas because you've born too many babes!"

Richard rose, lifting Gilliane with him and pulling his tunic down to cover her nakedness. " 'Tis a woman of Norman blood you have accused without cause." Turning to the housekeeper, who stood white-faced in the doorway of the ransacked house, he ordered curtly, "Take her inside—I'd not have her see what I would do." Bending to Gilliane, he promised grimly, "They will pay for every hurt."

Gilliane drew herself up and passed them proudly, daring to look in the faces of those who'd beaten and spat at her. And each turned away, not wanting to meet her eyes. At the front of the house they parted silently to let her by.

" 'Twas him—'twas Thorwald!"

The crowd that so lately had been a mob thrust forward a lean weasel-faced man, who shrank back against them. Richard picked up his sword and drew closer, his dark eyes hard. Lifting the point to rest at the bulge of the man's Adam's apple, he demanded silkily, "I'd know whom to blame, Thorwald—aye, else you'd die alone, you'd tell."

The man squirmed as the point pricked the skin of his neck. "I thought she was a witch," he managed to say, drawing his tongue over thin dry lips. "And she was naught but a whore, anyway." He let out a cry of fear as the blade dug in suddenly, and he fell at Richard's booted feet.

"Revive him."

Guy watched silently as Everard used his helmet to scoop up some of the foul water from the gutter and flung it over the unconscious man. Richard leaned to place Hellbringer's tip against Thorwald's breastbone as he awakened. "Who?" he repeated awfully.

"Nay," the man gasped.

"Speak now or die unshriven." For emphasis, he leaned on the hilt, pressing downward.

"Brevise—'twas my lord of Brevise." The man's eyes widened in terror as Richard did not lift his blade.

"Get him a priest that he may confess."

A murmur of apprehension spread through the crowd as everyone realized what he meant to do. There was no question of mercy—they'd taken a Norman girl of gentle birth and dragged her, bloodied and beaten, into the street. And now he would show them no more kindness than they would have shown her. They milled uneasily, wondering how many of them were to share Thorwald's fate.

Inside the house, the woman washed Gilliane's cuts and would have salved them, but was stopped. "Nay, but I'd have a bath first. Sweet Mary, but I thought to be killed," Gilliane whispered, still shaking from the horror of being nearly torn limb from limb by the mob. And then she heard the collective gasp from outside and knew that Richard had exacted a measure of vengeance for what had happened to her.

"Is she all right?" the strong, masculine voice asked.

She looked up to where Guy of Rivaux stood above her, and tried to nod despite the ache in her head where she'd been kicked. "Aye, I will mend." Her lips were stiff and her face sore, but she managed to inquire, "And Earl Roger?"

"He is dead."

"I am sorry for it, my lord."

"Nay, child, but he died as he lived, giving peace to those he left." He leaned to examine a cut on her forehead, murmuring, "We should not have left you here."

"I had not the right to go."

The woman tending her withdrew to see to the drawing of a bath, and they were alone. Guy moved away, pacing as though he would speak, and then he cleared his throat. "Why have you not spoken to Richard of the child?" Her heart seemed to stop at the question, and she sat very still, not answering, until he came back to her. "Gilliane, I have watched Catherine carry six of my babes, five to fruition, and I know."

"Aye." She sighed heavily and looked away.

"Do you mean to tell him?"

"Nay." It was scarce a whisper. "Nay, I'd not tear at him further for what he must do, and I do not think he would let me go if he knew."

"Gilliane—"

"He'd keep me and her both, my lord, and neither she nor I could bear it. 'Tis different for a man—he can lie with more than one woman to ease his body and yet think himself true. But we cannot share him—the pain would be too great."

"He has no wish to wed her."

"He cannot in honor refuse—and even if he could, Holy Church would not consider him free to wed me."

"Come to Rivaux, then, child. Cat and I would stand for you and the babe."

"And bear his bastard there? Nay, but I cannot—he'd know of it, and there would be that tie between us still."

"There is little else," he reminded her gently. "And bastardy is no bar to love for me—I'd welcome the babe and see it safe."

"I mean to go to the Priory of St. Agnes near Beaumaule, to the nuns there."

"Jesu! 'Tis no place for a babe, Gilliane." His heart went out to her for the sacrifice she would make, and he added in a gentler tone, "I'd tell him, were I you."

"Nay. 'Tis better to be a bastard in a nunnery than to be one in a household where there are legitimate sons, I think."

"Then come to Rivaux."

Tears scalded her eyes and threatened her composure, but she bit her lip until she could control the overwhelming gratitude she felt for this man who did not condemn her for what she had done. "If ever the need arises, I will remember what you have offered me, my lord."

He clasped her shoulder as one would a man's and then drew away. "Art a daughter to give a man pride."

"You will not tell him?" she asked anxiously.

"Nay, not if you do not will it."

Richard walked in, wiping Hellbringer's blade on a corner of his undertunic, and his anger at her injuries flared anew. "The one who first accused you is dead, Gilly. Aye, and others also. Jesu, but they cannot wait to accuse each other for what was done!" His eyes met Guy's, and there was no mercy in them. "Do you come with me to seek Brevise?" he asked grimly.

"Aye, but I'll warrant he has already fled. A man who attacks by deceit does not wait to be caught."

"I will follow him to Brevise itself then."

"Nay." It was Gilliane who spoke. "Richard, if he is not in London, he will not have gone there. Sweet Mary, but I'd not have you leave me this night."

In an instant he was there, leaning over her, brushing at the tangles in her hair with his bloodied hand. "Aye, if I find him not this day, I will return that you are not alone. And I leave full half my escort here, though I think there will be few foolish enough to accuse you again."

She reached up to hold his hand against her face, turning into it to press her lips into his palm. And she felt the fingers of his other hand tighten in her hair. Tears of impending loss brimmed in her blue eyes, brightening them, and he mistook the reason.

"Nay, I have not forgotten the oath I swore on Holy Rood, Gilly. If not this day, I will kill him yet."

"Aye."

The house was still after they left, the only sound being the hammering of those who would repair the door, as the servants and men moved about without speaking, each one of them lost in his own grim thoughts. There was not a man among them who had not asked to join in the search for Brevise.

Gilliane's body was bathed, her hair washed with care, and each and every cut was salved. The housekeeper hovered over her, afraid that Richard of Rivaux would ask how it was that she had not defended his leman. It was not until she drew the soft woolen undershift over the girl that she dared to ask, "You will not tell him that I fled when the door broke?"

"Nay, you would have been a fool to stay," Gilliane answered wearily.

"Demoiselle?"

"She is unwell!" the woman rounded on the servant who would interrupt them.

"The boy Garth—"

"Garth is here? Nay, but I would see him, then."

Still sniffing her disapproval, the housekeeper withdrew, admonishing the boy to speak his message quickly, that his mistress might rest. Travel-stained and weary, Garth looked around him in disbelief.

"God's blood, but what happened, Demoiselle?"

" 'Tis too painful to tell. But I'd know—did you find him?"

"Aye." He came forward and would have dropped on bended knee, but she shook her head. "I found him at Clifford's keep, and waited until your message was read to him by Lady Clifford's chaplain— three times he had it read, Demoiselle, whilst I waited."

"And his answer?"

" 'Aye—tell the Lady Gilliane I will await her as she asks on St. John's Day,' he said to me."

25

"He escaped."

He came through the repaired doorway and threw his helmet to the floor in disgust. His black hair glistened with sweat and his face was marked with the imprint of his nasal on his cheeks. The dark eyes that met hers glittered with the impotent fury he felt, and then softened.

"I am sorry, Gilly. I wanted to kill him for you."

"Aye, but you cannot be faulted for his fleeing," she consoled him, rising from her bench to take his heavy gloves. "Sit you down, that I may divest you."

"Nay—Walter can do that. 'Tis enough that you tend yourself." He touched a bruise that darkened her jawline, tracing it tenderly. "Does it pain you overmuch?"

"Not when I consider that God in His mercy let me live." Somehow, she managed to smile despite the soreness. "But you must be tired unto death, Richard, for I am told you did not leave Harlowe until yesterday."

" 'Tis but a bath and food I need."

"Then let me tend you."

His eyebrow lifted, but his faint smile betrayed his pleasure at the offer. He nodded and followed her into the small chamber they shared. She moved slowly, her body obviously hurting, and yet even as bruised and swollen as she was, there was an indefinable something about her that drew him to her. Nay, there were comelier girls to be had, but he'd not have them.

She divested him of his bloodied surcoat and his mail, reminding him of that first meeting at Beaumaule when he'd found her touch so pleasing. And, as if she shared his thoughts, she ran her fingers through the thickness of his hair, combing it, scratching his weary head, soothing it. He leaned back, overcome with the intimacy of her touch, of the feel of his head leaning back against her breasts. He'd wanted her from the beginning, but the intense love he felt for her was more than the mere slaking of desire. Any castle whore could do that for him. Nay, what he had of Gilliane de Lacey could not be gotten anywhere else.

"Art silent," she chided, rubbing his head with increased vigor. And then, bending over him, she sniffed and wrinkled her nose. "Jesu, Richard, but I have seen wet hunting dogs that smelled better."

"I'd see you put on a helmet and ride many leagues under a hot sun," he retorted, grinning. "Aye, we'd not smell your rosewater then." He reached upward, clasping her arms and pulling her forward over him. "But 'tis not my hair I'd have you kiss," he murmured, leaning back to look at her.

"Without a bath, there's naught of you I would kiss anyway."

"Gilly?"

"What?"

"How long has it been—how long since you knew you loved me?"

"I thought 'twas when we were at Rivaux, but I think now perhaps I was mistaken. Nay, but 'twas when I saw you among the smoke and flames at Beaumaule."

"Only then?" he teased.

"Well . . ." She appeared to consider the matter and then nodded. "Aye. Before that, I merely thought you rich and handsome."

"And you do not regret what is between us?" His

expression, which had been light, sobered, and the eyes that looked up into hers were intent. "I'd know, Gilly."

"I regret none of it," she answered solemnly. "May God forgive me, but I regret none of it."

"Nor do I."

Unable to bear the emotions that warred within her as she became acutely aware of his touch, his voice, his very presence, she forced herself to loosen his hands and back away. "If we speak much more of this, you'll not get your bath, my lord—and you cannot say 'tis not needed."

His men came in quietly, slipping back and forth to fill the heavy round tub, and then Walter of Thibeaux tested the water before pouring in a vial of perfumed oil. " 'Tis ready, my lord."

Richard stood, stretching muscles tired from two days of riding, and untied his chausses. Before he could stop her, Gilliane knelt awkwardly to unfasten the leather cross-garters. And as she struggled to rise, he was conscious again of the hurt she'd taken, hurt brought about by Brevise, and new anger coursed through him.

"I should not have left you here," he accused himself bitterly.

" 'Tis not your fault alone I am called a whore and a witch, Richard. Nay, but what I have become, I have done willingly."

"Gilly—"

"Nay, I'd not speak of it further, my lord."

"If I had but found Brevise!" he exploded.

"Then you would have killed him—aye, think you I do not know what you would do for me?"

She looked up at his naked body, seeing again the hard muscles of a fighting man, taking in the still-red and puckered scar that dented his shoulder. And then she looked again at his face, taking in the strong planes and curves, the clean, straight profile, and the eyes. Even if he had been ugly and mis-shapen, those dark, gold-flecked eyes would have made him beautiful, for to her they were a mirror of the man within. "Aye," she repeated softly, "you have given me much to love in you."

"Gilly—"

"And if you do not take your bath, I'll not be able to stay in this room with you," she added hastily as he stepped toward her.

He stopped, dropping his hands. "Aye. Jesu, Gilly, but art hard on my overweening pride. In one breath you tell me you love me, and in the other you say I stink." But incredibly, he was grinning. "I'd keep you with me if for naught else but to make me humble."

"Nay, you will have Cicely for that."

"Gilly, I'd not speak of her."

"Then take your bath."

He stayed up late, talking to his father about how best to take William of Brevise—whether he should seek royal redress for what had happened or whether he should search and fight his cowardly enemy and risk royal wrath. One course would again drag Gilliane's name before those who would judge her rather than her attackers, and the other might well send him into exile. In the end, Guy's pragmatism prevailed: they would wait for Brevise's next move and see that it was his last.

As the floating wick in the bowl of oil sputtered, signaling that it was about to drown, Guy finished the last of his wine and, setting it aside, leaned across the trestle table, his eyes intent on his son. For three whole days there'd not been a cross word between them, and he hesitated to strain their newfound peace. But he knew Gilliane de Lacey's situation was desperate, and he'd promised not to reveal her secret, so he'd try to aid her as best he could.

"You cannot keep her much longer, Richard."

"I cannot let her go, Papa."

"Think on it," Guy persisted, "and think on what

is right for her. This day she was almost murdered
because of what she is to you."

"I should have left more men," Richard retorted
defensively.

"And think of the shame she suffered at court—
would you condemn her to a life of that? Once you
are wed to Lincoln's daughter, her shame increases,
and you make her an adulteress."

"Jesu, Papa! Do not tear at me! I accept that I
must take Cicely! But I'd not abandon Gilliane for
her—I'd not."

"And what if she conceives of you? Would you—"

"Think you I have not thought of that also? I'd
acknowledge the child as King Henry did his, and I'd
love it for whence it came."

"Nay." Guy's voice was gentle, but the message
brutal. "Nay, you'd bring a bastard into a household
where it has no legal standing—you'd let a babe
suffer for the pleasure you have taken with the
mother. Ask your uncle—ask Brian FitzHenry what
'tis like to be a bastard, or Gloucester. And they were
royal bastards, Richard—yet both would say they have
borne much for their birth. If you believe it not, ask
Gloucester why he lies with none but Mabel, and he
will tell you he'd offer no child what he has had to
bear. Though he is the better man, there'd be few to
support him as king—because he is a bastard."

It was something that had tormented Richard when
he'd first taken Gilliane to his bed, but as the months
passed and it had not happened, he'd begun to think
it wouldn't—that mayhap she was barren. His duty
to Cicely of Lincoln was a cup of gall to be swallowed,
but his loss of Gilliane would be impossible to bear.
He stared into the dregs of his wine like a soothsayer
seeking answers.

Guy, knowing he'd planted the seed at least, leaned
across to grip his son's hand in comfort. "Think on
it—'tis all I ask. I have not the right to make such
decisions for you now—art a grown man."

"I'd not let her go, and she would not wish it,"

Richard decided finally. Rising slowly, he tried to ease his aching shoulders. "And I am too tired to think on anything tonight."

Guy remained at the table after he had left, wondering if there could not be some way, if there was not something he could do to ease his son. All of his life he'd fought and striven hard against so many enemies, and he had won. But all his wealth and all his power did not seem to matter in this, the happiness of his only son. The fact that he should have stood firm, stood against Gloucester in his opposition to the betrothal made no difference now. What was done was done in the eyes of the Church. Or was it? But there would have to be a reason, and even if he could find one, 'twould be too late. The Church moved slowly, and took years to resolve such things, and it was not likely that Lincoln would draw back from the betrothal, not when Richard stood but a pulse away from the earldom of Harlowe. Gilliane de Lacey could bear half a dozen children ere it could be determined that Richard's betrothal was invalid, particularly if Lincoln fought to enforce it. Nay, but as painful as it was to all of them, Gilliane was strong enough to choose the right path. And then he thought of Cat, his beautiful Cat, and knew how hard it would be for Richard to lose his Gilly. But he was not the only loser—already Guy felt a sense of emptiness knowing there would be a child born of them that they would never see.

Richard undressed in the darkness, taking care not to waken her, and eased his body into the deep feather mattress. The ropes and leather strappings groaned slightly with his weight, and she turned against him, proving she did not sleep. His arm slid around her, drawing her close.

"Are you in pain, Gilly, that you are awake?"

"Aye," she lied, grateful that he could not see her swollen eyes.

"Would you have me salve you again?"

"Nay."

He lay there stroking the softness of her hair against her shoulder, thinking of what his father had said. For a moment he considered asking her how she would feel if she conceived of him, and then he abandoned the idea. It would serve only to give her something else to worry her, and she needed no more pain. Instead, he stretched his body closer against hers and nuzzled the hair that fell forward over her temple.

He made no move to take her, choosing to hold her instead, and they lay in close embrace, savoring the warmth and nearness of each other. Finally, thinking he hesitated because of her injuries, she eased her hand from beneath the covers and reached to stroke the hardness of his shoulder.

"You need not fear to take me," she whispered.

"Nay." His arms tightened protectively around her as he shook his head against hers, and his breath was light and soft in her ear. " 'Tis for more than that I love you, Gilly. I can wait for you to heal."

In another time, it would have made her heart sing to hear him say it, but this night was different. She swallowed hard, thinking how soon it would be that she'd not feel his arms around her and not know the closeness of loving him again. As the time drew nearer to leave, she was loath even to sleep, lest she waste what there was.

The silence in the room was almost loud as neither of them slept, not daring to voice the thoughts that plagued them, until finally she roused slightly and asked, "I forgot—'tis the morrow that you swear to Stephen, is it not?"

"Uh? Oh, if 'tis the fifteenth of June," he murmured, yawning finally. "Aye, and I'd have you go to watch."

"Nay, I'd have none see me like this."

"You could go veiled."

"And have it said you brought your whore again to court against Queen Maud's wishes?"

"You are not my whore to me, Gilly, but I leave it to you to decide if you go. Now, try to sleep so that you will heal."

26

Neither Richard nor Guy spoke much as they rode back from Westminster, each feeling less than at ease with what he had done. For Guy it had been a difficult decision to swear to Stephen, and only the fact that the Empress had made no move to stop her cousin's usurpation of her throne had allowed him to do it—that, and the fact that he, like Gloucester, fully expected the pope to rule Stephen's claim invalid and reinstate the oaths they'd all taken to Mathilda. For Richard it was a different matter. He'd not sworn fealty to her and yet he was loath to give his allegiance to a man he neither liked nor respected. And it particularly worried him that somehow Stephen would find the means to be a threat to Gloucester.

"Well," Guy decided finally, " 'tis done, and there's naught to keep me here longer."

"Aye."

"I'd go home to Rivaux—it has been a month and more since last I saw your mother, and I'd be away from her no longer."

"Do you bring her to Harlowe?"

"Nay, not for a time. I'd find it hard to bear sitting in his place, and I am afraid your grandmother would think it necessary to leave, that Cat could rule in her stead."

"You do not think she will be lonely now?"

"Eleanor? Your grandmother is a remarkable woman, Richard. We spoke of that, and she said she could face whatever was left to her, knowing that she'd go again to Roger at the end. Besides, Aislinn stays with her for a time, seeing that she wants for naught."

They rode through streets so narrow that their escort followed in twos, each silent again until they turned into the small lane. And it was Guy who spoke again. "And you? Do you go to Lincoln now?"

"Next month." Richard squared his shoulders as though he faced a writ of execution. "For now, I take Gilly back to Celesin to spend these last days with her there. And once I am wed to Cicely, I suppose I must wait until she conceives before I go home."

"It is not right to leave your wife in her father's keep."

"Nay, and it is not right to break Gilly's heart," Richard snapped with asperity. "Jesu, Papa, but there is no right in any of it!"

"If I could, I'd break the contract for you, my son."

There was a genuine regret in Guy's voice that gave Richard pause. "Aye, I know it."

"But you are of an age, and I can think of no impediment. Loving elsewhere carries little weight with Holy Church."

" 'Tis a mull of mine own making, Papa. My greatest regret is that 'tis not just I who pay the cost of what I have done."

There was naught more to say on the matter, each having dwelled on it until he was sick of it. Stephen, the Empress's indecision, Richard's marriage, Gilliane—all weighed heavily on a newfound but fragile understanding. Richard leaned across the pommel of his saddle to touch his father's arm.

"I do not forget I am Rivaux—I'd not shame you."

"You never have."

Ostlers awaited them, ready to stable the horses. Still in court dress rather than mail, Richard swung down and walked toward the new door. And his

mood, which had been heavy since he'd placed his
hands between Stephen's, lightened. He'd tell Gilliane
they were going to Celesin, that he'd bargained for
more time.

He'd half-expected her to be waiting at the window, her needlework spread across her lap, but the
front chamber was empty. "Gilly!" he called out.
"Gilly!"

But the house was ominously silent. He strode to
the room where they slept, thinking perhaps she was
abed, still nursing her hurts from the day before.
But that room was empty also, and he experienced
an awful sense of dread. The hairs on his neck
raised, warning him.

"The Demoiselle bade me give you this."

He spun around to face the woman who'd tended
them during their stay, and one glance told him that
she was afraid to hand him the parchment in her
hand. He stared, unwilling to take it.

"Where is she?" he demanded hollowly.

"She left with the boy."

"And none stopped her? God's bones, but—" He
lifted his hand as though to strike, and then dropped
it. Nay, but after the vengeance he'd taken for those
who'd dared touch her in the street the day before,
none of his men would have wanted to restrain her.
And he'd taken those closest to him for escort to
Westminster, leaving but some of Guy's knights and
his wounded. Numbly he reached for the parchment, taking it now.

My sweet lord, I recommend me to you, and pray
that you will forgive me for seeking shelter with
the holy sisters, and that God also forgives me for
what I must do.

The Maid of Lincoln must be your wife in fact
as well as name, and you must honor her for what
she will be to you. 'Tis her right rather than mine
to have your love, and I have come to accept that.

I pray you do not regret what has been between

us, for I do not. Love me for what I have been and love her for what she will be. May God in His mercy care for you and keep you in His grace always. And I ask you to pray for me also. Fare thee well, Richard of Rivaux, from Gilliane de Lacey.

"This is all she left?" He read the letter again, his eyes scanning it with disbelief. "Nay, but she would not—she cannot have . . ." He turned to where Guy stood in the doorway and his fingers shook as he held out the letter. "Oh, Jesu, Papa—she has gone from here." He felt as though he'd been stabbed, that he stood a dead man waiting to fall. And then the ache in his chest tightened, intensifying until he could not bear it as he realized his loss.

Guy nodded. "I am sorry for it."

"Sorry for it! Sorry for it!" Richard's voice rose nearly to a shout. "Nay, but she cannot! D'ye hear me? She cannot!" He cast about wildly for some sign of her, moving to throw open first one cabinet door and then the other, experiencing an initial relief when he saw the rich gowns and then acknowledging that she'd taken but her plainer clothes. Picking up the chest that still held much of the jewelry he'd given her, he flung it across the room with such force that it cracked the plaster over the stone wall, splintered, and spilled its contents in a heap on the floor. Then, kneeling over it, he let the pieces slide through his hands before he leaned his head into the wall.

"Richard!"

"She took naught but the girdle and the heart." He spoke low. "She took naught else of what I gave her."

"Richard!" Guy repeated, reaching to pull him up.

"Art satisfied, Papa? You and Lincoln and Gloucester have your wish! She's gone!" He turned away, kicking viciously at a bench, sending it crashing against the floor. "Aye, I will take Cicely of Lincoln! May she not rue the day she has me in her bed!"

"Get him a cup of wine," Guy ordered the terrified housekeeper over his shoulder. "And bring the skin." Still holding his son's arm, he tried to calm him. "God's blood, but this does not answer, Richard! Would you force Gilly to stay against her wishes?"

Richard wrenched away with such force that he staggered into the heavy curtained bed, caught at the hangings, and tore them from the frame as he fell. "Aye!" he shouted back. "Aye, I'd keep her! She is mine, d'ye hear? Mine!"

Guy took the cup from the woman and moved to stand over him. "Drink this," he ordered curtly.

Brushing his father aside, Richard disentangled himself from the heavy curtains and struggled to his feet. "I do not want to addle my brain, Papa—I want Gilliane de Lacey back!"

"Aye, and she is a free woman! You have no claim!"

"No claim! No claim?" his son howled, and then he stopped and turned around. "You forget—Stephen confirmed me as her guardian. Nay, but I have but to go after her—to find her," he managed in a calmer voice. "Aye, and when I do, Lincoln can come for me in Byzantium, Papa."

"Where? There are a thousand nunneries and more—where do you think to find her?"

"I'll find her," Richard promised grimly. He reached for the cup and drained it, wiping his mouth on the sleeve of his crimson samite overtunic. Mastering himself, he picked up the letter she'd left him and read it again, this time aloud to his father. "I can feel the pain, Papa—I can feel what she must have felt. Jesu, but I thought I could wed Cicely and keep her, but I see now 'twas not so. Nay, she has the greater claim. Lincoln's daughter is but tied to me with parchment." He lifted the letter and held it beneath Guy's eyes. "Gilliane de Lacey is tied to me by my soul."

"You know not where she went," Guy repeated.

"Then I will look—if I have to seek every nunnery

in England. Nay, but she cannot have gone far, one girl and an unarmed boy."

"And if she does not wish to be found?"

"I will make her wish it."

"I would not speak of this to Lincoln yet, Richard."

"Nay, I'd not alert her enemies that she is alone and unprotected." He was outwardly calm now, but his mind raced ahead to the task that faced him. "There has to be someone who saw them leave. The old woman—someone has to know or to have heard her speak of this."

"I think you are wrong to do what you do," Guy murmured, pouring himself a cup from the wine-skin. "But if you wish it, I will go with you." For a moment he considered betraying what he knew, and then he thought better of it. When his son did not find her, he'd come slowly to his senses and honor his commitment to Cicely of Lincoln. Aye, if it were possible that he could wed Gilliane and give his name to her babe, it would be different. But no matter how painful it was now, it changed nothing.

"Nay. Go home to Maman. One of us has the right to be happy, Papa." Richard sighed. "And 'tis not your fault I have gotten myself into this coil."

"It will be dark within a few hours."

"Aye." Richard ran his fingers through his hair as he was wont to do when distracted. "I will send Everard and two others to question any who may have seen her and Garth leave. And on the morrow I mean to take to my saddle and look until I find her. There's little enough to be done on a moonless night."

Guy clapped him on the shoulder and turned to go back to the outer room. At the doorway he tried one last time. "Richard . . . ?"

"What?"

"Have you considered that after all that has befallen her, Gilliane is tired of being called your whore? That she has no wish to be beaten and spit on and humiliated further?"

"I'd wed her."

"Alas, you cannot—who would recognize the marriage?" Guy's hand lifted the latch and pushed the door open. "Think on it."

Suddenly weary of the incessant struggle within him, Richard picked up the skin and filled his cup again. Carrying the brimming goblet to the bed he'd shared with Gilliane, he sat for a time sipping his wine and thinking. There had to be a way. If Lincoln . . . Nay, Lincoln wanted the marriage. And his father was right: if he somehow found her, what had he to offer? If he wed her while still contracted to Cicely of Lincoln, his marriage would be invalid and his children bastards. He closed his eyes briefly and saw how Maud had received her, and then he saw again the terrible bruises inflicted by yesterday's mob. Jesu, he knew not how she could sit her horse, for she could scarce walk. Aye, she must have been terrified to have taken such a beating.

He drained his cup again and flung it to the floor, where it rolled, clattering against the wall. Mayhap it was wrong to go for her, mayhap he should free himself from Lincoln's daughter first. If Gilliane were under the care of nuns, there'd be none to harm her there, and if some miracle happened, if some impediment could be found to bar his contracted marriage, then he could offer her not only his protection but also his name. Aye, he'd find her direction, he'd know where she went, and he'd send money so that she would not be a poor penitent there. But what if she thought to take the veil? He did not think it likely, but then, he'd not thought she'd leave him. And then he realized that even if she had such an intention, 'twould be a year and more before she'd be received into any order.

With that comforting thought, he rose and walked to the door. Guy, who hunched over a table in earnest conversation with his own squire, looked up.

"Your pardon, Papa. I should not have accused you."

"You were overwrought."

"Aye." He moved into the room and reached to take a piece of cheese from the table. "I am decided to order a search for Gilliane, but I do not mean to go after her yet." He waited as Guy digested this sudden change, and then he nodded. "Aye—I am for Lincoln."

"Lincoln," Guy echoed, stunned.

" 'Tis time I became acquainted with Thomas of Lincoln and his daughter, I think."

27

It was St. John's Day—June 24, 1136, the day she'd chosen for her meeting with Simon of Woodstock. Gilliane rose early and dressed with care, choosing a plain blue gown and girding it about her waist with the golden chain Richard had given her at Christmas. Her red hair had grown past her shoulders now, but it still lacked the length to braid it properly. For a moment she considered weaving the false hair into it, but then it seemed somehow wrong to do it.

As the sun climbed higher in the sky, she began to worry that he would not come after all. And part of her feared he would. She paced the small cell, composing what she wanted to say to him. It would be difficult, she knew, for what man would accept such an offer? A landless man, she told herself fiercely, bolstering her flagging courage.

For ten long days she'd waited, torn between hope and doubt. And more than once she'd wanted to turn back, to seek out Richard of Rivaux and take what she could of life. Aye, and if she'd been the only one to consider, she would have done that. But there was Cicely of Lincoln and there was her own babe.

She heard riders then, and her heart stopped as it always did when any approached, but this time it was no large retinue to remind her of Richard of Rivaux. She drew her bench beneath the small high window and stood to peek outside as two men entered the walled courtyard. Nay, it was not Richard. These

men were shabby in comparison, dressed in dark
tunics pulled over dull and mottled mail. The one
lead dismounted, tying his horse to the iron ring in
the wall, and removed his battered helm. It was
Simon of Woodstock come on the appointed day.

His blond hair seemed lighter in the summer sun,
and his face darker, as though it had been weathered in sun and heat and rain. He looked toward the
bell tower, squinting upward, and then he frowned.
Leaving his companion behind, he walked slowly,
limping slightly, to the building where she waited,
and she could hear him ask of the prioress and be
directed there.

It was not long ere they came for her, their disapproval written on their faces. She smoothed damp
palms over her gown, drying them, and then took a
deep breath before following the two nuns down the
narrow corridor. And for the first time she believed
he'd deny her.

"Lady Gilliane."

The prioress, a dour woman who'd received her
grudgingly enough, motioned her forward. Turning
to the man who waited, she offered, "You may be
private here until the bells ring sext." And to Gilliane
she murmured almost by afterthought, " 'Tis Simon
of Woodstock who seeks speech with you." Brushing
past her so close that the rough cloth of her habit
touched Gilliane's gown, she left, closing the door
after her.

"Simon."

He started to kneel, but went only half down on
one knee, apologizing, "My leg was wounded in a
skirmish this spring and has not yet fully healed."

She took in his bared head, noting the sprinkling
of white with the blond, and passed a nervous tongue
over dry lips. "You look well."

"As well as can be in Clifford's keep."

"He is a hard lord?"

"He is a lean master who keeps his money to
himself. Thrice he would have cheated me of my

due had I not complained. But no matter." His blue eyes seemed oddly pale against his bronzed and lined skin. " 'Twas not to inquire of Clifford that you sent to me, I think."

"Nay." She clasped her hands together and then unclasped them, seeking to find the words to broach her business with him.

He cleared his throat, his own discomfiture obvious, and looked at her. "You look well also, Demoiselle."

"Simon . . ." She sucked in her breath and then let it out in a rush, blurting out, "You once asked me to wed with you, did you not?"

He stared and then nodded warily, wondering where she led him. "Aye, and I had not the right."

"But you loved Beaumaule," she prompted him.

"Aye."

"Rivaux has rebuilt part of it, Simon, but there is still more to finish." She turned her back to him, not wanting him to see her face as she confessed, sighing, "You once asked what Rivaux would have of one whose lands could scarce be bled."

"I should not have spoken thus."

"Aye, you should, for you were right." She closed her eyes for a moment and plunged ahead baldly. 'He wanted me for leman, Simon, and God forgive me, but I went willingly."

"And now you are here—he tired of you." The flatness in his voice betrayed that he took it for fact, that he did not question.

"Nay, I fled. Simon, would you have Beaumaule still? Would you wed and give your name to the babe I bear for the sake of Beaumaule?" As the silence between them grew until she could not stand it, she turned back to him. "I'd not bear a bastard, Simon, and I have Beaumaule to give."

In all of his years of warring and surviving, he'd thought he had seen and heard almost everything, but he could only gape at the girl before him now. Two things assaulted his rational mind: she offered him land and she carried another man's child. But his heart still leapt in his breast, and he knew he wanted her still. But he'd not appear too eager—no if he'd be master of her rather than her servant in this. And he'd punish her for what she brought to him.

"All a man leaves this world when 'tis done is his blood," he answered carefully. "Does Rivaux want the child?"

"He does not know of it, and I'd not send a bastard to live where there will be legitimate heirs. If 'tis a son, I want him to have Beaumaule."

"God's bones! And what am I, then—the mantle that cloaks your babe?"

"You will rule Beaumaule, Simon," she answered softly. "And you will claim my child for your son or daughter. If 'tis a son, your name will go on, and if 'tis a girl, then your blood will rule."

He faced her, taking in the bright hair and the soft, delicate skin, knowing that she would make him the envy of any man. "You will lie with me then?"

She swallowed, fighting the gorge that rose in her throat, and nodded. He moved closer and she steeled herself not to back away. A shiver of apprehension traveled down her spine as his callused hand cupped her chin, forcing her to look into his eyes, eyes that burned now with recognizable desire.

"You will be wife to me and lie with none other?"

"If we are wed, I will honor my vows."

His mouth came down on hers, and his mail-clad arms wrapped around her, crushing against her spine. There was no gentleness, no tenderness in this first kiss between them—only a hardened warrior's physical need. She stood still within his arms, letting him take what he would, and tried not to cry out as his mouth bruised hers.

When at last he released her, his breath came in harsh rasps. "Aye, Gilliane de Lacey, I'd be husband to you."

"So be it."

He looked down, his gaze falling to his shabby

clothes. "I'd have a bath and a barbering, but I've naught else to wear. You find the new master of Beaumaule yet a poor man, Demoiselle."

"I have sewn a tunic for you whilst I waited—aye, and chausses also."

"You knew I'd take you."

"I thought you'd take Beaumaule."

" 'Tis more than Beaumaule I'd have," he reminded her as his face twisted into a semblance of a smile. 'Aye, and I'd wed here today. I'll send Aldred into town to seek lodging for us for tonight, but we will have to travel to Beaumaule on the morrow."

"Aye."

He turned to leave, then stopped in the narrow door, his back to her. "And when does this son of my name arrive? Will all count and know?" he asked, his voice tinged with a bitterness he could not hide.

"Between Christmas and the new year, I think."

"I'd save my given name for the second one then. This one you can call any but Richard and I will not care."

"Simon?"

"Aye?"

"When we are at Beaumaule, I'd not have it known—I'd have my people think 'tis your child I bear."

An almost derisive snort escaped him. "I doubt me he will be blond." Then, realizing she could well change her mind, he added, "But I will spread it about that my mother was dark also."

"And I'd have you send for Alwina. She is at Celesin still, for Ri . . . for 'twas thought she was too old to travel to London."

"Aye." For some reason, that pleased him. He would be lord of Beaumaule when he had the priest write to demand the return of the woman. "Aye," he repeated.

Gilliane stood still for a time after he left, and felt a sense of unease about what she had done. Finally, telling herself that she was in no way worse than most of her class, that few had any choice in a husband, she shook off her misgivings. At least her babe would inherit Beaumaule.

Gilliane knelt beside Simon of Woodstock in the chapel of St. Agnes to receive the priest's blessing. Unlike Richard, who would wed Cicely of Lincoln amid great pomp and ceremony, she'd given her vows at the church door before asking God's blessing. She closed her eyes and prayed that in this hard, silent man beside her she would find something to love.

It was over quickly, this wedding devoid of ceremony, and she was wife to Simon of Woodstock for good or ill. The priest brought forward the marriage lines to sign, and she managed to scratch "Gilliane de Lacey, once Demoiselle of Beaumaule" beneath where the priest had noted "Simon of Woodstock, his mark."

They emerged into the priory courtyard, where the sun shone with a brightness that belied the sadness in her heart. Aldred and Garth led forward two horses apiece, while the prioress bade her good-bye and Godspeed, admonishing her to be a good wife and please God. Impatient to be gone, Simon cupped his hands and boosted her onto her horse, then mounted his own.

At the inn where he'd taken lodging in the stable loft, they shared a meal of roasted duck, cheese, and bread, washed down with ale, and he spent the last pennies in his purse, saying 'twas fitting as 'twas the only time he meant to wed. Then, to let the loft cool from the summer's heat, they walked through the town, winding through the merchants' stalls along a riverbank. Stopping to admire a bright silk scarf, he dug deeper within his purse and drew out a small broken brooch.

"The stones can be pried from it," he told the fat merchant who displayed his wares. "And I'd have that scarf for my lady."

" 'Tis not enough."

Simon's jaw worked as he fought his temper. "Nay, but 'tis a bridegift for her."

The fellow behind the table took in Simon's weather-roughened skin and his callused hands and relented. "Aye, 'tis fitting for a pretty lady." He dropped the broken brooch into the box where he kept his money and held out the scarf to Gilliane. "God's blessing on you this day, lady."

Despite the heat, Simon insisted on tying the scarf around her hair, saying that a married woman ought not to go about uncovered like a peasant. His hand dropped proprietarily to her shoulder, and she tried not to draw away, telling herself that she had given him the right to do what he would with her. But as she felt his rough palm catch in the cloth of her gown, she could not help but think of Richard.

They walked back to the inn slowly as the sun lowered, stopping to eat the rest of the cheese and bread he'd bought, and then climbing the ladder to the loft. It was still hot, and the straw felt steamy beneath her feet. Garth opened the wide doors used to pitch the hay into the courtyard below, and a warm breeze blew across, stirring dust in the closeness of the half-dark room. Aldred unrolled two pallets, setting one next to Garth's and the other near the open doors. It was then that the enormity of what she'd done came home to her—she'd share Simon of Woodstock's vermin-ridden sack of straw this night.

He looked up, catching her stricken look, and it angered him. "Nay—I paid a woman at Clifford's keep to wash and refill it ere I came. I like fleas no more than you."

Outside, the street grew quiet save for an occasional cart, and the summer insects hummed loudly. Below, the horses milled within their stalls, waiting as the ostlers pitched fresh hay and carried water to them. Gilliane moved to the loft doors, cooling herself in the breeze, and looked down into the darkened yard.

Behind her, Simon stripped eagerly, hungering for the feel of her flesh beneath his. For years at Beaumaule he'd watched her from afar, not daring to think of her thus, but now she'd turned to him, now she was to be his. And for this brief time he forgot that she came not a virgin to him, that she carried another man's child. Instead, he watched her gown billow from her body and his mouth was dry with desire.

"Come to bed."

He stood there like a stallion ready to mount a mare. She blinked, closing her eyes, as her face reddened with the realization that he expected her to lie with him in the presence of Garth and Aldred. When she did not move, he walked closer, bending so close she could smell the ale on his breath. His hand reached for the chain at her waist, unhooking it, as his other arm slid around her shoulders. Richard's golden girdle fell at her feet.

"Please." She swallowed hard, fighting revulsion at the crudeness of his embrace. "Nay, I cannot—not before them. I—" She tried to bring her hands up between them, pressing against his chest. "Oh, sweet Mary, but I cannot."

"Leave us then," he ordered over his shoulder, still holding her. Then, as their footsteps could be heard on the ladder rungs, he released her, staring at her with glittering eyes. "Take off the gown."

"Nay, I—"

" 'Tis my right, Gilliane—I've not given my name for naught."

"Aye, but, Simon, 'tis so sudden, and—"

"You cannot say you have not known a man before," he gibed cruelly, stung that she did not want him. His hand reached to cup a breast through the softness of her gown and he leaned to kiss her. "Take it off," he croaked as his mouth left hers.

This then was the price she paid for her babe. She turned her back to him and pulled off her gown, shivering in her undershift despite the heat. "Lie down and I will come to you," she whispered. "You will have your right."

She slipped the thin cambric over her head and walked to where he'd taken to his pallet. And despite the rebellion of every fiber of her being, she dropped to her knees beside him. She could hear the sharp intake of his breath and then felt him pull her down against the hard, lumpy pallet.

Willing herself not to cry, she let him explore her body roughly with his callused hands as they moved covetously over her shoulders, her back, and her hips. His mouth grew hot and insistent, his breath came in gasps. Without waiting for her acquiescence, he rolled over her and forced her legs apart with his knees, taking full possession of what his name had bought. She stiffened at the first hard thrust and then fell slack, lying beneath him passively until his body collapsed, his passion spent. There were no love words, no gentle easing when he left her. He rolled off as abruptly as he'd mounted her, and he lay staring upward into the darkness.

"I have lain with penny whores who have pleased me better," he muttered finally.

She swallowed back tears of humiliation and tried to conciliate him. "Simon, 'twas too soon. I cannot just—"

"I'll warrant you lay better for him. Aye, I doubt you lay like stone for him." He turned on his side to face her and twisted her hair cruelly, forcing her to look at him, and his eyes were hard in the darkness. "The time will come, wife, when you moan and pant beneath me as much as for your highborn lover— d'ye hear me?"

"Aye, and so will Garth and Aldred."

"I care not." He lay back, silent for a time, and then turned his back to her. "Get some sleep—'tis a long way to Beaumaule," he growled finally.

She turned away, seeking as much distance as possible on the narrow pallet. Tears spilled onto her cheeks and rolled unchecked as she dared to remember another time, another, kinder lover.

28

After years of poorly rewarded service in other men's households, Simon of Woodstock reveled in his newfound status as lord to even a small keep. Almost immediately he set about enforcing his authority over his wife, her land, and her people. From the moment they first sat outside Beaumaule's newly repaired gates, Gilliane realized she'd made his obsession reality.

He reined in, drinking in the sight of the small castle thirstily, straining forward in his saddle to admire what to another man would be as naught. Gilliane watched his pride lighten what had been a grim face most of the ride, and she followed his gaze. Even from the distance, she could see that Richard of Rivaux had ordered much done, for the blackened stakes of the old stockade were gone, replaced now by a new rock curtain wall that extended further out than the old one to take advantage of a rise in the terrain. And above the wall itself, Beaumaule's lone square tower still stood, its soot-blackened walls keeping vigil over less than one hundred hides of land.

"I mean to get back what your father and brothers lost," Simon said finally. "Aye, I will make Beaumaule what it once was. I'd be lord of more than this."

"Rivaux has done much," she murmured, scarce attending him as she studied the new wall.

"Rivaux—Rivaux," he mimicked sarcastically. "He has not done one-tenth of what Simon of Woodstock will do."

"His pennon still flies here." Her heart lurched at the sight of the familiar black hawk peering down from its crimson banner, and for the first time she worried about her welcome in her own keep.

" 'Twill not fly there long," Simon muttered grimly. "Aye, I'd have naught to remind me of Rivaux here."

"Stephen confirmed him as my guardian."

His eyes narrowed, growing cold as they raked over her. "Your husband guards you now, Gilliane de Lacey. And I'll not wear the horns of a cuckold for you."

"And you'll not speak to me thus," she responded with equal coldness. "Without me, you'd have no claim to Beaumaule."

"I mean to have it all, Gilliane—the land and you."

He turned away from her, leaning across his pommel to watch the few sheep that grazed on the gentle slope of a grassy hill, and his expression changed abruptly. It was as though he counted each one, coveting it, letting his eyes wander over the wattle-and-daub huts slowly, exultantly.

"Aye, I mean to have it all—and more," he half-whispered. "I'll not be a beggar in Clifford's keep again."

Then he seemed to catch himself, and straightened. Clicking his reins and nudging his horse with his knee, he approached the closed drawbridge, stopping only at the spiked timber bridge nest. Across the narrow moat, a red-shirted guard hailed him.

"Nay, but who comes?" he called out.

"Simon of Woodstock, lord of Beaumaule by right of marriage to the Lady Gilliane! I am come to take possession of what is mine!"

Had it not been for the authority in his voice, they would probably have laughed at him, for there were but the four of them—two men, one boy, and a girl. But Rivaux's man looked down at them curiously, and then turned to confer with another guard on the wall.

"There is a man here who knows the lady!" he shouted back again. "Have her uncover her hair!"

The muscles of Simon's jaw tightened until they twitched, and his hand went to his sword, an impotent gesture for one on the outside. Finally he nodded. "Show your head," he ordered Gilliane curtly.

"Aye." She lifted off the scarf, baring the coppery waves. Raising her arm, she waved to the men on the wall. "Let us in, good people. 'Tis I—'tis Gilliane de Lacey!"

Simon reached across to knock her arm down roughly. "Nay, but I'd not have you overfriendly," he hissed at her. "You will conduct yourself as befits my lady."

Stung, she retorted, "Art unused to ladies, Simon of Woodstock, and cannot instruct what you do not know."

For an instant she thought he meant to strike her. But at that moment the bridge began to lower, distracting him, and he merely dropped his hand. Taking her reins, he urged his horse in front of hers, leading her into her own keep. And, once inside, when one of Rivaux's men stepped forward to dismount her, Simon brushed him aside to lift her from her saddle.

As she slid down, her body against his, he leaned into her and growled, "I'd have none other touch what is mine, and I'd have you remember that."

"I told you at St. Agnes that I'd honor my vows," she retorted, pushing him away.

"Aye."

For the moment, it seemed she'd pacified him, and he turned to the man he took to be in charge. "You may deliver the keys to the castle to my wife."

The fellow hesitated. "We received no word of your coming, and my lord of Rivaux—"

"She is the last de Lacey," Simon snapped, "and you cannot deny her right to be here—nor mine as her husband."

"Aye, but—"

"Simon . . ." Gilliane laid a restraining hand on his arm and hissed in a low underbreath, "We are but

four, Simon, and have need of their goodwill. Tell
him you will write to Rivaux of Celesin."

"Gloucester is overlord here," he muttered.

"Aye, but he supported Rivaux for guardianship."

"I'd ask Richard of Rivaux for naught."

"There is no other way."

Finally Simon nodded grudgingly and spoke aloud.
"I will write to your lord of what has passed," he told
the red-shirted man. "Aye, and whilst we wait for his
answer, I'd take the lord's lodgings here." The two
guards looked blankly at each other. The one who'd
been silent spat on the ground and considered the
matter. "Well, there's naught but the one tower for
sleeping, sir, and all are bedded there."

"How many?"

"We are but thirty garrison."

"How many from Beaumaule?"

"Seven."

"Jesu! And thirty men built this wall in a matter of
months?" Simon demanded incredulously.

"Lord Richard granted relief from rent for services and the villeins have done the heavy work."

His hand still resting possessively on Gilliane's shoulder, Simon looked around the small courtyard where
the stable, the granary, and the main hall had been
cleared away, leaving a blackened open space where
once they'd stood. A rough shed at the other end now
served for a stable; wooden stalls that had been leaned
against the base of the single tower appeared to be
used for everything else. The second man followed
Simon's visual inspection of the yard and nodded.

"Aye, there is not much left save the tower and the
chapel, is there? Lord Richard has ordered that new
windows be fitted over the chapel and a carved stone
over the boy, but they are not done yet."

Simon noted then the small stakes driven into the
packed earth to mark off portions of the yard. "And
those?"

"A new kitchen and a new hall. We have lived
poorly here whilst rebuilding, but I was told that

Lord Richard himself is determined to build another two towers inside the wall and to connect them with upper walkways. Would you see the drawings he has sent?"

"Nay," Simon muttered tersely. "I'd see to the clearing of a chamber for my lady and myself." Then, looking at Gilliane, he squeezed her shoulder, and his eyes warmed. " 'Tis not meet that she should sleep in a common room with the others. She should have a bed with a mattress of feathers and hangings to keep out drafts."

Clearly, he viewed such a thing as a great luxury, but it nonetheless touched her that he would want her to have it. For the second time in the day and night they'd been wed, she felt sympathy for him. In his own way, he was trying to give her something beyond what he himself had experienced. But later, when she tried to thank him for it, he merely shrugged and said if she had no stature in the keep, then he had none.

While Simon sought out the garrison's chaplain for the purpose of drafting a letter to Richard of Rivaux, Gilliane unpacked his meager possessions, carefully folding his two tunics and laying them within the ancient cabinet. Despite all that had passed since that cold December day, she felt a sense of homecoming as she surveyed the tiny solar she'd once thought relatively fine. But that had been before she'd seen Rivaux or Celesin or the Lombard merchant's house. Yet, despite all she'd seen, Beaumaule was still the place of her childhood, the place where she'd fought and teased and played with brothers and sisters now gone. Her place. Aye, for good or ill, she was mistress of Beaumaule now in fact as well as in name.

The old bed that had been dismantled when she'd left was found and put together with new ropes. And one of the villeins' wives aired and beat the mattress to freshen it, but Gilliane had little hope that it would not still smell of smoke. Her small tasks done, she dismissed the woman and moved about, idly opening and closing boxes and cabinets, thinking she would have to see what, if anything, of Geoffrey's could be made to fit Simon. In the last box there was a scrap of the crimson velvet and some tiny pieces trimmed from the precious vair, remnants of the cloak she'd sewn so carefully for Richard. She stared, thinking it seemed so long ago now, that so much had passed since then.

She heard heavy steps on the stairs and hastily closed the box, turning around guiltily as Simon stooped to clear the low archway of the door. He stood, not speaking, watching her.

"Did you send your message?" she asked warily.

"Aye, and if the priest wrote what I asked, I expect to hear again from Rivaux of Celesin forthwith." He stepped into the room, kicking a bench aside. "The fellow didn't want to write what I asked."

Her stomach knotted uncomfortably, but she managed to keep her voice calm. "You should have brought it to me—I'd have written it for you."

"Aye, I'll warrant you would," he gibed. "Would you tell him that you lie with me now, that you've given his bastard my name?"

"I'd not have him know of it, Simon. I'd not have you tell him."

"Aye," he sighed. "And I did not. I'd not have it said that the babe you bear is not mine—I'd have no man's pity."

"What did you write to him, then?"

"I told him that I wedded you and that I'd be lord of Beaumaule now. Aye, I said all that was right and meet to say, Gilliane, but it pained me to say it." He moved closer and reached to twist a strand of copper hair around his finger. And he felt her flinch at his touch.

"God's blood, but is he that different from me?" he demanded, pulling her head closer by the hair. "I'll warrant that you did not jump away when he touched you, else you'd not have gotten a babe."

"Simon—"

"This is Simon of Woodstock, Gilliane—not a fool! For six long years I watched you here, and I wanted you even then, but you had no eyes for one beneath you. Aye, you did not even know how many years I had—I was naught but your brother's poor captain then. But now you have as much need of me as I of you, and if you'd have me cover your shame, you'll lie as willing for me as for him." His voice dropped low as he released her hair and let his hand drop to trace the bone along her shoulder, eliciting an involuntary shiver. "Nay, Gilliane, but you'll not deny me what you gave to him."

She was suddenly frightened of the rough man before her, but she knew she dared not show it. Instead, she broke away and moved to the window, hoping he would not follow. "I did not deny you what was your right, Simon."

"I want more than that." He came up behind her and turned her around, forcing her chin up so he could look in her eyes. "I want what you gave Rivaux."

This time she did not flinch. "I had but one maidenhead to give," she answered evenly. "And I have lain with you."

"Lie with me now then, and show me what you did for him. I'd feel you alive beneath me."

She wanted to cry out that she could not, that she did not love him as she loved Richard, but she dared not. But neither could she give him what he wanted. She met his gaze soberly and exhaled slowly. "If I am dead beneath you, Simon, 'tis because my heart is sore. Give me time, and I will be a good wife to you."

"There is no time, Gilliane," he told her hoarsely, his hands moving to her shoulders. "Before your belly grows, I'd like to pretend that mayhap I could have put the babe there—then mayhap I will not hate it as I hate Richard of Rivaux."

His arms went around her, holding her against him, and his mouth sought hers hungrily, his teeth gnashing against hers, forcing her to take his tongue.

For a moment she thought she would gag, for she felt no passion. But she tried; she twined her arms around his neck and molded her body into his, thinking that somehow it would be possible to feel something. But it was as though he was doing what he did to someone else.

His mouth left hers to croak, "I'd have you show me how you lay for him, Gilliane." With one arm still around her, he picked her up and carried her toward the bed. Then, laying her down and working her gown upward to expose her legs, he straddled her and undid his chausses, while very fiber of her body revolted against what he was doing.

It was over quickly—a few angry thrusts and then he cried out. He drew back on his haunches and stared hard into her open eyes. " 'Tis no wonder he left you," he muttered. "Or is it that I am not good enough for you—that you think yourself too fine a lady to lie with me?"

The acute queasiness she'd been feeling rolled over her like a wave, engulfing her. She barely had time to scramble from the bed to vomit into a basin. She leaned over, holding on to the rough stone wall for support as she retched until there was naught left to bring up. He rose from the bed and retied his chausses before dipping a corner of his tunic in water. Pulling it up, he tried to wash her face.

"I am sorry that this crude touch of mine sickens you," he told her bleakly. "I'd not wanted it this way."

She caught her breath finally as the last of the sickness passed and managed to shake her head. "Nay—'tis but the babe."

And in that moment, Simon knew he hated Richard of Rivaux's unborn babe as much as he hated the man. Between the two of them, they'd cheated him of his dreams.

29

It did not take long to discover that Richard's greatest ally was Cicely of Lincoln herself. Although the earl had welcomed him openly, his daughter was far more subdued and disinclined to his company. In fact, whenever it appeared likely that she would be expected to entertain him, she managed to plead illness, so much so that Lincoln was fast losing all patience with the girl, telling his wife, "If she persists in this nonsense, I will beat compliance into her."

But Richard did not realize the depth of her aversion to the marriage until the second week of his sojourn there, when at supper Lincoln allowed that they'd waited far too long to tarry further—that he'd have the marriage solemnized the day after Lammas, August 2. Richard almost choked on his food, and a quick, covert glance at Cicely revealed that all the blood had drained from her face. For some reason, the girl was loath to wed him.

It took him two more days to discover her alone. As he emerged from the armorer's stall within Lincoln Castle, he caught sight of her crossing between the garden and the kitchen, the skirt of her overgown held up to form a bag for the roses she'd gathered. He hastened to catch up with her, waiting until he was almost even to call out, "Demoiselle, I'd walk with you!"

She started guiltily, releasing her skirt and dropping the roses at her feet. Gallantly he bent to retrieve them, collecting most of them from the ground and handing them to her. She flushed, taking the flowers reluctantly, as though they'd somehow become tainted, and she backed away slightly. It was the first time in his memory that he'd met a girl who had not openly admired him from the beginning.

"If we are to wed, do you not think it wise that we should at least speak?" he murmured, reaching for her elbow. "Come, I'd speak with you where we can be alone."

"I'd not be alone with you, my lord."

His black eyebrow rose slightly. "Am I wrong to think you've no wish to wed me?"

She was very small and delicate, beautiful in a fragile way, and his sun-bronzed hand seemed huge on her arm. She looked down at it as though she were held by a serpent, and then she glanced about them to see if any could hear.

"Nay."

"Then I'd walk alone with you and hear why you have taken me in dislike."

Her color deepened against the fairness of the pale gold hair. "I'd not speak my foolishness to you," she managed, shaking her head.

"Cicely, if you would talk in riddles, I cannot aid you."

"I want no aid of you!" she cried out, wrenching away from him. "Do you think kind words can make me forget what you will do to me?"

"What I will do . . . ?"

She'd started walking quickly away from him, but he was even more curious now. He caught her from behind, pulling her back between the kitchen and the garden wall, covering her mouth as she opened it to cry out. He could feel her whole body shudder beneath his hand.

"Listen to me!" he hissed, his palm still stifling her protest. "I know not what I have done to you, but I am sorry for it." He leaned closer and her eyes widened like a cornered animal's. "Jesu! You think I wish to bed you unwilling? Nay, but I do not wish to bed you at all, Cicely of Lincoln!" He released her then and stepped back, ashamed of himself for frightening her.

"But you will, because 'tis necessary."

It came home to him then what scared her and, God aid him, he meant to use that fear. "Aye, I will have to. A man must have heirs, Cicely."

She looked up, swallowing hard. "Art so big."

"Smaller girls than you have carried babes in their bellies," he reminded her.

"And died."

"You are afraid to wed me because you think you will die carrying my babe?" he asked incredulously.

"Not just that." She glanced downward below his belt and then looked away quickly, repeating, "Art a big man, my lord."

"And you are afraid to lie with me also."

"I have heard Maman's tiring women speak of what happens, and I—"

"And you are afraid I will tear you apart."

This time her face was as red as the roses she carried. "Aye," she whispered, mortified.

He was torn between trying to allay her fears in the case that he did have to marry her and trying to give her such a disgust of him that she straightway refused to wed him. "A marriage is not binding without your consent," he reminded her softly.

"And you think I have a choice in the matter?" she cried, showing more spirit than he'd expected. "Nay, but I do not! When I would speak of this to Papa, he is angered! 'Nay Cecy,' he tells me, 'but I have found you a handsome husband—'tis up to you to please him'—and he will hear no more! Even Maman thinks I should be happy to have a man twice my size in bed," she added with a tinge of bitterness.

"Aye, you are small," he agreed, feeding her fear of him.

"And I have heard you have a wondrous temper, my lord—that you can be as fierce as your father."

"Sometimes fiercer," he admitted. "But so long as you please me, I'll not beat you."

"And that you have killed many men."

"In battle."

"That you tore a man's head from his body with one blow."

"Jesu, which one was that? Did I use Hellbringer or my ax—or did you hear 'twas my bare hands?" he asked, scarce hiding this amusement.

"Hellbringer?"

"Robert of Belesme's sword."

"You carry Belesme's weapon?" She stared at him in horror, wondering whether to believe him or not.

"Aye. Would you wish to see it?"

She shook her head. "Nay, 'twould be accursed."

"Cicely . . ." He tried to speak patiently now, fearing to push her too far just yet. "I am a hard man—as hard as my father before me—but I am no ogre. If we are wed, I will take my rights of you, but I will try not to harm you any more than necessary."

"Can you not delay?" she asked desperately. "Can you not tell Papa that you'd wait?"

"Nay."

"My lord, I'd not wed with you."

"Alas, but there is no help for it—I have to take you or break my oath."

"And what of the de Lacey? What of your whore?" she cried out. "Would you not lie with her instead?"

His eyes hardened, darkening, and the sudden fury in his face backed her up against the garden wall. "Gilliane de Lacey is no whore!" he spat at her. "A whore lies willingly for any man with the penny to pay her, Demoiselle, and that cannot be said for Gilly!" His hand snaked out, grasping one of her blond braids. "But what sort of wife would want her husband in another woman's bed? Wed with me and I will be in yours!"

"And tear me asunder!" Tears welled in her eyes as she looked up at him. "Aye, you will hurt me in the taking, and make me bear sons for you!" She slid down slightly and slipped beneath his arm as he released her hair. "I do not want to wed with you!" she flung at him as she ran away.

"You tell the wrong man!" he shouted after her. He looked down at the spilled roses on the ground and felt an overwhelming ache for Gilliane de Lacey. Bending down, he picked one up and crushed it between his thumb and forefinger, rubbing it until he smelled the sweetness that reminded him of the rosewater on her copper hair. And he wondered if she missed him too.

Supper had ended, and the harpers played whilst the jongleurs tuned their lutes and vieles in a corner of the hall. Richard beckoned a servant over to pour him more of the honeyed wine and then sat back to sip it pensively. At his side, Cicely of Lincoln remained silent, staring at the huge signet ring on his hand. Throughout the meal he'd taken every opportunity to emphasize what she feared most—his size. He'd laid his hand next to hers, had brushed against her arm while cutting her meat in her trencher, and had moved his thigh to touch where her gown lay over her leg. And each time, she'd recoiled. Telling himself that he did it as much for her as for him, he played the lover she did not want.

A page approached Lincoln and whispered to him something about "a man from Beaumaule," only to be shunted away with a frown. But Richard's interest was piqued on the instant.

"Beaumaule? God's bones, but I'd hear any who comes from there, Thomas."

" 'Tis but a messenger." Lincoln shrugged and motioned the boy back. "Bring him here, then."

Richard recognized the man wearing his colors immediately and beckoned him forward, certain that he brought ill news—that Brevise had attacked again before the earlier damage was repaired. The fellow pulled off his red felt cap and went down on bended knees to deliver Simon of Woodstock's letter.

Breaking the wax at the end, Richard opened it and began to read, his face darkening as his eyes traveled down the page. Heedless of his host or the company, he exploded with a string of oaths that bordered on blasphemy and rose furiously, knocking the bench from behind him with such force that it flew off the dais.

"I will kill him! Afore God, I will! Jesu, but the impudence of the man!" His fingers shook as he scanned the letter again, and then he flung it away. "He'll not keep her—not so long as there is breath in this body!"

"My lord—"

He turned on Lincoln with full fury then. " 'Tis because of this accursed marriage that she left me! Nay, I'll not stand for it, d'ye hear? He can wed her, but he cannot keep her!"

The hall lapsed into stunned silence as he pushed past those still seated at the long trestle tables and left. Everard of Meulan rose from his seat toward the back of the hall and followed him. Lincoln bent to pick up the discarded letter, then signaled to his steward to bring on the jongleurs while he read. Turning to his wife and daughter, he could not contain his glee at Simon's message.

"You need fear the witch's spell over him no longer," he chortled. "Aye, the whore of Beaumaule has wed!" He sat back in his high-backed chair and reread Simon of Woodstock's curt message. "And whether it angers him or no, there's naught Lord Richard can do about it." Leaning past his wife to address his daughter, he crowed, "Aye, Cis, but the last impediment to your marriage is gone. When young Rivaux realizes she is lost to him, he'll wed."

The girl blanched and her supper rose from her stomach. Covering her mouth, she left the table and ran for the door. Lincoln stared after her in disbelief. "God's blood, woman, but your daughter acts as though good news makes her sick. 'Tis time you schooled her in what is expected of one who will be twice a countess! Aye, and I'd have you cease filling her head with foolish notions," he grumbled, turning back to his wine.

His own countess sighed, cognizant of the ingratitude of the girl. "She would be a nun, she says."

"A nun!" he fairly howled with indignation. "A nun! Madam, you have raised a fool! Look at the man—sweet Jesu, but there's not a maid in Christendom who'd not have him if he had nothing! Nay, but your daughter has no wits!"

The morning was still early when the Earl of Lincoln was summoned to his daughter's bed, and his temper was already strained. A brief unsatisfactory interview with his prospective son-in-law had been for naught, and the young man was leaving for Celesin forthwith. That he found Cicely lying amid pillows with a basin beside her, looking as wan as if she'd been ill a month and more, was almost more than he could bear.

"Get out of that bed and bid your betrothed farewell with a pleasant countenance," he growled. "I'd have him come back for the wedding ere long. Aye, and if he does not choose a day soon, I will appeal to King Stephen."

"I am too sick, Papa."

"Pinch her cheeks and put on her best dress—I'd have him remember her thus," he ordered her tiring woman.

"Nay." Cicely lifted her hand and let it fall wanly. "I am sick, I tell you."

He moved closer, eyeing her suspiciously. "You were well enough yesterday."

" 'Twas supper mayhap."

"You ate of the same trencher as Rivaux."

"I feel as though I am poisoned, Papa. Nay, but I cannot be in the same place with him without this, I tell you." She raised up to spit into the foul-smelling mess in the basin. "I'd not wed him."

"Aye, you will. I have a contract—"

"He sickens me, Papa—he frightens me!"

"God's blood, girl! What nonsense is this?" Lincoln exploded. "You'll get out of that bed if I have to pull you out! Aye, and you'll dress in your finery and—"

"Nay, I will not."

"Leave her be, Thomas," the countess spoke up. "Would you have him see her whey-faced and ill ere he leaves? He does not appear overeager for the match as it is," she reminded him. "Would you give him cause to withdraw, saying she is unhealthy?"

" 'Tis no cause!" he snorted. "There's naught wrong with the girl that a good beating would not cure!"

"Aye," she agreed mildly, "but will he know that?"

While he doubted it possible to annul the betrothal on such grounds, since the girl was neither diseased nor badly blemished, he had to admit that Rivaux might attempt it. "Very well," he snapped. "Then let her stay abed until she is well. But I warn you, Cecy, that I mean to send to Rivaux as soon as you are well, demanding that he honor his oath to take you."

"Aye, Papa," she managed weakly.

He moved closer, reaching to touch her head, which was cold and clammy, and then looked into the contents of the pan and nearly retched himself. " 'Tis but something you ate," he muttered finally, retreating.

The countess followed him out, leaving Cicely with the woman who had attended her since her birth. The girl pulled herself up in bed. "Take this away—I know not where you got it, but it smells."

" 'Tis the gorge of a man who had too much wine."

Cicely pulled out the wet cloth from beneath the covers and tossed it onto a bench. "Well, I think they believed me, Ada."

"Aye—this time. But he will come back, Demoiselle."

"And when he does, I shall take to my bed again—if I have to spend the next three years in this bed, I'll not wed him. I'll not be torn apart bearing babes for a man whose temper frightens me. Ever have I been the dutiful daughter, but I cannot do this. Nay, but I will be sick at Lammas also."

30

Autumn came to Beaumaule, bringing it with cooler, crisper weather that made Gilliane's pregnancy easier to bear. The sickness had subsided, but her belly had grown and the child had quickened within her, taking on new meaning to her. As she could feel it move, she began to love it intensely, praying daily for its safety and health.

And a big belly was not without its blessings, for as she grew ungainly, Simon ceased making demands on her body, turning his attention fully to Beaumaule itself. She rose, restless now despite the fact that she had a full two months more to wait, and walked to the narrow window. The cool, almost chill breeze blew her skirts about her legs as she surveyed the changes he had made.

The moat was wider, deeper now, having been dredged completely and refilled. And a new garde-robe had been built out over the side of the tower, flushed by new pipes that had been built into the wall from the cistern above it. Wooden scaffolding embraced the beginnings of another tower, and fresh lumber still smelling of its sap lay seasoning in the yard for next spring's rebuilding of those structures that had burned. Simon worked ceaselessly—she could not deny that—lavishing all of his love and care on Beaumaule, taking all his pride in the keep.

Already new timbers crossed like skeletal ribs ready for a roof where the old hall had been. She felt a pang of regret remembering how she'd met Richard

there, the way he'd looked as he pulled her after
him, his face cold and impassive beneath the shadow
of his nasal. She'd thought him the enemy then. But
he was neither cold nor an enemy—not then anyway.

His reply to Simon had been terse—he'd ordered
his small garrison to fall back to Ardwyck for the
winter, leaving the protection of Beaumaule to "Simon of Woodstock, husband to the Lady Gilliane."
That was it—there'd been no recriminations, no other
word even. The only others who'd appeared to be
interested in Simon's assumption of lordship over
the keep had been Stephen, who'd charged him but
five sheep in relief or inheritance tax, and Brevise,
who'd taunted him with "You and the whore you
have wed cannot hold it once Rivaux is gone."

For once, Simon had shown sense over pride and
sought out Gloucester, giving his oath and securing
the earl's writ of protection, a copy of which he'd
had carried to Brevise. So long as Gloucester remained in England and continued his uneasy truce
with Stephen, Brevise dared not move against them.
But as always, rumors of an impending rift abounded.

Reluctantly she closed the shutters against the breeze
and turned back to her needlework. She sewed almost incessantly now, making things for her babe,
the finest things she dared afford for this son of
Rivaux. What she could not obtain in fabric, she
made up for in intricate embroidery, taking care that
each small garment had lavish borders.

"You'll go blind without light."

Simon came in and pulled up a bench to watch
her, keeping his eyes on her hair and the chiseled
profile of her face. He could not bear to look lower
now, and he longed for the day when she no longer
carried the unwelcome reminder that Rivaux had
had her first. He burned now, burned with the wanting of her, but whenever he ran his hands over the
swell of her belly, whenever he felt the kicking of the
bastard within, he felt so cheated that the lying with
her was worse than the wanting. He rose and moved

behind her, where he could no longer see the advancing pregnancy.

His callused hand smoothed the red hair that shone like a torch in the dimness of the room. "I think your hair is what I like best," he murmured. "I was used to dream of it even when you were but a little maid."

She tensed, fearing that he meant to bed her, and he felt it. "Nay, I would not," he muttered, dropping his hand. "I will wait until you drop your bastard."

He'd long since fallen into the habit of referring to her babe thus when they were alone, and it rankled her. "My bastard," she reminded him evenly, "is all that ensures your lordship here. Were there no child, there'd be no claim."

"I'd get my own babe of you."

"Simon, 'twas the bargain we made—you accept my babe and gain Beaumaule."

"Aye, but I did not know it would be like this. I did not know that the babe would be all to you, and I would be as naught."

"You have Beaumaule."

"I want no more than that."

It was the way he said it more than what he said. There was a yearning there that she could recognize, for 'twas what she herself had felt when she knew Richard would wed. And she felt guilty for what she could not give him. "Aye," she sighed. "Mayhap when the babe comes 'twill be different between us."

"Aldred asked me what I would name it," he mused aloud.

"They think it your right."

"Even the old priest says it should be named for me, Gilliane, but I could not bear it."

"What did you tell him?"

"I said I've leave it to you, that I thought you meant to name it for one of your brothers that died, and that I did not object to it."

"Simon, 'twill be yours by birth—there's naught you can do now to deny it. Holy Church holds that unless it can be proven that we did not lie together in the year before its birth, 'tis yours."

"Aye."

"I'd have you cease calling it my bastard then."

Her needle darted expertly, making bright, intricate stitches around the neck of the tiny bleached linen shirt. With an effort he tore himself away from her and dropped again to sit on the bench. Even though he was lord now, even though he could claim Gilliane, the gulf between them was as wide as ever, and he felt it acutely.

"How much longer?"

"Until the babe comes?"

"Aye."

"I have hopes of Christmas. Alwina says she judges 'twill be then."

"Jesu! 'Tis two months and more," he complained.

"Lady Gilliane?"

Both of them turned to where one of Beaumaule's men stood in the stairwell. When Gilliane nodded, he emerged to hand her a parchment case. Irritated that there were still those who looked to her, Simon reached across to take it, opening it.

"Fetch the priest."

"Nay, I can read it," she murmured, her heart leaping as she recognized Richard of Rivaux's seal.

"From whence does it come?" he asked.

"I know not," she lied, fearing she'd not see it again.

That she could read and he could not bothered him greatly, and he did not like to be reminded of it. But there was no telling how long it would take to find the old priest, nor how long it would take that ancient to climb the tower stairs. He handed it over and waited.

"Nay, read it to me even as you read it to yourself," he ordered.

But she was already racing ahead, paling as she read. It was not until she realized that he meant to take it from her that she cleared her throat and began again, trying to keep her voice even and her hands from trembling.

To Simon of Woodstock, lord of Beaumaule, greetings. Be it known now and from this day forward that Robert Fitzroy, Earl of Gloucester, has ceded to Richard of Rivaux, lord of Celesin, Ancennes, Ardwyck, and lesser possessions, the suzerainty of Beaumaule for the sum of two hundred pounds, transferring all rights of fees, aids, and guardship to him.

Be it further known that Richard of Rivaux accepts homage for the manor of Beaumaule no later than Christmas Day, 1136, at Ardwyck.

Attested to this day, 20 October 1136, by Bertrand de Geurlin, clerk to Richard, Rivaux of Celesin, witness his seal affixed.

"Rivaux is overlord here? Nay, I'll not believe it!" He snatched the parchment away from her, staring at it as though he could read, and then he left in haste to seek the priest. Gilliane sat still, too shaken to think. And then it slowly took on meaning. Richard of Rivaux sought revenge for what she had done. As suzerain to Beaumaule, he would still have power over her.

His fears confirmed by the priest, Simon spent the better part of a day and a night considering what Rivaux could possibly want with Beaumaule, particularly what he could want enough to spend two hundred pounds to get. And over and over again, the only answer he had was Gilliane. It was not enough that the rich and powerful lord had had her first, it was not enough that he'd gotten his babe on her— nay, but he must want her still.

And, as the second day wore on, his sense of ill-usage grew, redirected at his wife. Everything that he would have of her, he got after Rivaux—her body, the heir, Beaumaule. He drained the wineskin he'd been nursing steadily since morning and lurched to his feet. Weaving, he managed to climb the tower stairs to the solar.

She was sewing again, another garment for her precious bastard, no doubt. With an effort, he walked across to where she sat and reached to take it from her. It was a beautifully worked christening gown made of softest cambric, bleached white as snow and trimmed at neck, sleeves, and hem with tiny gold leaves.

"You waste gold thread on your bastard," he muttered thickly, tossing the gown to the floor.

"Your heir," she reminded him firmly as she leaned to retrieve it. " 'Twould be remarked if we did less."

"My heir," he mimicked sarcastically. "Aye, a black-headed whelp that all will know cannot be mine."

"None will gainsay him if you do not."

"I'd have you sew for me instead, Gilliane—aye, I'd have you make me something half so fine. I'd not put my hands between Lord Richard's at all, but if I must, I'd not go as a beggar."

"I have made you much, Simon. You've no cause—"

"Aye, you have made me things fit for Beaumaule! Nay, I'd have something finer!" He ran his fingers through his hair as though he could clear his head, and stumbled toward one of the lacquered boxes that held what she'd brought with her. Strewing her plain gowns about the rushes on the floor, he dug until he found what he wanted. He lifted the one dress she'd been unable to part with, the gold-shot purple samite gown Richard had given her the Christmas before, and held it up to let the light catch the richness of the fabric. "Aye, you have no use for this now, Gilliane—'tis more befitting a countess than a whore."

She flinched and turned away, unable to look again at the gown. But he was not to be denied. Carrying it to fling it against her swollen belly, he stood over her. "When I place my hands between his, I'd wear this—d'ye hear? This!"

"My gown? Sweet Jesu, but I think you mad!"

"Mad? Nay, I'd have him see that I wear what he gave you—I'd have him know you are mine now! You will make me a tunic from this and naught else!" His hand caught in her hair, forcing her head back painfully. "Aye, I'd wear the finery he gave you, Gilliane!"

"Art drunk with wine."

He hit her then, turning her head with the blow and leaving his palm print against her cheek. Both of them stared as she caught at the stone wall behind her bench for balance, and then he was on his knees before her.

"Jesu, Gilliane, but I did not mean—"

"I will make your tunic, Simon."

The flatness of her voice was not lost on him. He leaned forward awkwardly and tried to put his arms around her, pressing his head against the offending belly. And the babe within protested, shifting beneath his face. "If I could tear this child from you and you would live, I'd do it," he mumbled into her stomach.

"I said I would make the tunic."

She did not move beneath him, but sat very still. "You still love him." It was a statement rather than a question.

"Aye."

"And there's naught you feel for me."

Despite his gibes and the fact he'd just struck her, Gilliane's heart went out to this rough man she could not love. Her hands crept to clasp his head against her, holding him there, and her fingers caressed his graying hair as though they soothed a child.

"It was wrong of me to wed you, Simon. I did but think Beaumaule a fair exchange for my babe, but now I can see 'tis not."

"I'd not lose you—art the only beauty in my life, Gilliane."

"When this babe is born, we have to look forward, Simon. You have to accept it and try to love it as

ours, and I have to accept you are my husband and
ry to bear others for you."

"I know not if I can."

Her hand moved from his hair to the stubble of
his beard. He turned his head into her palm and
ressed a kiss there. "Art the only beauty in my life,"
he repeated, whispering into her hand.

"You've not slept since word came from Rivaux,
Simon," she murmured gently. "Let me undress you
and put you to bed ere you are sick."

He sat back on his knees and nodded, suddenly
embarrassed by his weakness. "Aye."

"And I will make you as fine a tunic as I have seen
even at Stephen's court."

"With gold embroidery and banded sleeves?"

"With whatever you wish."

He lurched to his feet, using her shoulder to brace
himself, and turned away, staggering for the bed. "I
am too tired to undress," he mumbled, falling within
the curtains and lying across the mattress.

Sighing, she picked up the purple gown and
smoothed it lovingly over her rounded stomach, remembering when she'd gotten it. But that part of
her life was over and gone, and she had no use for
such a gown now. Brushing at the lone tear that
dared trickle down her cheek, she reminded herself
that she'd sworn to be Simon of Woodstock's wife for
good or ill. And the skilled seamstress in her looked
critically at the material, seeing now how it could be
cut to fit a man, how it could be embroidered to
show the richness of the cloth to advantage.

31

With the lord gone to pay his homage to Richard of
Rivaux, there was no Christmas chairing and very
little gift-giving at Beaumaule. New robes made by
Alwina and Gilliane were passed out among the household, two sets for each man and woman within the keep,
and a dinner consisting of a roast boar, a stout mut-
ton stew, roasted chickens, fish dumplings, peas and
beans stewed with onions, and dried fruit was served
to household and the invited villeins alike, and then
the soaked bread trenchers were collected for distribution to those too aged or infirm to come. In the
center courtyard, vats steamed with spiced wine and
wassail, and people brought their own cups to dip
from them.

Gilliane ate sparingly, her appetite dimmed by the
room taken by the babe, and withdrew early, leaving
the others to enjoy the traveling jongleur she'd hired
to sing for them. But once in bed sleep did not
come, and she felt slightly nauseous. It was the dumplings, she decided, for she felt the first stirrings of
cramps.

But as they intensified, she suddenly realized her
time had come. She pulled herself up from the bed
and walked, pacing before the fire in the brazier to
ease the pains that crossed her abdomen and settled
in her back. The babe within her ceased the almost
incessant kicking that had plagued her for a week
and more and grew still. She should be afraid, but
she wasn't. A sort of detached calm descended as she

alked back and forth again and again, pressing
gainst her mounded abdomen, rubbing it to ease it
fter each pain. Below, she could hear the music and
evelry of Christmas.

"My lady?"

The old woman, breathless still from climbing the
eep, narrow stairs, stopped at the entrance to the
oom. At that moment Gilliane felt the warm gush of
aters pour forth, soaking her undershift and stain-
ig the rushes at her feet. "I think," she gasped as a
arder pain hit, "the babe comes."

"Aye." Alwina turned back to the stairs and called
ut as loudly as her old voice could manage, "Annys!
nnys!"

Between them, the two women stripped Gilliane's
oaked shift and laid a thick padding of clean rags
ver the mattress before helping her to bed. Alwina
oured water from a ewer into a basin and set it on a
ow table nearby, while Annys cleaned a knife and
laced it on a stack of folded linen. More logs were
ragged to the brazier to warm the drafts that stirred
ie tapestries Gilliane had made for the walls.

The labor was neither swift nor hard. As Alwina
at beside her and cooled her face with wet cloths,
illiane tried to concentrate on relieving herself of
er burden. From time to time, Annys pressed hard
n her distended abdomen, pronouncing that the
me had not yet come. Gilliane's back hurt worse
ian the pains, aching as though it would break, and
ie strained to push downward, ready to be done
ith this.

"In time, lovey," Alwina whispered, wringing out
ie cloth yet again.

Annys washed her hands and felt for the babe's
ead. " 'Tis turned right, but the pains do not come
uickly enough."

"So long as 'tis turned right, 'twill come," Alwina
romised. She went to the cabinet where she kept
er simples and mixed dried pennyroyal with a little
ur wine, carrying it back to the bed. " 'Twill make

the pains harder," she offered, holding the cup to Gilliane's lips.

"Arghhhh." It was bitter and sour at the same time, but somehow she managed to swallow it.

The cock crowed ere Gilliane's stomach tightened as the pains intensified. Beads of perspiration dampened her forehead and were patiently washed away by Alwina. And still they waited.

"Sweet Mary, but I'd sleep," Gilliane murmured. "I tire."

"Aye, but 'tis soon now."

An intense, searing pain racked Gilly then, followed closely by another, and Annys unfolded a sheet of linen and moved to crouch at the bottom of the bed. Biting her lip until it bled, Gilliane grasped at the bedpost and gave one final push, expelling her burden into Annys' waiting hands, and then fell back, exhausted, listening to the indignant wail of new life. Annys picked up the knife and cut the cord carefully.

" 'Tis not over," Alwina reminded her. "Nay, but we are not done." Moving to knead at Gilliane's stomach, she felt for the next few contractions, pressing down to force out the spongy afterbirth. Gathering it into a basin, she examined it. " 'Tis all there—there should be no fever."

Gilliane's eyes were closed and her breathing labored from exhaustion. She'd borne Richard's babe, and it lived. God had given her that at least. She could hear Alwina and Annys washing the child, murmuring as they cleaned the eyes and mouth.

" 'Twas an easy birthing—I've seen none easier," Annys murmured.

"Aye, and God be praised, for 'tis, a daughter."

A daughter. But she'd striven so hard to bear a son. Swallowing hard to hide her disappointment, Gilliane tried to tell herself that it did not matter. The son she'd wanted so badly, Richard's son, would only have made Simon more bitter.

Alwina carried the crying babe back to the bed.

lacing it in the crook of Gilliane's arm. " 'Tis a
retty one. Look on her, for she is much as I remember you."

Already Annys was lifting Gilliane's tired legs, pulling the soaked wadding from beneath her. "Aye, my
lady, but she is as pretty as her mother."

"What do you name her?"

Gilliane forced herself to look down into the face
of the child she and Richard had made. The babe's
feet and hands waved wildly and its whole body
shook as it cried loudly, its face almost purple with
seeming rage. But it was whole. She reached a fingertip to touch the rosebud mouth and was rewarded
by a noisy sucking.

" 'Twill be the morrow before there is milk, but I'd
put her at your breast."

"Nay, I'd look at her."

She reached with her other hand to smooth the
soft, faint reddish down over the small crown, both
saddened and relieved that her daughter did not
have Richard's black hair. The babe stopped crying
and blinked, its slate-colored eyes solemnly regarding her. And suddenly Gilliane did not care that it
was a girl. It was her babe and that was all that
mattered.

"Her birth name," Alwina persisted.

"Amia. Aye—Amia, for love."

"Nonsense," she heard the old woman mutter.
"Born of sin, she should have a Christian name to
guide her."

"One day, Alwina, you will speak too much," Gilliane
retorted. "If Simon does not care what I name her,
you have no complaint." Still awed by what had
come from her body, she looked again at her babe.
"Will she have blue eyes also, do you think?"

" 'Tis too early to tell, but I have hopes of it."

Owing to the ease of the birth, Gilliane healed
quickly, rising from her bed on the second day despite Alwina's dire warnings, refusing to give her

daughter over to a wet nurse. Her milk came and the babe sucked noisily, easing the painful fullness. Gilliane sat for hours stroking the soft hair on the small head, singing softly, reveling in the newfound fulfillment of mothering her child, until Alwina chided her that she would make the babe too demanding.

Finally, she did what she dreaded most—she wrote her husband of the birth, couching the news in the most positive words:

> To my lord husband, Simon of Woodstock, I recommend me to you, and tell you I am safely delivered of a daughter, born with little travail and named Amia in honor of our Lord Jesus, who loves us all. Should you wish to add to her birth name, I'd have you advise me of it.
>
> The child is well, and shows promise of fairness, my lord, although 'tis feared she will have hair as red as mine. And I think her eyes will be blue, even as are yours.
>
> I have given alms to our people in honor of my deliverance, and ten pence to the priest for his good blessing. We await your direction as to godparents and christening.
>
> God return you safely to your wife, Gilliane de Lacey.

Dispatching the letter to Simon at Ardwyck, she gave instructions that it was to be delivered to none other, and she fervently prayed that her husband would not speak of the babe there. It would take too little for Richard to surmise from whence Amia of Beaumaule had come.

Across the room, Annys moved about the solar listlessly, and for the first time Gilliane noted her pallor. She'd been so concerned with her advancing pregnancy and the birth of her child that she'd missed the girl's sickness. Laying the sleeping Amia in her cradle, she rose to study the little maid as she dropped to a bench.

"Art unwell?" she asked solicitously.

The girl's forehead was moist and her face ashen, ut she shook her head. "Nay—'twill pass." But she'd o sooner gotten the words out than she retched iolently, bringing up her supper onto the rushes at illiane's feet. It was then that her mistress remem- ered 'twas not the first time the girl had been sick tely. Turning her head away, Annys stared misera- ly at the floor as Gilliane lifted her skirts and moved sit on the other side.

"Annys . . ."

The girl swallowed visibly and kept her head verted. "Nay, but I'd not speak of it, my lady," she umbled.

"How long since you have had your courses?" illiane persisted.

"I know not—three months mayhap."

"And you are with child." She slid her arm about e girl's shoulders to comfort her. "I'd not have my omen debauched here, Annys—you have but to ame the father to gain a husband."

"I'd not have him," the girl whispered, her voice low that Gilliane had to strain to hear her.

"If you liked him well enough to lie with him, ou'll like him well enough to wed," Gilliane told her rmly. "You cannot wish to bring forth a bastard."

"I have never liked him."

For a moment Gilliane thought she'd not heard ight, that the girl's anguish obscured her words. You have never liked him? Sweet Mary, but—" She opped guiltily, thinking that in her own troubles, e'd failed to protect her serving maid. "Annys," she sked gently, "are you saying he took you against our will?"

Silent tears welled and spilled from the girl's eyes, ickling down her cheeks. Nodding, Annys stared gain into the mess on the floor. "Aye."

Gilliane rose, pacing angrily at the thought that ny would dare ravish a maid in her keep. "Why did ou not come to me? Why did you not accuse him to

me? I would have seen him punished! Sweet Jesu,
but I'd have no maid forced at Beaumaule!"

"Nay—"

"How many times—how many times did he lie
with you against your will?" Not waiting for the girl
to answer, she continued to pace. "Aye, but he will
answer for this! If you want him not, I'll have him
brought before my manor court—aye, he'll appear at
hall-mote and I'll have him castrated for this! I'll not
have a ravisher at Beaumaule!"

" 'Twas not often at first—only when he quarreled
with you."

Gilliane stood still, her stomach knotting within
her. "With me?" she asked hollowly, not wanting to
believe the awful suspicion that was taking root in
her mind.

"But when your belly grew—"

"Jesu!" Gilliane exploded finally. "You accuse
Simon—you accuse *my husband?*"

"I did not come to you because I did not think you
would wish to hear it!" Annys cried out. "And he
said if I told, he'd deny it! That he'd have me sent
away—or condemned for a whore!"

"Does he know of the babe?" Gilliane's voice was
suddenly hoarse. "Did he think to hide it?"

"He knows."

"And what did he say? What said he to this?"

"He said I lied—that I'd been with others." The
girl turned a tearful face to Gilliane, and her voice
rose. "But I have not—I swear I have not, my lady!
And I'd not go to a serf's hovel for this!"

"Of course you will not," Gilliane said soothingly.
She sat down heavily beside Annys and stroked the
girl's thick blond braids. "Of course you will not."

She believed the girl. Too often Simon had flung
out of her solar, saying he'd find a more willing
woman. But he'd found Annys instead, and Annys
had been less than willing.

"I'd not go to a serf for wife." The girl cried softly
now, her face turned against Gilliane's shoulder.

"Nay, lovey, but I'd not let it happen."

"He'll send me away."

"Of a certainty he will not." With a comforting pat, Gilliane straightened the girl away from her. "Nay, dry your tears and seek your bed until you are better. You have naught more to fear of Simon, I promise you."

"He'll beat me," Annys sniffed.

"He will not—he'll not touch you again."

The girl rose uncertainly, hesitating before blurting out, "You do not hate me?"

"Why should I hate you for what you cannot help?" Gilliane countered. "Nay, if any should be faulted, 'tis he."

Gilliane walked to the shuttered window and threw it open, letting the cold, snow-laden air blow in. Drawing a deep breath of it, she remembered how she'd first met Richard of Rivaux. Had he not wed, she'd have stayed with him, warm and secure in his love for her. But instead she'd made a bargain for her daughter, one she now regretted bitterly. The chill wind tangled her hair, whipping it about her face as she stared below at the piece of land that had once been everything to her. Slowly she closed and relatched the shutters, replacing the rags that had shut out the draft.

She crossed the room to where the babe lay, full and warm, in the cradle near the crackling fire. The tiny fingers curled even in sleep, drawn close to the small, perfect face. The red down of her hair contrasted brightly to the pale, lightly veined skin, and the rosebud mouth moved silently, as though she still sucked. Amia of Beaumaule, born of love and claimed as daughter by a man who already hated her.

Dropping to the bench beside the cradle, Gilliane rocked the basket gently, almost absently, and considered what must be done. With her determination to love Simon gone with Annys' revelation, she could not bear the thought that he would touch her again.

And yet a woman could not deny her husband. For a moment she considered fleeing, leaving Beaumaule behind, and taking her babe to Guy of Rivaux. But in doing so, she would openly admit her daughter's bastardy, jeopardizing the babe's claim to Beaumaule.

She sat thinking long, her mind in turmoil. Too many people depended on her now—too many for her to be weak. Nay, but she would fight for her babe, for Annys, and for her people.

32

Richard of Rivaux recognized the gold trim of Gilliane's favorite dress as Simon of Woodstock placed his hands between Richard's, and he felt a surge of anger and bitterness. As he looked down on the bent, graying head, he wanted to draw away, to strike a blow rather than accept the man's oath. The man before him, poor as he was, had what Richard wanted most—Gilliane de Lacey—and he could think of naught else as he felt the callused fingers beneath his. Try as he had, he could not conceive of what had made her prefer Simon of Woodstock over him. Not even marriage seemed enough of an answer. He felt betrayed still, as much now as when he'd heard she'd wed. And those roughened hands that touched his now touched Gilliane de Lacey at will.

Simon, his own hatred of the man who stood above him barely contained, managed to get out the accepted words, muttering so low they were scarcely audible, "I promise by my faith that from this time forward I will be faithful to Richard, Lord of Celesin, Ancennes, Ardwyck, and lesser possessions, and that I will maintain toward him my homage entirely and against every man."

"In good faith and without deception," Everard of Meulan prodded.

His color rising, Simon fought the urge to spit at Richard. "In good faith and without deception," he repeated, adding, "saving in matters that conflict with my allegiance to my lord king, Stephen of England." He felt small relief when the other man's warm palms released his hands.

"So be it, then," Richard managed tersely. Taking the baton from his herald, he tapped Simon's shoulder, intoning in sharp, clipped cadence, "Having received such from my lord Robert FitzRoy, Earl of Gloucester, I hereby invest you, Simon of Woodstock, with the manor of Beaumaule, secured to you and your heirs so long as you keep your faith to me and mine."

Instead of raising Simon according to custom, Richard merely dropped his arms, growling, "I'd forgo the kiss of peace—'tis enough that you have sworn."

It was done, then. Humiliated, Simon struggled to his feet, facing his new overlord. That Richard of Rivaux was of taller stature, physically stronger, and certainly handsomer than he did nothing to improve his temper. He stepped back, his jaw tightening visibly at the insult Richard had offered him.

"I'd return to Beaumaule with your leave," he grunted.

"I'd have your castle-guard here."

Simon was surprised and not a little chagrined at the order. While it was Richard's right to take his feudal obligation in service as part of a garrison or as escort in time of peace, and certainly as soldier in time of war, Simon had not expected to be called so soon. "If it please your lordship, I'd serve later." Then, deliberately baiting the man who rivaled him in Gilliane's heart, he added, "My wife is with child, and I am loath to leave her."

The thought of Gilliane de Lacey's bearing this rough man's babe was almost more than Richard could stomach. Every feeling revolted, and for a moment he thought he'd be sick. He waited, trying to master his rising temper, and lost the battle within.

"You lie!"

"Nay, she bears the heir to Beaumaule," Simon spat back at him.

The desire to punish Simon of Woodstock and

Gilliane overwhelmed him, and he struck out with the means at his disposal, not caring what it would do to him also. "Very well, then," he snapped. "Tend your . . . wife"—it was an effort not to choke on the word—"but afore God, I'll have your service ere the year is out. You'll come to me here again in May, bringing your lady with you then." He turned away, muttering, "I'd not have it said I deprived you of her company."

Simon paled. He'd meant to taunt Richard with Gilliane, but he had no wish to bring her to Ardwyck, where she'd see her lover again. "Nay, the babe—"

"Bring the babe also." Richard caught the disapproval in Everard of Meulan's face and shook his head, dismissing it. "Nay, bring forth the next man who owes me fealty this day."

Surrounded by men loyal to Rivaux, Simon had no choice but to withdraw with what little dignity he could manage. He turned stiffly and walked the length of the long audience hall, hating his new lord and wondering how many there knew he'd taken Richard's leman for wife. And suddenly the rich samite tunic she'd made him counted for naught—he was still but Simon of Woodstock, lord of but Beaumaule. And his wife's lover, the sire of her babe, held power over him now.

"My lord . . ."

He saw the boy Garth waiting for him, his plain cloak wrapped about him, his face ruddy from the cold, and Simon knew why he had come. He held out his hand for her letter, dreading that she'd borne a son. Moving into the small antechamber, he looked to see that none watched him, and then he took the letter case from the boy's hand, opening it.

"Do you know what it says?" he asked, not wanting to admit that he could not read.

"Nay."

"But the babe came?"

"Aye, Lady Gilliane was delivered of a daughter

two days ago at Beaumaule, my lord, and she would have you know of it."

He should have felt relief at the news, but he didn't. Instead, he took the letter and went in search of a clerk who would read it for pay. So the bastard had turned out to be a girl—how that must have rankled Gilliane, who'd probably thought to cheat him of Beaumaule with her babe. Well, she had not, and any sons she bore would now come from him.

He paid a penny to have the fellow read it thrice— once to hear what Garth had already said and twice more to verify that the babe was fair rather than dark. Amia—Jesu, did she think him a fool? Amia for Christ's love? Nay, she'd chosen the name because she yet loved Richard of Rivaux. The daughter he was forced to claim—the daughter he already hated—was named for her love of his new overlord. Aye, and as poor as his Latin was, he knew it.

He left the clerk's small office and almost collided with Everard of Meulan, captain of Rivaux's mesnie. "Ill news?" Everard inquired.

"Nay." Simon rolled the parchment and tucked it inside the neck of his tunic, unwilling to have it known that Gilliane had borne Richard of Rivaux's babe. Aye, even a man-at-arms could count and surmise. Instead, he managed a semblance of a smile. "My lady wife would have me at home."

"How fares she?"

He eyed Richard's captain suspiciously for a moment and then shrugged. "She is as well as can be, I suppose."

"You are fortunate in your lady."

This time, Simon was certain he detected a hint of sympathy in the other man's voice. "Aye," he growled, unable to bear that Meulan knew he had taken Rivaux's leavings.

"Give her my greetings then—tell her she has my regard."

Richard's captain moved on, leaving Simon alone with his resentment. Bring Gilliane here? Nay, but

he'd not do it. He'd not risk being cuckolded for all
to know. He'd say she was unwell—anything to keep
her away from her lover.

"Methinks you like Rivaux no better than I do."

Simon spun around guiltily, wary of the intrusion,
and faced a thin, hake-faced man, who glanced fur-
tively about them before moving closer. "He is overlord to me," Simon responded cautiously.

"Aye, I have taken service with him also."

Curious, Simon stared openly at the man before
him, taking in that he wore the red shirt of Rivaux
over the black hose of a household knight. "Art a
mercenary then?"

"I serve him who pays me best—as should you.
Those of us not born to the wealth of Rivaux must
make our ways as best we can."

"Aye."

"I think him overproud—Guy of Rivaux's whelp—
and without his great sire, he would be as nothing."

"He'd still be rich," Simon muttered.

"A new king can raise a poor man."

The hackles raised on Simon's neck, telling him to
be wary, not to betray his hatred of Richard of Rivaux,
and yet he was intrigued that one of Rivaux's own
men would dare to speak so openly. "How are you
called?" he asked, stalling while he tried to determine a motive.

"Talebot."

"Methinks you are rather bold to speak thus of
your master, Talebot."

"You also like him not."

"Aye."

"You'd not serve him had you the choice," Talebot
persisted.

"Poor men have no choices," Simon retorted bitterly. "We serve whoever claims suzerainty over what
little we have."

"There is always the choice."

The younger man spoke softly, but there was no
softness in the eyes that scanned Simon's face, and

Simon felt a chill, as though he ought to move away. "I put my hands between his—I swore to him. Nay, my feelings mean naught in the matter."

"You swore homage save in matters pertaining to allegiance to your king," Talebot reminded him smoothly.

"I have naught of the king—Beaumaule matters little to Stephen."

"Would you be lord of more than Beaumaule?"

"What manner of question is that?" Simon snorted. "Aye, I'd be lord of the world if 'twere possible. But I am not a fool. If I break mine oath to Rivaux of Celesin, I will not even have Beaumaule."

"Walk apart with me in the yard," Talebot urged. "Aye, but there is more than one small fief to be had, Simon of Woodstock—there are lands for men such as you and me."

Simon drew back, feeling very much like Satan tempted him. "I am not an oath-breaker."

"Whom would you serve first—Richard of Rivaux or Stephen? Who can give you more?"

"Nay."

"If Rivaux were dead, there'd be none to remind you that your lady wife lay with him also."

For a moment Simon considered hitting the man before him. Instead, he turned to walk away. 'Twas too dangerous to listen to such talk.

"My lord of Brevise would reward you—as would the king."

Again the hackles on Simon's neck warned him, but he stopped, unable to resist hearing Talebot's offer. Reluctantly he turned back, knowing he should leave instead. "Aye, I will walk with you, but I'd mistrust Brevise. William of Brevise wants but Beaumaule."

"Nay—he aims higher now."

Talebot held the door and waited for Simon to pass before him. As they traversed the gloomy corridor to the outer steps of the keep, neither man spoke. At the bottom of the stairs Talebot waved away a sentry and turned to Simon. "We cannot be heard here, I think."

"Aye, only a fool would stand outside in the cold."

"A fool or a cautious man."

Talebot's next words stunned him. "Brevise has little interest in the likes of Beaumaule—'tis this keep he would have. Aye, he would share in what Richard of Rivaux leaves after him."

"Then he is the fool!" Simon retorted, disgusted that he'd listened to the man's nonsense. "You yourself said Lord Richard is Guy of Rivaux's whelp!"

"Count Guy will declare for the Empress—King Stephen is certain of it—and when he does, his lands will be forfeit. And the old lion, Roger de Brione, is dead."

"Everyone remembers 'twas Guy of Rivaux that brought down Belesme!"

" 'Twas years ago. Nay, but Count Guy is not so well-known in England—people know not of whom they sing."

"God's bones," Simon muttered, "and this is supposed to concern me?"

"Unless you are a fool also."

"You forget Gloucester. He would rise if any threatened either Rivaux. They are close allies."

"Dead men do not rise—not on earth, anyway."

"King Stephen would move against Gloucester?" Simon stared in disbelief. "Nay, the earl is too powerful."

"Alive." Talebot leaned closer, dropping his voice so low that Simon had to incline his ear to hear. "Stephen will not move openly against him—'twill be treachery."

"It concerns me not."

"Aye, it does. With Gloucester and Richard of Rivaux dead, there are lands, rich lands, to be divided among those who serve King Stephen. My lord of Brevise already offers me ten manors to spy on the whelp. He would do the same for you." He caught at Simon's arm to stay him. "Aye, if you were in his mesnie, when the time is right, you could strike the blow that takes Lord Richard from this world."

Simon shook free angrily. "You would make me an oath-breaker and a murderer!" he hissed at Talebot. "You would rob me of mine honor! I ought to betray you!"

He turned and strode halfway across the courtyard, his heart and mind torn by what he'd heard. Behind him, Talebot spoke clearly. "Nay, you will not, Simon of Woodstock. When all is considered, you will join me."

33

imon thought it odd that Gilliane did not come
own to greet him on his return to Beaumaule, but
hen assumed 'twas because she still ailed from birth-
ng the babe. Taking off his helm and gloves and
ivesting himself of his sword belt, he handed them
o Aldred before crossing the yard to the tower. The
teps were as steep as ever, but there was an eager-
ess to see her that made the climb easier than usual.
lready his pulse quickened at the thought of her,
er body now slender, relieved of the babe that he'd
rown to hate.

She sat as always, drawn close to the light of the
inter sun diffused through the oiled parchment
he'd placed over the unshuttered window, her head
ent over her exquisite embroidery. He stopped, his
houlders just clearing the stairwell before the open
oor, and watched her hungrily. Her red hair was
nbound, still drying from a washing, and it gleamed
rightly where it fell forward over her breasts.

"You should not sit close to the window when 'tis
old," he chided her, his mouth dry with rising de-
ire. "Draw your bench to the fire instead." Negotiat-
ng the last step, he entered the solar.

She looked up then, and he was taken aback by
he coldness in her blue eyes. There was no welcom-
ng smile, no pleasure in his arrival. Setting aside the
loth she stitched, she rose gracefully, and he could
ee by the lacings of her gown that she was as slen-
er as ever—save for the fullness in the breasts. But

instead of walking toward him, she went to the cradle by the fire and picked up the babe, smoothing the soft red hair that fuzzed like down on the small head. For a moment she held the child close, nuzzling it and speaking softly. Then she carried the babe past him, calling down the stairwell, "Alwina! Come tend Mia for now!"

Mia. It sounded neither French nor Latin, but he liked it better than Amia. With an effort, he forced himself to look over her shoulder at the babe, wishing it were his, wishing he could love it.

" 'Tis small," he offered.

"Most babes are."

"I received the letter."

"Aye."

It was as though, close as they were within the room, an abyss gaped between them. He laid a hand on her shoulder, moving the back of it to rub against her neck. "I am glad 'tis fair at least. 'Twill not be said that she cannot be mine."

She ducked beneath him and called down the stairs again, "Alwina!" Then, turning back to him, she eyed him with utter contempt. "Well, I am not—I'd have rather had a dark son."

He groped about for an explanation, something to give meaning to her coldness. "But you wrote—"

" 'Twas before I knew about Annys."

"Annys?" He knew dread then. His stomach knotted, sickening him, but he tried to keep his voice light. "What of her?"

"Sweet Mary! Dare you to ask?" she demanded. Alwina rounded the top step and Gilliane thrust the babe into her arms quickly. "Take her down whilst I speak with my . . . my husband."

Her hesitation was not lost on him, nor was the loathing inflection she placed on the word. He steeled himself, considering how best to excuse what he had done. Stalling for time now, he walked to the brazier and held his cold hands over the fire.

"By rights, you should be castrated!" Gilliane flung

at him. "Aye, you should be taken before the hall-
mote and charged!"

"For what? What lies does the girl tell you?" he
managed to ask, keeping his voice far calmer than he
felt.

"Do not try to lie to me, Simon of Woodstock!"
Her face flushed, she moved to face him across the
fire. "This is Gilliane de Lacey to whom you speak!
For twenty years I have known you!"

He cursed himself for a fool under his breath—he
ought never to have left the girl there. "I know not
what she has told you, Gilliane, but I swear—"

"Do not swear to me! On St. John's day last, I wed
with you, Simon of Woodstock, putting aside all else,
promising to be wife to you and none other!" Her
red hair caught the light from the fire, forming a
soft bright halo about her, making her even more
beautiful. Her voice dropped low, coming as a force-
ful whisper as she reminded him, "Aye, I gave you
Beaumaule, Simon, and I gave you my body in this
marriage!"

"Not willingly," he muttered, suddenly unable to
meet her eyes. "Nay, you never lay willingly for me."

"I never denied you—I gave you all I had left to
give."

"You wanted a name for your bastard—'twas all
you would have from me."

"Aye, and you knew it from the first. I never lied
to you."

"You cheated me! You bore his bastard!"

She reached across the fire and slapped him hard.
"Nay, you gave up the right to call her a bastard the
day we wed, Simon! Whether you like it or no, Amia
of Beaumaule is as legitimate as you are! Aye, 'tis the
price I paid—my body and Beaumaule—for your
name! Every time you call her bastard, you shame
your own honor!"

He flushed and clenched his fists as though he
would hit her back. "She's not mine."

"Nay, but she is mine, and she bears the blood of the masters of Beaumaule."

"And that atones for what you have done to me?"

For a moment they faced each other, each flushed from the heat of argument. Gilliane's eyes flashed with anger as she shook her head. "Nay—I've naught to atone for to you, Simon of Woodstock, and well you know it. What is it that you think I have done to you?" she demanded awfully. "I wed you, Simon—I gave you my land. Without Amia, you would still be in Clifford's keep!"

"You think of me as naught but a common soldier, Gilliane. You care only that I hide your shame," he charged back.

"I made my bargain in good faith, and I have tried to honor you as husband. But 'tis hard—'tis hard to learn to love one who calls my babe a bastard." And then she remembered her earlier anger. "But that is not so important as Annys just now. You forced a maid—you ravished a girl in my house."

"She was willing enough," he grumbled.

"Nay, she was not—you took her unwilling and got a babe of her."

"I said she was willing!"

"Jesu! What a fool you must believe me! Think you I cannot remember the bruises? Think you I cannot recall the excuses she gave me for them? She was afraid of you, Simon—you ravished her!"

"I am lord of Beaumaule," he muttered defensively.

That was too much for her. She stared incredulously across the darting flames, wondering how she could ever have thought to give him her land. "Sweet Mary," she breathed finally. "And you think that makes it right? What were you going to do with her ere I discovered it?"

"I'd have taken care of her."

"How? By making her wife to a serf she loathed?" Noting the dull red flush that crept upward to his face, she nodded. "Aye, 'twas what you would have done."

"I will wed her to Aldred! He'll be glad enough of wife," he maintained stoutly. "Aye—he'll take her."

"Nay. I'd not wish such a thing on another woman ving, Simon of Woodstock! I'd not have him call er a whore and your babe a bastard as you have one to me!"

"If I turned to her, 'twas because you were cold to e!" he retorted hotly. " 'Twas because your belly as filled with Rivaux's babe! 'Twas because you did ot want me in your bed!"

"Neither did she!"

"I burned, Gilliane de Lacey! I burned for you— nd you were cold to me." He unclenched his fists nd moved around the fire to her. "I wanted you for ears, Gilliane, and you never noted me."

"You cannot excuse rapine by blaming me, Simon."

"Since you were scarce more than a maid, I have ain awake on my pallet and thought of you. Long lid I dream of taking you, of having you beneath ne, and you never knew it, did you? Aye—ever have loved you."

It was the first time he'd ever used the word be- ween them, and it sickened her to hear it now. "I annot love you, Simon, I've no love left in me now."

"Because of him!"

"I should not have wed you. I should have stayed vith the nuns at St. Agnes' priory." She felt drained nd empty, as though there was naught more to say o him.

"I want you still, Gilliane."

"Nay." She turned her back and went again to the vindow, tearing the oiled parchment away from the opening. Looking down on a land as cold and bleak s her heart, she shook her head. "Annys will stay ere unwed, cared for by me since you blame me for he lust that got her babe, and I will keep the child he bears. If somehow we should prosper, you will provide for the child when 'tis grown."

The tonelessness in her voice was more frighten- ng to him than her anger, and he sought the means to placate her. "Gilliane . . ." He came up behind her and tried to put his hands on her shoulders, but she wrenched away. "Nay, I'll not lie willingly again for you either—if you would have me, 'twill be as you had Annys," she told him coldly.

"You dare not deny me, Gilliane—I am lord of Beaumaule and your husband." His finger twined in a strand of her hair, curling it. "Nay, you'll not deny me."

"There is a difference. Before this, I was willing to try to learn to love you, Simon."

" 'Twill happen."

"I cannot forget what you have done to Annys."

"I'll make you forget it—I'll give you no other cause for complaint of me. Lie with me, Gilliane—lie with me this night."

"I could not if I would—'tis too soon after the babe."

Unreasoning anger surged through him. It was still the babe between them, the babe that cheated him of what he wanted. "You'd have me acknowledge her, would you not?"

"You will."

"Only if I am your husband in fact as well as name, Gilliane. I'd rather bear the shame of telling that she is not mine than of sleeping alone in mine own keep." His hand closed over the hair that hung down over her neck, pulling her head back roughly. "Nay, 'twas not for this that I gave you my name."

"You wanted Beaumaule," she reminded him evenly.

" 'Tis not enough!" He turned her around and pulled her against him, his mended mail cutting into her skin through her gown. Forcing her head back with fingers tangled in her hair, he bent to kiss her, bruising her mouth. "Nay, Gilliane de Lacey," he whispered when at last he lifted his head, "the first time I had you, you carried his babe. The next time, you will carry mine."

"I will not come willingly to you."

"You will." He released her then, almost flinging her away. "There will be a time when I am great in your eyes, a time when I am a rich man, Gilliane, and then you will come willingly to me." He dropped to a bench and pulled off one of his heavy boots. "I'd have you divest me now."

"Nay."

He reached out and grasped her arm, twisting it painfully. "I am lord here—aye, and you'll remember it."

She flinched from the pain and shook her head. "Release me, else I shall call for aid, and we shall see who rules Beaumaule. I was born to this manor, Simon—would you see whom they'll follow?"

"I'll beat you," he growled.

"And they will turn on you."

"Whore!"

"And you'll not taunt me again thus, or I will appeal to Rivaux to have you tried for what you have done to Annys."

It was an idle threat, one that she dared not attempt, for she'd not see Richard again, but he did not know it. She thought she saw fear in his eyes, and then it was gone.

"I'll say the wench lies," he growled.

"And I will say she does not." She jerked her hand away and went back to the stairs, calling out, "Aldred! To your master! To Woodstock!"

"Nay, I'd rather undress myself," he decided wearily.

Aldred emerged from the stairwell, but Simon shook his head. "Nay, I have no need of you now— 'twas a mistake." He waited until the man's steps receded, growing fainter, and then he turned again to Gilliane. "One day you will love me as your husband, and I can wait." When she did not answer, he dropped the other boot and nodded grudgingly. "Aye, and it shall be as you say about Annys."

"And you will never again call me whore nor my daughter bastard?"

"I will claim the child." It pained him to do it, but

he knew nothing less would satisfy her. "Aye, I will hold the babe at its christening, giving her name to the priest myself."

"And you will never again touch Annys or any other unwilling woman in this keep?"

"Nay."

She moved behind him then and reached to unfasten the hooks of his coif. "I will divest you and see to your bath, Simon. I'd not have either of us shamed further."

As he felt her fingers work the hooks deftly, he dared hope that she would come to forgive his lapse with the girl. He leaned back to give her better access to his shoulder and closed his eyes to pretend that they were like any other husband and wife. Her touch soothed him now, relieving him of the discomfort of his armor.

"You did not ask of Rivaux."

Her hands stilled briefly and then grasped his surcoat beneath his arms. "You will have to sit up and raise your arms, else I cannot do this, Simon. And I did not ask because I do not want to know. That part of my life is over."

He waited until she'd pulled the woolen overgarment over his head and finished unfastening his hauberk. " 'Twas bitter gall to swear to him, and he did not even have the courtesy to raise me. Aye, one day he will pay for what he has done to me."

It was idle boasting, but she had no wish to confront him further. Ignoring it, she lifted off the heavy mail, discarded it onto the floor beside her, and unlaced the padded gambeson beneath. This time, he leaned forward when she yanked it over his head.

"Art rough," he complained.

"No rougher than Aldred, I'll warrant."

"The fool thinks I will bring you to Ardwyck when I go for castle-guard in May."

She'd knelt to unfasten his cross-garters, and her hands trembled on the leather bands. Keeping her head bent and her face averted, she managed to ask, "What fool?"

"Rivaux—Count Guy's whelp." He moved his leg impatiently. "He bids me come again in May and tells me to bring you and the babe."

"Sweet Mary!" she gasped. "You did not tell him of the babe, surely?"

"Nay. Richard of Rivaux would be the last man I'd tell of that," he muttered.

"I cannot go, Simon. I'd not see him again."

"Truly?"

"Truly."

He relaxed slightly, easing his shoulders forward again. "Well, I do not mean to take you anyway, so you worry for naught." But it pleased him that she'd not see Lord Richard again. "Nay, 'tis enough—I will finish them myself," he murmured gruffly, feeling again the intense yearning as he looked down on her copper hair. "If you would mend from the babe, you should rest." He loosened the chausses as she rose, facing his nakedness.

She looked at his lean, hard, battle-scarred body and felt nothing. "Wrap yourself in a blanket whilst I have them fill the washing tub."

He stretched and scratched before her, flexing his tired muscles, and then reached for the folded blanket in the cabinet. She turned away, wondering how one man's body could inflame and another chill her, when all men were more or less alike in that. And the old, familiar longing washed over her, the ache that Simon of Woodstock could not ease.

34

By the time spring thaws came, Gilliane was glad of them, for then Simon occupied himself with hunting and planting and managing his small manor. The winter months had been a strain between them, with him waxing surly one day and pleasant the next, depending on whether the babe took her time or whether he thought to lie with her. And despite her threats, she did lie with him, for the priest had intervened, saying a woman could not deny her husband. But she suspected he got as little satisfaction as she did from it.

But spring had eased the tension somewhat—except where the babe was concerned. Once he'd held the screaming child for her christening, he'd considered his duty done, and now he carped frequently that Amia was overindulged, that she should have a wet nurse, and that Alwina should tend her. Now, more often than not, he made oblique suggestions that perhaps the babe should be reared for the Church, or, failing that, then perhaps she should be sent away to another house to learn to be a lady as soon as she was old enough. Gilliane rejected both ideas flatly, declaring that Amia was heiress to whatever she had and would learn to be mistress of Beaumaule when the time came.

Already the infant showed promise of beauty, something that even Simon could not deny. The soft, fuzzy red down had turned to a rich, deep red, and the slate-blue eyes were fading to a green that reminded Gilliane of Elizabeth of Rivaux's. And, much as Simon could have wished it otherwise, the babe was bright and healthy.

Gilliane finished tying the laces of Amia's exquisite gown and set her, propped on pillows, on a blanket near the brazier's small fire, handing her the great ring of keys to occupy her attention. As usual, Amia jingled them and gurgled happily. Gilliane settled onto a bench and prepared to sew a new tunic for her husband, something to take when Rivaux called him to service.

Despite the muddiness of his boots, Simon entered the solar and handed Gilliane a sealed message bearing the imprint of Richard's signet in the wax. "Read it," he ordered curtly. And then he unbent enough to explain, "Father Gerbod is with a villein named Dedric, whose beast has trampled him in the field."

"Aye." Despite the fact that it had been ten months since last she'd seen Richard of Rivaux, her whole body trembled as she broke the seal and drew out the letter. But Simon, pacing before the small fire that kept the babe from chilling, failed to note it. Gilliane cleared her throat of its sudden hoarseness and began to read:

> To Simon of Woodstock, liegeman, greetings. Be advised that your suzerain returns to Ardwyck this day, 20 April 1137, and orders your castle-guard for the three months beginning 1 May of this same year. You will bring with you two knights, your wife, and one body servant in fulfillment of your obligation to me. Richard, lord of Celesin, Ancennes, Ardwyck, and lesser possessions, over-lord to Beaumaule, as witnessed by his seal.

"Jesu!" Simon exploded. " 'Tis all he said? Just that I am to come to Ardwyck in less than ten days?"

" 'Tis all." Gilliane slid the parchment back into the case and held it out to him. "I'd not go, Simon."

"Aye. 'Tis no place for you—he'd have us bed in a common room, no doubt."

"I'd have you tell him I am unwell and cannot travel—anything."

"You've really no wish to go?"

"Nay."

"You are content to remain here?"

She could not tell him that she'd be grateful to see him gone. Instead, she nodded. "Aye—there is much to do, and I'd not leave. One of us should remain to command what garrison is left here."

"Aye."

She could see his relief. He reached to brush back her hair, much as Richard had been wont to do, and she had to choke back tears. His blue eyes were sober as they searched her face, and then he clasped her to him, crossing his arms at her back. "I'd not have you cry for me, Gilliane," he murmured over the crown of her hair. "Nay, it may not be three months even ere I am home."

"I am all right," she managed.

" 'Tis not like you to weep." He held her back and looked into her eyes. "You do not think you could be . . . ?" he started to ask hopefully.

"Nay."

"I hope the first babe has not made you barren." He glanced down then to where Amia sat propped amid pillows on a blanket, and he frowned. "Mayhap if you got her a wet nurse—I have heard 'tis harder to conceive while you give suck."

"Nay, I'd let none other feed her."

"She draws your strength."

"She is but a babe, Simon."

It was an old argument, one they'd had many times over, one that he never won. He'd even gone into the small village and found a woman who'd lost her own babe and brought her back to Beaumaule, but Gilliane would let none but herself and Alwina and Annys tend her precious Amia. Nay, but Richard of Rivaux's babe required the best of what

Beaumaule had to offer—the best of the silk, the finest of the wool—the child even slept in a silk-cushioned cradle. And he resented everything Gilliane did for Amia of Beaumaule.

His arm still around Gilliane's slim waist, he moved closer, rubbing against her suggestively, sliding his other hand over her back and down to cup her hip. He could feel her body tense, but she did not push him away. She never pushed him away anymore, but her lack of enthusiasm usually cooled his ardor. This time it did not. This time he meant to make her want him even as he wanted her.

He stroked over her hip through her gown and whispered, "Hold me, Gilliane—I'd feel you pressed against me."

She slid her arms around his neck and stood still within his embrace, waiting. He brushed her lips with his, tasting lightly, telling himself that it was perhaps that he was always too eager for her. He held her closer, feeling the thrust of full breasts against his chest, and every fiber of his being came alive with the wanting of her.

"Mia," she murmured, bringing her hands down to hold him back a little.

"Aye."

He released her then and walked to stand over the babe, who'd been grasping at the iron ring of castle keys. The green eyes stared up soberly and then she grinned, waving the keys at him. He reached down and picked her up, carrying her to the stairwell and calling down, "Alwina! Alwina! Come tend—come tend your mistress's babe!"

But it was Annys who came, easing her swollen body up the steep stairs slowly, her belly so full that it looked as though she could drop twins even though it was not near her time. She reached for the babe gingerly, as though she feared to touch him, and immediately Amia began to cry.

"Give her to me," Gilliane ordered.

"Nay, take her," Simon countermanded.

"Hush, lovey," Annys crooned, jostling the babe until it settled down. "Nay, lady, but she is all right." Brushing past Simon without looking at him, the girl carried the child out.

Simon cursed the girl under his breath, cursed her for again reminding Gilliane of what he'd done. Following her to the stairs, he closed the heavy door and threw the latch. When he turned back, Gilliane had moved to stare out the window, her back rigid.

"Nay, sweeting." He came up behind her and tried to turn her around. When she resisted, he held her against him, moving his stomach against her back as heat rose again within him. His hand moved from her waist to touch her breast as his mouth sought the place where her hair parted and fell forward from her neck.

"I'd have you love me, Gilliane."

He did not think he'd ever wanted anything as badly as he wanted her now, but she broke away, moving several feet toward the middle of the room. "Have me, then, but—"

"Nay, do not say it—I'd not hear it."

He advanced on her and she felt cornered despite the openness of the room. Willing herself to let him touch her, she waited. This time, when he caught her to him, he did so roughly, kissing her hard, hoping to evoke a response in her. But the feel of her body against his made his pulses race and his loins ache unbearably. He bent her backward, lifting her, and carried her to the curtained bed, undressing as he went. She rolled into the mattress and turned away rather than watching him. He saw her avert her eyes, and it rankled him that she showed no eagerness for the coupling. But determined that this time would somehow be different, that if he gave her time to respond, she would, he eased his aroused body down next to hers and drew her close to him. And then the babe's insistent wails floated up from below. As he stroked the rich, silky hair over Gilliane's shoulder, he could hear Amia crying harder,

reaming as though in a rage. He began untying the
ces beneath Gilliane's arms and slid a hand up the
de sleeve to cup a breast.

His body was unbearably hot with wanting, but she
y still beneath his hand. And as the babe's screams
tensified, he could feel Gilliane's body stiffen, and
knew 'twould be no different this time—that she'd
beneath him still as stone, receiving his body and
s seed, but she would not love him. Cheated and
ustrated, he rolled away.

"Jesu! A man has a right to expect better than this!
o tend the brat!"

" 'Tis not Mia, Simon—'tis not Mia who takes away
y desire," she responded, sitting up to retie the
ces that fitted her bodice. " 'Twas Annys."

"And how do you think it is for me?" he countered
ngrily. "If I judged you as you judge me, I would
ever look at you again, Gilliane de Lacey! Aye, I'd
ink of Richard of Rivaux and hate you!" He lurched
om the bed and groped for his discarded chausses,
rsing her as he pulled them on. "Damn you,
illiane! Damn you! You care for everything and
eryone in this keep more than you care for me!"

When she did not answer, he grasped her arm
ughly and pulled her up to face him. "You lay for
ichard of Rivaux like a stinking whore, Gilliane!
ou let him get a babe of you! But you have naught
r your husband! Answer me!"

" 'Twas not a question!"

"Afore God, there will come a time when you are
ot cold to me!" he shouted in her face.

He'd lifted his other hand as though he meant to
rike her, but she did not flinch. And strike her he
d—her head snapped back and her cheek and jaw
ung from the impact of his palm when he hit her.
tunned by what he'd just done, he stared, speech-
ss at the reddening print of his hand on her face.
or a moment, neither of them spoke. Her blue eyes
et his steadily, holding them, until he had to look
way. Then, flinging her from him with such force

that she staggered and lost her balance, he picked up
one of the benches and threw it against the wall. I
skidded across the floor, sending rushes flying, and
crashed into the masonry, splintering and shattering
on impact. Gilliane shielded her face from the piece
of wood and stood.

"I think you are mad, Simon," she told him simply

Her voice was quiet and dispassionate, but it car
ried across the gulf between them, echoing in hi
mind. Knowing he'd yet again turned her from him
he reached out his hand helplessly before dropping
it to his side. And he felt anew the surge of impo
tent, defensive anger.

"The time will come, Gilliane de Lacey, when yo
want me even as I want you!"

He cast about wildly for something else to vent hi
wrath on, and finding nothing, he turned, picked up
his heavy boots with one hand, and strode for th
door. Throwing the bar, he hit the wooden cross
piece so hard that the hinges banged against th
frame, and then he was gone. Ignoring her stil
stinging jaw, she bent over and began picking up th
pieces of the bench, tossing them into the brazier. A
dog yelped and Simon cursed belowstairs, and the
she heard him shouting in the courtyard.

Sinking wearily to her seat by the window, she fe
an acute sadness for him and for herself also. It ha
been a mistake to wed him—she knew it now, but a
the time it had seemed the best course. What sh
had not known then was that she could not lov
him—that no matter how many years passed, n
matter what distance separated them, she would a
ways love Richard of Rivaux and none other. And
had been wrong of her to think if could be otherwis

Simon stomped across the yard, his scowl sendin
everyone and everything out of his way, until h
reached the small chapel. "God's bones, but is he n
back yet?" he demanded of the boy who studied wit
the priest.

"N-nay."

"Then I'd have you go tell him I have need of
m," he snapped tersely. "Aye, tell him I'd have him
rite to a man at Ardwyck this day."

"Aye, my lord."

Simon watched him flee, and then he turned his
tention to his rebuilt chapel. Gone were the cracked
indows, replaced now by thick panes of amber glass,
d the sunlight that streamed golden through them
ll on the flagged floor, illuminating the graves of
e de Laceys buried there. He stared down, feeling
ke an intruder, and his resentment of Gilliane grew.
she'd accepted him as her lord, every man in
eaumaule would have also, but he suspected that
vas not so—that 'twas Gilliane rather than him they
llowed. Well, that would change, he'd see to that.
ye, and with Richard of Rivaux dead, she'd have to
rn to him.

"My lord."

He swung around to face Beaumaule's chaplain.
)id you have to bury the man?"

"Aye."

"I could scarce afford to lose him." Unable to meet
ather Gerbod's eyes for the guilt he felt, Simon
unched his shoulders and turned his back to the
d priest. "I need two letters written to Ardwyck,
ther—I'd send to a man called Talebot—aye, and
Richard of Rivaux also. I'd have him know she
pes not come."

35

Simon of Woodstock's letter, couched in terms th[at]
bordered on insolence, had said that Gilliane cou[ld]
not come, and Richard of Rivaux was furious wi[th]
the both of them. Nay, he had to see her again—he[']
thought of naught else for days as May drew near—
and he'd not be denied. He had to see for himself,
hear from her lips that she'd chosen the hard, lo[w-]
born Woodstock for husband. He'd not paid Glouce[s-]
ter two hundred pounds for suzerainty to Beaumau[le]
for naught—nay, he'd done it to bring her into h[is]
power again, to punish her for leaving him, f[or]
inflicting the pain he still felt whenever he thoug[ht]
of her.

"I see our wall stands," Everard muttered dry[ly]
beside him, drawing him back to reality.

Richard stretched in his saddle, relieving achin[g]
muscles garnered in a hard two days' ride, and su[r-]
veyed the wall he'd had built at Beaumaule. "Ay[e,]
and the ditch is widened also."

"Would you that we sound the approach, my lord[?]"

"Nay. I'd be at the gate ere I warned them," h[is]
lord decided grimly. "I want to see their faces whe[n]
they look over that wall."

" 'Twill not be an easy task to take it now that 't[is]
done."

"For all that I dislike him, I do not think Woo[d-]
stock a complete fool," Richard snapped, betrayin[g]
his impatience. "I am his suzerain, Everard—he da[re]
not deny me and keep his land."

"Aye." Casting a furtive look at his master's scowl, he captain felt it incumbent to remind him, "She is is lady now, my lord. If he would not bring her—"

"I have a right to visit what is mine, and I choose o visit Beaumaule."

Knowing the famed Rivaux temper lay barely concealed beneath Richard's hard, set face, Everard wisely hose to hold back further comment on the matter. To him, it was beyond belief anyway that any woman ould so overset a man, but Gilliane de Lacey, gone en months and more, still held power over his young ord. Aye, he'd seen it all these months past—the lisbelief, the anger, the pain, and finally, the bitterless over what she'd done. And instead of healing, he wound festered beneath the surface, poisoning he man.

Garth was the first to see them from where he tood on the outer stairs of an unfinished tower. quinting into the spring sun, he made out the red- nd-black banner of the younger Rivaux, and he felt surge of gladness. Too long his mistress had la- ored to please her sullen, bitter husband. And as imon of Woodstock was gone to Devon for the rdering of a new hauberk in the absence of an rmory at Beaumaule, Garth regarded Richard of ivaux's arrival as an omen of better things to come. le hastened down the stone steps and made his way o the gatehouse.

"Lower the bridge!" he shouted. " 'Tis Rivaux!"

"Nay, Sir Simon—"

"The lord is gone, but he'd not dare deny his uzerain!" Garth yelled when the gateman hesitated. You'll not be thanked if you turn Rivaux of Celesin way!"

"Aye," the fellow growled in answer. "I suppose is his right." He climbed to the guardpost and veri- ied the black hawk that sat staring proudly from its ed silk pennon, and then without seeking further ermission swung down to release the wheel that >wered the wood-and-iron bridge.

Gilliane, hearing the commotion as the armed reti
nue crossed over it, hurried down from her solar. A
quick glance, obstructed by the scaffolding of the
new tower, revealed only that the mesnie in her yard
was far too large to be her husband's. Alarmed, she
ran from the tower, ready to urge whatever defense
could be mustered in Simon's absence.

And then she saw him. He still sat astride hi
horse, his tall body in full mail, his red-and-black
surcoat whipping about in the late-spring breeze, hi
face hard and set beneath the shadow of his helme
nasal. She cast about wildly for the means to escape
to run, to hide from him, but as he dismounted, she
stood rooted to the hard-packed earth of the yard
Her whole body shook as he removed his helm and
pushed back his sweat-dampened hair with his gloved
hand. Tossing the helm to Walter of Thibeaux, he
pulled off the heavy gloves with his teeth and tucked
them beneath his saddle. And when he turned around
his look as his eyes met hers told her that he hated
her now.

His step was slow and deliberate, his spurs clink
ing as he walked to face her. Raking her with dar
eyes so cold that the golden flecks were gone from
them, he took in everything from her copper braid
to her slender waist.

"You do not appear unwell to me."

"Nay, I . . ." Unable to face him like that, she
dropped to make her obeisance to her husband'
overlord, mumbling, "Welcome to Beaumaule, m
lord. You find us unprepared—nay, *astonished* b
your arrival." Then, not daring to feel even th
touch of his hands again, she hastily arose and backed
away.

"Where is Woodstock?"

"He is not here—he has gone to see to a new coa
of mail ere he enters your service."

"And your . . . babe?" It was an effort for him t
ask her that, for he hated the thought that she'
borne a babe for Simon of Woodstock.

Wiping suddenly damp palms against the coarse, plain wool of her gown, she tried to keep her voice from shaking as she answered him. "Amia of Beaumaule is well, my lord."

"Amia." He gave a derisive inflection to the word. "You waste your Latin on Woodstock, no doubt—I'll warrant he knew not what it meant."

Her stomach knotted at the coldness in his voice, making her almost sick. "He knew." She held her breath, praying that he would not ask to see the child, and then was disappointed when he did not. With an effort, she forced herself to ask politely, "For how long do you honor us with your presence, my lord?"

"I am undecided in the matter."

"Beaumaule's larder is small, and . . ."

The black eyebrows rose above the cold eyes. "You would deny your suzerain the hospitality of the keep you hold of him?"

"Nay, but . . . my husband is not at home, my lord!" she blurted out desperately.

"Aye, so you have said." His eyes met hers again, sending another shiver down her spine. "I will wait that he may accompany me back to Ardwyck."

Her heart cried nay—that she would not, could not be at the mercy of this stranger before her, that her dreams of him would crumble in the face of his coldness, and her memories of him would be as ashes from the fire that had once been between them. But aloud she managed to murmur, "Then we will see you are attended whilst you are here. I will send to Dover to my husband, apprising him of your arrival."

Tearing himself away from her blanched face, he looked toward his men. "Aye, I'd have a bath and a bed myself, and quarters for my men."

She ran her tongue over suddenly parched lips and shook her head. "There is a dearth of beds here, my lord. Only—"

"As overlord here, I will take Woodstock's cham-

ber," he cut in harshly. "You and the babe ma
remove to the lower floor."

"Aye." She had not the right to argue with him
Instead, she inclined her head respectfully and nod
ded. " 'Twill be as you wish, my lord. I will see to th
ordering of a bath for you whilst you are divested o
your mail ere you come up." Bobbing a hasty curtsy
she turned and fled.

"Nay, it cannot be as I wish it," he muttered unde
his breath as he watched her walk away from him.

He paced the narrow confines of the small sola
restlessly, waiting as the men carried steaming pail
of water to pour into the heavy tub, waiting for he
to come up. He'd been a fool to come, and he knev
it. She belonged to Woodstock now, but he'd had t
see her again. The old pain of her leaving washe
over him, and he wanted to strike out, to make he
pay for what she'd done to him.

Somewhere below he heard a babe cry, Wood
stock's babe mayhap, and his bitterness over he
betrayal was almost too much to bear. Amia o
Beaumaule. God, but what a fool he had been—she'
lain with the likes of Simon of Woodstock and born
a babe of the man, living proof that she'd shared he
body with her lowborn husband even as she ha
once shared it with him. And then she'd named th
babe for love. Revulsion flooded him, sickening h
soul.

"My lord?"

He spun around at the sound of the old woman
voice and shook his head. "Nay, Alwina, I'd not hav
you tend me. Seek your mistress and bid her come i
haste—I do not mean to wait for her."

"She thinks it unseemly, my lord."

" 'Tis my right to be attended by the lady of th
keep!" he snapped angrily. "Remind her whom sh
would refuse!"

"Nay, but—"

"Now, old woman—I'd have you tell her *now!*"

Clearly he was in the devil's temper, and Alwina was no fool. She backed away, bobbing obediently. "Aye, my lord, I will speak with her."

He followed her to the stairwell, calling out loudly enough for those below to hear, "Tell your lady I'd punish her lord for her insult!"

Gilliane winced at the fury in his voice. Laying Amia in her cradle, she covered her bared breast and looked to Alwina. "I know not which is worse," she half-whispered in anguish, "whether 'tis better to risk his anger or Simon's. Sweet Mary, Alwina, but I'd not face him alone."

And for once, the old woman's face softened. "Nay, tell him of the babe, and he cannot but understand."

"Nay! I cannot—and you must not either, Alwina! I'd have your word that you will not! 'Twas for my daughter that I left him—I'd have her heiress to Beaumaule rather than bastard to anyone! Do not make what I have done be for naught, I pray you."

"Aye." The old woman turned to place a sugared rag in the unsatisfied babe's mouth, hoping to still her crying.

"Give me your word, Alwina."

"He'll know—even a man knows enough to count."

"If he sees her not, he'll not know when she was born."

"Aye, I'll not tell him."

Gathering her skirts about her as though she gathered courage, Gilliane started up the steps. Her mouth was dry and her palms wet, and her stomach seemed to have risen into her throat. With thudding heart she managed to make the last turn in the narrow, winding stairs.

Stepping just inside her solar doorway, she faced him. "My lord, I'd not undress or bathe you in my husband's absence. He—" She got no further, as he'd crossed the room to tower over her.

"I did not ride two days to hear you gainsay me, Gilliane de Lacey!"

Her hands clenched in the folds of her skirt as she

raised her eyes to his. "Then why did you come?"
she asked with a calmness she did not feel.

"To see for myself that you have taken Woodstoc
for husband! To hear from you that you chose hir
over me!" His hands reached to grab hers, forcin
them open, lifting them before him. "Look at you
self, Gilliane de Lacey, and tell me I did not offe
you better than this!"

She stared downward into her roughened palm
palms that had helped scrub and clean and rebuil
Beaumaule. "He wed me, my lord."

"I loved you, Gilliane." He dropped her hand
and looked away. "Aye, I clothed you in silks, drape
you in jewels, and gave you my heart, Gilliane d
Lacey—all for naught."

His voice had dropped, but it carried as clearly a
if he'd still shouted. She swallowed hard, attemptin
to speak over the awful aching lump in her throat. "
am sorry for it, my lord."

"Sorry, *Sorry*?" he hissed intensely. "Nay, but yo
are not half so sorry as I mean to make you and th
husband you have taken!"

"My lord, 'twas not my intent to wound!"

"Wound!" he howled, his voice rising again. Hi
eyes raked her contemptuously, his mouth curvin
in a sneer. "Holy Jesu, but you know not the mean
ing of the word!"

"I swear I am sorry for the pain," she whispered
turning to stumble for the stairs.

"Nay—we are not done, Gilliane." He lunged pas
her, blocking the doorway with his body. Then, fac
ing her, he reached behind him to throw the latch
bar. "I'd have my bath and more of you this day."

"You'd dishonor me, and I—" His face blurre
before her, blotting out all else as his hand graspe
her arm painfully, pulling her close. And she fel
again the hard strength of his body, but this tim
there was no gentleness in him. She closed her eye
tightly, squeezing out tears of humiliation, as hi
mouth came down on hers as brutally as Simon's

Twisting her head away, she managed to gasp, "You would take me for revenge."

"Revenge? Nay," he whispered back, his lips again seeking hers, his arms closing about her body, his anger fading to hunger and desire.

He'd been unprepared for the feel of her, for the softness he'd nearly forgotten in his bitterness, and the old fire flared unbidden between them. One of his hands caught at her braids and cradled her head while the other moved incessantly along her spine and down over the curve of her hip, seeking to mold her closer. And all the time, his lips sought, teased, and took, moving to trace increasingly urgent kisses from her earlobe to the sensitive hollow of her throat. And she responded ardently, arching her head back to give him access, pressing her body achingly close. And for a moment she allowed herself to experience the desire she'd thought had died.

But it was wrong to let him touch her again. With an effort, she broke away and clutched at the door-jamb for support. "I . . . I cannot. Sweet Mary, but I cannot!"

"I thought I hated you," he rasped, staring at her from where he stood, "but part of me would love you still."

"I swore my marriage oath to Simon, Richard, and 'twas not lightly given."

"Why? Why did you take him over me, Gilly?"

" 'Twas not over you! 'Twas never over you!" Her voice rose almost hysterically as she cried out, "I wanted to be more than a rich man's leman!"

"And are now but a poor man's wife!"

"Aye, but I am wed—in the eyes of Holy Church I am wed, Richard! My sons will not be bastards! If my sons cannot stand beneath the banner of Rivaux, they can rule Beaumaule!"

"Beaumaule. Sweet Jesu, but 'tis naught, Gilly! I could have given our sons lands far greater than this scrap of ground you value so highly."

"But could you have given them your name? Nay,

but I'd have borne babes with naught but a Fitz t
your name!"

"I told you when you first came to me—when firs
we lay together—that I would wed you if I could
Gilly."

"Aye, if you could—but you could not!"

"As well you knew from the first!" He took a ste
closer and held out his hand. "Nay, I'd not quarre
with you, Gilly, not when there's so little time here.
He spoke softly now, reaching out to her. "I'd lie i
your arms again and remember love."

She wanted to take his hand more than anything
but she dared not—to touch him again would destro
what little resolve she had. Instead, she backed agains
the door and lifted the bar. "Nay, but 'tis my hus
band's honor as well as mine own."

"Gilly, I cannot live like this. You have cast me int
hell. At night I burn, wanting you, and by day I hat
you for it."

"Please—"

"You would tear at my very soul for that which
cannot help, Gilly."

She thought he meant to move yet closer, and sh
knew she wanted him as much as he wanted he
Turning the iron latch handle, she backed out ont
the step. "As hard as 'tis to say, my lord, I'd tell yo
what I tell myself: if you burn, lie with your wedde
lady. Lie with Cicely, Richard—only she has the righ
to your love."

"I did not wed her, Gilly. Unlike you, I could not."

"Simon of Woodstock gave my babe a name
Richard."

She'd not meant to tell him, had sworn to hersel
she would not, and yet the words had escaped. Tak
ing advantage of his shock, she turned and ran dow
the steps, not stopping at any landing until sh
reached the safety of the ground. And then sh
stood shaking against the hard, rough stones of th
tower wall.

Too stunned to call her back, he stared after he

as the realization came slowly that he had a daughter, a babe born of his blood and Gilliane de Lacey's flesh. Amia of Beaumaule was his babe also. Amia— named for love. And then he followed her, running down the winding steepness of the stairs and catching up to her in the courtyard below, where she stood, her tears spilling down her cheeks and wetting the soot-streaked yellow limestone.

"Gilly . . ." He spoke gently now, his hands reaching to touch her shoulders and turn her around. "Why did you not tell me, sweeting?"

"You saw how I was received at court—you saw what those people in London did to me. Nay, but I could not bear a bastard child, Richard." She raised reddened eyes to his face and met his gaze squarely. "I did not wish my babe to grow to hate me for what people said I was."

"Jesu!"

"I thought to give my son legitimacy—and Beaumaule. I thought I owed him that. But 'twas a daughter."

"And Woodstock knew?" he asked incredulously.

"Aye." She sighed heavily and looked down again, digging at an embedded twig with the toe of her slipper. "He wanted Beaumaule. To you 'tis naught, but to a landless man 'tis everything."

"Gilly, bring the babe and come with me."

"Nay. When I wed him, I swore to Simon I would lie with him and none other. I cannot go with you."

He knew defeat then. He searched her face for hope and found none. And then he noted the bruises he'd mistaken for shadows earlier. He lifted a hand to brush back an errant strand of copper hair, and he studied the discolored marks.

"He beats you," he observed soberly. "The swine beats you, Gilly."

"Because of what I was to you. I was glad you called him away to your service." She pulled away from his touch and traced the outline of a stone with her fingers. "Please—for whatever love you bore me, Richard, I'd have you leave ere he returns."

"If he touches you in anger again, I will kill him," he promised her grimly. "If you will not come now, you have but to send to me."

"Aye."

"And I'd still punish Brevise also."

"Nay, I absolve you from the oath, my lord. Brevise rises too high in Stephen's favor to attempt his life now."

"The day will yet come, Gilly. I did not take the oath lightly." He squared his shoulders and squinted up at the brilliant sky, wondering how the sun could shine so brightly when his heart was so empty. "If you will but feed us, then, we will leave and seek lodgings elsewhere. I'd cause you no further pain."

Her heart cried out within her, but somehow she managed to nod. "Aye."

He spoke low. "God aid me, Gilly, for I love you still."

"Then may God aid me also, Richard."

Unable to bear the pain that caught beneath her breasts, she ducked beneath his arm and started back inside. As her hands wrenched the heavy door ring, she felt his cover them, and her will crumbled. "Sweet Mary, but I cannot stand this," she whispered, turning into him.

His arms closed around her, holding her close as the spring wind whipped the sleeves and skirt of her gown around them. He stood, locked in her returning embrace, his heart breaking.

"Nay, 'tis not right what I would do," she choked into his shoulder. "You will have to go."

"Gilly . . . Gilly."

"Please." With an effort, she drew her arms from about his waist and brought her hands up between them to press at his chest.

"I'd kill him, Gilly."

"Nay. I could not live with his blood between us."

Reluctantly he released her and stepped back. "I'd see the babe at least—would you give me that?"

She started to say that 'twould serve no purpose, but then relented. Sighing, she nodded. "I'd not have you claim her, Richard—I'd not have wed for naught."

He followed her inside and up to the second landing. Alwina looked up as they entered the sleeping room, and her lined face betrayed her surprise. Then, without a word, she crossed to where the babe lay in its cradle and picked her up. Turning back to Richard of Rivaux, she brushed the soft, bright hair on the child's head with her veined hand and held it out to him.

"She was christened Amia—for Christ's love," she told him with a perfectly straight face. "Aye, and she is as fair as any."

He hesitated before accepting the squirming babe and then held his daughter as though she were made of eggshells, cradling her gingerly in a warrior's arms. Looking down, he felt a surge of pride.

"Amia."

"She is called Mia also," Gilliane murmured behind him, "for 'mine'."

"She is that. Jesu, Gilly, but she's got your hair."

"And your sister's eyes—I think they will be green when she is grown."

The child blinked solemnly, regarding him with those widened eyes. "You know not what to make of your sire, do you, little one?" he whispered to his babe. Then, returning to Gilliane, he met her misting gaze. "You had not the right to keep her from me, Gilly—I'd have found some way to have you both with me." And in his arms, Amia began to squirm and fret.

"Then she would have been naught but your bastard." She reached to take Amia from him, holding her easily against her shoulder. "She is not used to being held as though she were an uncooked egg, my lord."

He took another look at the daughter that he could not claim. "My mother would have cherished her, Gilly—aye, and my father also."

"And Elizabeth would have cosseted her." Unwilling to allow herself to think further of what could not be, she asked instead of his family. "Your lady mother is well then?"

"Aye."

"And your lord father?"

"Equally so. He comes to England within the week as Stephen quibbles over the relief fee for Harlowe, saying that my father is overgreedy if he would have the Condes, Rivaux, and Harlowe also. I think Papa means to counter that he has already relinquished all claim to Nantes in my mother's name. He wrote that he should reach Dover by midweek."

"I would that I could see him," Gilliane sighed wistfully. "Aye, he was ever kind to me."

"And would be still, Gilly—he loved you as a daughter."

The child in her arms stirred, turning its head against her breast and wetting her gown with its mouth. "She grows hungry, my lord, and would eat."

"I'd watch."

She shook her head. "I'd have no milk. Go down and I will sup with you ere you leave."

He had to be content with that, he supposed. He smoothed the rich red hair over the babe's crown, knowing full well that 'twould be the last time he saw his daughter. "Fare thee well, Amia of Beaumaule," he told her softly.

After he had left, Alwina watched Gilliane bare her breast and set the babe to it. "Your husband will not like it that he has come, I fear."

"Aye, but there is no help for it," Gilliane sighed. "Surely when he learns that Richard did not stay, he will know I turned him away."

She looked down at Amia and wished it could have been different, that this small babe could have grown in Richard of Rivaux's love, that he could have called her daughter. Amia of Beaumaule would have been Amia of Rivaux, and she herself would have been his wife. But it did no good to think such thoughts. Resolutely she forced herself to once again accept what she had done.

36

"Whore! Red-haired witch!"

For a moment Gilliane tried to waken from her nightmare, and then she realized she was not dreaming. Before she could raise her arms in defense, her husband hit her, smiting her so hard across the face that her head snapped backward against the pillow.

"Jesu . . . what . . . ?" She rolled away, only to be pulled up roughly from between the bedcovers. His hand struck her mouth with enough force that her own teeth cut her lip.

"You lay like a bitch in season for him! You damned whore!"

"Nay, I . . ." She wiped the blood from her face with the back of her hand and tried to rise from the bed. "Simon, I swear I did not—I swear it!"

"Lying harlot!"

He stood over her, his fists clenched to strike her again. His whole body shook with uncontrollable anger, and Gilliane knew fear. " 'Twas not so—he came for you!"

He hit her again, this time catching her shoulder, and she collapsed back into the depths of the feather mattress. Raising her arms now to shield her face, she cried out, "You have no right to accuse me thus! I have done nothing!"

"Nothing!" he shouted at her. "Nothing? What call you Rivaux's brat? Deny to me how you got her!" His fist caught her arm, knocking it away. "Aye, tell me that!"

"You knew when we wed!"

"You swore to me, Gilliane—*swore* to me that you'd lie with me and no other then!"

"And I have not! Simon!"

His hand struck her full in the temple. She rolled away and struggled, panting, to her knees. "For the love of God, Simon! I tell you I have done naught!"

"*For the love of God!*" he mimicked cruelly. "Aye, for the love of God, Gilliane—tell me again how you came to name the babe!"

"She was born at Christmas!"

"I'll teach you not to gainsay me!"

He hit her again, this time with his closed fist, in the ribs. Doubling over in pain, she managed to roll onto the floor behind the bed, crouching warily. He grasped a bedpost to move it out of the way, and she lunged toward the cold, empty brazier, reaching the poker before he reached her.

She'd had enough—whether it was his right as husband to beat her or not, she'd not let him kill her. Clutching the poker behind her, she waited for him to strike her again. And this time when he raised his hand, she aimed it, swinging hard and catching him in the groin. He doubled over and went down in a heap at her feet, rolling and howling in pain.

"Jesu," he gasped, "you have hurt me!"

"Aye," she panted over him. "May you never get another child!"

"Witch! Whore!"

She raised the poker again. "Call me either one more time, Simon of Woodstock, and 'twill not be your manhood that suffers, but rather your brain!"

"Whore!" he spat at her.

The poker caught him across the brow and he collapsed as though the breath had left him. He fell forward, his face buried in the rushes, his body sprawling motionless. She stared, stunned by what she had done, and then dropped the poker and screamed, "To me! To me! To de Lacey!"

She could hear running footsteps below and then

the door burst open, admitting Aldred and the others. Alwina caught at her hands, holding them, while Simon's squire and Garth knelt beside him. Aldred shook his head in disbelief as he turned his master over and noted the already darkening bruise on his forehead.

"Is he dead?" Gilliane asked numbly, heedless of her nakedness.

"Nay, he stirs. God's bones, but what happened lady?"

"I hit him."

They all turned to her, and even Garth looked shocked until Alwina reached to touch Gilliane's swelling face. "He hit you first, I think."

"Aye, I was afraid."

Annys moved closer to peer down at Simon, her hatred evident in her face. "I would that I had done it," she murmured.

Simon groaned and tried to sit, but Aldred pushed him back. "Get some water—'twill waken him faster."

Alwina was the first to move, walking over to where a ewer sat in a basin. Picking it up, she checked to see that it was full, and then she turned and threw it in Simon's face. He coughed and choked and struggled to stand.

"Jesu!" He looked down to where his chausses were tied. "You would have ruined me, Gilliane de Lacey!"

"You beat me without cause!" Gilliane retorted.

"Aye, I remember." His face twisted with anger and he lunged for her again. "Aye, and I will teach you to play me false! Get out of here—all of you!" he shouted as he caught her by the shoulders and pushed her to the floor.

The boy Garth was the first to reach them, and he tried to pull Simon away. With his greater weight, Simon flung him against the wall and turned back to Gilliane, catching her in the side with his heavy boot.

"Aye—lie there like a bitch on the ground," he panted. "God's bones, but what a fool you think me.

Turning away, he staggered to where the babe wakened in her cradle, and he kicked the side of it with such force that it turned over. Amia of Beaumaule began to squall loudly.

"Bastard!" he spat at her. "Art naught but a fancy lord's by-blow, you little witch!" He raised his foot again as though he meant to stomp on the helpless babe, and Garth caught him off-balance, butting him from behind. The two of them fell to the floor and rolled, knocking over benches and a cabinet. As Simon tried to shake free of him, Garth cried out, "Save yourself, lady!"

But Gilliane could scarce move. Holding her ribs with one hand, she crawled toward her babe, reaching it just as Simon regained his footing, Garth still on his back. The men of Beaumaule, many of whom had watched in uneasy silence, unwilling to interfere between a man and his wife, stirred now. Aldred grasped Simon's sword and raised it to strike at Garth, but Alwina and Annys both caught at his arms and cried out.

"To your lady! To Beaumaule!" Annys screamed, holding desperately onto Aldred's sword arm. "Sweet Jesu, can you not see they would kill your lady? To her! To her!"

Only two men tried to intervene when the rest tackled their lord, bringing him down. Garth managed to fall free and came to his knees. "He tried to kill her," he gasped. "He tried to kill them both!"

" 'Tis his right," Aldred muttered, his arms pinned between two other men.

"Nay, she is blameless! He accuses her falsely because he would rule Beaumaule alone!" Garth disputed. "Look to your lady! See what he has done!"

It was no light thing to turn on one's lord, but as each one of them saw the blood that trickled from Gilliane's mouth, the swelling of her eyes, and the bruises on her naked body, the collective mood grew ugly. She sat, her pain evident, and cradled her babe against her, trying to soothe its frantic cries. Alwina moved to throw a sheet over her mistress's body to cover her.

"Kill him," someone urged.

"Nay, let Rivaux do it," another argued. "The king's justice is hard on one who kills his lord."

Gilliane tried to focus on Simon through eyes that were already swelling shut. "You would have killed her," she whispered. "You would have slain an innocent babe." Then she touched her face gingerly, feeling the cut on her lip. "Why, Simon—*why?*"

"I received word that he came here, and I rode all night," he muttered sullenly, cowed now by the ugly looks of his own men. "I told you I'd not wear horns for you."

"Simon, 'twas *I* who sent you word—'twas my own hand that wrote it."

Annys walked over and stood staring at him for a long moment. And then she spat in his face. He struggled to free an arm, but neither man released his grip. "If 'twere asked of me, I'd have you dead," the girl told him. "Aye, I would."

His anger replaced by fear now he appealed to Gilliane. "Nay, Gilliane—"

"Nay."

She handed Amia up to Alwina and then sought her feet, lurching to stand, her face ashen and damp from the sharp, searing pain in her ribs. " 'Tis the last time you will beat me, Simon. The next time you think to do it, I'll see you dead."

She spoke tonelessly, but he knew she meant it. And he knew that with the exception of Aldred, she had the loyalty of every man in Beaumaule. What he had sought so long to command, what he held now was still not truly his.

" 'Twas my anger, Gilliane," he offered lamely. " thought—"

"You have made it plain to all of us what you thought," she interrupted coldly. "And now I'd have you leave Beaumaule while we both yet live."

"You cannot deprive me of my right to this place."

"Nay, but neither do I have to live with you. I'll not gainsay your right if you will go."

"You need me to hide your shame," he gibed, realizing now that she meant to hold Beaumaule without him.

"Why? Have you not shouted to the world that Amia of Beaumaule is my bastard? Have you not called me harlot and whore before my own people? Nay, Simon of Woodstock, but there's naught left to hide."

"Rivaux—"

"He knows now. In your anger, you sent a letter certain to bring him here, and it did. He has seen her, Simon, and if you harm either of us again, he will see that you do not live." With an effort, she dragged her aching body to face him, and he had to turn away from her bloodied face. "Nay, look at me."

"I did not mean—"

"I do not forgive you." She nodded to the men who still restrained him. "Let him go that he may ready himself to leave—he takes service with Rivaux the first day of May. Until then, I care not where he goes."

"Jesu, lady!" Garth protested. "You cannot let him go!"

"Nay, he will not harm me now—he knows he has no further power over me."

There was a grumbling among the men, but Alwina shook her head. "He knows he will not leave Beaumaule alive if any harm comes to her or the babe now."

Simon shook free of his captors and tried to touch Gilliane's arm, but she shrank from him. Wordlessly he dropped his hand and stepped back. "Aye, I'll go," he decided finally. "Aid her to bed."

Still grumbling, they set up a watch over her while Alwina put her to bed and drew the heavy curtains. For a long time Gilliane lay and stared up at the canopy over her, scarce listening as her husband moved about the chamber gathering what he would need at Ardwyck. Aye, she admitted to herself, if 'twere not for the pain he'd given her, she would have felt nothing at his leaving.

Disheartened and ashamed of what he'd done, Simon searched silently for his things, seeking the fine tunic she'd made him for his last journey to Richard's keep. Finally he turned toward the bed, asking, "Where is the purple overtunic?"

"In the large chest."

Again her toneless voice unnerved him. "Gilliane, when I am come back, 'twill be different between us."

"Nay."

"If you could have ceased to love him—"

"I could not."

He flung open the chest and began throwing out those things which were not his until he came to the tunic, its rich, deep purple samite carefully folded with a linen cloth between. And as he reached for it, the faint light reflected on the jewels beneath. His fingers closed on the filigreed heart and pulled it out. When he opened his palm and saw the winking stones, he knew from whence they had come.

He held it up to the light, charging, "He brought you this!"

Without looking, she knew what he'd found and her heart tightened within her breast. "If you have discovered the necklace, my lord, I have saved it for Amia these many months past."

"Amia—Amia! 'Tis always Amia! There have been times when I had not the money to buy so much as a new helm—and all the while you had this!"

"Put it back."

The necklace still in his hand, he walked behind the bed and threw open the curtains before any could stop him. "Put it back? So you can give a babe what by rights you should have brought to me?" He dangled it before her, waiting for her to reach for it. " 'Tis mine, Gilliane."

"Put it back, Simon."

"Else you'll call out again?" he taunted. "Nay, you have the babe if you would remember him." Then, just as they reached him, he dropped the jeweled heart to the floor and ground it into pieces beneath the heel of his boot. It crunched against the hard floor as it collapsed.

He'd expected her to plead, to cry for this last treasure from her lover, but she lay quietly within the feather mattress and said nothing, cheating him again of revenge. He bent to pick up the crushed pieces and flung them into the cold brazier, not seeing the wet trickle of tears that coursed silently over her swollen cheeks.

He finished his packing then, rolling his clothing into a blanket much as he'd done when he was but a mercenary. "When I return to you a great lord, we will speak again," he muttered. "And then you will love me as you love him."

They followed him out, closing the door and leaving her alone. She stuffed her fist into her mouth and bit her knuckles to stifle her sobs. With the loss of her necklace, she had naught left of Richard of Rivaux—naught but Amia. Aye, and as much as she wanted to die from the pain that tore at her heart as well as her body, she could not. God might punish her for her hopeless love, but he'd given her Richard's babe to love. Slowly she mastered her tears and lay quietly, listening to the sounds of the bridge lowering and Simon riding out of Beaumaule.

After a time, Alwina brought Amia to nurse and bathed her cuts and bruises while the babe sucked. "I think he may have broken your ribs—they will need to be wrapped to heal."

"Aye—Sweet Mary, but he hurt me."

" 'Twould be safer if you took her to a convent," the old woman murmured, rubbing balm into places where he'd cut Gilliane's face.

" 'Tis no place for a babe—and they'd ask why I came. I'd have none beyond here know he repudiates her." She sighed and felt her ribs ache.

"Would you that we put her to a wet nurse now? It must pain you to bear her weight."

"We are together in this, Alwina, and I do not mind it." She rubbed the silky hair lovingly and looked down at her daughter. "I pray her red hair does her more good than mine did me."

"Red hair had naught to do with it," the old woman retorted. " 'Twas loving unwisely."

The child's small mouth worked noiselessly, drawing its very existence from her, and its greenish eyes were almost closed now. "Nay," Gilliane whispered, caressing the soft skin, "never that."

She lay awake a long time after Alwina took the sleeping babe from her breast, unable to ease her broken body. She heard the door creak inward and footsteps cross the floor.

"My lady?"

Garth pulled a bench closer to the bed and peered anxiously between the hangings, his face mirroring his concern. She tried to see him through the slits and managed a painful smile.

"Aye. I think I owe you my babe's life, Garth."

" 'Twas naught." He leaned closer and drew out a parchment roll. "A rider bearing this came just after Lord Simon left," he told her, lowering his voice.

"For Simon?"

"Aye, and I'd have you read it."

" 'Tis not mine—it should be sent to Ardwyck to await him."

"The man bearing it serves Brevise."

"Sweet Mary, but you cannot know that, Garth." Nonetheless, Gilliane attempted to sit up, holding her covers to hide her nakedness.

"I know—I saw him when we were overrun. The man comes from Brevise."

Gilliane felt a cold chill of apprehension spread through her. "Art certain—you could not be mistaken?"

"Nay."

"Open it then, and light a candle so that I may see it."

" 'Tis lit." To prove it, he drew the heavy candle spike closer, and then he slit the wax covering with his knife.

"Jesu, but I cannot see still."

The boy nodded and peered closely at the words on the heavy vellum, reading aloud slowly and haltingly:

To Simon of Woodstock, lord of Beaumaule, I give you greetings. As I spoke at Ardwyck, so it comes to pass. My lord king bids Gloucester and Rivaux of Celesin also to accompany him into Normandy to discourage rebellion there. Already all is in readiness, and my lord of Brevise does but wait to strike the first blow at Gloucester with King Stephen's goodwill. As the earl is well-liked in England, 'twill happen once they are there.

If you still would strike at Rivaux also, my lord of Brevise offers not only Beaumaule but another of Lord Richard's keeps as well, both to be held of him when King Stephen confirms them to him. He further offers one hundred silver marks on Richard of Rivaux's head, the same to be paid in addition to what you have already had of him.

"There is no seal, nor name given either," he observed, turning the letter over in his hand.

"Art certain 'tis what it says?" Gilliane asked hollowly. "You cannot be mistaken?"

"Nay, Father Gerbod teaches me to read—and 'tis what it says." He held it closer for her to make out the beginning.

"Holy Jesu." Brevise plotted with Simon against Richard and Gloucester, with King Stephen's blessing. 'Twas certain why 'twas unsigned, for it was a dangerous message. Aye, and it explained more than she cared to believe—Simon's sudden ability to pay for new mail and his boasts that he would come back a richer man.

"Garth, I'd have you ride to Ardwyck," she decided suddenly.

"And if Lord Simon is already there?"

"Oh—aye. Nay, 'twould not serve, for it tells not how they mean to take him, does it? And if the king supports them . . ." Her voice trailed off as she held her aching head and considered the problem.

"He will turn on you again," Garth warned. "Nay, I'd have you safe ere I rode, for if 'tis discovered the message I carry, more than one of us will die."

"Not if 'twas Count Guy who warned Richard," she mused slowly. "Garth, I'd go to Count Guy."

"In Normandy? Sweet Mary, but 'tis a long way, and you are unable to ride," he protested. "Nay, I'd seek sanctuary closer—at St. Agnes mayhap."

"If Richard could ride with an arrow broken in his shoulder, I can ride with sore ribs. Nay, we seek him in Dover, Garth—Richard says he comes this week."

"Then I will ride to him, but you—"

"He might not believe you."

"Aye, but—"

"And he once told me that I could turn to him if the need arose. I am taking Amia and going to him."

37

When it was discovered that she could not in truth ride, it took two days to build a makeshift litter for her, and still the men of Beaumaule were uneasy about her journey. In the end, she left the small keep with far better escort than the two men Simon had taken with him. Parting the curtains, she took a last look back at her childhood home. It had not the same memories for her now; in the last ten months she'd lived there, it had become almost a prison.

The constant jostling between the pack animals made for an arduous trip, and Gilliane's ribs pained her greatly and tired her beyond bearing. Still she managed to sing soothing songs to Amia and keep the babe reasonably quiet. From time to time Alwina took the child, but it was all that Annys could do to ride by herself. As it was, her huge belly made it impossible for her to see her own saddle.

They had to break their journey into short distances to allow for the litter, making Gilliane fear that they'd miss Richard's father at Dover. Richard had said midweek, and already 'twas Tuesday, and if they were too late, all might be lost.

"You are certain he would pass this way should he have already left for Harlowe?" she questioned them often.

"There's not so many roads, my lady—aye, he'll come here if he goes directly there. If he means to stop in London or Westminster, he'll not," was the best answer any could give her.

"Then I'd not stop again."

Garth edged his horse closer to the pack animals and offered, "I'd recognize his standard and him also. Would you that I rode ahead and sought him out? If he is in Dover, I will find him," he promised solemnly.

She was torn by the knowledge that only he shared fully in her plans, and if he was taken . . . Nay, she dared not think it. But she did have the letter from Brevise's man to carry to Harlowe if necessary. And for all her brave words, she doubted she could go much further. Finally she nodded. "Aye. Go, and God speed you, Garth. I'd see you knighted one day for this."

"Nay, 'tis not for me. If you would do anything, I'd have you place me with the clerks." He flashed her a boyish grin and leaned over to confide, "I'd live to be old and gray over my books rather than have my brains spilled by an ax."

"I'd seek a place at Rivaux for you then—I'd not part with you." She managed a tired smile, knowing he did what she could not—that the cough that plagued her was growing worse and sapping her strength.

He rode on, leaving from that first abbey where Richard had taken her nearly a year and a half before, while Gilliane and her small party broke their journey there. The fat abbot bade them less than truly welcome, taking in the frayed surcoats and the mended mail on the men. But when she produced the stones that had once been set in her necklace, he relented sufficiently to offer them food and shelter.

"Humph! That one wins few souls, I'll warrant," Alwina grumbled under her breath.

Gilliane unwrapped the heavy veil from about her battered face and lay wearily upon the cot provided her. She'd thought three days sufficient to ease her pain, but her sides still ached unbearably, and now she was coughing far too much. Alwina reached to touch her brow, and shook her head.

"Nay, but you will have to stay some time, my lady. Annys, she has fevered—see if there is any skilled in simples here."

"I am all right," Gilliane managed before she choked in a fit of coughing. "Jesu, but it hurts, Alwina—it hurts."

"Aye." The old woman sat down beside her and stroked back the bright hair from her forehead and temples. "Aye, but you must rest."

Gilliane rolled miserably onto her side and drew up her knees, hugging them, and did not see Alwina's worried frown. She slept, she knew not how long, but when she wakened, it was dark and her thirst was unbearable. She tried to croak out a request for water, only to discover that Alwina still sat beside her. The gnarled and veined hands slid behind her, easing her upward, and someone handed her a cup. She drank deeply and fell back.

"Sweet Mary, but we must go on," Gilliane whispered. "On the morrow."

"Aye—on the morrow."

She slept again, her body aching and racked with a fever that broke from time to time into a heavy sweat, only to rise again. But each time she woke, the old woman was there with a cup and a cool cloth to ease her. And then she plunged into a netherworld of demons, a world where she knew nothing but heat and pain, a world tormented by visions. Richard lay dying at her feet, Simon laughed over him, and Cicely of Lincoln wept. And a hundred babes wailed somewhere. When she struggled to sit, she was pushed back into the abyss. She screamed for Richard again and again, but no one heard and no one came.

"How long has she been like this?"

Alwina looked up and her tired old eyes brightened at the sight of Guy of Rivaux. "Two days and more."

He walked into the room, dominating the small cell, and stood above Gilliane. Her face was swollen beyond recognition, her eyes were blackened closed,

and her lips cracked and bleeding from her fever
He reached down and lifted the blanket to see the
ugly purple and greenish bruises on her body, and
his jaw hardened. "This comes not from a fever."

"Nay. Her husband beat her."

"The boy did not tell me she fevered."

"He did not know it when he left her."

He eased the cover back over her shoulder and
turned away. It was one thing to see a man broken
and battered in battle, another to see a girl beaten
thus. "Do you think 'tis from the injury she has
taken?"

"I think he broke her ribs," she answered. "If 'tis
the reason or not, I know not."

"Aye. And what of the babe?"

"The abbot found a woman of the village to give
her suck, and she is well."

"And you look like the mask of death, old woman
Nay, get you to your own pallet."

"And who would tend her? Annys nears her time
and—"

He silenced her with a wave of his hand. "Nay, I
will see to her." He went into the narrow corridor
and called out to someone, "Bring me a bench that I
may sit."

Gilliane thrashed restlessly, murmuring his son's
name. He took the bench and drew it close, leaning
over her to take her hand. For a moment her eyes
tried to open but could not. "Richard?" she croaked

"Aye."

She stilled somewhat then. Alwina gaped at the
sight of Guy of Rivaux sitting there, his strong hands
clasping Gilliane's. She hesitated, unwilling to leave
her mistress in any hands but her own, but the ache
in her old bones was undeniable.

"You may put a pallet here also. We are not enemies in this, I think."

He sat there more than half the night, holding the
girl's hand, answering her when she called to his son
There were so many fevers to take one from this

rld, and he knew not whether this was one of
em or whether she would mend. But he did know
at she'd once meant everything to Richard.

When she coughed, he raised her to ease her
eathing, and when she thirsted, he held the cup to
r swollen lips. Jesu, if there was ever a man in
ed of a lesson, 'twas this Simon of Woodstock
e'd wed. But he understood why she'd done it—
e'd wanted to give her babe what his son could
t.

The abbot, who'd been such a reluctant host be-
re, could not do enough now—he'd not realized
e girl was anything to the likes of Rivaux, he'd
ologized to any and all of those who would listen.
d when he'd heard Count Guy himself call her
ughter, he worried she would complain of him
er. But Jesu, who could have guessed that one so
orly accompanied as that was anyone at all?

No expense was spared for the girl now—herbs
re brewed for her fever, broths were made to
urish her, and precious poppy juice was given to
se her pain. Finally, when nothing seemed to be of
e, the abbott had her moved to his own bed and he
nt to another chapter house for a physician skilled
fevers.

Guy considered for a time that he ought to send to
rdwyck to Richard, but her husband was there also.
d as much as he knew Richard loved her, he
ondered if the bitterness between them was yet too
eat. Besides, he had hopes of the new monk's
ring her, for unlike so many, he wanted neither to
rge nor to bleed her. Instead, he brewed bark
ought from the East, making a bitter draft, and
rced it down her, stopping when she choked, and
instakingly trying again until the cup was gone.

It was a strange alliance—a ruling count, an old
oman, and a silent monk. But by day, 'twas the old
oman who bathed and spread balm over her wounds,
d by night, Guy himself took the task, telling him-
lf that he could do no less for her.

As dawn broke the third day after his arrival, G
dozed with his head braced against the wall. Gillia
bathed again in sweat, turned her head, and the fi
thing she saw was the red silk of his overtunic,
front brightly blazoned in black and gold. She w
safe—she'd not been dreaming.

"Richard?" she whispered into the soft, rosy ligh

His hand tensed in hers and he leaned forward
push back her tangled hair. The wild, half-craz
expression she'd had ever since he'd arrived w
gone. Rubbing her cheek with the back of his han
he answered, "Nay—'tis Guy."

"Guy? Nay, but—"

"Gilliane, would you that I sent to him?"

"Oh, Jesu. Nay." She swallowed hard to hide h
disappointment. "I must have dreamed. I . . ."

"You were taken ill on your way to Dover,"
prompted her. "You sent the boy Garth to me ther

"Garth." And then she remembered. "Oh, nay
Simon means to kill Richard," she croaked. "Ay
and Stephen plots with Brevise." She closed her ey
again. "So tired."

"How came you by this?" he asked, leaning clos
to hear her. "Gilly, how came you by this?"

"Brevise sent to Simon. Garth knows . . ."

He released her hand and rose, stretching his t
frame, letting his tired muscles tense and then rela
Then he walked to where the old woman lay slee
ing on a pallet by the foot of the bed. Nay, there w
no need to waken her yet. Instead, he went to th
door and ordered the sentry, "I'd see the boy Garth

Still sleepy, his hair rumpled, Garth stumbled in
the abbot's chamber and tried to make sense of beir
awakened. At first he thought perhaps his mistre
was worse, but she seemed quieter, and yet he cou
hear her breathe.

"Nay, she mends." Guy of Rivaux looked yea
older now, his black hair flecked with gray, but th
green-gold eyes were alert and intent as he faced th
boy. "And I'd hear more of this plot against my sor

Garth swallowed, wishing she were awake also,
d then nodded. "Aye. But hours after Lord Simon
parted Beaumaule, a letter was brought for him.
, I knew the one who carried it came from my lord
Brevise, 'twas decided to read it."

"And?"

"It offered Lord Simon money and land to take
rd Richard when they go into Normandy." The
y hesitated, uncertain as to what Gilliane would
ve told him.

"Go on—I'd hear the rest."

"Aye. If 'tis to be believed, Stephen means to ask
y lord of Gloucester to accompany him to Nor-
andy, and Lord Richard also. And when they ar-
ve, they are to be beset and killed, with Brevise
fering Lord Simon and others their lands with
ng Stephen's knowledge and will."

"Jesu! And you have the letter still?"

"Nay, but Lady Gilliane had it in her litter with her
d the babe. She meant to carry it to you."

"When? When do they go to Normandy?"

"I know not, my lord—'twas not said."

It made no sense, but Guy knew Stephen was
ore affable than wise, and he did not doubt at all
at he'd be glad enough to have Gloucester gone.
hat surprised him most, he supposed, was that an
steady king would risk his rising—and rise he
uld if any thought to harm his only son. Aye, and
 would Mathilda—he'd see to that if he had to
omise Geoffrey of Anjou half his lands.

But why had Gilliane come to him rather than
chard? Aloud he merely asked the boy, "Why did
oodstock beat her?"

"Because Lord Richard came to Beaumaule." Garth
oked at the floor, uncertain as to whether to tell
e story, and then decided that surely Guy of Rivaux
ust know most of it anyway. "Lady Gilliane wed
mon of Woodstock to give her babe legitimacy, my
rd."

"You've said naught I did not know."

"Aye, but she thought he'd be content with Be[a]
maule, but he was not. He could not forget that s[he]
came not a virgin to him or that she bore L[ord]
Richard's babe. It made him more than a little m[ad,]
I think."

"And when my son left, he beat her."

"Aye. He means to kill Lord Richard that she [would]
love him no more."

"But why did she not go to my son?" Guy had [to]
know.

"Because she feared for the babe, I think. L[ord]
Simon nearly killed Amia of Beaumaule in a ra[ge]
ere he left, and he is now at Ardwyck too. And s[he]
said you once told her she could turn to you." Ga[rth]
squared his shoulders and met Rivaux's strange ey[es.]
"I think she thought you had the power to end t[he]
plot."

"I can scarce accuse the king," Guy retorted. [...]

Then, seeing the boy's face fall, he relented. "[But]
I can warn my son and Gloucester—aye, and I c[an]
go with them, that they are not taken by surprise.[."]

Garth brightened and his face broke into a smi[le.]
"Then 'twas right that she came to you."

"Aye, 'twas right." Guy turned back to whe[re]
Gilliane lay, her body bathed in sweat as she aga[in]
seemed to sleep. "I know not how she came this [far]
like that—Jesu, but she has the courage of a ma[n,]"
he observed to himself.

"She did but want to save Lord Richard, my lo[rd.]
She knows you brought in Belesme—and William [of]
Brevise is no Belesme."

"Of a certainty he is not," he admitted, his expr[es-]
sion sobering. "But I cannot tarry, for you know [not]
when they mean to leave for Normandy." He look[ed]
again to where Gilliane lay. "The monk thinks s[he]
mends, though I doubted it until this morning. [I'd]
have her stay here until she is well enough to tra[vel]
further, and then I'd send her to Rivaux. If Steph[en]
means to move to Gloucester, 'tis safer there than [...]

ngland. Tell her that I have written to Cat—to my
dy—and that a welcome awaits her."

"And you will see Lord Richard safe."

"Aye, and tell her also that she should rewax and
al the letter and send it to Woodstock. I'd not warn
em lest they devise another plan."

"Aye, my lord."

"And tell her not to worry ere she is well—Richard
a man grown and can defend himself. Now . . ."
e flexed his shoulders again to ease them. "Now, I
ould see the babe born of my blood ere I ride."

38

Unable to sleep, Simon of Woodstock moved uneaily about one of the several small campfires th dotted the Norman hillside. After years of hatir Richard of Rivaux, he had his chance to take him, strike a blow against the man who had everythir he'd wanted. But it was not an easy thing to despite Talebot's urging.

They were all there—King Stephen, Glouceste Richard of Rivaux, Brevise, and a host of others—come to Normandy to suppress the uprisings th spread throughout that troubled land. Aye, and the were even more murmurings of discontent in E gland. For a moment Simon wondered if his rewar would be worth the certain anarchy that would fo low the death of Robert of Gloucester.

"Art about late."

He spun around to see Richard of Rivaux stan ing in the darkness between the tents. Not that l could be mistaken for any other, for he stood tall than any save his own sire, and he had a voice th carried well. As he stepped closer, his dark ey reflected the firelight eerily, making Simon sudden afraid. There was that about the younger Rivar that was oft said of his father: if he fought not at a he would still command men.

"Aye," Simon muttered, unwilling to look at tl overlord who had so much. "As are you."

Each man eyed the other warily, one knowing tl other meant to kill him at some appointed time, tl

her fearing to do the deed. Simon measured him,
king in the fact that he was armed but not mailed,
at only the stiffened leather *cuir bouilli* protected
m, and the tension was unbearable. He considered
s chances of getting it over with, of striking him
w, but Richard of Rivaux's fighting skill was greater
an his own, greater mayhap than even his sire's.
d he would face certain punishment.

"You carry the sword of Belesme, I am told."

"Aye. It has served me well." The warning hairs
Richard's neck stiffened as he faced the man
o'd beaten Gilliane so badly that his father had
t recognized her, and he too was tempted to end it
tween them then and there. Too long he'd waited
r Brevise to move, too long he'd let Woodstock
e. "Would you see it?" he asked.

Jesu, but the man had not blood in his veins to
fer to disarm himself like that. In another man,
ould be said he was but a fool, but Simon realized
at Rivaux baited him, offering him the advantage.
d as Simon looked at him, he thought he saw
llfire in the gold-flecked eyes. He nodded.

The sword flashed quickly, reminding Simon yet
ain what he faced, and then it was proffered hilt-
st. The dancing flames caught and were reflected
the strange symbols etched the length of the blade.
unes," Richard noted softly. "They are said to
otect whoever wields it—even you now."

Simon gripped the hilt, curving his palm against
e crosspiece, feeling the weight of it in his hand.
Tis heavy."

"For the striking of a better blow. 'Tis called
ellbringer, for it has sent more than one man there."

"Aye."

He raised it then as though he would strike, and
w the glitter of the other man's dagger as it re-
cted firelight. He hesitated, and then dropped the
ade, driving it into the ground at Richard's feet,
ightened by what he thought he saw in those eyes.
"Nay, I'd not use it," he muttered.

"And I'd not let you." Richard of Rivaux sheath his dagger and leaned to retrieve his sword. "But hoped you would try—I'd thought the greater leng would make you bold. Alas, I was mistaken."

Simon gaped after him as he disappeared ag between the tents and his insult sank in. In so ma words, he'd called Simon a coward. With an eff Simon shook off the fear he'd felt, telling himsel was but the effect of Robert of Belesme's swo Aye, it had bewitched him, its master's evil reachi from the grave.

"What did he say to you?"

Simon jumped at the sound of Talebot's voi "Jesu, but you would frighten a man," he complain "He said naught."

"I am come to tell you 'tis the morrow—when t sun rises high and they are tired and thirsty, Brev means to strike." Talebot clapped a hand on Simo shoulder "Aye, tomorrow you make yourself a ri man."

"I mislike it. I'd strike when they are unarmed."

"Nay, it must appear we have been beset by rebe Woodstock, else the cry will be too great. That only our enemies that fall will not be noted so eas then."

"Aye, but I think he knows."

"Rivaux?"

Simon nodded, his unease growing as he reme bered the way Richard of Rivaux had looked him—as though killing him would be a pleasu "He knows," he repeated.

"Nay, only a fool would come if he knew it, a Rivaux is no fool. Besides, he cannot know—ther none to tell him of it."

"There was your letter."

"But it reached you still waxed and sealed, did not?"

"Aye." Simon closed his eyes and thought Gilliane, wondering if she could ever be brought forgive him for what he meant to do. The messag

d had written to her were unanswered, and there'd
en no word except Talebot's letter. Jesu, but if she
ly knew what she'd done when she sent the letter
opened.

"Tomorrow night we will join in mourning him."

"Aye."

"And Gloucester also. God's bones, but what there
here for the taking. You will return lord of far
re than Beaumaule, Simon of Woodstock."

And Gilliane de Lacey would learn to love him.
th Richard of Rivaux dead and buried, she would
rn to love him. Simon exhaled slowly and nodded.
) be it then."

Robert of Gloucester led the way, his banner un-
led in the hot summer's wind, followed by Rich-
l of Rivaux and their combined mesnies. King
phen had stopped to pay his respects earlier at an
bey he'd founded, saying he would rejoin them
er in the day, and William of Brevise brought up
e rear of the small host.

Richard reined in beside him and looked down
er the crest of the hill to where the road disap-
ared between thickets. "I mislike the place," he
ittered. "Too much can be concealed there."

"Aye." Pulling up, Gloucester leaned closer, speak-
g low for Richard's ears alone. "Art certain Guy
lows?"

"His men have come and left our camp at will
der my badge. He lies somewhere between us and
e king."

"Stephen will not come this way—he'll want to
pear blameless," Gloucester hissed back.

"If we are attacked, we divide, making them do the
ne, that we are not surrounded. You ride for
en and I for Varaville."

It had been discussed and decided before—Robert
d support at Caen, the town of his birth, and
uld be expected to raise troops there if the need
ose. Varaville, on the other hand, could be counted

on to support Guy of Rivaux and therefore his
also. Gloucester nodded and clicked his reins, o
again moving the column forward.

William of Brevise rode up, impatient at the p.
and growled, "God's bones, but I'd sleep in a bed
night, my lords." Then, looking down to where
road narrowed, he feigned concern. "I mislike tha
I'd not go through there in a column—nay, but
could be picked apart and routed." Turning in
saddle, he waved his men forward. "We'll take
outside for your greater protection, my lord,"
addressed Gloucester.

It was what Richard had been waiting for. He
back a few paces, leaving Brevise with the earl,
found Walter of Thibeaux. Raising his hand to
helm as though to feel the heat, he gave the sig
Walter nodded and dropped back in the column
though to seek water from the packs, ready to
for Guy of Rivaux. And as the last of the colu
dropped below the crest and out of sight, he whi
his mount and rode, spurring furiously.

His palms sweating beneath his heavy gloves,
mon of Woodstock came up closer to Richard.
aught amiss, my lord?" he asked.

"Nay."

They moved slowly, deliberately down the hill, f
abreast now on the narrow road, with Brevise's n
crowding Gloucester's, and Simon of Woodstock bes
Rivaux, taking care to keep his lord between him
Everard of Meulan. Meulan exchanged a warn
glance with Richard and his hand crept closer to
mace he carried across his saddle. Talebot, who ost
sibly served Richard, rode forward to speak to Brev
and both men dropped back to wait for Rivaux.

Richard caught the glint of metal from within
trees ahead and the hairs on his neck prickled
every fiber of his body was now alert to the dan
The wait was nearly over, and the tension he felt
unbearable. And yet he had to ride as though
were unaware they planned his death.

"Jesu, but 'tis hot," Brevise complained loudly. "I'd op soon for a drink ere I stew in mine own sweat."

"Nay, we ride through this ere we stop," Glouces-r muttered, feeling the strain build.

"I thought you misliked the place," Richard re-inded Brevise grimly.

Behind him, Simon grasped the hilt of his sword, ady to strike.

The road darkened abruptly, the tall trees casting ep, straight shadows, and the cool smell of musty rth and leaves closed in about them, shutting out e bright summer heat. And then the road came to e under a hail of arrows that stampeded the ani-als amid the shouts of attackers. Richard drew ellbringer as his own horse reared.

"For Rivaux! For Rivaux! For Saint Agnes and vaux!"

Within the narrow confines of the road, they ap-ared surrounded as men shouted and horses ighed frantically. Richard kicked viciously at a horse at came too close, and turned in his saddle to ward f a blow. Simon raised his arm to strike, then sitated, knowing full well that Gilliane de Lacey uld hate him forever for it.

"Fool!" Brevise shouted at him furiously, waving s battleax.

"Watch out!" Richard shouted in warning.

But he was too late—Brevise's ax caught Simon's oulder with full force, nearly severing his arm. ood spurted from an artery as Simon slumped rward, the surprise of death in his glazing eyes.

Already Gloucester had managed to outdistance s attackers, drawing off a full half of them. Rich-d turned back to face Brevise, muttering a prayer at Hellbringer would bring him down. New shouts "For Rivaux! For Rivaux!" brought up the rear, nicking those behind William of Brevise.

"Holy Jesu! Nay, we are attacked! 'Tis Rivaux o!" Those who could not escape easily began throw-

ing their weapons down in surrender, choosing to sa
their lives.

"Whore's whelp!" Brevise spat at Richard, cuttin
through the air with his bloodstained ax. Richa
leaned away, but the ax crunched through the mu
cle, bone, and gristle of his horse's neck, sending it
its knees. Falling free of his stirrups, Richard car
up to crouch, his sword still in his hand, behind t
dying animal, and waited for Brevise to swing agai

"Come take me, William!" he challenged. "Fa
me! Art not so brave when you do not face a
fenseless girl! Come on—I have but my sword!"

In another, William, would have taken it for fo
hardiness, but 'twas Guy of Rivaux's son he face
and even on the ground that made a difference.
he looked into the fierce, glittering eyes that taunt
him, Brevise was afraid. Flinging the ax away,
turned to flee.

"Nay, I think not!" Everard blocked the road w
his horse and raised his mace. Bringing it do
heavily, he knocked Brevise from the saddle by t
force of the blow glancing off his shield.

"And now you are even!" he shouted down at hi

"Nay—I am unarmed! Take me for ransom
pray you!"

"Not this time." Richard rose, holding his shi
before him and carrying Hellbringer. "Arm hi
Everard."

But one of Brevise's own men kicked the swo
he'd surrendered to his overlord. "Aye, lead us,
lord!" he taunted bitterly. "Show us how you
make us rich!"

Richard poked Brevise with the tip of Hellbring
prodding him. "Pick it up."

"Nay! I'd not die, my lord." He licked his dry l
and backed away from the sword as though it we
an adder. " 'Tis my right to be ransomed!"

"Pick it up."

"Nay! 'Twas I who saved you from Woodstoc
blow!"

" 'Twas you who killed my horse. Nay, but the
choice is yours, William: you can fight me for your life,
or you can hang from one of these trees." Richard
circled him, Hellbringer in front of him. "I give you
a better chance than you gave Geoffrey de Lacey,
William."

" 'Tis no chance at all!"

"Fight for how you would die then."

Richard's voice was deceptively soft, coaxing al-
most, and it sent a shiver up the other man's spine.
"He was naught to you, my lord," Brevise croaked.
"Jesu, your mercy, I beg you."

"I have no mercy for a coward who strikes from
behind, William. I'd give you the same mercy you
gave others—is that what you would have of me?"

Brevise cast about him wildly for the means to
escape, and read the contempt on his own men's
faces. Then he glanced from the sword that lay in
the dirt road to Richard of Rivaux's impassive face.
"Jesu, but what manner of man are you?" he asked
desperately. "Ransom me."

"Nay." Richard stepped back and waited, but Brevise
made no move to take the sword. Finally Richard
turned his back and nodded to Everard. "Hang him
slowly."

Desperate, Brevise lunged for the sword and raised
it to Richard's back, but he was not quick enough.
Richard spun around, a grim smile on his face, and
caught Brevise's blow with the side of his own blade,
deflecting it with such force that the older man reeled.
"I am not that great a fool, William."

He fought a mortal man, Brevise told himself in
desperation—both Guy of Rivaux and his son tied
their chausses like any other men. He dropped to a
half-crouch and waited warily for Richard to move.

"Nay, I can wait also."

Jeering broke out around them, until Brevise
snapped, "I'd see any of you fight him!" Goaded into
action by their derision, he finally brought up the

sword and swung it, glancing a blow off Richard
shield. And the battle was joined between them.

With each thrust, Richard's anger grew. The ma
before him had burned and killed for a piece o
ground that was nearly worthless, and he'd murdere
Simon of Woodstock also, striking one who did his bio
ding. Richard let Brevise land blows, catching then
with his shield, tiring him, and all the while h
taunted him by dropping his guard and letting him
think he could deliver that final thrust. But eac
time, his reckless courage proved but cunning, thwart
ing the older man.

The tension around them grew as victors and pri
oners alike watched in complete silence, a silenc
broken only by the sounds of steel against steel an
steel against sheathed wood. Both men sweated heav
ily from the heat, and William of Brevise felt h
strength ebbing with each blow he gave. Finally h
swung wide, trying to come up beneath Richard
arm, beneath the heavy shield, and Richard saw h
opening. His own blade flashed in the sun before
found his target, and then there was only the sicker
ing sound of ripping mail and Brevise's sudden screa
as Hellbringer took him home.

Brevise collapsed in the dirt, dropping first to h
knees and then falling to lie in the blood that flowe
freely from the wound in his chest. Richard wipe
his blade with grass and then turned William o
Brevise over with the toe of his boot.

"Wh-why?" The man formed the words slowly a
his life's blood ebbed.

"For Gilliane de Lacey," Richard answered hir
"Aye, for what you have done to her."

There was a gurgle and a half-cough as foam
blood welled from Brevise's mouth before his hea
lolled and his eyes took on the vacant stare of deat
Everard leaned over him to listen, passing his har
over the man's nose, and then he straightened.

"He is dead, my lord."

"Aye."

Richard squinted up into the brightness above them nd saw his sire herding those who'd sought to flee efore him. And the black hawk spread its wings on he crimson field, flapping them from its standard. t was a welcome sight. He bent down and loosened he jeweled buckle from Brevise's belt while he aited.

Guy swung down and embraced him, holding him lose. " 'Tis done then."

Richard clasped his arms and nodded. "Aye. Wood-tock is dead by Brevise's hand, and Brevise is done y mine. Gilly has naught to fear again from either f them."

"Do you go to her then?"

It was a question that had plagued Richard ever nce he'd first known of Simon's treachery. He'd reamed the answer both ways—that he would take er again to Celesin, and that he'd let her go. But he'd paid too dearly for loving him, and he would ot ask it of her again.

"Nay," he answered finally, stepping back. "She is afe with you and Maman."

"She loves you still."

"I cannot give her what she deserves, Papa." He ooked back to where Simon of Woodstock fell and ay facedown in the road. "Tell her he died not by y hand."

"Richard—"

"I'd not have her called whore again when she is ot, Papa. If you will keep her at Rivaux, I will pay r her and the child."

"Nay, she costs me naught that I cannot afford." uy draped an easy arm about his son's shoulders nd turned to where Everard and Gloucester counted risoners. "I let enough get away to carry the tale to tephen."

"I know not what Robert will do," Richard mut-red grimly, looking around him, "but this breaks the oath between me and Stephen—I'd not serve a king who plots with mine enemies."

"Nor would I." Guy's arm tightened, squeezing Richard, and then he released him. "Lincoln will be disappointed in us both, I think."

39

Gloucester knelt in prayer at the Abbey of St. Stephen in Caen, the abbey his grandsire the Old Conqueror had built on his marriage, and considered his oath of fealty. And when he rose, he knew the time had come to send to his half-sister in Anjou. And to his uncle, King David of Scotland.

Both Richard of Rivaux and his father had already sent dispatches to the Empress, but they had not so much to lose. Robert, on the other hand, held as much land as Stephen in England. But, like Richard, Gloucester would not serve a man he could not trust.

"My lord . . ."

"Aye?"

"There are those come from King Stephen as would seek speech with you. Already they meet with my lords of Rivaux and Celesin."

"Who comes?"

"The earls of Lincoln and Mowbray, my lord."

A rare smile flitted across Robert of Gloucester's face as he considered how Stephen must have felt to learn his plot had gone awry. And now he'd sent two of Gloucester's friends to seek peace with him. Jesu, what could Stephen say? That he knew not of what Brevise had planned? That 'twas but chance that he stopped to pray? But he'd hear them—if for naught else but the amusement it would afford him to hear Stephen's tale.

"Aye, I will see them."

Richard looked up at the sound of bootsteps on

the stone walkway, ignoring Lincoln's attempts at conversation. Across the room, Guy sat, leaning against the wall and sipping of some sweetened wine. Neither of them had responded at all to Lincoln's plea, but Richard was as anxious as his prospective father-in-law to hear what Gloucester meant to do.

"My lords," Robert murmured in greeting as he entered the room.

"You are unhurt then?"

"You may tell my cousin Stephen that I suffered not so much as a single cut, Thomas."

"He will be relieved to hear of it."

"I am certain he will," Robert responded dryly. "If one means to kill an enemy, 'tis best done cleanly."

"You accuse your king? Nay, but he—"

"Let us not play chess between us, Thomas," Gloucester told Lincoln coldly. "We have the letter that was sent Simon of Woodstock by Talebot, an agent of the king. And in it he promises to divide my lands to reward those who struck against me."

"He professes to know none of this, Robert," Lincoln protested.

"Aye, I'll warrant he does," Richard cut in sarcastically. "It must be difficult to face those you would murder when it becomes known."

"Nay, my lord. Stephen denies—"

"Aye, he denies! What else is he to do—say 'your pardon, dear cousin, but I'd have you dead'?" Richard demanded. "And what can he say to me? 'I have promised your lands to your enemies for your head'? Jesu, but what fools he must think us!"

"He'd meet with Earl Robert—he'd make amends for what has happened," Lincoln tried desperately. "Aye, and with you also—both of you."

"Nay." Richard shook his head, his dark eyes chill and devoid of any gold. "I am done with Stephen."

"You will be forsworn," Mowbray warned him.

"He is forsworn to me!"

"Nay, but I'd speak with him—I'd reason alone."

Lincoln appealed to Mowbray. "You'll not say you heard him speak thus, I pray you."

"Would you that I repeated it?" Richard asked Mowbray. "I renounce my oath to Stephen of Blois—to him who would call himself king of England. Aye, and I offer my sword this day to the rightful heiress."

"Jesu!" Lincoln gasped. "Nay, you know not what you say. You have not heard—" Turning to Guy, he stretched out his hands. "Tell me that he dare not—"

"He is a man grown."

Lincoln stared in disbelief. "God's blood, but are you both mad? There is Harlowe and more to risk in this folly! Aye, and his head also!"

Guy rose then, towering above Mowbray. "Leave them then that Lincoln may speak plainly. As one with a bond to my son, he has that right at least."

"Aye." Mowbray sighed regretfully. "But I'd not fight either of you."

Gloucester held the door, ready to follow them out, but Richard's eyes met Guy's. "Nay, Papa, I'd have you stay."

"You have no need of me, my son."

"I'd have you hear what I say."

Mowbray shrugged and passed beneath Gloucester's arm. "I care not what he says, Robert—Stephen but charges me with you."

The door had scarce closed behind them ere Thomas of Lincoln rounded on Richard. "If you care not for yourself, my lord, you must consider those of us allied to you by blood!" He snapped. "Would you cast suspicion on all of us?"

"My overlord plotted my death!"

"You cannot know that!" Seeing the famed Rivaux temper rising in the younger man's face, Lincoln lowered his voice and attempted once more to conciliate. "Stephen needs you, Richard—aye, and Guy also. Full half of Normandy and England will rise in your wake if you choose to set yourself against him. Your father—"

"Leave my father's name from this! 'Tis I and I alone who repudiate Stephen in mine own name!"

"And what is the king to think when he hears? What is he to think of me? Listen to me, Richard of Rivaux!" Lincoln pleaded. "Sweet Jesu, but I hold my lands of him!"

"Then you will face me at lance-point, my lord, for I mean to fight for Henry's daughter!"

Lincoln whitened. "Nay, you dare not. 'Tis treason you speak, Richard. Nay, but there is a bond of blood between us. Richard, you cannot—"

Guy had risen to face the window, his back to them. "Do you know what blood you would share, Thomas?" he asked, interrupting Lincoln's tirade. "Do you know what blood you would so eagerly give your heirs?"

"Papa!"

"Do you think we are afraid of Stephen? Do you think we fear anything you have said?" Guy continued harshly. "Nay, but we are born of the blood—"

"Nay, Papa! I'd not have you do this for me!" Richard burst out.

Thomas of Lincoln stared from one man to the other, seeing not the wealth and power of Harlowe, Rivaux, Celesin, and the other places they held, but the danger they represented to him. And for the first time, he bitterly regretted the alliance that probably would cost him all he had. He'd schemed and plotted and badgered his daughter in hopes of gaining for his heirs lands so vast that not even Gloucester could match them, and now Stephen would take it all back from him.

"Nay, I'll not mix my blood with yours!" he spat at Richard. "Long have I thought there was a violence in you, but I was prepared to overlook it for the marriage, Rivaux of Celesin! But no longer—nay, no longer." His voice dropped as he faced the younger man. "My daughter goes to the Church, where she was promised first."

Time stood still for Richard as Lincoln's last words sank in. "You repudiate the betrothal?" he asked finally.

"Thomas, 'tis binding," Guy reminded him. "They were pledged."

Lincoln turned to the elder Rivaux and shook his head, his bitter disappointment evident. "Nay, 'tis not—the girl won't have him, my lord. I have beaten and berated her, and yet she maintains that she pledged her heart to the Church as a little maid. I'll not stand against her in this longer—I'd rather have her a nun than wife to a traitor."

Guy looked over Lincoln's shoulder at his son and then back to the earl. "And if we sue to claim her?"

"Her chaplain will swear she chose holy orders first."

"You are certain of this? You knew and you forced her to give her oath to my son also?"

Stung by the censure in the other man's voice, Lincoln retorted, "What was I to do? Gloucester proposed the match, and 'twas a good one—my girl could have been countess to much. And I did not know 'twould come to this! Nay, I thought I allied myself with honorable men!"

"You sold your daughter against her will."

"Bah! What choice does a girl have, I ask you, but to bend to the will of her father?"

The import of Lincoln's revelation was not lost on Richard. Recovering from his shock, he managed to hide the surge of elation he felt. "You are telling me that my betrothal is not binding, my lord—that Cicely has bound herself to Holy Church?"

"Aye."

"Will you repeat this in the presence of Gloucester and Mowbray, saying there is no betrothal between us—that there is no bond of blood?" Richard asked coldly.

"Will you absolve me of blame in the matter, saying I did not know at the time?" Lincoln countered.

"Aye. I'd take no wife who found me abhorrent—I'd have no unwilling woman in my bed."

"So be it then," Lincoln answered bitterly. "I'd have no treason in my blood."

"Then there's naught more to be said between us,

my lord." Walking to the door, Richard reached for the latch. "Swear before witnesses, and 'tis done."

The earl pushed past him, muttering, "I'd tell them ere you make them think me as false as you."

"Call me false, Thomas of Lincoln, and I'd meet you now," Richard responded coldly.

The earl paled visibly, and backed down. "I will tell them she had a prior pledge and I did not know of it."

Guy leaned past Richard to push the door closed behind Lincoln, and then chuckled. " 'Twas one of those rare times when cowardice brought forth truth, I think."

"Aye." Nearly overwhelmed with relief, Richard turned to face his father. "I know what you would have done for me, Papa, but I could not let you do it."

Guy's divided eyebrow lifted over his strange, flecked eyes. "It matters not now whose blood I bear, my son. If I keep Harlowe and Rivaux, 'twill be by battle anyway. I'll hold them by right of arms rather than blood."

"Aye, I doubt the Empress cares whether 'tis a Belesme or a Rivaux who supports her."

"Do you care?"

"Not at all."

His face breaking into a grin, Guy reached an arm around his son. "Do you go to Rivaux with me to tell Gilliane?"

"Nay, and I'd not have you tell her either, Papa. Too many times the Church courts have ruled slowly or not at all—and when I come for her, 'twill be to wed. I mean to carry Lincoln's sworn statement to Rouen and ask that it be ruled I am free ere I come home." Richard turned into his father's arms and held him. "And whatever blood I carry to my sons, 'tis yours that gives me the greatest pride."

"Nay. I tell you what Roger de Brione once told me: you are what you make yourself, not what blood you bear."

40

Castle of Rivaux Normandy— Christmas Day, 1137

Outside, the wind whistled through the courtyard, rattling the shuttered windows and swirling heavy snow into drifted peaks and valleys over the hard-packed earth. Inside Gilliane de Lacey had withdrawn with Elizabeth to the quiet of the small chamber they shared to finish the last work on the fine Christmas robe they made for Catherine of the Condes. Drawn close to the blazing hearth for both heat and light, the two of them plied their needles rapidly, one stitching an embroidered band at the hem of the garment while the other finished the wide sleeve. And with the hammering on the mummer's stand in the hall below and the ringing of the chapel bell as it pealed out the hour of tierce, neither heard the bridge lowered, nor did they hear the riders cross below.

For Gilliane, her work was a labor of love, some small thing she could do to repay Elizabeth's mother for her many kindnesses. Indeed, in the seven months she'd been at Rivaux, she'd truly been received as a daughter of the house by all of them, welcomed and tended lovingly while her wounds of flesh and heart

healed. And they had all adored Amia from the day
she had ridden in with the child, treating the babe a
a treasured grandchild, petting and cosseting her
until Gilliane feared they would spoil her beyond
bearing. But Amia loved them back wholeheartedly
and there was not a day that passed that she did no
beg to be taken up on her tall grandsire's shoulder
and carried about the great castle. Nay, but Gilliane's
cup was nearly full—she had everything she desired
except Richard. And she had long since accepted the
impossibility of that.

He wrote her often, inquiring about her and the
child, but he had not come to Rivaux when Guy had
returned home, nor had he come as she had half
expected for Christmas. Swallowing her pride, she'd
managed to ask Guy why, saying she was sorry that her
presence kept him away. But he shook his head, reply
ing that Richard was busy pursuing a matter in the
courts. She had to be content with that, she sup
posed, but she still ached unbearably when she al
lowed herself to think of him. And, try as she might
she thought of him far too often for her own peace
of mind. Wrenching those thoughts from her mind
she smoothed the rich, deep green samite of the new
gown she'd donned almost hopefully earlier, and she
turned resolutely again to her work.

Elizabeth finished the last stitch of the hem and
rose to stretch, holding her hands toward the fire
"God's bones, but if Mary were in the stable this
night, she'd freeze."

" 'Tis warmer in the Holy Land," Gilliane reminded
her.

"Aye, I'll warrant it is." Elizabeth reached for a
poker and thrust it into the coals to heat. "I'd mul
some wine to warm us—would you have it spiced or
sweetened with honey?"

The bells stopped abruptly and the sound of Amia's
squeals of delight carried up the stairwell. Gilliane
looked up, frowning. "I'd take it spiced, but do you

not think I ought to fetch the babe here? Your father—"

"Papa probably makes her do it, if the truth were known, Gilly," Elizabeth cut in, exasperated. "And if she makes too much noise, there is Maman or Alwina to calm her. Nay, but I'd finish this yet this morning." She poured from the wineskin into a pitcher. "Cinnamon and ginger?"

"Aye. Is it still snowing?"

Elizabeth walked to the window and lifted the rug to peer through the crack in the shutter, and her heart quickened at what she saw. " 'Tis blinding," she managed, turning back. "But there's no cinnamon —I'll fetch some whilst you finish the sleeve."

Gilliane's spirits lowered. She'd known Richard would not come, but now the weather made it impossible even if he would have tried. She dropped her head and appeared to study the intricate pattern she'd embroidered, hoping that Elizabeth could not see her disappointment. Taking another careful stitch, she nodded, "Aye, go on."

In the courtyard below, Richard of Rivaux removed his snow-caked helmet and pulled off his heavy gloves, handing both to Walter of Thibeaux. Despite the howling storm, the yard was filled with people come to share their lord's table, and many huddled around small fires sheltered by stretched hides. He pushed his way through them, acknowledging greetings as he passed, until he reached the warmth of the lower hall. It too was crowded by those who would share the wassail bowl. Rather than fight his way across it, he ducked up the back stairs to his mother's solar, stamping the snow from his feet as he climbed.

Already there was an assemblage of his father's lesser vassals come to feast, and many had gathered in this, the warmest room in the castle. His eyes still blinded from the snow glare, Richard tried to make out Gilliane but couldn't. Guy saw him first and lifted the child he held on his knee as his face broke into a grin.

"Come see your sire, little one," he murmured, settling Amia on his shoulders. The babe squealed with delight, one hand grasping at the thick silver and black hair, the other clutching his face while she bounced against his neck. Guy's eyes met Richard's and his grin broadened. "You behold one born to ride—ouch, you little vixen—'tis your grandsire you would blind."

Despite the ice still on his boots, Richard crossed the room to face his daughter. Her green eyes sparkled impishly and she reached a chubby hand toward him.

"Take her," Guy urged. "She knows no fear, this one."

Richard hesitated, but the child leaned forward, arms outstretched. "I am wet and muddy."

"She likes the red cloak."

Richard lifted her gingerly from his father's shoulders and stared at her, taking in the deep red of her hair and the brilliant green of her eyes. "Jesu, but she is beautiful," he breathed, feeling the softness of her cheek with his knuckle. "My hands are cold, Amia of Beaumaule, but if you will wait for them to warm, your sire intends to become better acquainted with you." To his father, he added, "Gilliane—she is well?"

"Her body mended long ago—her heart mends today."

"You received my letter, then?"

"Aye, and 'twas hard not to tell her of it, but I did not—that I leave to you."

"Richard!"

He half-turned into Elizabeth's welcoming arms, hugging her with the babe between them. "Jesu, Liza, but what ails you? If I'd thought you meant to greet me like this after all these years, I'd have come sooner," he teased.

"Mayhap living with Gilly has made me see you

through her eyes," she retorted, tiptoeing to plant a kiss on his wet cheek. "She still loves you, you know."

"And I her—where is she?"

"In my bedchamber—I'll take you up, Richard. Sweet Mary, but I'd see her face when she sees you."

He set her back from him, shaking his head. "Nay, you take Amia, Liza—I'd see her alone. Aye, I'd surprise her."

"She thinks I am come down for spice for the wine—I'd take it up first, then."

"I'll take it." He eased the babe into her arms, teasing her with, "Practice holding her—mayhap 'twill make you want to wed again."

"Never. Maman and Gilly have the good men, brother."

He paused at the landing to remove his soaked boots and finished his climb in his hose, hoping to take her unaware. At the last step, he reached within the folds of his crimson and vair cloak and felt again the parchment case that contained his freedom, and he toyed with the thought of just giving it to her. But he had to see her first.

He cleared the stairwell silently and stopped. She sat close to the fire, her back to him, her hair plaited into a single braid that hung down like a copper rope over the rich emerald of her green and gold samite gown, and he watched her, feeling suddenly humble. Her love for him had cost her her honor in the eyes of all but his family, and yet she loved him still. And it came to him yet again how very blessed he was to have her. She worked quickly, the gold bands that trimmed her wide sleeves catching the firelight as they dipped to brush over the woven mat as her fingers moved deftly with each stitch. Jesu, but she was so beautiful in her shimmering Christmas gown that it made him loath to disturb her.

"Your poker is hot, Elizabeth," she observed, bending still lower to knot the golden thread and break it with her teeth. "Did you get the cinnamon? If you

did not, I'd be glad enough with just the heated
wine."

His throat ached with what he felt for her, but he
managed to step fully into the chamber, asking softly,
"Would you be willing to settle for me, Gilly?"

She sat very still, not daring to move for fear she'd
but dreamed she heard him, and then she forced
herself to turn around. He stood there almost diffidently, his handsome face wearing the faintest of
smiles, his black hair still dusted with melting snow,
his dark eyes intently watching her. And her heart
pounded at what she read in those eyes.

"Sweet Mary," she whispered as time stood still.
And then she rose, letting Cat's magnificent robe
slide to the floor. "Richard!"

"Aye." He smiled crookedly, his eyes misting with
tears, and he opened his arms. "I'd wed you, Gilly."

She mistook his meaning as she was caught tightly
in his embrace. "Aye, I know you would, but it matters not anymore, Richard—'tis enough that you love
me." She leaned into him, folded into the soft warmth
of the fur-lined mantle she'd made him, and rubbed
her cheek against his blazoned surcoat, feeling the
hardness of the man and his mail. "I was so afraid
you would not come," she choked out. "The weather—"

"Nay, I'd cross hell for you this day, Gilliane de
Lacey," he murmured into the shining crown of her
copper hair. His hands rubbed over her back as
though to make certain she was really there, and
then his arms tightened about her again. "I would
have been here sooner, but 'twas not ruled for certainty until two days ago."

"Your father said 'twas a court case that kept you,"
she whispered into his shoulder.

"Aye." Abruptly he released her, setting her back
from him, and he reached beneath the heavy cloak
to draw out the parchment case. When she looked
perplexed and disappointed, he handed it to her,
urging her, "Read it—'tis the archbishop of Rouen's
seal that witnesses it." Then, not waiting for her to

open it, he took it back, broke the seal, and shook
the rolled document out for her. "Go on."

She glanced up at his eager face uncertainly. "The
archbishop—but what—?" Then she unrolled it and
looked down, reading aloud.

Know ye all men that it has been adjudged this
day, 22 December, in the year of our lord 1137,
that the betrothal contract between Richard of
Rivaux, lord of Celesin, Ancennes, and lesser possessions, and Cicely, daughter to Thomas of Lincoln, is found null, voided by said Cicely's dispar-
agement of her vows to Holy Church.

Gillian'e hands trembled until the parchment shook.
"Richard, what does this mean?" she asked, unable
to read further.

"It means that Cicely would not wed with me."

"Would not wed with you? Nay, but—"

"Aye, she feared to be crushed beneath me in the
marriage bed, and finally her fear of me exceeded
her fear of her father. Cicely of Lincoln, my love,
goes to be a nun."

She stared, too stunned for speech, as he began
rerolling the document that had given him freedom
from the unwanted marriage. "Aye, Gilliane de Lacey,
and since yours are the only sons I want, I'd have
them stand tall beneath my standard. Our sons,
Gilly—yours and mine—will one day rule Rivaux
and Harlowe and the Condes—and anything else I
can win for them. And our daughters will wed into
great houses."

"Amia—"

"I'd not mantle her—'twould brand her for my
bastard when she is legitimate in the eyes of all now,
but I'd dower her with as much as any of them." His
dark eyes were heavily flecked with gold as they
studied her. "What say you—would you wed with me
this day? Would you pledge to me at the chapel door
now, Gilly?"

She could not speak for the lump that formed in her throat. Tears welled in her eyes and overflowed as she nodded her assent.

"You are dearer than my life to me, Gilly," he told her, watching her still. "Sweet Jesu, but I do love you."

"And I you."

She turned her head into his chest and slid her arms beneath the mantle to encircle his waist, savoring the feel of his body against hers. The drops of water from the snow that had melted on his black hair dripped on her, but she cared for nothing but to be held by this man. Her heart sang and her mind repeated over and over, "He is yours—Richard of Rivaux is yours," until it sank in.

"I'd have you unbind your hair, Gilly—I'd have you wear it down like a maid's. I'd see it the way it ought to be worn on your wedding day." One of his hands came up to work at the silk band that held the single plait, loosening it, and then his fingers gently combed through the braid until her hair streamed in waves over her shoulders. "You cannot know how often I have seen it thus in my dreams of you."

Her hands twined in the heavy swordbelt at his waist, the one she'd made in what now seemed another lifetime, and then she was conscious of the sharpness of the buckle where it pressed against her. Looking down, she saw the winking stones and felt overwhelming gratitude for what he'd done for her.

"You had this of Brevise," she murmured, touching it.

"Aye." He loosed her arms briefly and stepped back for room, grinning boyishly as he felt for the leather pouch that hung from his belt. "In my gladness, I almost forgot—" He fumbled with the flap and then drew out a large cabochon emerald, holding it so it dangled from an exquisitely wrought gold chain. " 'Tis your bridegift, Gilly."

"Nay, but I—"

"It pleases me to give you things, Gilly." Still grin-

ing, he reached to clasp it around her neck, lifting
er heavy hair to hook the chain. "And 'tis beautiful
vith your gown."

She fingered the green stone where it nestled at
he crevice between her breasts. " 'Tis—'tis beautiful,
Richard," she managed as her eyes misted over. "But
have naught to bring you—I have naught to give
ou."

"Nay, you bring me Amia—and you bring me love,
Gilly, making me richer than any man I know."

His arms tightened around her, holding her close
nce again, cradling her against the hardness of his
nailed chest. Looking up through tear-sparkled eyes,
he met the warmth of his gaze and was overwhelmed
y the love she saw there. And naught else mattered,
he decided as she lifted her lips to receive his kiss—
he could face the coming wars and separations, she
ould face anything now, secure in the knowledge
hat she loved and was loved also.